Riven

A.J. McCreanor

Constable • London

CONSTABLE

First published in Great Britain in 2014 by Constable
This paperback edition published in 2015 by Constable
1 3 5 7 9 8 6 4 2

A CIP catalogue record for this book
is available from the British Library.

ISBN 978-1-47211-231-6 (paperback)
ISBN 978-1-47211-236-1 (ebook)

Typeset in Great Britain by SX Composing DTP, Rayleigh Essex
Printed and bound in Great Britain by CPI Mackays

Constable
is an imprint of
Constable & Robinson Ltd
100 Victoria Embankment
London EC4Y 0DY

An Hachette UK Company
www.hachette.co.uk

www.constablerobinson.com

For Don

Friday, 13 December

William MacIntyre took advantage of the shift change at Glasgow's Royal Infirmary. The nurses were congregated around the desk at the far end of the ward. The day shift was ending and the night shift was beginning. It was eight o'clock, and, outside, icy sleet fell in sheets from the sky. At the hospital entrance, a diverse group of smokers huddled in the rain, sucking tar deep into their lungs and holding it there before reluctantly exhaling. MacIntyre ignored them and shuffled on, his head bent against the sleet. His movements were slow but eventually he reached his destination.

The bridge.

Pulling his coat tight around him, he swayed slightly before finding his balance again. Christ but it was cold. He clamped his jaw shut to stop his teeth from chattering. Despite the methadone, pain had started to gnaw at his kidneys. Instinctively he put his right hand over them and rubbed the three stumps where his fingers had once been, over the pain, kneading them into his back. Under his coat the flimsy green hospital gown crackled against his paper-thin skin. Above him, sodium streetlights bled over the wet concrete, staining it nicotine-yellow. He tried to take a deep breath but the night air was coated with ice. MacIntyre inched closer to the edge, heard the constant thrum of the traffic beneath him. Castle Street fed into the High Street, one of Glasgow's main arteries, and the road below him snaked around the Victorian facade of the infirmary, past the gothic cathedral and the crypts of the Necropolis where the official number of bodies entombed lay at 50,000.

At the bottom of the High Street, a bus pulled away from the stop and gathered speed. MacIntyre waited until he saw the driver's face before scrambling over the barricade. Screwing his eyes shut, he muttered a curse before stepping into air.

'Christ, that was brutal.' Andy Doyle sat at a table in the Victorian bar in the Bluestone Theatre. 'I thought pantos were meant to be a laugh.'

His companion, Smithy, nodded in agreement, making the deep folds of fat around his neck wobble. 'Aye, it wis garbage right enough.' He took a sly glance at Doyle, wondering whether or not to risk a comment. 'Thought Stella was good though.' Waited for the response.

Doyle stared at him until he looked away. 'Stella's way off limits to you.'

Smithy realised his mistake and tried to make amends by digging himself a bigger hole. 'Am just saying though, she looked great up there on the stage. Great part that.

Back of the chorus line, right enough, but she's a real talent though, eh?'

'Mibbe,' Doyle replied, but his attention had shifted to a skinny boy who had come into the bar. The boy wore a ripped cagoule and filthy jeans and his face was scarred with acne. Doyle turned to Smithy. 'Piss off. Go wait in the car.'

The boy approached the table and stood waiting, dripping rainwater onto the floor.

Doyle sipped his drink. 'Well?'

'Okay Mr Doyle?'

Doyle looked across to the bar. 'What've you got?'

'Bit of news, thought you'd want to know.' He clawed at the track marks on his arm. 'Guy jumped off a bridge earlier on in the night.'

'Anybody important?'

The boy raked his nails through his skin, drawing blood. 'MacIntyre. William MacIntyre did a flyer off the bridge near the Royal.'

Doyle sat back in his chair. 'Thought he was in the hospital. An overdose?'

The boy stopped scratching, began clenching and unclenching his fists, shifted from foot to foot. 'Aye, but he left. Just walked out the door – nobody stopped him or nothing.'

'Is that right?' Doyle gave the boy his full attention.

'Aye.'

'So he just walks out of the Royal and then he jumps?'

The boy nodded then made a downward gesture with his hand. 'Splat.'

'Nasty.'

'Very nasty,' the boy paused, tried for a smile, almost succeeded. 'Baxters.'

Doyle glared at him. 'Come again?'

'He's soup.'

Doyle smiled. He saw Stella come into the bar and scan it anxiously for him; he raised his hand. She smoothed down her silver dress and made her way towards him, high heels clicking on the wooden floor.

The boy gave a shaky thumbs up. 'Right then,' he paused, 'I'll be off then Mr Doyle.' He waited.

Doyle kept his voice low. 'Tell Smithy I said okay. One bag. He's round the corner.'

He watched Stella teeter towards him. The news of MacIntyre's death made up for him having to sit through her atrocious performance.

She reached the table and held onto it to steady herself on her heels, stuffed the chewing gum into her cheek before asking, 'Well babe, what'd you think?'

Doyle put his hands together and made a little clapping noise. 'Great, Stella, you were wonderful.'

'It's okay then that I go out with my pals to celebrate?'

Doyle looked at her, saw the blush, saw her look away. Kept his voice calm. 'Of course, I need to go see Weirdo for a wee chat. Business. Need to tidy up some lose ends.'

Stella's face relaxed. 'Great, we'll hook up at home later? Have a good meeting.'

'You have fun,' he grinned, watching her. Saw her smile fade for a second before she pasted it back on. For someone going out to celebrate, she didn't look too happy.

Chapter 1

Monday, 9 December (four days earlier)

It was early evening and the sky over the East End of Glasgow was gunmetal grey, solemn and cold. Beyond the stone wall, the old graveyard stretched out, the dead earth waiting patiently for the turn of the year and then later, spring, when longer days and shorter nights would see a thaw and the rebirth could begin. Gravestones that had been toppled long ago rested in shrouds of lichen and moss. The trees were naked, their branches stretched heavenwards in despair at the desolation surrounding them. Beyond the graveyard stood a solitary house, silently hoarding its secret, its back door ajar. Waiting.

The two youths stood in the rain peering at the door; through the slit they could make out a dark hallway. Alec Munroe was the smaller of the two. He wore a yellow shell suit, trainers and black woollen gloves. His dark hair was shaved close to his head. He spoke first. 'Am no sure, Rab. What if someone comes?' The tremor in his voice gave him away.

'You shittin' it wee man?' Rab Wilson tried for a laugh but it was a hollow sound. A head taller than his friend, he assumed the authority in their relationship. He wore denims, a fleece jacket and old, battered trainers. He hadn't bothered with gloves, but had wound a long red scarf around his throat. His thick blond hair was dark with rain.

They waited, listening. The wind moaned around the house, breathing into cracks and gaps. Rab glanced back at the dirt track. Empty still. Much of the noise from the traffic on the London Road was muted by the heavy rain but he heard the occasional roar of a lorry on its way to the English capital. Rab wondered how his father was doing in London and if he would ever see him again.

Alec folded his arms tight across his chest to stop the trembling. 'Ye sure there's nobody about? That his car over there?' He nodded in the direction of a blue Ford Focus parked a short way from the house.

'Fuck knows, but there's naebody here. There's nae lights on. Come on ya numpty.' Rab pushed open the door and paused, waiting for the creak to die away before stepping into the hallway. 'See, it's empty. Let's have a wee shuftie and mind we're only takin' what we can carry.'

'God, it's mingin',' muttered Alec.

'Aye well, we'll mind tell folk that old Gilmore's hoose stinks.'

'Dis stink but.'

'What kind of a cunt would live in a hoose like this?' Rab tiptoed to the sitting-room door and tentatively pushed it open. They were there to steal what they could from Gilmore's house. A wee bit of thieving and money in their pocket if they could sell it on. It was the way forward. A career of sorts and the only one open to them at present. Rab knew Gilmore worked at Watervale Academy and that there was a parents' night that night at the school. All the staff would be there. Rab stepped into the shabby room and adjusted his eyes to the dim light. 'Noo just grab stuff an' remember—', but he didn't finish his sentence. Instead he stood transfixed by the image in front of him. The bloated body was hanging from a hook on the wall, its neck almost completely severed by the rope. Its blackened eyes bulged at them from a face livid with bruises.

James Gilmore was still at home.

Alec wrapped his arms around himself, swallowed hard, tried but couldn't look at the body.

Rab moved towards it and stared into the dead man's face for a full minute before turning his back on the corpse. 'Alec, my wee pal?'

'Aye.'

'Call the polis.'

Chapter 2

A voice, angry, accusing, bellowed into the darkness.
'STAY WHERE YOU ARE! DON'T MOVE!'
The sound of gunfire.
Silence.
In the People's Theatre, in the middle of the third row, Kat Wheeler held her breath.
'STOP!'
More shots.
Then silence.
Wheeler felt the familiar rhythm of her heart, heard her breathing return to its usual pace, soft, gentle, unwilling to disturb the silence.
Darkness and silence.
Then the beat of a single drum. The glare of the searchlight trained on the audience. The sound system, loud.

'YOU!'

'STOP!'

The blinding light, too harsh after the cool of dark, scanned the audience. She blinked hard, felt the familiar vibration begin on her leg, small and tremulous but insistent. She wriggled, tried to extract the phone from her jeans. Two fingers flailing. Failed.

'FREEZE!' bellowed the voice.

She shifted uncomfortably in her seat.

The vibration stopped.

'ARE YOU READY TO DIE?'

She hadn't thought too long and hard about it.

'YOU CAN'T ESCAPE DEATH!'

The searchlight off. Welcome darkness. Silence.

The vibration returned; this time she was ready and yanked the phone from her jeans, its glow a solitary prick of light in the darkness. The too-familiar number blazed silently on the screen.

The searchlight was back on, scanning the room. 'WELL?'

Her voice less than a whisper, 'I have to take this.'

Beside her, Imogen's reply, 'Have to? Or choose to?'

Wheeler stumbled over feet, pushed past knees, finally forcing a large woman in a red dress to stand to let her through. Wheeler mouthed a silent apology while noticing the stubble around his lipsticked mouth, saw the Adam's apple move.

'WHAT'S IT TO BE?'

She saw the gold necklace, a pentagram. He smiled as she pushed past him. She flickered a smile in return, noticed his hair, a short undercut with a bit of a quiff on top, a haircut identical to her own. She wondered fleetingly if they went to the same barber. She moved on, ignoring the scowls and huffs of disapproval from the other people in the row, until finally she lurched through a door and heard it close behind her. In the corridor she leant against the wall, flipped open her phone and punched in the number. Kept her voice low and controlled. 'This had better be good.'

Five minutes later she had texted her apologies to Imogen and was driving out towards Carmyle Police Station in Glasgow's East End. The station was in the centre of the triangle between Auchenshuggle, Mount Vernon and the South Lanarkshire border. Twenty-eight minutes later she barged into the station, took the stairs to the CID suite two at a time and was rounding the corner just in time to hear a familiar sound. One of the team whining.

'Weather's shite.' Detective Constable Alexander Boyd nodded towards the window before slurping black coffee from a chipped mug.

Acting Detective Inspector Steven Ross shuffled papers together and crammed them into his in-tray, smoothing them down with a satisfied smirk. 'The game might get postponed.'

Boyd shrugged. 'Personally, I don't give a toss.'

She stood behind Boyd. 'Me neither; I think the murder takes precedence here.'

Boyd swivelled round in his chair, spilling coffee onto his wrinkled white shirt. 'Sorry, didn't hear you come in.'

Ross stood, hastily pulled on his leather jacket and automatically smoothed his dark hair. 'Ready when you are.'

'Well get a bloody move on – I had to leave a night out for this.'

She was at the front desk signing for the pool car when he caught up with her.

Tommy Cunningham, the desk sergeant with ninety-seven days left at the station before he retired, sucked air through pursed lips. 'Dearie me,' he said in a soft Irish accent, 'tell me you're not taking that eejit with you?'

''Fraid so TC.'

'See that he keeps it on the road this time, won't you?' Cunningham sounded doubtful.

Ross shook his head. 'Can't believe you fuckers are still going on about it. Accidents happen all the bloody time.'

Cunningham sighed. 'Shit happens to some more than to others, son. See, I think that maybe you're jinxed. Did you even pass your SDT?'

Wheeler smirked; all officers had to achieve at least seventy-five per cent in order to pass the Standard Driver Training Course.

'I got ninety per cent,' muttered Ross, 'but thanks for asking.'

'And now we've a pool car with a rare big dent in it, because of you,' Cunningham grinned at Ross.

Ross didn't return it. 'Adds to its character.'

'You're a bloody eejit, son.'

Wheeler made for the door. 'He might be, TC, but he's our eejit.'

'Right enough.' Cunningham shook his head, his voice resigned, 'he's ours.'

Ross kept his silence and followed her out.

Wheeler closed the door behind them, trapping the sticky heat in the station. Outside, a freezing Glasgow downpour was well under way but she strode ahead, oblivious to the rain, her blonde hair plastered to her head.

Ross strolled beside her, long legs easily keeping pace. 'Nightmare this weather. Last night's storm nearly took the roof off my flat.'

'Here, catch,' she tossed the keys at him, 'you're driving.'

'How come?'

'Weather's shite,' she paused, 'and apparently you need the practice.'

Ross hauled fourteen and a half stones of honed muscle into the driver's seat. Settled himself. Pointedly said nothing.

The car started on the second attempt, the engine growling malevolently, windscreen wipers smearing a gentle coat of grease across the screen. Ross groaned. 'Christ, I can hardly see a thing.'

Wheeler pushed the seat belt into place and waited for the click before answering, 'Quit whining and try to focus on the task in hand.'

'I know, *the poor sod who's been battered* . . . I am a professional.'

'A professional numpty.' Wheeler's mobile rang; she wasn't in the mood. 'Yeah?'

The person on the other end paused before asking, 'Kat?'

'I can't talk now Jo, I'm on a case.' Wheeler switched off her phone.

He glanced at her, 'Family?'

'Flipping yes. Again.'

'Lucky you.'

'Aye, lucky me.'

A few minutes later they were settled on the A74, London Road, linking Hamilton Road at one end to the High Street in Glasgow's city centre at the other. On their right were blocks of flats, many with their windows illuminated with Christmas trees dripping with tinsel, fairy lights and shiny baubles, bright against the dark of night. On their far left the River Clyde meandered through the city from its source in the Lowther Hills, out into the Firth of Clyde and into the Irish Sea. The Clyde was over a hundred miles long and its waters held some of the city's darker secrets.

Ross navigated the road carefully; visibility was poor. As he concentrated, Wheeler reached across, turned on the radio and listened to the local news.

'. . . The father of a twenty-four-year-old man who was attacked by a gang outside a gay nightclub last weekend has made a plea for more information to be brought forward. William Johnstone was beaten to the ground and left unconscious as the gang ran off towards the city centre. His father, Alan, issued this appeal: "Someone has to know who these men are – they are someone's son, brother or husband. Whoever is shielding them should share their blame." William remains in a critical condition in the Royal Infirmary.

'. . . A fight in a south-side pub between rival football fans has resulted in one man being taken to hospital, where his condition was said to be stable. A twenty-year-old man has been arrested in connection with this incident and is due to appear in court . . .

'. . . A woman has been charged with child neglect after leaving her three-year-old daughter alone in a house in the Springburn area of the city for three days. The thirty-three-year-old woman, Bernadette Malcolm, stated that she had been to a series of parties held over one weekend and had "forgotten to go home" . . .'

Wheeler let the news wash over her and thought of the murder scene they were about to visit. She watched the Christmas trees in the windows of houses and hoped that, despite the gloomy news, most residents of the city would have a happy Christmas.

The radio continued its report.

'. . . The release of notorious Glasgow criminal Maurice Mason from Barlinnie prison on Friday, after serving only half of his seven-year sentence for manslaughter, has sparked an outcry from the family of the victim. Scott Henderson, thirty-nine, died shortly after a frenzied attack by Mason. The controversial decision to release Mason came at a time when pressure to—'

'All good news,' she sighed, reaching forward and switching the radio off. 'And Maurice Mason's out in time for Christmas.'

'Cheer up, it'll soon be the holidays and let's positively reframe it, think of Maurice Mason being let out as a wee early Christmas present for us. What could be cosier?' Ross grinned. 'And talking of Christmas pressies, you got mine yet?'

Wheeler stared ahead. 'Thought we'd agreed that we wouldn't bother with presents? Just do the Secret Santa thing with the rest of the station?'

Everyone at the station did a 'Secret Santa' dip for anything around ten pounds and the usual rubbish turned up – joke aprons, flavoured condoms, plastic nonsense that would end up in the bin by January – but it was about as familiar as Wheeler wanted to get with most of her colleagues.

'But aren't we more than that?' asked Ross.

'Like what?'

'We're partners.'

'We're not in an American cop show, we're part of the team.' But she knew what he meant; they were closer and they did work better together than with the others.

'Suppose.' Ross indicated and switched lane. Ahead of them, the security lights from the whisky distillery glowed in the darkness. Ross turned off the road and bumped the car down a single-track lane which was so rutted Wheeler felt the car lurch to the side. Ross drove on, past the walls encircling the old cemetery, the mossy gravestones slick with rain. Wheeler opened the window and a rush of cold air filled the car, bringing with it the smell of damp vegetation. The cemetery had been closed for years and languished, neglected. Finally, at the end of the lane they stopped beside a shiny new BMW, the colour of congealed blood. Personalised plates told her that CA11UM was on duty.

Ross turned to her. 'You okay?'

'Why wouldn't I be okay?'

'You know, dead bodies, that kind of . . . stuff.'

'You worried you'll faint?'

He smiled. 'Might do. Will you pick me up?'

'No chance,' she muttered, getting out of the car, 'but I'd stomp over you to get to the case, would that suit?'

She watched him grimace before striding through the rain. She ignored the downpour, knowing that her hair was already flattened, that her skin would be pale with the cold.

Across the drive, a scene-of-crime officer was examining a Ford Focus. She shouted to him, 'That his car then?'

The man nodded, water dripping from his nose.

'Get anything useful?' she asked but she already knew the answer.

'Too early to say.' The man turned away and concentrated on the car.

She looked at the house. Once it would have been a solid building, but the old stones had suffered decades of neglect; stained-glass windows rattled in rotted frames, slate tiles gaped obscure patterns across the roof. The door was too wide for the house, and the garden, an anarchic knot of weeds, had long since gone wild. 'Would've been lovely once.'

'Aye.' Ross shifted from one foot to the other, distracted. 'Shit.'

'What's up with you?'

'Cramp.'

11

'For goodness' sake.'

'Still, but it's sore.'

She stared at the house. 'It looks close to derelict now.'

He shook his left leg vigorously. 'Seen worse.'

Fluorescent police tape twisted and snapped in the wind, catching the light from the open door. She ducked under. 'Come on smiler, let's go join the party.' Ross followed, his limp pronounced. Up ahead the familiar scene was being re-enacted. Assorted SOCOs, each contained in their own world, were moving silently like spectres, searching the ground, gathering information, bagging evidence.

A young detective sergeant walked briskly towards them, his thin lips stretched into a tight smile. His navy-blue suit was pristine, his dark hair smoothed into a side parting and his brogues held a dull sheen. A hit of lemon aftershave arrived ahead of him.

'How does he even do that?' She tried not to sound impressed. 'I look and smell like wet dog.'

'Freak,' coughed Ross.

Detective Sergeant Ian Robertson greeted her with a polite nod, while ignoring Ross.

'What've you got?' Wheeler asked.

'Male, deceased, fifty-four years old. Looks like he lived alone. One toothbrush, only male clothes in the wardrobe, nothing to suggest anyone else lived there.'

'And?'

'He was an educational psychologist. He was peripatetic, travelled around different schools across the city.'

'And?' Wheeler sighed; it was like drawing teeth. 'Got a name?'

'James Gilmore.'

She held out her hand. 'Gimme those, Robertson, it'll be bloody quicker for me to read them.' She scanned the neatly written notes. Two boys had found the body. It was a far from pleasant sight as it had 'shown considerable signs of beating'. The boys were in shock and the body was waiting for her inside. She thrust the notes back at the sergeant – 'Fine,' – turned, 'Well, Ross, if you're ready?'

Robertson held up his hand, neat, manicured nails, broad gold wedding band gleaming. 'There's something else.'

She paused. 'Go on.'

'I knew him.'

Wheeler whistled. 'Geez, was he a friend?'

Robertson flinched. 'No, nothing like that. We weren't close. I didn't know him well at all; I only met him once, twice maybe, that's all.'

She waited.

He studied his shoes. 'We met at one of the schools he visited.'

'Which one?'

'Watervale Academy.'

Wheeler recognised the name. The school was in the north of the city, slap-bang in the middle of a run-down shambles of a scheme. She knew that the school's nickname was Waterfuck and having Academy tagged on was seen by some as a cruel joke thought up by the heid high yins in Glasgow City Council. Watervale catered for some of Glasgow's most challenging kids.

'The school for kids with behavioural problems?' She looked at Robertson.

Robertson nodded. 'Some have special needs too.'

'Aye a special need to kick the shit out of anyone who gets in their way,' muttered Ross.

Wheeler ignored him and addressed Robertson. 'You there on police business?' Like a lot of schools in the city, uniformed police sometimes had to visit. But CID

13

was another thing. And it wasn't even their area. She was curious why Robertson had visited the school. She waited. He hadn't answered her question. 'So why were you there?'

Robertson looked at the ground, the rain damping his hair. Still it remained in place. He glanced at Ross, winced, 'Personal business.'

She saw his discomfort. Felt the tension between the two men deepen. Decided to ignore it – they were meant to be grown-ups and she wasn't their mammy. Heard her mobile ring. Checked the number. Her sister. Ignored her too.

Wheeler watched as a SOCO passed, his suit rustling as he walked, before turning back to Robertson. 'And the two boys who found him, how're they doing?'

'They're both very upset, as you can imagine.'

'I'll bet. I hope they're not still here?'

'Course not. I had them taken to the station.'

'Good. So, what do we know about them?'

Robertson checked his notes. 'Alec Munroe and Rab Wilson, both nineteen and both ex-Watervale Academy.'

'So they knew the victim?'

'Only that he visited the school. They'd left before he started there. But they knew his name – they still hang out with kids from the school.'

'At their age?'

He nodded. 'Said all their pals still went there. They came to the house on the off chance it was empty.'

'All the way across the city? That doesn't seem right.'

'On the bus.'

'On the bus,' she repeated, 'because?'

He glanced at his notes. 'Parents' night at school – they thought all the staff would be there. They were going to rob the place.'

She whistled. 'Geez, they broke in and found a body – bad luck there boys.'

'*Technically* they didn't break in,' he corrected her, 'the door was already open.'

She looked at Robertson, then at the house, trying to imagine the scene. 'Uh huh. And how'd you find out about the intended robbery?'

Robertson beamed. 'They told me.'

'Christ,' Ross spluttered, 'they're no Butch Cassidy and the Sundance Kid, are they?'

Robertson kept his voice low. 'Humour's hardly appropriate, given the grave circumstances.' He busied himself rereading his notes.

'Fuckin' amateurs! On the bus!' Ross was still sniggering.

She glanced at Ross, took in the fitted jacket, purposely tight over a taught six-pack. His body was gym-toned, hers ex-army-honed. He had long legs, broad shoulders. Dark hair, pale blue eyes, long lashes. She knew that if he was chocolate he'd eat himself. He was also loud and routinely inappropriate. That said, she still liked him. She looked at Robertson, noting how a faint smir of rain seemed to hover over his suit, while her trousers were already soaked.

'So our boys aren't the brightest . . . anything else I should know?'

He returned her smile, patted his notes, his ring catching the light from the police vehicles and reflecting it. 'I think that's a pretty accurate assessment of the situation.' His mobile rang. 'Excuse me.' He passed his notes to Wheeler before he moved off, but they could hear him hissing into the phone, 'Yes, I'm still on the job; I'll probably be here all night . . . because it's important work.' A pause while he listened. 'Oh for pity's sake Margaret, I'll be home whenever I can; go on up to bed and for goodness' sake stop fretting.' He clicked off the phone and turned back to them.

Wheeler and Ross studied the notes intently, Ross smirking.

Robertson blushed, aware that they had overheard him. 'I'll be out here if you need me.'

Wheeler stepped forward. 'If you need to get home, go now. There are enough of us on duty.'

'But DCI Stewart said that—'

Ross cut him off. 'Stewart's got two days off. I think between us, we can manage till he gets back. Even without you being here.'

Robertson shook his head and walked back towards his car.

She watched him leave then turned to Ross. 'Is there a wee problem between you two lovebirds?'

He shrugged. 'Problem's with him.'

'How's that?'

'PB.'

'Sorry?'

'He's Plymouth Brethren. No drinking, whoring or swearing.'

'Christ, really? No swearing?'

''Fraid so. Fuckin nightmare.'

She could imagine Robertson's welcome at the station. 'Just another bloody division in the team,' she muttered.

He straightened to his full six foot three, looked hurt. 'The rest of us are okay.'

'You think?'

He shrugged.

'Well then, let's refocus: the two boys walked in through the back door intent on robbing the place, instead they found the body and, rather than scarper, they did the concerned citizen bit and called it in?'

'Sounds about right,' said Ross.

'Let's go see it then.' She walked ahead of him, careful of her steps, keeping to the tread plates, conscious that there may be evidence still to be collected, some tiny piece that may help them find the killer.

She was first through the door. Boots and muddy wellingtons were piled inside and an old wooden coat stand held a good-quality Berghaus outdoor jacket. A camera tripod was propped against the wall. Four oak doors led off from the hall, all open. Through the nearest she could see the body laid out on a tarpaulin and kneeling beside it a stout man with a goatee beard. Professor Callum Fraser.

She stood in the doorway. 'Smells like rancid meat in here.'

Fraser turned from the body, looked her up and down and grinned, 'DI Wheeler, how very lovely to see you but I thought DCI Stewart might have shown a face.'

'Stewart's on leave.' Ross tried not to look at the corpse. Held his breath, turned red in the face.

'Ah. Lucky man being on leave; wish I were off doing something nice.'

Her mobile rang; she checked the number before answering and instinctively turned away from the body as she spoke briefly to the caller.

'Stewart *was* on two days' leave,' Wheeler corrected Ross as she clicked off the phone. 'He's on his way into the station. Says he'll meet us there.' She turned to face the body.

'Watch your feet please, detectives, there's still a lot of evidence to be collected.'

'This much blood, Callum, tell me there's a decent set of footprints?' Wheeler sounded hopeful.

'Not your lucky day I'm afraid; there are no crisp outlines. Looks like the killer bound his or her feet with something to distort their prints. Towels maybe? The splatter's been soaked up in places. The footprints are quite indistinct. Except for those excellent specimens.' He pointed to two sets of fresh, clear prints a short way from the body. 'But apparently they belong to the two boys who discovered the body.'

Wheeler moved carefully towards the corpse. Close up she could see the dead man's face was a mass of pulp, the skin broken and raw. 'He certainly annoyed somebody.'

The pathologist nodded. 'He did that. He was already dead by the time the killer hung him up. A lot of extra effort – a dead weight like this would take a considerable amount of strength. Either that or the killer was bloody angry; the adrenaline in anger can give us almost inhuman strength.'

'Somebody wanted to make a point.' Ross glanced at the body and away again. 'A warning maybe?'

Callum nodded. 'Could be.'

'What ETD do you have?' Wheeler could smell stale blood and cupped her hand around her mouth before coughing discreetly into it.

'Well, decomposition's beginning and rigor's advanced, so I'd say we're talking about some time last night. Can't be more specific at this time; I'll know more when I get him back to the mortuary.'

'He hardly looks human,' she sighed. 'So we've got his name and where he worked. Bit strange though, an educational psychologist ending up like this.'

'Usually more gang-related,' Ross said, 'this kind of thing.'

Wheeler peered at the body. Dark eyes bulged back at her. 'You think he got on the wrong side of one of the Glasgow families?'

Ross held out his hand, counting off each finger. 'If it was drugs, the McGregor crew, or the Tenant clan, both are at loggerheads. Or one of the independents? Doyle or Jamieson? Any one of them could do this in a heartbeat.'

'An educational psychologist though?' Wheeler pursed her lips. 'Are that lot not a bit out of his league?'

'You thinking mistaken identity, somebody got the wrong guy?' asked Ross.

She pointed to the corpse. 'I think this was more personal. This amount of blood, they took their time.' She looked around the room; it had morphed from someone's home into a crime scene – everything was being photographed, bagged and tagged. She tried to see beyond the gore, tried to get some idea of who James Gilmore was, hoping that his home would give up some of its secrets. But there wasn't much homeliness to the room; it appeared that, even before Gilmore had been murdered, the place had been slowly dying. The sofa was ancient, torn cushions exposing the inner foam padding. A threadbare carpet, filthy curtains. Everything old and worn and neglected. She turned away. 'Whatever they're paying educational psychologists these days clearly isn't enough.' She turned to Callum. 'I don't suppose they left the weapon behind?'

'Nothing found in here I'm afraid Katherine – maybe they'll find it out in the garden somewhere.'

'If you had to guess . . .?'

'If I had to guess, and I don't like guessing, then I'd say the weapon was some sort of a bat, possibly baseball, and most certainly wooden, considering the presence of these splinters.' He tweezered a tiny shard of wood from a pool of blood and held it up. 'Could be made from ash, that's the most usual, or if our killer went upmarket for his bat, it could be made from maple.'

19

Wheeler shook her head. 'With so many baseball bats in circulation in the city, is it not about time we had a few actual teams going?'

'I'm done here.' Callum stood with a groan. 'Want a lift back in Jessica? I don't mind detouring to the station. For you, Katherine, anything.'

Wheeler tutted. 'You still naming your cars, Callum? Is that not a wee bit immature?'

'I name all of my vehicles.'

'Thought you'd have grown out of it by now. Thanks, but I'll go back with Ross.'

'Suit yourself, but I'll keep her on the road.'

Ross groaned. 'It was an *accident*.'

'Ignore him,' said Wheeler, 'he's feeling tired and emotional. We'll be at the PM tomorrow. What time?'

'I'll let you know – we're backed up just now, but I'll try to give him priority. Although,' he paused, 'I think it's obvious . . .'

She cut him off, 'I know, I know, *it's obvious what happened.*'

'Indeed it is. A man was battered to death. All you need to do is find out the "who" and the "why".'

She chewed her bottom lip as she followed him into the hall. Her phone bleeped again. She pulled it out and glanced at the screen – her sister again. She flicked it off as she passed three young SOCOs. Overheard one whisper to Ross, 'Haddy, get it? Short for haddock.'

Behind her Ross tutted, 'Aye, I get it. Fish tea. He's been battered.'

At least their laughter was subdued.

Outside, Callum pointed at the house. 'You see the extra-wide doorway?'

She saw it.

'This place was the old slaughterhouse and that's where

they herded the cattle in for slaughter. Of course it's been renovated since then and that stained glass put in. It's totally out of character with the building. Not that there's much left of anything really – it's all a bit of a wreck. But the hook the body was found hanging on is an original feature and would have been used to tether the animals before they were killed.' He smiled at her. 'Are you absolutely sure about that lift, Katherine?'

'Sure.' She watched Callum lumber towards his car, felt herself breathe in the cold damp air and was grateful to be out of the house, away from the atmosphere of evil. She inhaled again, deeper this time, bringing the freezing air low into her lungs, enjoying the shock it gave her system. She watched the crime-scene photographer come out of the house and continue taking pictures before she half turned back to the house and opened her mouth to yell, but he was already striding towards her, long legs covering the ground easily. 'No need to shout,' Ross said, 'I'm here already. We're going to interview the two boys. Right?'

She smiled at him. 'Bingo.'

Chapter 3

Ross turned the car into the station car park and braked sharply. 'Christ, I nearly killed the wee shite'.

The wee shite in question, Graham Reaper, was chief reporter with the *Glasgow Evening Chronicle* and he flashed a crooked smile before signalling to his photographer to get a picture of the cops. He already had the headline in mind: *Gruesome Find in Glasgow's East End! Murder Inquiry Begins.*

'You ever wonder how Grim gets here so fast?' Ross parked the car, pausing to smooth down his hair before releasing his seat belt.

'Aye, he's being tipped off and if Stewart ever finds out who the hell's doing it, they'll be fucked.' She glanced at him. 'You always so worried about your appearance?'

'Well, if I'm going to be in the paper . . . there's no harm in looking my best. You never know who'll see it.'

'You single *again*?'

'I know it's hard to believe.'

'What happened to the last girlfriend – what was her name?'

'Sarah.'

'Aye, her. What happened?'

'The usual.'

'The usual in that she woke up one day and realised that you're a numpty?'

Ross tried for a hurt look. 'The usual in that she started blethering on about rings, future plans, kids. She even mentioned coming off the pill. That sort of shite.' He mimed putting two fingers down his throat and gagging.

'You not want a wee "mini-you"? Thought that would be right up your street.'

'No way. I'm too young. In my prime.' He threw open the door, blinked back the flash from the camera. He fixed a 'no comment' smile to his face and made for the door.

She had already reached it when the reporter caught up with her. 'So, a murder inquiry, Inspector Wheeler – any comment?'

'You know better than to ask for anything at this point, Grim; there'll be an official statement later and if you're really lucky Stewart will throw you a press conference by mid-week.'

'Aye but is it gang-related? It must be, surely? Drugs? A turf war? What's your take on it?'

'See the above answer.'

'Got anything to do with Maurice Mason being released?' he persisted. 'Christ sake hen, gimme something.'

She smiled.

'Come on, eh? Man needs to make a living here. Give me a break, I'm only doing my job.'

'Well, okay Grim,' she stopped and turned towards him, 'but you first. You tell me who called you about this, who's giving you the heads up on these cases?'

Grim gave her a sly smile. 'You know I cannae reveal my sources hen. It wouldn't be professional.'

'That right?' she asked, holding open the station door to let Ross go inside.

'Aye,' Grim made to follow her, 'but maybe we could have a wee chat, off the record like?'

Wheeler walked into the station and slammed the door, heard Grim curse her. Shrugged, 'Let the ugly wee runt get soaked.'

'Still but,' Ross stood beside her, shaking his head like a dog who'd just returned from a walk in the rain.

She stood beside him, the rain drops from her boots leaking onto the cracked linoleum. 'I know, I know.'

'Mason,' said Ross.

Tommy Cunningham sat behind the desk. 'That bastard got out early.'

'Aye, he did, TC,' she agreed. 'I wonder what he'll be up to now he no longer has his own rent-a-thug empire.'

Cunningham scowled. 'He'll be up to his old tricks again.'

She walked to the desk and was signing the pool car back in before she continued, 'Mason gets released from Barlinnie and James Gilmore gets battered to death in what was his territory. We already know Mason expresses himself best with his knuckles.'

'Who's Mason got history with?' Ross continued. 'The Tenant clan? McGregor's lot? Or a freelancer, maybe Andy Doyle or Roddy Jamieson?'

'Mason's always been a freelancer, can't seem to get on with folk. Saying that, he's probably got history with half the freelance thugs in the city, Jamieson and Doyle included.'

'Doyle's the most ambitious,' said Ross. 'His star's on the ascendant.'

'True. But he stays on his own turf. Well, so far.'

'The others?'

'The Tenants and McGregors are way more insular. Unless Mason's become part of their setup and I doubt that; it's family members only. He'd have to marry in, it's that tight-knit in both families.'

'Okay but I still can't help thinking it's a hell of a coincidence. Mason gets out and someone gets murdered.'

'Trouble is, this part of the city has a bit of an overlap. Tenants to the north, Jamieson's crew to the south – around here's a bit of a no-man's-land.'

'Bandit country.'

She stopped in the corridor. 'Besides, Mason's gone AWOL. He got out of the Bar-L okay, but apparently he never made it home to his beloved.'

'A blonde tart named Lizzie Coughlin,' Ross said. 'Apparently she's stayed faithful, turned up for weekly visits, played the supportive partner all these years.'

'Any relation to Kenny Coughlin?'

'His daughter.'

'But Mason skipped the big reunion. Why? After all that time, where does he have to be that's so important he doesn't make it home? Unless someone got to him first?'

Ross pursed his lips.

'Exactly my point. It's suspicious.'

'Does it have to be? He was never a class act from what I heard, so maybe he's out drinking and whoring. Three and a half years is a long time to be celibate.'

'You think he's out partying?' Wheeler thought about it. 'Maybe, but he could be in more trouble than suffering a bit of a hangover.'

'Well, wouldn't you be out on the razz if you'd been locked up for years?'

'I think he'd still want to see Lizzie, especially if he's been celibate for all that time.'

'True,' agreed Ross. 'What's the point in paying for it when you can get it for free?'

Wheeler slapped his arm. 'God, it's a wonder a romantic like you is still single.'

Ross started up the stairs. 'I think he's involved – it's too much of a coincidence. Mason gets out, then there's this.'

'Okay, so let's go have a chat with the two boys, see if they give us anything. See if there's a link from Mason to Gilmore.' She pushed open the door to the CID suite.

'Or to one of the other lot.' He followed her.

'That would be a result.' She looked at Boyd. 'The two boys ready?'

'DCI Stewart's going to interview them, says there's another interview he wants you to do.'

She dumped her wet coat on the back of a chair; she'd learned in the army how to take orders. Her mobile rang. She recognised the number – her sister again. Wheeler heard it beep. A text. She glanced at it.

Why r u not answering? Jason's not returning my calls. I'm SICK with worry. I think he's in TROUBLE.

'Problem?' asked Ross.

'My bloody sister's paranoid about her son Jason, going off to Glasgow University and into the big bad world. We've never been close and now that he's in Glasgow she pretty much wants me to stalk him.'

'I take it you're not one big happy family?' Ross asked.

'We're not close.' She turned away, unwilling to explain. Their father had died in a road accident when they were toddlers and their mother died when they were teenagers.

26

After her mother's death Wheeler had her first tattoo done, in gothic script between her shoulder blades – *Vita non est vivere sed valere vita est* (life is more than merely staying alive) – and enlisted in the army. Years later, after her last tour of yet another war-torn country, she'd celebrated leaving the army with a final tattoo, *Omnia causa fiunt* (everything happens for a reason). It was a fairytale she hoped would negate the reality of what she'd seen. Too much had happened for no reason. Meanwhile, Jo had met and married Simon Thorne, a Somerset farmer, and twenty years of polite distance between the sisters had followed, until now, when Jason had landed on Wheeler's patch. Wheeler watched Ross leave the CID suite, then she deleted the text.

Chapter 4

Detective Chief Inspector Craig Stewart bumped into Ross in the corridor just outside one of the interview rooms. Stewart's grey hair was shorn as usual, to a peak, and was still damp from the rain. His slate-grey eyes were shrewd. He wore a dark-blue suit, a pink-gold Rolex and a broad gold wedding band. He nodded to Ross. 'I've a few minutes before my meeting with DI Wheeler. I've already interviewed the Wilson boy.'

'Anything?' asked Ross.

'He was giving it the whole "I'm completely innocent" spiel. He should've thought that argument through before admitting that they were there to steal.'

'He made a bad choice there,' Ross muttered, 'but do you think they're in the frame for the murder?'

Stewart frowned. 'I'm keeping an open mind. They've

not a speck of blood on them and they have an alibi for last night, a Christmas party at the youth club. Apparently it's all been uploaded onto Facebook; should be easy enough to check with the other kids who were there. We're already on it. They've never been in trouble before and seem like okay kids, but you never know.'

'Bloody bad luck if they just chanced on a dead body.'

'Certainly it's a coincidence.'

'Confident?'

Stewart shrugged, 'He seemed a bit fazed but not like you or I would be in their place at their age.'

'Can't imagine they did it – they're surely not that stupid that they'd go back the next day and call it in. Then confess all to Robertson when he turned up.'

'Agreed, so even if they're just two boys intent on thieving, I'll give them a bit of a fright, see if it manages to persuade them to get back on the straight and narrow.' Stewart's eyes creased. 'You hear about them being on the bus?'

Ross sniggered.

'So, I'm thinking that boys like that aren't career criminals. Neither of them would last a day in the Bar-L.'

Ross made a cutting gesture across his throat. 'They'd have no chance if they were put in with folk like Maurice Mason.'

Stewart's lip curled at Mason's name. 'Agreed, so it's our job to change the course of their lives. Sit in the observation room if you like. Give me your take on the wee lad. See if that body-language course you took has paid off.' Stewart walked off, leaving a vaporous trail of aftershave lingering in the corridor.

Ross turned to his left. A few seconds later he settled himself into an uncomfortable moulded plastic chair and stared through the one-way mirror. Beside him, Robertson was already ensconced in an identical chair, toe tapping impatiently, staring ahead. Neither greeted the other.

After a few minutes, the interview began.

Alec Munroe sat hunched over a desk which was pock-marked with gouges and graffiti, an untouched mug of weak tea in front of him. He was picking at a weeping cold sore on his top lip. Every few seconds the tip of his tongue appeared, collecting a stray drop of blood. He swallowed hard. His eyes stayed on Stewart as he entered the room, sat at the desk, adjusted his cuffs and fiddled with one of his cufflinks. Boyd lumbered across the room, opened a package and put the tape into the machine. Burped loudly. Didn't bother excusing himself.

Stewart began immediately, speaking clearly, noting the date, time and the participants in the room. He stared at the boy, kept his voice low. 'So Alec, why don't you start by talking me through the events leading up to you and your pal, Robert Wilson, finding the body of James Gilmore. I know that you've already told DS Robertson, but just humour me. Talk me through it.'

Munroe swallowed and looked first at Boyd, then back to Stewart. 'Is there no supposed to be a lawyer here?'

Stewart gave a sorrowful smile and held out his hands, palms up. 'Are you requesting legal representation now, son?'

'No, but . . .'

'But what?'

'Nuthin', jist, see on the telly . . .?' Munroe looked at Boyd. Boyd studied the floor.

'You're not on the telly, son,' Stewart continued, 'you're not even being charged, we just want to know how you managed to stumble on a dead body. Remember your size eight and your pal's size ten footprints are all we have at the scene of a murder.' Good cop. Tone reasonable, but foot tapping impatiently on the lino. A clue to the bad cop about to emerge.

Alec Munroe started to snivel; small hiccupping sounds echoed around the room. He wiped his eyes with the back of his hand, wet running across self-inflicted, amateur tattoos – an eagle, a badly smudged creature which looked like it might have been intended to resemble a snake. All a mess.

Stewart leaned closer, whispered, 'How did you manage to stumble upon a battered-to-death body?'

Silence.

'How did you even know where Gilmore lived?'

Alec sounded confused. 'We jist walked around a bit. It was jist . . . he told a few of us about the area he lived in . . . we walked around a bit,' he repeated, 'till eventually we found it.'

'Do you understand what I'm saying here, son, 'cause this is serious stuff?'

Alec sniffed. Hiccupped. Wiped his hand across his eyes.

'A dead body is the worst sort of trouble you can be in, you know?'

'This wisnae meant tae happen.'

'Okay, tell me what was meant to happen.'

'Naw!' Alec put his head in his hands.

Stewart leaned in at the boy and kept his tone even. 'You will tell me what was meant to happen in that house, son. You will tell me everything. You understand?'

Munroe kept his head in his hands, refusing to look at Stewart.

Stewart leaned across the table, his voice cold. 'And get on with it.'

In the room next door, Robertson was leaning forward in his seat, elbows resting on knees, engrossed in what was happening through the wall. He licked his lips, head bent a little to the side, his features frozen in concentration, following Stewart's every move.

On the other side of the glass Stewart sensed a change in the atmosphere, knew what it meant. Munroe had stopped snivelling, had decided to talk. Stewart stared at the boy and waited. He had all night if need be.

Eventually Munroe began, his voice a whisper. 'We knew where he lived – he'd told some of the folk at school. No exactly the address but it's a wee rutted track. Easy enough to find.' He sniffed quietly.

Stewart sat back in his seat. 'Go on.'

'So we decided, that since he was going tae be at the parents' night, that we'd go and—'

In the next room Ross's chair scraped across the floor when he stood. He'd seen enough.

He was back at his desk in seconds.

'Where've you been?' Wheeler asked.

'Watching Stewart in action, trying to change the course of the two boys' lives or scaring them into a confession. Not sure which; either way, it's not how I'd go about interviewing potential suspects.'

Wheeler sat back in her seat. 'Right, so how he's going about it? Good cop, bad cop stuff – I've seen him do it. It's effective, Ross.'

'Trouble is, it muddies the waters. What if one of them says he did it?'

'Why would they, if they're innocent?'

Ross pursed his lips. 'Maybe they know who did it and they're scared. Maybe it would be safer for one of them to cover for the killer. It's too early to call. The boy's body language says he didn't do it.'

Wheeler chewed at the stray rag nail on her thumb as she

looked at the few notes she had jotted down about James Gilmore. 'I don't think they'd hang around if they were guilty. They might be a wee bit slow but they're not stupid.'

Ross sat at his desk, powered up his computer. 'I think I pissed Stewart off.'

'How so?'

'I mentioned Maurice Mason getting out of the Bar-L. Stewart just about spat when I mentioned his name.'

'How come he's so pissed about Mason?' asked Wheeler.

'Mason got off with manslaughter.'

'So? It's a result. He was put away.'

'Not the one Stewart was looking for – it was his case, remember? You know he has his own moral compass and according to it, Mason should have been done for murder. The boss is going for promotion and the top brass have long memories.'

Wheeler sat back in her chair, looked around the tired room, the flaking paint and the worn furniture and wondered how it was meant to inspire success. She rubbed her eyes. 'Anyway, how long's the interrogation going to be?'

'Not long; it looked like Alec Munroe was just starting to unravel.'

'Wee soul . . . what a nightmare, finding a dead body when all you're trying to do is lift something to sell.'

A cough from the doorway cut her off. Stewart squared his shoulders. 'I think you'll find some of them are a wee bit more savvy than they appear, DI Wheeler. I think that Alec Munroe could get an Oscar for his performance in there, snivelling and sighing like a professional actor. If you're right and they are just lost souls, then we should try to help get them back onto the right path. But let's remember that they were there to thieve; they're not innocent bystanders.

He managed to talk to Robertson at the scene. Why?' He beckoned to her. 'A moment?' He led the way to his office, settled himself behind his desk.

She stood waiting, glanced at the framed photographs on his desk. Him looking like a film star in every one. And his wife, Adrianne, looking the same.

Stewart steepled his fingers, pointing his manicured nails at the ceiling. Then he watched her for a second, licked his lips. 'Wheeler, I think we need to focus on the school. Maybe the two wee muppets back there aren't involved at all, but,' he stared hard at her, 'we still need to keep digging.'

She waited.

'I think that *probably* the two boys aren't involved but in that case we have to eliminate them. Their prints are in the house.'

'But we can explain that.'

'Let's just hold it for the time being. I want you to go make a home visit.'

She knew what was coming even before he said it. A woman's job.

'We're getting someone from Education Personnel out of their beds to get Gilmore's records. Meantime the good news is that Watervale's head teacher, Ms Paton, has been located; the bad news is she's off to a family wedding in Canada first thing in the morning and so she needs to be interviewed tonight.' He handed her a scrap of paper with an address scrawled on it. 'The head teacher's also supplied us with Gilmore's next of kin – his mother lives in a care home in Milngavie.'

'Boss?'

'She's just coming round from an operation and is still groggy. The doctor says to wait until tomorrow when she can understand things a bit more.'

'Surely she should be told first?'

'Not while she can't take it in. You can take Boyd or Ross with you to interview the head teacher. You know you're great at getting information.'

She looked at him. 'Woman's intuition?'

He smiled. 'What? I know you have your own way of working,' he paused, 'but for now though, let's just agree to go with mine? Give it a go?' He held eye contact a fraction too long.

Wheeler tried not to get involved with the smile, stared through the eye contact, telling herself that she was imagining it, that he did trust her to do a good job, that he wasn't just giving her the soft option. But, a jaunt to the West End to interview the head teacher was taking her out of the loop, so she kept her voice equally smooth. 'With respect, boss . . . I'd rather stay here and—'

He didn't bother trying another smile. 'I like your enthusiasm, Wheeler, but the team are already on to it. They're good cops; if there's anything there, they'll spot it.'

'And I wouldn't?'

'Wheeler, we both know you're headed for the top – maybe give others a wee chance to shine? Anyway, the briefing's first thing in the morning, seven a.m. sharp. We'll share all the information we've collected then.' He paused. 'And Wheeler?'

She sighed. 'Boss?'

'The head's waiting.'

She gave a terse nod and closed the door quietly behind her.

They drove west on London Road, past the dirt track leading to Gilmore's house, out past the new housing development, Belvedere Village, houses that replaced the old Belvedere

Hospital, past the huge, looming structure that was the Sir Chris Hoy Velodrome, built for the Commonwealth Games. Out through Bridgton Cross and rows of tenement buildings, past the deserted Barras market, a ghost of itself when closed. They drove along the Gallowgate and the Trongate with its steeple inscribed *Nemo me impune lacessit* (no one provokes me with impunity) and on through the city centre, until they saw the Kelvingrove Art Gallery and the bohemian West End.

A few minutes later they stood in the rain outside Nancy Paton's home. The wind was up and Wheeler shivered inside her coat. Her knock was loud.

Ross whistled. 'Big difference between this and Gilmore's place.'

'Big difference.'

The red sandstone townhouse stood back from the road in its own neat, ornamental garden. Like Gilmore's house it had stained-glass windows, but this time they were all intact, an orderly repetition of Mackintosh-type roses arching across each pane. The frames were painted green to match the door, which had a brass knocker in the shape of a lion's head. A light went on in an upstairs room. They waited.

'Classical architecture this, not like the station,' Wheeler muttered, teeth chattering.

'Aye, the station's brutal. Bit like this weather.'

'Dead on, Ross; I'm impressed.'

'How come?'

'Know how the station's all concrete?'

'Aye, so?'

'When it's built with poured concrete like that it's called Brutalist architecture.' Wheeler hugged her coat to her. 'Thought you'd like to discuss some culture, seeing as we're just standing out here freezing our arses off.'

'Aye, it's a comfort right enough, but I'd rather be inside getting a cup of tea and a heat.'

They saw a light go on in the top-floor landing and a few seconds later the hall light was switched on. The door was finally opened by a brittle-looking woman in her late fifties. She was small and scrawny and her cashmere cardigan hung around her thin frame. Her dark eyes were pitted in a face criss-crossed with lines. On both hands blue veins snaked towards her cuffs and ten curved talons were painted the same red as the slash of colour across her mouth. Her voice was the voice of someone with a lifelong love affair with nicotine. 'Police? A Detective Chief Inspector Stewart called earlier and explained what has happened,' she rasped. Paton studied their ID cards for a few seconds before finally, reluctantly, standing back. 'Dreadful business all this. I suppose you'd better come in.'

'Thanks.' They followed her into a large reception hall.

'This news about James, I can hardly believe it. Just awful, but as I explained to your colleague, I don't really see how I can help.'

She crossed the hall, heels clicking on polished wood; the air was lemon-scented. A huge vase of silk roses dominated a slim glass-and-steel console table. She led them into a sitting room with bow windows offering a view across to the houses opposite. Paton fixed her bony spine on one sofa and beckoned for them to sit on the one opposite. No tea was offered. Wheeler sensed Ross's disappointment.

'So, the CID are visiting me at home about one of my staff.'

'A dead member of staff,' said Ross.

'Suppose you tell me what it is you need to know.'

Wheeler edged forward on her seat. 'We just need some

background on Mr Gilmore, a bit of an insight into what he was like.'

'Well, he usually came in on a Tuesday or a Friday – it depended on his timetable. He stayed an hour or so; I often didn't see him at all. He typed up his reports on the children he was working with, left them in my tray for me. Usually the reports were fairly accurate.'

'Was he married?'

Paton paused. 'Never mentioned it. Only mentioned his mother once.'

'In a home in Milngavie,' said Wheeler.

'Shouldn't you be out there now?'

'She's just coming round from an op. We'll speak to her first thing in the morning.' Wheeler paused. 'What about the children Mr Gilmore was working with; what were they like?'

'He came in to see George Grey,' she paused. 'He'd seen a few of the others in the past, but he's only working with George now.'

'Because?'

'What?'

'Only working with George because . . .?'

Paton lit up a cigarette and sucked angrily on it, the ridges around her mouth gathering together like a concertina. 'We wanted James to work longer sessions with George, to look at building up his self-esteem, to try to get his confidence up to a reasonable level.' She gnawed at the cigarette. 'There are some concerns about George; he's become very withdrawn and uncommunicative recently. Become a bit of a shell. Difficult area, as you can appreciate, getting weans to talk.'

'But there's been something wrong just lately. Any ideas what it might be?'

'Could be anything, knowing his background. You know

the kind of kids we get at Watervale – their lives are usually very difficult.'

'Neglect?' asked Wheeler.

'Neglect in one form or another. Sometimes it's economic, sometimes emotional, sometimes unintentional, but it can be deliberate. On a few occasions it's been worse than just emotional, it can be physical too. We know our kids and George has been acting out of character, becoming tight-lipped and defensive if we ask him what's wrong. Not like his usual chatty self.'

'More than just teenage angst?'

'I wouldn't have asked James to work with him if that's all it was, would I? But George has a hard enough life at home. I wanted to know what was bothering him. See if we could either support him through it or sort it out.'

'George is sixteen?'

She nodded. 'You got kids Mrs . . .?' Another suck on her cigarette, inhaling smoke and tar with relish. 'Or is it Miss Wheeler?'

'Detective is fine. Might it be girl trouble with George?'

'I doubt it.'

'Because?'

'George isn't interested in girls.'

Ross looked up from his note-taking.

'Or boys for that matter.' Paton sucked harder on her cigarette.

'And you'd know?'

'Three of our girls got pregnant last year. Twelve, thirteen and fourteen. There are worse stats out there, but I'm sure you're aware of them. George just didn't show any interest in girls or boys.' She looked at her cigarette, watched the dying embers fade. 'James Gilmore was one of the good guys; he tried to help the kids.'

'So did Mr Gilmore get anywhere with George?' asked Ross.

Paton shrugged. 'Nothing specific, nothing we could use. Said he needed more time. He worked slowly, gained their trust, built up the relationship bit by bit. Things like that take time. George Grey has an awful home life – both mum and her partner are heroin users; they're both off their faces most of the time. It's a bloody minefield. And if we challenge them about the way they bring up George,' she snorted, 'it's their human rights we are violating.'

'Are social workers involved? Can't they do anything?'

'Social worker's been off sick for six months. She's having a breakdown. Her man left her, then hanged himself. Poor cow doesn't know what day it is.'

'Is there going to be a replacement sent out for her?'

'Might get one in a month or two. Cutbacks dictate what will happen.'

'I see what you mean about it being a nightmare.' Ross had got over his need for tea.

'Welcome to my world. End of the academic year and George is out of school and that's that.' Paton looked like she was about to cry. 'And now James has been murdered.' She ground her cigarette stub into a silver ashtray.

Wheeler sat back in her seat. James Gilmore had been battered to death and his body left as a warning. A very disturbing warning. Was it something he'd uncovered in connection with George Grey? Paton lit another cigarette, sucked hungrily on it, then exhaled. She flicked ash towards the ashtray – most of it landed there but the rest settled like silver dust on the polished floor. 'I don't know what'll happen to wee George now. I thought he was really beginning to trust James, that they were establishing a bond. I thought we might be getting somewhere.'

Ross kept his voice neutral. 'What kind of a boy is George, Ms Paton?'

'Nice, he's a nice wee boy,' she squinted through a whorl of smoke at Ross. 'I hope you're not thinking he had anything to do with this?'

Ross pursed his lips. 'I'm sorry, but we need to consider all angles. And also the two boys who found Mr Gilmore, Alec Munroe and Rab Wilson, we need to ask you about them.'

Paton glared at him. 'George Grey has had a shite life. I'm trying to help him and James was trying to help him. Rab and Alec weren't much better off – have you any idea how difficult their lives are?'

'But they were there to steal from Mr Gilmore,' Ross reminded her.

Paton looked to the floor. 'These weans think stealing is nothing; you've no idea what their lives are like. Lifting a few odds and ends from someone's house, even a member of staff, well, we all know better than to take it personally.' She paused. 'You've seen the places they live in? The families they come from? Getting caught stealing's the least of their worries. Besides, Detective Stewart says they called the police when they found the body. Why would they do that if they were involved in James's death?'

Ross and Wheeler let the question hang.

The head teacher got it, her eyes widening. 'You've got to be kidding, a double bluff? They're toying with the police? Good God, Alec can hardly read or write. The only thing he was good at was painting – he helped to paint the backdrop to the Christmas play. I thought he might get taken on with a painter and decorator in the area but nothing as yet. That's where his strength lies. Academically he was very poor, though. As for Rab, he was good at PE, got some awards for boxing – you can tell by his build he'd be a good fighter. I think he took it up for a while, fought a few local fights. Again, not that academic but better than Alec. Rab was also pretty good at drama; he was in the school Christmas play two years hard running. Like us all they had their strengths and weaknesses, but to do this kind of thing? Never.' She sucked on her cigarette and exhaled the smoke through her nostrils, glaring at them like a tiny, angry dragon.

Wheeler watched as the woman seethed then smoked some more, finally calming herself. 'But it was George that Mr Gilmore saw most recently?'

Paton shifted on her seat, crossed then uncrossed her legs, trying and failing to get comfortable. 'George is a lovely boy but he's too distracted to do well. James tried hard with him and, given time, I'm sure he would have found out what was troubling him.'

Ross kept his voice gentle. 'And now James is dead.'

Paton didn't bother to hide her anger. 'You're wasting your time if you think George could do anything like that.'

'Who does George hang out with – is he in with a bad crowd?'

'No, some of the kids at our school are violent, he's not.' She stubbed out the half-smoked cigarette in the ashtray. 'If anyone wanted to kill poor James, I'd be looking at some of the thugs running about Glasgow.'

'We're looking at everyone.'

'Why would Mr Gilmore be involved with thugs?' Wheeler asked.

'He wouldn't; he was trying to do good but sometimes these things are just random,' Paton looked at Wheeler, 'aren't they?'

Wheeler studied the floor for a second, thinking of the time and energy someone invested in beating Gilmore to death. 'Maybe he got to know something he shouldn't have?'

'Like what? If he knew anything important, why wouldn't he come to you? No, I can assure you, this tragedy has nothing to do with either my school or any of the pupils.'

Ross kept his voice level. 'James Gilmore's death was savage.'

Paton shuddered. 'Yes, your DCI Stewart outlined the circumstances.' She moved to the edge of the sofa. 'It has to be a mistake. It's just awful but I'm sorry, there's not much I can tell you. I already told your DCI, there's no way either boy is connected *in any way at all.* I'd bet my whole career on it. Have either of you two met them?'

Wheeler shook her head.

Ross answered, 'No, not yet and I know you're fond of the pupils but to be fair Ms Paton—'

That was it – the head teacher lost her patience. 'FAIR, SON? What age are you?'

Ross stared at her then looked to Wheeler.

Paton continued, 'I'll bet you that I've been a teacher since you were in nappies. I was born and grew up in Glasgow, taught in schools that practically streamed some of the weans towards Barlinnie and you think I've never come across a murder before? Are you serious?'

Ross looked at Paton, swallowed and glanced across at Wheeler.

Wheeler ignored him, recognised the strategy, thought he was pushing his luck.

'Thirty-odd years teaching in Glasgow and you think this is a one-off?' Paton was still angry; her vowels had changed from clipped head-teacher-speak to working-class Glasgow. 'Do me a favour.' She stood. Conversation over. She turned to Wheeler. 'It's not like I'm an unfeeling old bitch but there really isn't anything else I can add. Alec and Rab had nothing to do with it. Neither did George Grey. It's terrible that poor James is dead but you should be out there finding his killer, not going after some poor weans.'

'Was there anything unusual in the days or weeks leading up to this?' Wheeler spoke quickly, aware that Paton had finished with them.

Paton shook her head, 'Nothing out of the ordinary. Well, James did mention that he thought some old correspondence might have gone missing from his briefcase, old bills, that sort of thing. Reminder for a bill or something. Nothing important.'

'Did he report it to the police?'

'What do you think? He wasn't sure, just a couple of old envelopes, a receipt maybe. Not worth the bother. If they were taken at all and he'd not just mislaid them. He wasn't that sure.'

Wheeler kept her voice gentle. 'Thanks anyway. If you remember anything, you know where we are. We'll go into school tomorrow and have a wee word with George, but it'll be a quiet word.'

Paton tapped her arm. 'You see that it is. I won't be there, I've got to go to a wedding, but I'll hear about it. George Grey's a poor wee soul, you see and remember that.'

They retraced their steps into the lemon-scented hallway.

Paton leaned in to Wheeler. 'Even when they were in the first year, so, somewhere between eleven and twelve,' she explained, as if the police might struggle to work it out, 'sometimes Alec and Rab struggled to do up their own shoelaces. They are not capable of this,' she paused, 'unless someone has set it up to frame them. If they have, you find the evil bastards.'

Wheeler paused. 'Did Mr Gilmore work at any other schools?'

'Two others, St Austin's and Cuthbertson High. He used to do a lot more but he was scaling back and had gone part-time. As far as I know he had worked city-wide nearly his whole career so his CV and all his records will be kept at Glasgow City Council, Education Department. We should have copies in the school office. If we haven't lost them. Our filing system's shite at the best of times.'

'Someone from the Education Department is coming out tonight; they'll send us a printout. Were there any friends or colleagues Mr Gilmore was particularly close to?'

'Not that I know of – he stayed to have a coffee now and again in the staff room, but didn't say much. I went weeks without meeting him if I was out and about. I've no idea about his home life.'

Wheeler opened the door and turned back, handed the head teacher her card. 'If you think of anything at all, Ms Paton, will you call it in?'

Paton took the card, glanced at it before slipping it into the pocket of her cardigan. 'If I think of anything I'll call.'

They said their goodbyes. Wheeler and Ross were almost at the pavement when she called after them, 'And if you find out who did this, you'll call me right away, okay?'

Wheeler turned. 'Of course.'

The door closed.

Outside the rain hurled itself against them; the temperature had gone well below freezing. As they walked to the car, Wheeler turned to Ross. 'Well you certainly charmed her.'

'Bit touchy.'

Wheeler walked ahead of him, suddenly exhausted. And hungry.

He read her mind.

'I'm bloody starving. Chips?' Ross looked hopeful. 'My treat?'

'The chippy? Is that the best you can do?'

'God, but you're hard to please. What do you suggest, taking me home and cooking me dinner?'

'Aye, in your dreams muppet, but since this is reality, you can buy me a bar snack and a glass of something chilled.'

Chapter 5

James Weir paused outside the office door and spat into the palms of his hands before smoothing his purple-tipped Mohican into shape and knocking sharply, *rap rap rap*. He waited. Rotated the metal stud in his tongue, felt the new stud in his nipple sting against the heft of his leather jacket and hoped the piercing wouldn't bleed again; his last shirt had been ruined.

He waited some more.

Finally, 'Come.'

He opened the door, walked into the room, his biker boots soundless on thick carpet. The smell of fresh coffee hit him: a top-of-the-range stainless-steel Gaggia gurgled in the corner, hot coffee foaming gently into a single cup. An oak desk the size of a boat took up half the room. He fought the urge to gnaw at his nails. Instead he closed his mouth and let his tongue switch the steel stud against the roof of his mouth. Somehow internal flagellation felt comforting.

He held out a trembling hand. 'Mr Doyle.'

Doyle ignored the hand, let a moment pass before answering, 'Weirdo, how goes it?' Watched the six-foot-four man with warrior piercings twitch.

'Fine, Mr Doyle. Aye great.'

Doyle sighed, 'Wish I could say the same.' He crossed to the coffee machine. 'Need my fix. You're okay for drinks.' A statement.

'Oh aye. Sorted.'

'I've a wee problem; it's no much but it's irritating.'

Weirdo waited, his left leg jerking involuntarily.

'See, Weirdo, I've been watching you and you're making progress. But selling dope to wee university students is child's play and I thought, mibbe you're more ambitious, keen to get on in the organisation?'

'Aye, definitely.' Sweat formed in his armpits; he wiped his nose with the back of his hand. 'Anything you want, Mr Doyle. Consider it done.'

'That's what I thought.' Opening a drawer, Doyle took out a photograph of the house. The address was scrawled at the bottom of the page. 'How's your memory?'

'Excellent.'

'Remember this then.'

Weirdo stared at the address, blinked hard, swallowed.

Doyle gave him a second. 'Nothing much to it. It just needs to be . . .' he put his hands together and made the sound of an explosion, '. . . gone.'

Weirdo nodded.

'Here,' Doyle chucked a brass Yale key at him, 'catch.'

Weirdo grabbed it, ran his finger over the rough of the edge. 'Consider it done.'

Doyle flicked open a lighter and held it under the photograph, watching it burn before tossing it into a metal wastepaper bin. He turned back to Weirdo, stared hard for a second. 'You still here?'

Biker boots stumbling silently across thick carpet.

Chapter 6

The Kelvin wine bar was busy, the music just loud enough to complement but not drown out the chat from the mixed clientele. Wheeler was squashed into a booth in the back room, trying to ignore the braying noises from a group of pinstriped London businessmen who'd escaped from their hotel rooms for a night out in the city. Ross brought back the drinks. 'Overheard one of them ask the barman "Where's the best place to go flirt with the local fillies?"'

She nearly choked on her drink. 'Christ, they'd better watch where they go, they'll be eaten alive. What'd he tell them?'

'Told them to go visit The Sandy Shack Nite Club.'

'The shit-shack? Oh God, they've got no chance of coming out alive. He's an evil git, telling them that.'

'I know, we'll find their bones picked bare in the morning.'

The food arrived and they settled into munching on olives, patatas bravas, hummus, tortilla and the varied contents of the huge bread basket.

'Best pub food in the West End,' said Ross, munching happily.

'You ever put on weight?'

He shook his head. 'Never. Metabolism's too fast.'

'Freak'. She sipped her wine, sat back in her seat and felt the tension slip from her knotted shoulders. 'So, what's your take on the head teacher?'

Ross scooped up an olive. 'I think she knows her kids pretty well.'

'And maybe she sees them through rose-coloured specs?'

'She's a tough old bird; I don't have her down for the sentimental kind but she's convinced none of them are involved in the murder.'

'So, if we take her word for it then James Gilmore's death isn't linked to the school or either Alec Munroe or Rab Wilson.' Wheeler speared a potato.

'Yep. Totally coincidental.'

'Or George Grey for that matter,' Wheeler said.

'Or George Grey.'

'But only as far as she's concerned and she must have a bias towards the kids – you saw how defensive she was.'

'Okay then, let's assume she's wrong.' Ross sipped his Coke.

'You think he was abusing the kids?'

'Could be – there's a hell of a precedent in place, a loner guy who works alone with vulnerable kids. What do you think?'

'I'll keep an open mind but Nancy Paton seemed pretty sure of him and I don't take her for someone who wouldn't be on the lookout for suspicious behaviour. And there are a lot of quiet guys working with kids who are completely trustworthy.'

'Okay, point taken. So what or who are we looking for?'

Wheeler sipped her wine. 'Who else could be in the frame for something this sustained and brutal? It wasn't just a quick attack – he wasn't stabbed in the heat of the moment.'

'Okay. If we look at some of the big players – Tenant, McGregor, Jamieson and Doyle – then I can't honestly see how he'd even know them. But traditionally, a beating like this would be a gangland signal giving out some kind of a warning. It would fit their MO.'

'So, which one of the rogues' gallery uses this way of communicating? What's your gut instinct?' Wheeler attacked the olives. 'McGregor or Tenant? Mason?'

Ross thought for a moment. 'I don't know. They're all definitely capable of it but also they're all complete professionals; they're career criminals. I think if it was McGregor or Tenant, Gilmore might just quietly have disappeared. They'd get rid of the body and move on. They're very subtle about their methods. Remember the two nutters who tried to gatecrash the party and muscle in on the local drug scene a few years back?'

'The newbies? The charming young men from just south of the border who were somewhat overly ambitious and decidedly naive?'

'Those two, exactly. Pete Thorton and what was the other one called, the one with only half a nose left?'

'Osborne, Douggie Osborne. Wee fat thing, looked like a slug.'

'That's them. Well, they disappeared PDQ didn't they?'

'Yep. But they could have just been given a friendly warning and trotted back down south, couldn't they?'

'Or they could be part of the hard core underneath some of our newer roads. What do you think's most probable?'

Wheeler sighed. 'The city's full of gangsters or wannabes.'

'You didn't answer my question,' he prompted. 'Where do you think Thorton and Osborne are now?'

'Gone to sleep somewhere quiet. Subtly spirited away to their resting place by a concerned Glasgow thug playing God.'

'Dead then?'

'Dead,' she repeated, 'dead and buried under a pile of rubble and concrete.'

'Agreed.' Ross clinked his glass to hers. 'So leaving Gilmore's battered body behind has nothing to do with subtlety and everything to do with a warning.'

'Uh huh, I'd say that it was very personal. So, if it was Doyle or Jamieson? Gilmore would have to have known one of them, but how would he? Where would you meet someone like Andy Doyle or Roddy Jamieson? Or Maurice Mason for that matter, and he's only just been released.'

Ross shrugged and scooped up another olive, ate it and then took a slice of bruschetta and dipped it into the oil. 'Maybe happy-clappy Robertson or lovesick Boyd will get lucky with their part in the investigation. Or there might be something interesting in Gilmore's diary. Some event that would link him with one of the big guns. Glasgow's a small city sometimes.'

'Or one of Gilmore's keys might open a Pandora's box of secrets.'

'Aye, and if we're fantasising, there will also be a big long letter written in blood and telling us who did it.'

'So, let's back up here – what was that comment . . . the lovesick Boyd?'

'What?'

She dipped the bread into the last of the hummus and took a large bite before answering, 'Lovesick. You tell me.'

'Boyd's not quite on the ball at the minute.'

'How so?'

'He's in luurve.'

'And that's a problem because . . .?'

'He's in love but it's not with his wife. His eight-months-pregnant wife.'

'Shite.'

'Aye, exactly. It's getting complicated. The poor boy got distracted by a big burlesque dancer he met on his mate's stag do.'

'A what?'

'She's a burlesque dancer at Foaming Frothies.'

Wheeler tried to stop the laugh, but too late it was out. 'Frothies? Fuck.'

Ross wagged his finger at her. 'Not the most upmarket place, I grant you, but the boy's got a wee secret life going on at the minute. In fact . . .'

She held up her hand. 'I don't need to know any more, thanks. As long as he concentrates on the job in hand. But I hope he sorts it out with his wife. I met her once; she seemed . . .'

'Butch?' suggested Ross. 'I met her too; she's ex-navy. He's a brave man two-timing her.'

'Focused,' she corrected him, 'she seemed a very focused woman, given Boyd's so shambolic. Let's hope they work it out, at least for the sake of the child. And anyway,' she smiled at Ross, 'you're not bothered about Boyd being in love because you love Robertson.'

He munched on the last olive. 'Aye, but that's unrequited.'

Wheeler drained her glass. 'Think James Gilmore had a secret life?'

Ross smiled. 'Doesn't everyone?' He held her gaze. 'Even you?'

Wheeler looked away, 'What about the letters, if they were even stolen and not just mislaid? You think there was something incriminating in them?'

'Useless stuff, the head teacher said, old bills or receipts. He could've just lost them. If it had been important to him, surely he'd have reported it to us?'

'What's on a letter, even just an old bill?' Wheeler asked.

'His address, but the boys knew where he lived, said he mentioned it to others at school.'

'I'm not talking about the two boys. If they're not in the frame then I'm talking about someone who might have known where Gilmore worked but needed more information. Someone who wanted to find out where he lived. I'm talking about the killer.'

'Why not just follow him home?'

'And get caught on CCTV trailing someone who winds up battered to death? Wouldn't be clever and whatever else the killer is, he's been clever enough not to leave footprints or much else behind in the house.'

Ross pointed to her glass. 'Same again?'

She shook her head. 'We'd better not, Stewart's scheduled the briefing for seven sharp tomorrow morning.'

'Pity.' Ross pulled on his jacket.

'Yeah, but we're professionals, remember?'

Ross dropped her outside her flat in the Merchant City. She lived halfway down Brunswick Street and Ross slowed before the heavy wrought-iron gates that led to her home. She flicked the remote and the rusty gates rolled back, sighing and creaking to reveal an inner courtyard of old stone, mossy and damp, and worn copper tubs of evergreens and ivy. Her home. In the heart of the arty area of Candleriggs, not quite as trendy as the West End but close. Champagne bars sat alongside the Italian Centre, the Scottish Youth Theatre HQ and a myriad of designer shops. Alongside these were boarded-up shops, half-demolished buildings and enough swaggering hooligans to prevent the area from tipping too far towards gentrification. She turned to him. 'See you in the morning smiler,' then closed the car door and waited until he had reversed the car through the gates before clicking the remote and watching the gates lock.

Inside her flat she kicked off her boots, dumped her coat over the hallstand, the sole piece of furniture in the hallway. She walked through to the lounge: one white sofa, one small glass coffee table, a CD player and a collection of paintings and prints. Her flat had been described as minimalist by one friend, spartan by another, but she liked the austerity of few possessions and felt suffocated by too much furniture or too many belongings. Except art. Wheeler had left the army with everything she owned crammed into one rucksack – that was as much as she needed in her life. She felt the same about relationships: easy, light and temporary suited her best. She crossed to the window and saw below her the streets glistening with rain, darker where it had pooled into shallow puddles. Lights from other windows illuminated the night but the sky seemed to press down on the city. Christmas trees twinkled from numerous windows and reminded her again to buy decorations. She checked her phone. A text from Imogen – apparently the show had been wonderful. Two more texts from her sister, Jo. Jason was still AWOL, could she go and *FIND HIM*? Wheeler glanced at the clock; it was half past one in the morning. She deleted the texts, went through to the fridge and poured herself a large glass of sparkling water. Flicked through the late-night

TV stations. Nothing. Opened the novel she was reading and realised she was too wired to read. Flicked through her collection of Thelonious Monk CDs and chose *Monk's Dream*. She sat on the sofa sipping her water. Decided to text Jason, not expecting an answer.

She was right.

By two o'clock she was tucked up in bed, snoring gently.

In the East End of the city, in a ground-floor flat in Haghill, Lizzie Coughlin pressed the stub of her cigarette onto an upturned saucer, taking the time to grind the ash into tiny flecks before reaching for her mobile phone and checking for missed calls. There were none. No texts either. Nothing. She took the phone across to the window and stared out. Haghill was deserted at this time of the night except for a thin dog, its ribs clearly visible through its coat, wandering through the rain and stopping for a moment to sniff the air before deciding which way to continue. Behind her, her canary, Duchess, moved a little on her perch. Coughlin's voice was scratched with nicotine when she spoke to the bird. 'It's okay Duchy hen, you go to sleep, I'll see you in the morning.' Coughlin scrolled down the numbers on her phone, stopped at Mason's. She started texting furiously: *M where the fuck r u? Get ur arse back here.* Pressed send and heard the chirp of the phone tell her the message had been successfully sent. She waited for a few minutes but heard nothing. She cursed Mason loudly before opening the door to her bedroom and going inside.

Chapter 7

Like other sprawling European cities, Glasgow's ongoing renovation and regeneration had encountered problems. Changes had been enforced in the city and some of the new-world, architecturally envisioned incentives perched nervously beside the resistant old-world buildings. In various parts of Glasgow, shiny new buildings were thrown up in isolation and conflicted with the barren wastelands and derelict tenements that often sat a short stroll away. In the progress-versus-tradition argument, the old pub sat firmly on the traditional, wasted-to-fuck side. Its boarded-up windows were doubly secured with wire mesh and the reinforced door bore the scars of a recent unsuccessful arson attempt. The area was almost desolate; empty premises mourned a displaced or long-dead community and rain battered on corrugated iron nailed across shop fronts. What sign of life there was, came in daylight hours when the bookies and the cut-price booze shop were open and then pale, wasted bodies slipped in and out of each establishment, carefully counting out money to be lost or slugging hard and desperately from bottles encased in brown paper bags.

Maurice Mason stood in the shadows across the road from the pub. He was wearing a second-hand navy-blue imitation-Crombie coat, black chinos, black DM boots and a thick gold bracelet around his wrist. He was bald and drops of rain clung to his skull, like sweat. His hands were stuffed into the pockets of his coat. His pallor was grey. He studied the pub entrance. A few of the neon letters over The Smuggler's Rest had been smashed and the sign now read 'The muggers Rest'. Crudely stapled to a noticeboard were four A4 photocopied sheets of paper advertising nightly pole-dancing, *Girls, Girls, Girls*, until three a.m. Mason waited. The pub door opened and a couple staggered down the side alleyway. They were soon followed by a second couple. The women in both couples were identical twins. Heather and Shona Greg had followed their mother into the profession. And their mother had followed her own mother before that. The twins both wore silver platform boots and Shona was already hiking her miniskirt up around her waist as she entered the alley. Two minutes later Shona walked back out, the man walking ahead of her, zipping his fly and turning away from the pub. Shona turned into the doorway, shoved a five-pound note into her plastic handbag and tugged her skirt back into place. A few minutes later Heather emerged behind the second man. As he walked away, she bent over and spat heavily on the road before following her sister back into the pub.

Mason crossed the road and went inside. Behind the bar

an obese man, his face smothered by tattoos, looked up. 'Mason you old bastard, you out already?'

'Looks like it, Sonny.' Mason smiled, baring his teeth.

Sonny returned the same smile. 'Time flies, eh?'

'Aye, it does.'

'How goes it?'

Mason tried to keep his voice even. 'No too bad.'

'Nah, been in for longer myself. The Bar-L's no the worst of places.'

'Not the worst,' Mason agreed.

'Cosy wee place.'

'Aye, sometimes gets a bit crowded though. And I fucking hate that you can't wear your own gear.' He patted the lapel of his coat as if stroking a kitten.

In the corner of the bar the sound system cranked into life and a small, skinny woman in her late forties took to the floor, gyrating around a steel pole. After a few seconds she began tugging at the red nylon Santa outfit she was wearing.

The barman shook his head, 'Fucking mental that Gail. Told her it's one size fits all but can she stop clawing at herself? Can she fuck. It's no hygienic and it puts the punters off.'

'Mibbe she's got worms?' sniggered Mason.

'Naw, it's worse,' said Sonny.

Mason watched Gail dance. Recognised the signs: features exhausted by a long and committed diet of alcohol, drugs and violence. A jagged scar ran from thigh to knee. Thin strands of peroxide hair clung limply to her misshapen skull as she gyrated against the pole. Her eyes were already dead.

Mason glanced around the room. 'That Gail looks knackered.'

'Well spotted, Mason.'

'Can you no dae any better than that, Sonny?'

'Nabody else willing to dae it, wages we pay.'

'You one of they not-for-profit organisations then?'

'Aye very funny. I've got overheads like every other fucker in this business.'

Mason risked another furtive glance. 'Anybody still knocking about these parts or have things moved on since I was inside?'

'Jamieson or McGregor or what? Who are you looking for?'

Mason's voice was low. 'Either or. Mibbe no one. Just trying to get the lie of the land, that's all.'

'Okay, well Weirdo took a look in earlier. On the hunt for somebody. Didnae say who. Doyle I haven't seen for donkey's and the rest don't bother – they like tae be seen in classy wine bars. A bit more upmarket, where the money is.'

Mason licked his lips.

'But there's been a wee upset lately.'

'Oh aye?'

'Course you've probably heard.'

'Go on.'

'Guy name of Gilmore got mashed.' He studied Mason's face, waited for a response, maybe recognition. Got nothing. Gave up. 'You been hame yet tae see Lizzie?'

Mason shook his head. 'Cannae be arsed. I fancy becoming a freelancer, flying solo.'

'That right?'

'Aye, commitments just drag ye down.'

'Totally agree, Mason. Family and commitments, can't see the point of either myself. I had tae clear my old man's house last year after he died. House was full of shite. Should've just put a match tae it and watched it burn.'

'Aye, you should've just torched it,' Mason agreed, watching Gail claw at her crotch.

'Took most of it to the skip. A few bits and pieces I sold. Hardly worth the bother.'

'Nae inheritance tax tae keep ye up all night worrying then, Sonny?'

'Nuthing keeps me up at night, Mason, it's called a clear conscience. Whit about you? You got big plans with all this talk of freelancing?'

Mason felt the package in his pocket. 'I've got a wee plan. A friend of mine in the jail's got me ontae something.'

'Oh aye, whit's that then?'

'Let's just say that I've come intae a bit of merchandise; it'll give me a wee income.'

'Merchandise?'

'Aye, I think it might roll and roll.'

'And I suppose it's top secret?'

'Correct.'

'You staying for a pint or are ye just farting in the wind?'

'Might as well have a pint, if the coast's clear. Pint of heavy.'

He paid and took his drink to a table at the back of the room. Mason made a point of sitting with his back to the wall, giving him a clear view of the door. He took out the package and looked inside. Saw the home-made video his cellmate Davey Tenant had made all those years ago. Smiled. Piece of luck Davey and him sharing a cell and Davey telling him where to find the video when he got out. They were splitting the money 50/50. Mason paused, thought about the money, what he could do with it, then he put the package back in his pocket.

'All in good time,' he muttered to himself. He sat back, ignored the come-on from the twins and watched the scarred Gail gyrate and twirl, lost in a world of her own.

Outside the rain fell in sheets against the building, hammering on the roof and pouring from the gutters as if the water were trying to sluice the old pub from the city and make room for something cleaner and less contaminated.

Chapter 8

By four a.m. the rainfall, which had waned temporarily, began increasing again and with it the wind. Rows of street-lights struggled to emit their glow as the weather settled in over them and to walk any distance from their dim light meant that visibility was poor. No matter, Weirdo knew what he was doing. He parked the car in a residential street a quarter of a mile away and walked back to London Road in the downpour, his biker boots squelching over concrete pavement. Eventually he stopped at the edge of the graveyard wall and breathed in. The night air was heavy with earth and wet and decay. The wind shrieked and howled past his ears and pawed at his coat; his Mohican lay crushed and flat under his black beanie hat. Raindrops fell on his skin and rolled down his face. He took a few steps back and then half jogged, half ran towards the lowest part of the wall and began clambering over. Lichen had woven itself through the stones, making it difficult to climb, and he slipped and slithered over the wall.

On the other side he landed heavily, rasped a cough and doubled over trying to get his breath. The bottle rattled against the lighter in his pocket and the smell of petrol cut through the sodden air.

He crept on through the graveyard, stumbling over toppled headstones and discarded debris, empty bottles and syringes nestled beside tinfoil and used needles. His biker boots crunched on broken glass and the sound reverberated around the abandoned graveyard.

He paused.

Waited.

Listened.

Nothing.

Weirdo started on again. Felt the rain smear his face. Heard the wind wail through naked trees and wind its way around ancient headstones, loud enough to summon the dead.

Finally he reached the far wall and scrambled over. He fell hard on the frozen ground and heard the crack of his knee against stone. 'Fuck Fuck Fuck.' He felt for the pain, blood on his leg, designer jeans ripped at the knee and then he whispered a curse to a man already dead, 'You cunt, Gilmore. Fuck you to hell and back.'

Weirdo limped on, taking a wide skirt around the dirt track where the police car was parked. He kept under the cover of shadows until he was at the back door of the house. Christ, his knee hurt. He felt for the knife in his pocket, slashed the air silently. The police tape offered no resistance to his blade. He slid the Yale key into the lock. Once inside, he stood in the darkness, listened to the silence, waited for his heartbeat to slow, then he quickly stuffed the rag into the bottleneck, flicked his thumb on the lighter and when the flame caught, hurled the bottle against the wall and heard it shatter. The flames rose, catching the hem of the filthy curtains and devouring them in seconds, then searched greedily for more to consume.

Weirdo bolted, running and gasping through the freezing night air, the metal stud raw against the tender flesh of his nipple. Bleeding hard. Like his knee. Pain, adrenaline, the fire already blazing behind him. On he went, cursing and running. Not looking back. Trusting himself and the job he had done.

But there was no need to look back.

Out front, the light flicked for a moment before beginning to spread. First the hall erupted into a fireball and then the rest followed. Weirdo was halfway across the graveyard when he heard the sound of shattered glass as the windows blew, belching black smoke into the wet night.

He stood for a second watching the scene, before running through the graveyard, over the wall, limping to his car and climbing inside. He headed home the long way, ignoring the distant wail of a fire engine. Felt a rush of pleasure. Andy Doyle would be pleased.

Job done.

DREAMER

The Dreamer turns in his sleep, eyelids flickering, unaware of the rain falling outside the window. Instead he is reliving another night, hearing the rain on another roof, the sound of breath leaving another man's body. The groan of the wind outside. The night he had killed Gilmore had been the stormiest night since records began. He had watched the water course from the roof tiles as if the weather itself were trying to wash the house free from blood. The Dreamer moves in his sleep as images flash across his mind, blood mixed with matter. Blood and water. The blood of sinners mixing in some unholy communion.

Chapter 9

Tuesday, 10 December

It was six a.m. when Wheeler returned from her morning run. She showered, dressed and was out of the door twenty minutes later. On the way to the station she listened to a CD, humming along to Sonny Rollins while she systematically revised all the evidence they had gathered so far in the case. By the time she drove into the station car park, she had come to no new conclusions as to why James Gilmore had met with such a brutal death but she knew that the team would uncover more and more pieces of the jigsaw, until they had the complete picture. She opened the door to the station and felt the familiar sense of anticipation that descended on her at the beginning of each case.

She was early for the briefing and sat nursing a black coffee, waiting for the others to arrive. The room was chilly; a forlorn halogen heater rotated mutely at the front of the room, giving off a bright light but precious little heat. The station would heat up as the day progressed and be sweltering before midday. Wheeler looked out of the window: it was still dark outside. Inside, the room was in a seventies time warp. It was a large room, walls the colour of vomit, the skirting a peculiar sludge shade. The parquet flooring had suffered over the years and was now chipped and pieces that were missing had been ignored, leaving the floor uneven. The obligatory fluorescent light flickered lazily overhead. By seven a.m. the room was full and the whole team was assembled; those on night shift were bleary-eyed, needing their beds, while the day shift were yawning, not long out of theirs, but Stewart had requested that everyone attend.

Stewart strode to the front of the room and placed his notes on a desk, patting them firmly into place as if that would create some kind of order from the chaos of their predicament. He cleared his throat and looked at the team, keeping both his voice and his gaze controlled.

'Can anyone tell me how in God's name James Gilmore's house got torched last night?'

Some of the team looked at him, some looked at the floor, others studied the wall. All of them said nothing. Wheeler waited. She knew that the two uniformed cops who'd been in the patrol car were going to be *severely reprimanded* and that Stewart was going to *personally* investigate. And after that the two officers would still face disciplinary action. Wheeler, like the rest of the team, knew that the shit had hit the fan and was about to drip all over them.

Then Stewart let himself go. 'Did you hear what I said?' he bellowed, banging his fist on the desk. In front of him, officers shifted uncomfortably on their seats but didn't voice what they were thinking, that last night's debacle had nothing to do with them. They were part of a team, and somewhere down the line of command someone had messed up and now they were all complicit.

'But surely the evidence had already been removed.' Ross spoke clearly, attempting to move the briefing on. 'So, nothing of any note could have been lost in the fire.'

Stewart turned on him. 'Nothing of any note was lost? Forgive me, Ross, I didn't know that you were psychic. A wee talent you've kept hidden?'

Ross's blush moved from his neck to his cheeks. 'What I mean, boss, is that—'

But Stewart cut him off. 'Is that meant to make me feel better? That at least we managed to collect *some* evidence before the place was torched? And since you're psychic, perhaps you'd like to tell us who managed to get by two of Strathclyde's finest and burn the bloody house down?' Speckles of spit escaped from Stewart's mouth and landed on his notes.

Ross kept his eyes on the floor. Said nothing.

Stewart turned from him and addressed the team. 'So, despite our best efforts and you will admit they haven't been *sterling* so far, the killer or killers managed to murder James Gilmore, then sneak back into the house *under our noses* and destroy whatever else it was they didn't want us to find. But thank you, *acting* DI Ross, I'm gratified that in your opinion we've no cause to worry.'

Nervous sniggers spread around the room. Stewart ignored them. 'So, let's move on. Who was James Gilmore?'

Wheeler spoke. 'James Gilmore, age fifty-four, lived alone. Unmarried. Worked as an educational psychologist peripatetically in Glasgow schools.'

Stewart continued, 'A victim who was found by two former pupils of Watervale Academy beaten to death in his own home.' Stewart glanced behind him; photographs of the body had been pinned onto the board. He waited for a few seconds, letting the team take in the horrendous images. Watched the faces scowl in concentration as they registered the bloody purple of Gilmore's battered flesh and the hook on which the body had been hung.

'Okay. Now we know what we're dealing with, I want you to think about who would do something like this.' He looked around the room then continued, 'What do we have?'

Silence.

'Well, let's get updated. Someone must have seen something. Let's start with door-to-door enquiries.' He pointed to a uniformed officer in the second row. 'Well?'

'Door-to-door gave up nothing helpful, boss. It seems that Gilmore's house is too remote for him to have anyone just passing by. A few neighbours knew him by sight and said that they were on nodding terms with him but nothing more. There were never any invites round for drinks or dinner; apparently he never socialised with any of his neighbours. Not even a card at Christmas, nothing. He kept himself very much to himself.'

'A ghost,' muttered Ross.

'What was that?' Stewart turned towards him.

'Nancy Paton, the head teacher at Watervale, made it sound like Gilmore came and went so quietly it was like he was a ghost,' he paused, 'albeit, according to her, a benign one.'

Stewart pursed his lips. 'So, he came and went without any real presence? Your take on him, Ross?'

'The guy was a bit of a loner – he'd no wife or girlfriend and he worked with kids on a one-to-one.' He paused, letting the possibility hang in the air.

'Any evidence?'

Ross shook his head. 'Nothing.'

Stewart looked at Wheeler. 'What's your gut instinct about the head teacher? Do you think she trusted him?'

Wheeler nodded. 'Absolutely. She said he was very good with the kids.'

'Then keep an open mind.' Stewart glanced around the team. 'Last known movements?'

More silence.

Wheeler spoke again. 'Hard to tell – he wasn't due at Watervale until today. He had two other schools on his rota,' she checked her notes, 'St Austin's and Cuthbertson High. I'll call them today. Send someone over to interview the staff.'

He looked at her, the tension easing from his face. 'Good and check receipts, find out where he did his shopping, get CCTV from the stores. Where did he buy his petrol? They must have CCTV in the forecourts. Which garage did he use to get his car MOT'd? Check all of the usual background information.' He paused. 'Education personnel have emailed Gilmore's file and it chimes in with what Ms Paton said about the other schools. James Gilmore's mother is in a home in Milngavie. She's recovering from a minor operation but I've sent two uniformed officers and an FLO to break the news to her.'

'The death knock,' muttered Ross.

'And DI Wheeler will go see her today,' said Stewart. 'Now, did you get anything else from the head teacher?'

Wheeler glanced at her notes. 'Nothing much, boss. She said James Gilmore was one of the good guys, tried to help the kids at school. He worked with one child in particular, George Grey. Gilmore had no real conflict with any of the kids, no run-ins, he was generally seen to be on their side,' she paused, 'and Ms Paton was particularly adamant that neither Alec Munroe nor Rab Wilson could've been involved in his death.'

'She said she'd bet her whole career on it,' added Ross.

'Well that's understandable, given that she was their head teacher, but let's not just take her word for it – let's try to keep an open mind, shall we?' Stewart steepled his fingers. 'They're neither in nor out of the frame. At this point good police work is about gathering information and evidence – it's too early to eliminate anyone unless we know conclusively that they had no involvement in the murder.'

Wheeler drummed her fingers on the side of her chair. 'The kids definitely couldn't be involved. No blood spatters, boss, no scratches, nothing.' She'd spoken her thoughts out loud.

'Remember, Wheeler, theirs are the only footprints we have at the scene,' said Stewart.

'The killer was careful, boss, wiped the place down before he left. He's a pro. These kids are less than amateurs,' said Wheeler.

'But they could've known whoever did it,' suggested a female uniformed officer sitting at the back of the room. 'It could've been one of their pals – a school like that, who knows?'

'Or a brother, father, uncle,' agreed Boyd. 'Gilmore could have upset someone associated with the school.'

'It would have to have been a very bad upset to result in a murder,' Ross said.

Stewart tapped his fingers on his notes. 'So for the moment it's too early to dismiss the idea that the murder isn't linked in some way to the school. What do we know about the place?' He looked around the room, 'Anyone have any direct dealings with Watervale Academy in the past?'

Only one person nodded.

'Well, spit it out Robertson.'

All eyes were on him and Robertson flushed. 'It was personal business, sir.'

'Not now it isn't. Go on. Shoot.'

'Outreach, sir.'

'Sorry, come again?'

'My hall—'

'Your hall?' Stewart interrupted.

'The Gospel Hall I belong to, sir, we do outreach. We go into schools, give a wee talk about God and try to get to know the kids. We spend a bit of time telling them how to accept God, try to get them to listen to . . . the right side of things.'

'And that's it?'

'Well, we also encourage them to come to Sunday School and Bible-study class. To turn to the Lord and be saved.'

'Bible-bashers,' said Ross under his breath, 'happy-clappies.'

Stewart looked at Ross. 'Unhelpful.'

'So did anyone from Watervale come to the classes?' Boyd asked.

'A few,' Robertson replied, 'but not recently. This was over a year ago. A couple of kids came for a few Sundays, then they tailed off. By that time we were recruiting in . . . I mean we were visiting . . . other schools.'

'And Gilmore?'

'I only met him once or twice, in passing. We didn't have a real conversation.'

'He didn't want to be saved then?'

Sniggers around the room.

Robertson ignored them. 'He'd no interest in our work, sir, none at all.'

Stewart grunted before turning to the rest of the team. 'Moving on, I want you all out there. I want someone to go pay a visit to the local youth club.' He checked his notes. 'It's being run by an ex-con name of Malcolm Miller, known as Manky. Apparently there was a party the night of the murder. DI Wheeler, you get back to the school, get a feel for the place, find out what sort of a guy Gilmore was and check out the kids, see if any of them had a grudge against him. See if there were any incidents reported.' He held up his hand, palm facing the team. 'And no, I'm not convinced Alec Munroe or Rab Wilson had anything to do with this, but as mentioned they all have big brothers, dads, uncles. Remember the scheme the school's in – a fair few of the residents are candidates for Barlinnie and Manky Miller was inside himself.' Stewart looked at the team. 'Okay?'

Nods and agreement.

'And while we are on the subject of Barlinnie residents, Maurice Mason's been released and according to our snitches he's gone AWOL. Mason gets out of Barlinnie and someone is found murdered; let's just be aware of the coincidence.' He clapped his hands together. 'Okay, let's get to it. I want to know everything about James Gilmore by close of play today, at the latest. DI Wheeler will dish out your chores. And I want the case done and dusted by Christmas, not hanging over me when I'm lying on a beach sunning myself. Okay?'

More nods and grunts of agreement all round. Stewart shuffled his large sheaf of papers into a semblance of order and marched out.

Wheeler walked to the front of the room and pointed at Boyd. 'Go through Gilmore's address book; call everyone in it. Follow up every lead, no matter how small.'

He grabbed his jacket. 'Aye, of course, but first off, a coffee and a minute to eat my breakfast roll, though. I'm starving.'

'God almighty, if you must, but be quick,' said Wheeler.

'I've been up all night,' he smirked.

She remembered what Ross had told her about Boyd's new girlfriend. 'Too much information, Boyd – I don't need to know.' She turned to Robertson. 'You take the sets of keys, find out what they open and where. He must have secrets somewhere; there was sod all in his house.'

'He must have a secret life,' Ross chimed in.

'Maybe there's no secret life,' said Robertson sourly. 'Believe it or not, not everyone has one.'

'In which case, you're fucked,' Ross answered, 'so you'd better start *praying* the keys are to a Pandora's box of goodies leading us to the killer.'

Robertson flushed.

'Ignore him, Robertson, he's on his period.' Wheeler glanced at the list of objects found in Gilmore's house. 'There are a couple that don't look like house keys. Sort through them, find out what they open. And search through his diary, see where he's been, who he's spent time with, go through his mobile, ring all the numbers stored on it. Find out who he called last. Double up with Boyd and split the lists.'

'Already onto it.' Robertson held up a list of names and numbers. 'So far all the calls have been to schools and his mother's home.'

'Okay, good. Keep at it. And both of you take a trip out to the youth club. Speak to Miller, try to get some idea of who was at the party on Sunday night and find out if Alec Munroe and Rab Wilson were there all night.' She spent the next few minutes issuing orders, trying to galvanise the day shift while hoping to keep the sleep-deprived night shift inspired. Then the briefing was over.

As she gathered her notes, two uniformed constables walked past her and one muttered, 'I think the two lads are definitely in on it.'

'Nah,' the other said, 'breaking and entering. That's about the height of them. Criminal fucking masterminds they're not. Poor weans were white with shock. I heard that wee Munroe laddie started crying. Wanted his mammy. Christ, no way he could've battered anyone to death.'

'You'd be surprised. Delayed shock maybe? Good actor?'

'Nah. You're talking shite. They're innocent.'

'Want to bet on it?'

'Fair enough, how much?'

Wheeler watched them leave the room and thought that their conversation accurately summed up the team. Divided.

Ross turned to her. 'Watervale it is then? But can we stop off for coffee on the way? I'm starving.'

'Can't think why – you had loads to eat last night.'

'That was a whole other day away. Besides,' he said, patting his stomach, 'I need to keep myself refuelled.'

'We don't have time and anyway, you're not a bloody racehorse, Ross.'

She was out of the door and down the corridor before he'd finished saying, 'See myself more as a stallion, Wheeler.'

Chapter 10

Tuesday, 9 a.m.

'. . . And why was that?' The woman stared at him.

No answer.

The wall clock tick-tocked softly in the background. Outside the window the steady thrum of traffic from Clarkston Road passed underneath the second-floor office. Rush hour, mothers dropping children off at nursery, school, playgroup, childminder. Folk going to work. Day shift driving in to start the day, night shift driving home. HGVs in for the long commute across Europe. A world busy with itself, the everyday noise only mildly dampened by the constant beat of rain against the window pane.

Dr Sylvia Moore sat in a leather and chrome Le Corbusier chair, her long legs crossed, her red hair shorn tight to her head. She wore a fitted black trouser suit, a heavy gold watch and flat patent leather brogues. Her face was free from make-up.

She repeated the question, 'Why was that?' adding, 'Do you think?'

This time an answer. 'Why was what?'

'Why did you feel you couldn't reach out to her?'

Doyle shrugged, 'Who knows?'

Her voice hard, 'You do, Andy. You know why you couldn't reach out to her.'

His fist on the side of the Le Corbusier, skin on chrome, harsh, beating. 'She's a fucking woman, I don't know! I don't understand you lot.'

'Us lot?'

'Fucking women. I mean, I buy her stuff, anything she wants. I paid to go to a charity do, paid to get sat at the same table as some fucking art-house producer who needs "investment" for his next project, some play about fuck-knows-what. All for Stella.'

'But that's not enough, is it? She wants more . . . what is it she wants?'

'Fuck knows.' He paused. 'She wants to be a star but she's got fuck-all talent.'

'If Stella was here what would she say? Apart from you buying her stardom, or at least a part in a play, what else does she want from you?'

Shrug.

The gentle tick-tock of the clock; outside a police siren screamed past, its wail fading in seconds.

'Is she in love with you?'

A shrug. 'Mibbe. But I don't understand her.'

'Do you want to understand Stella?'

Another shrug.

'Would it be different if you were in love with her?'

'Probably.'

'But you're not?'

'No.'

'Then you're just stringing her along?'

'Love isn't what I need.'

'Most people need to be loved, to feel wanted, appreciated, connected.'

'Good for them, but I'm not most people.'

'No.' Moore watched him, saw the anger leave him. 'So, what is it you need, Andy?'

She waited while the pause stretched over several seconds.

He glanced at his watch. 'Time's up. I'm out of here.'

'We're not finished.'

'I am.' He stood.

'Then you're bailing out.'

'Christ.' He sat down again.

'You need to look at your actions, take responsibility for yourself and your interactions with others. You're not a child, you're a grown-up. Stop acting like a spoilt child.'

His eyes glittered, one darker than the other, his voice a whisper, 'I do fucking take responsibility for everything I do. And I am always a fucking adult. And I am not a spoiled child.'

'We need to work with this.'

'You need to work with this.'

'What is it you need from others?'

'One word. Loyalty.' He stood, had reached the door in a second.

'Same time, same place,' she called after him.

Heard the sound of the door slamming.

Moore stood, crossed to the window and opened it wide, letting the cold, damp weather seep into the room. She breathed in deeply, held the icy air in her lungs for as long as she could before exhaling. The city was bathed in a grey glow made colourful by the umbrellas bobbing beneath her window. Moore crossed the room and lifted Andy Doyle's untouched water glass, took it into the next room and began to rinse it under the tap. Watched as the water ran clean and cold.

Chapter 11

Watervale.

Ross drove. The scheme was similar to dozens of schemes across the city. Rows of council semis lined the streets; a few empty houses had their windows boarded up, metal grilles securing the doorways. A low one-storey building had a hand-painted sign on plywood: *'Watervale Youth Club.'* A skinny cat shot across the road into a garden littered with broken glass. Dog shit dotted the pavement. A group of boys huddled together in the cold, their staffie-cross straining at its leash. As Wheeler and Ross drove past, the boys turned and stared hard at them. Wheeler smiled. They gave her the finger.

'Fucking clichés,' Ross grinned, turning into the school car park. 'They look like they're auditioning to be in a Peter Howson painting.'

'Bless,' said Wheeler, 'making their wee mammies proud.'

Watervale Academy was a two-storey building thrown up in the seventies and then forgotten. It was covered in graffiti and the windows had a protective covering of wire mesh, through which crisp and sweet wrappers had become entangled together with assorted plastic bags. The door was locked. Wheeler pressed the buzzer beside the intercom and heard a voice ask who they were. She spoke into it, heard the door click open and they were through to the reception area where a small woman with a round, kind face held out her hand. 'Pleased to meet you. I'm Margaret Field, the deputy head teacher.'

They showed her their ID.

'It's dreadful news about James Gilmore. Just awful. Nancy Paton called me – what a nightmare.' She pushed a book across the desk. 'I'm afraid you'll need to sign in, just name and time. Rules.'

They signed.

'I've set up an interview room for you; I hope it'll be okay.'

'Great, thanks,' said Ross.

'Every class has a classroom assistant,' she continued, 'so I've arranged for each teacher to come and speak with you, then go back and then the assistant will come. That way you get to see everyone, but the class remains covered at all times. Does this suit?'

'Perfect,' Ross said.

'Did you know Mr Gilmore?' Wheeler asked and she could feel the woman draw away from her.

'No, not really. A hello now and again. Tuesday was his usual day. I take assembly on Tuesdays, so I was never in the staff room much. He seemed to just pass in and out.' She gave a nervous laugh. 'What is it about the police that always makes me feel a bit guilty?'

'Everyone feels a bit like that.' Ross gave her a wide smile.

They walked through the main corridor; there was pupil artwork on the walls and a glass case with two large silver trophies. Wheeler glanced at them – they were two years out of date. She saw various framed photographs of winning teams at other presentations. Again out of date. A few Certificates of Merit were more recent.

'I hope you don't think the death is connected to the school?' The deputy's smile didn't reach her eyes. 'The kids here can be a handful but none of them would do that. I'm sure of it. Neither Alec Munroe nor Rab Wilson had anything to do with this awful mess.'

'Ms Paton's already told us as much.'

'I'm sure she did and she was right to.'

'Do you know the boys well?'

'Alec needs to be getting an apprenticeship for painting and decorating; it's his best chance of work. Rab could do a few things, loves drama, always nattering on about NCIS or the other shows. He was a good boxer too. They are good kids who are struggling with different challenges. This place was their refuge against a hostile world. It becomes home to many of them, when their own home is a place of neglect or hostility. We do our best to make the building as welcoming as possible. Except the exterior – the council are refusing to come out and paint over it again. Seems we've been vandalised once too often, taxpayers' money, accountability, that kind of rubbish response.' The deputy head wasn't happy. 'How can the kids feel safe and protected when the council won't even paint the place?'

'About Mr Gilmore,' Wheeler reminded her.

'Yes, sorry, I didn't really know him well – he was peripatetic.'

'But you must have had meetings, surely, about the children?'

'Of course, but they are usually multi-departmental and I'm often called away. He was a quiet, professional man who seemed content enough in his job. Not someone who made waves. He wasn't loud or challenging. He seemed decent enough . . .' she trailed off.

Three hours later and they'd heard the same thing a dozen times, different variations on Gilmore's lack of presence.

'I didn't really know him – he just came in and out of the school. A couple of times he came to meetings with the social worker, Mary Burns; she's off long-term sick. Stress. Her husband . . . poor soul.'

'No idea he lived alone. Never really knew him. Sent a note to class when he needed to interview any of the kids, then I'd send them off to him. Hardly had any dealing with the man. Mary Burns might know, but she's off sick.'

'Seemed a nice enough man. Was he married? Leave any family? It's a tragedy, isn't it? We were all in shock.'

'Just awful. No, I never really spoke to him. Just sent the kids he wanted to work with along to him and then he sent them back, typed up his reports and emailed them to me.'

'He could've been a ghost, weaving his way in and out, not leaving a trace.' They were alone together and Ross sipped the coffee the school secretary had brought them. He helped himself to another chocolate biscuit from a plate piled high with biscuits, cake and fingers of shortbread. He saw Wheeler look at him. 'What? I'll work it off at the gym. Right now I need to refuel.'

Wheeler heard the frustration in his voice. They'd seen the desk James Gilmore had used; nothing personal had been stored there. They'd asked to speak with George Grey. 'George is off sick today. When he didn't come in this morning we called home. He said he had a bug.' Wheeler had copied down his address – a wee home visit was in order.

Finally she stood. 'Let's go, Ross, nothing much's happening here.' She took the tray back in to the secretary. 'Thanks for the coffee and biscuits.'

'Awful shock about Mr Gilmore.'

'Did you know him?'

'Only to say hello to when he signed in and out.'

Figured.

'Not one to talk about his social life then?'

'I think he did mention his mother once, said that she was quite poorly.'

Wheeler put the tray on a table. 'Yes, we're on our way there now. Did he say much about her?'

'Only that she was often poorly. I said mine was too. It was just in passing.' The secretary screwed up her eyes in concentration. 'I think she's in a home out by Milngavie. I can't be sure but I got the impression it was out that way. I could check if you like?'

'We already have her address thanks,' said Wheeler.

They walked to the car in the rain. Wheeler spotted him first. 'Looks like we're being watched.'

Ross looked at the boy who was sitting on his bike, watching them. His knuckles showed white as he gripped the handlebar. His hood was pulled tight around his face; only two dark eyes and a scowl were visible. Ross walked towards him, but immediately the boy pushed off on his bike and a second later he had disappeared around the corner of a house.

'Too old to be a schoolie.'

'So are Alec Munroe and Rab Wilson but they seem connected to the place.' Wheeler stared at the houses. 'You think there are kids behind those curtains watching us?'

Ross glanced down the road; he could feel eyes watching but there was no one in sight. 'Probably – we're the pigs, remember.'

'Come on,' Wheeler opened the car door, 'let's go to Milngavie and speak to James Gilmore's poor old mother. I hope she's not too much of a wreck.'

'She's bound to be in pieces. Her only son's dead. I just hope she can hold it together long enough to talk to us.'

A few minutes later they were on their way.

Chapter 12

The car was idling at a red light on the road to Milngavie. The radio was on, a debate about the recent spate of violence against the lesbian, gay, bisexual and transgender community in Scotland was just finishing. Wheeler reached for the volume and turned it up. She knew Callum Fraser was very active in the community and may have been interviewed for the programme.

'Shocking statistics have just been revealed which suggest that hate crimes that target individuals because of their sexual orientation are on the increase. The number of reported cases of homophobic abuse, including violent attacks, has increased dramatically in the past four years.

'Strathclyde Police spokesperson DI Andrea Sinclair had this to say: "We are aware of the on going struggle to bring the perpetrators of these crimes to justice, but we are committed to doing so. We firmly believe that, while the statistics show an increase in attacks against the LGBT community, there is also an increase in convictions. We work hard with the LGBT community and hope that all incidents are reported. This way, a firm message is sent out to the wider community that these kinds of hate crimes will simply not be tolerated. Prejudice, whether based on gender, race, religion or sexual orientation, has no place in a modern Scotland."'

The lights changed. The programme ended and a jingle advertising The Sandy Shack Nite Club began. Ross reached forward and switched off the radio. 'You think Gilmore might've been gay?'

Wheeler stared out of the window, watched the grey clouds scudding across the sky. 'Could have been. Nothing seems to point at much in the way of relationships, either way.'

'But he wasn't openly gay, like Callum. I mean, no one even hinted at anything at Watervale.'

'No, but I'd imagine it wouldn't be easy to come out if you were part of the educational establishment.'

'Especially when you're working with kids who might give you a bit of a hard time.'

'Yep, it wouldn't be just a bit of joking from the kids themselves. The usual prejudices might emerge from the other teachers or parents. It could've been tough going and maybe he preferred to keep his sexuality private.'

'Do you think it might have been a hate crime?' Ross asked.

'From a group of anti-gay vigilantes? Doubt it somehow.'

'Or maybe an ex-lover? Or back to square one and keep an open mind?' Ross stopped the car at a red light.

'Square one for the time being; until we gather more of the pieces of the jigsaw, we can't see a pattern emerging.'

Ross watched the light change to green, moved the car forward.

She reached across and touched his shoulder.

He glanced at her, 'What?'

'Is that dog hair on you?' She picked off the offending piece of fluff.

He ignored the question. 'Do you think that maybe instead of going to visit old Mrs Gilmore, we should go see George Grey? Gilmore was working one-to-one with him. Maybe they chatted; maybe Gilmore let something slip. Or maybe wee George isn't quite the angel Ms Paton made him out to be and he's going to do a runner. What do you think?'

'I think we go see George Grey later. Let's go visit Gilmore's mother first – she deserves it.'

'Okay, but I'm glad Stewart delegated it to uniform. Telling an old dear that her son's been murdered ranks up there with the crappiest part of this job.'

'Stop being so bloody sensitive. Maybe she can shed some light on who Gilmore was; we've not got much of a picture to go on. If he was a ghost to his colleagues, I'm hoping that he will have meant much more to his mum. And besides, while poor Boyd and Robertson get to visit Manky Miller at the youth club, we get a nice old lady in Milngavie. So stop whining.'

They drove into Milngavie. According to their directions the home was just off Mugdock Road and close to Tannoch Loch. 'We're looking for The Courtyard Retirement Community,' said Wheeler.

'Death's waiting room.'

'Hold that thought,' Wheeler said, 'here's the turning.'

Chapter 13

'That heater's fucked. It's boiling in here.' Boyd's shirt showed signs of sweat under his armpits as he parked the car outside the youth club and killed the engine. He had deliberately kept the sports news channel on full volume for the entire journey, which meant that conversation between him and Robertson would have been impossible. He glanced across at Robertson, noting that despite the heat, Robertson's navy-blue suit and white shirt remained in pristine condition. His hair retained its dull sheen and today's aftershave was lime-based.

'Look.' Boyd pointed to the end of the road. A group of boys stood huddled in the rain, hoods up close around their faces, watching them. Boyd waited for a couple of seconds until the boys moved off, then he opened the car door and stepped into the drizzle. He breathed deeply, theatrically.

'Christ, Robertson, your aftershave is a bit strong in an enclosed environment.'

Robertson ignored him and strode ahead towards the club. 'Let's get this over and done with; if Munroe and Wilson were involved in Gilmore's murder, then this place might hold some of the missing information.'

Boyd lumbered along beside him, wheezing hard. 'Aye, maybe. Hard to tell if they were involved but there's not much chance that anybody from round here's going to talk to us.'

'If the two boys are not directly involved, then they know something – they're not the innocents they pretend to be.'

'How come you're so sure?'

'A hunch.'

'Aye, right. A hunch didn't do much for Quasimodo, but knock yourself out, Sherlock.'

As they approached the building the sign suggested that it was open. The padlock around the gated entrance told them otherwise.

Boyd glanced around, noted that the group of boys had returned and were watching. 'A wee audience for us.' He ignored them, read the sign: *Watervale Youth Club* and in smaller letters, *Support, advice and mentoring for those struggling in society*.

'Shite.' Boyd shook his head, felt a burst of annoyance. 'I've seen what vicious criminals can do, how they ruin lives. Folk like Manky Miller think every fucker has rights – the *marginalised* have a right to get enough support to live within a society they hate.'

Robertson watched a figure turn into the road and saunter towards them.

Boyd built up steam for his argument, his voice rising.

'Helping the marginalised, ignoring the law, encouraging and supporting people to live outside the law? This Manky's an ex-con and a spineless cunt.'

The figure approached. Malcolm Miller scowled at them. 'You the polis?'

Boyd and Robertson flashed their ID cards. Boyd could smell the body odour from the man. 'We'd like a word if it's convenient, Mr Miller.'

'It's not. I'm just on my way out.' Manky checked his watch.

'You're not even in the place yet, Malcolm,' said Boyd.

'Mr Miller – we're no pals.'

'Mr Miller,' Boyd corrected himself, 'we'd still like a chat.'

'I'm just here to collect some information, then I'm off. I've things to do, folk to help. Folk who've been intimidated by some of your lot in uniform.'

Boyd sighed, 'Good of you to invite us in out the rain – we won't keep you long.'

They waited until Manky had reluctantly unlocked the door, then followed him into an open-plan office. Robertson busied himself looking at the photocopied sheets that had been stuck around the wall offering advice. Boyd pulled a plastic chair over to Manky's desk and made himself comfortable. 'We won't keep you long, Mr Miller. We just need some information.'

'Information on what?'

'The people who use this place, specifically the people who were here on Sunday night, the night of the Christmas party.'

'Oh aye?'

'In particular Rab Wilson and Alec Munroe – were they at the party all night?'

Manky stared at him. 'And you're sitting here asking

93

about them because . . .? Suddenly you care about the kids round here? How's that then?'

'Because of recent developments,' said Boyd.

Manky snorted. 'You mean the murder? The old guy who worked at the school, the one who copped it?'

Boyd shifted in his chair. 'So much for sympathy or compassion.'

Manky smirked. 'I'm fresh out. What dae they call it, "compassion fatigue"? Think I'm suffering from a wee dose of that myself. And I can't tell you anything about the two kids who found the body. They might've been here, hard to tell. It was a busy party, know what I'm saying?'

'We'd like a list of the folk who were here.' Boyd tried for a patient tone, failed. 'Just print out your contacts list.'

'Printer's fucked.' Manky studied his filthy nails. Chewed on a rag nail. 'And there's nae money tae repair it. And I cannae remember who wis here. Folk running in an out all night.'

Robertson walked over to the printer; it was in pieces.

Boyd leaned forward, his voice a hiss. 'We want a list of names, Malcolm.'

Manky waited a minute before yawning in Boyd's direction. 'And you think one of the weans must automatically be a killer because they live round here? Nice detective work. No prejudiced thinking, jist clean solid police procedure and hard evidence.' He leaned towards Boyd. 'You dae *have* evidence?'

Boyd sucked his teeth.

'Aye, I thought so. Sweet fuck all.'

Boyd sat back in his seat and slowly crossed one leg over the other. 'I'm just asking for some *information* on people who attend the party, folk who use this place. At the moment that's all.'

'Not *some* folk, *vulnerable* folk.' Manky took his time shifting papers, organising his in-tray, making sure he let them wait. Eventually he continued, 'You wouldnae be here grasping at straws if you'd any leads. I imagine that the heid high yins are delighted with your lack of progress; it shows just how shit the polis at Carmyle station are.' He pointed his finger at Boyd. 'And instead of getting something concrete, you come in here sniffing about for some wean you could stitch up for the murder. Am I right?'

Boyd stood. 'So, were you here all Sunday night yourself?'

Manky sniggered. 'You want tae blame it on me now? Talk about clutching at straws. Have you nae imagination? I wis here all night. Ask anybody.'

Boyd walked to the door.

Robertson approached Manky.

'Whit now?' Manky was impatient.

'I think you should reconsider. There's a killer who is watching, waiting. He's in this community and at the moment he's getting away with murder. Even your clients aren't safe.'

'Our wee community looks after its own.'

'A few names are all we're looking for.'

'No can do. You heard about client confidentiality? Well, if my clients cannae trust me, who can they trust? Certainly not you lot.' He stared at Robertson. 'This here is all those weans have,' he paused, 'so mind you two muppets shut the door on your way out.'

Robertson's voice was harsh. 'So you're telling me that you can vouch for all of your clients on the night of the murder?'

'I didnae say that.'

'No you didn't because you can't, can you?'

'You've no reason tae suspect any of the weans here. Or

me. This is polis harassment. If you've got anything in the way of evidence then let's see it.' Manky reached out his hand. 'Well?'

Robertson ignored the hand, sweat breaking out on his forehead. 'You're okay with the idea that you might be harbouring a murderer?' He leant towards him. 'You're *absolutely sure* you're okay with that?'

Manky grinned, showing a row of dark mercury fillings. 'You're fucking pathetic. I'm not *harbouring* anybody. Now get going.'

Robertson pulled out a card and dropped it onto the desk. 'If you hear anything, anything at all. You call me.'

Manky didn't do them the courtesy of waiting until they were out of the room before he picked up the card and dropped it into the wastepaper bin.

Outside, Boyd stalked ahead to the car. The rain had started again and he was soaked before he'd even opened the door. 'Fucker knows more than he's letting on.' He settled himself into the driver's seat and barely waited until Robertson had closed his door before he shot off.

'Definitely lying,' Robertson said.

They drove to the end of the road, turned and felt a hail of empty cans hurtle into the back window. Robertson gasped. Boyd ploughed on. 'Bastards.'

The group of boys stood laughing and pointing as the cop car retreated. At a house at the end of the road, at an upstairs window, Rab Wilson stood in his bedroom and watched.

Chapter 14

'Hope it doesn't have that old-folk smell of piss,' Ross said.

Wheeler squinted at the cheerfully painted sign which read 'Welcome to The Courtyard Retirement Community.' Ross turned the car into the gravel drive. The Courtyard was a long, two-storey brick building set well back from the road in its own grounds. In the gardens pruned roses and hydrangeas bowed to the wind and shivered in the rain; only the heather looked like it was coping. Ross pressed the intercom, a man's voice answered and they were buzzed through to the reception area, where a plump middle-aged man in a too-tight suit introduced himself. 'Hello, I'm David Line. I'm one of the managers here at The Courtyard.'

Wheeler and Ross both flashed their ID and the three of them moved through to a stuffy office. Wheeler took off her coat and sat opposite the manager. Ross took the seat beside her, picked up a brochure from the desk and began fanning himself.

Wheeler began, 'You know why we're here?'

The manager shifted on his seat and rearranged his hands into a nervous knot of twitching fingers. There was a sound of knuckles cracking. He swallowed twice before speaking. 'DCI Stewart called last night and again earlier this morning and outlined what happened. The two policemen and the family liaison officer arrived this morning. This is dreadful news about Mrs Gilmore's son. Really, just awful. I can't imagine . . .' His voice drifted off, his face tortured with the images of a dead man. 'And you know that she's just out of hospital?'

They both nodded, paused for a second before Wheeler spoke. 'Did you ever meet James Gilmore, Mr Line? Was he a frequent visitor?'

'I'm afraid I can't help you there; I never met the man. I've only worked here for a few months. That's not to say he hasn't visited his mother during this time – he has on a number of occasions. We have a system whereby everyone has to sign in and out. I checked the book and it records him being here last month, on the twenty-eighth; he arrived at 8.20 p.m. and left around 9.30 p.m. He was her only visitor. As far as I know, she has no other living relatives.'

'Is there anyone who would have known him well? A member of staff, perhaps?'

'I asked the carers but no one seems to have known him. A few saw him come and go, but by all accounts he kept to himself. "Self-contained" is how one carer described him, and,' he added, 'extremely polite. His mother is fastidious about manners.'

Wheeler rose. 'Thanks for your time, Mr Line. Maybe we should go and speak with Mrs Gilmore now?'

'Of course. Helen, the family liaison officer, is waiting in the coffee lounge. We can collect her on the way.'

'What's Mrs Gilmore's first name?' Wheeler asked.

The manager seemed baffled. 'Moira, why?'

'Sometimes it's better to use first names when giving someone bad news.'

'It's more personal, less formal,' Ross added, as if he had remembered the section on dealing with bereavement in the handbook and could deliver it verbatim.

The manager hesitated. 'As I said, Mrs Gilmore is a stickler for manners and I'm certain that she wouldn't approve of you being so familiar.'

They made their way down a thickly carpeted corridor; the walls were painted a sunny yellow shade, in contrast to the grey sky visible through the windows. Ross sniffed. There was no smell other than a faint mustiness coming from the bowls of dusty pot-pourri that were dotted on occasional tables. They passed the coffee lounge where the FLO was waiting. She was heavyset and sat with her plump hands resting on her lap, sturdy legs crossed at the ankle. Her hair was cut in a short, business-like bob. She stood and introduced herself as Helen Curtis. Wheeler held out her hand. 'Glad you're here. Mrs Gilmore will need support.' Curtis shook hands and smiled and fell into line behind them as they trooped on down the long corridor, finally stopping outside a closed door.

Line paused. 'Shall I come in with you?'

'Might be an idea.'

Wheeler knocked, heard an impatient voice announce, 'Let yourself in – I'm recovering from an operation, remember?'

The manager opened the door.

They were following him into a small hallway when Wheeler's phone bleeped a text message. She hung back while Ross and the FLO and the manager all went into the apartment. She glanced at her phone. *Jason.* She quickly scanned the message, got the gist. *Hung over. Party. Feeling ill. Will call later. Promise.* She slipped the phone back into her pocket, walked into the apartment and waited while everyone seated themselves. She glanced around, took in the pictures, was drawn to one in particular. The drawing was small but the line was unmistakable. The subject, a young woman, her hat drawn over her face, was typical of one of the Scottish Colourists. It was an original J.D. Fergusson. Wheeler felt a pang of avarice flit through her. She heard a sharp cough and turned from the picture to a woman in her late eighties. She wore a pale blue dress with a dark blue cardigan and a rope of pearls hung from a wrinkled neck. On each wrist she'd stacked slim gold bracelets and her gnarled fingers held enough bling to impress a rapper. Her white hair was set in stiff waves.

'Mrs Gilmore?' Wheeler asked.

The old woman sighed. 'Of course. They've already been here, the boys in uniform.'

'I'm sorry.'

'I knew the minute I saw them that something had happened, that it was bad news.' She spoke with authority, someone who was used to giving orders. She glanced at Ross, then back to Wheeler. 'Which one of you is in charge?'

'Both of us actually,' Ross smiled gently.

Mrs Gilmore turned her face from the smile and Wheeler noticed how translucent the old lady's skin was, a thin layer of gauze stretched tight over ancient bones.

'I knew that something had happened to James.' There was nothing ancient about the sharpness in Mrs Gilmore's voice. 'A mother's instinct.'

'Would you like a glass of water?' Wheeler moved

forward. The woman stared at her. Wheeler watched the woman study her, saw her take in her scuffed boots, the short hair, saw that she had been judged. And found lacking.

Mrs Gilmore leant on the arms of the chair and curled her fingers around the wood before letting out a long breath. 'No.' She met Wheeler's gaze head on. 'Well, sit down and let's get on with this. What else have you come to tell me?'

Wheeler perched on the end of a plump sofa and kept her voice gentle as she told the mother some of the circumstances around her son's murder.

Mrs Gilmore sat in silence for a long moment before speaking. 'I can't say I'm surprised. Saddened, yes, but surprised, no.'

Wheeler inched forward on the sofa. 'Not surprised?'

'Those people did it.'

'Those people?' Wheeler prompted.

Mrs Gilmore paused. 'Scum. My son worked with scum. I imagine you do too.'

The FLO fussed around the old lady. 'You're in shock, Mrs Gilmore . . .'

'On the contrary!' Mrs Gilmore snapped. 'I've just told you that I wasn't surprised. The only surprise is that it didn't happen years ago.'

'You're just out of hospital; I'll make you a nice cup of tea.' The FLO walked towards the kitchen.

'You will do nothing of the kind. Do not touch anything of mine until I tell you. Now sit down.'

The FLO sat.

'When exactly did he die? The uniformed police suggested Sunday or Monday. Which is it to be?'

'His body was found on Monday evening but we think he was killed sometime the previous night.'

'My son went against my wishes and left academia to

work with . . .' she paused, searching for an appropriate word, found it and continued, 'he left a university position to work with trash.'

'You didn't approve of his career?' Ross asked.

'No. I never wanted him to do that sort of work. He should have followed his father, god rest him, into academia. His father was worried that this would happen one day.' Her voice hardened. 'That's why he gave it to him.'

'Gave him . . . ?' Wheeler prompted.

The old lady patted her throat. 'My husband, Murdo, gave James a St Christopher medal to keep him safe – a stupid, sentimental gesture but there you have it. My husband was somewhat emotional. I was the disciplinarian. Nevertheless I should like both the medal and the chain returned to me.'

Wheeler was pretty sure they hadn't been listed among the items retrieved from the house. And James Gilmore had certainly not been wearing it when they found his body. 'Can you describe it for us?' she asked.

'Twenty-four-carat gold – the medal is about half an inch wide, quite a chunky piece. It previously belonged to Murdo. And before that, to his older brother Duncan. Poor Duncan died of tuberculosis. People did in those days, you know.'

Ross glanced across at her and Wheeler met his eye. The old woman's bitterness was a shock. Although it was one way of processing her grief. And she had suggested another possible motive for the death: theft.

Mrs Gilmore stared hard at Ross, her eyes bright and cold. 'I would like the piece of jewellery returned immediately. It's of considerable monetary value.'

Wheeler kept her voice neutral; there was no point in giving the old woman false hope. 'We'll have a look at . . . what we found in Mr Gilmore's house and get back to you.'

'But it would have been with him at the time – he always wore it. It was a talisman. Murdo told him to always wear it and I know he listened to his father.'

Wheeler nodded. 'I'm sure he did but . . . when we discovered the body . . . there didn't seem to be . . .'

Mrs Gilmore narrowed her eyes. 'It wasn't on his body, was it?'

'No, it wasn't.'

'Was it found with his personal effects?' Mrs Gilmore asked.

Wheeler shook her head. 'No, I'm pretty sure it's not listed.'

The old lady's eyes glinted. 'It was stolen, wasn't it? Whoever killed James took it.'

Wheeler looked at the floor. 'I'll double-check if it was listed.'

'You do that and get back to me immediately.'

Ross changed the subject. 'Did James have a girlfriend?'

Mrs Gilmore shook her head. 'He had a fiancée when he was in his early twenties. Angela Meek. She was a timid soul, frightened of her shadow as I recall. She died in a horrible accident; he never recovered.'

'No one recently?' Ross persisted.

'None. That was it. After Angela died, something in him just seemed to curl up and die with her. He was his father's son.'

'In what way?' asked Ross.

'He was a martyr to emotional nonsense.'

'Were there any close friends that you know of, maybe a colleague he got on particularly well with?' Wheeler hesitated before adding, 'Or a gym buddy or anyone he went on holiday with?'

Mrs Gilmore pursed her lips. 'Never anyone that I knew

of. After his bereavement he withdrew into himself – he was a quiet man who was far better than those he served.'

'When did you last see your son, Mrs Gilmore?'

She sniffed. 'The twenty-eighth of last month. He was extremely busy. He loved helping . . .' her lips dipped into a scowl, 'those kind of people.'

'Those kind of people.' Wheeler echoed the words. 'The children at Watervale?'

'Delinquents, every one of them. Even if they've got parents, they're useless. Feral brats that should never have been born. James was too soft.' She peered at them. 'What about his house – somebody has to go and make sure it's secure. I gather you'll attend to it?'

Ross coughed, looked at Wheeler.

Wheeler grimaced.

The old lady caught their exchange, her eyes darting between them. 'What is it? What are you withholding?'

Ross told her and watched the wrinkled lips purse in disapproval; the beady eyes shone as she turned on them. 'Well, well. The police fail to secure a crime scene and allow evidence to go up in smoke. My son's house is lost to me, all his memories.' She paused, lips drawn tighter in a deep scowl. 'My lawyer will be in touch with the Strathclyde police force.'

Mrs Gilmore began quietly issuing orders: the manager was to contact her lawyer, the FLO was to pour her a sherry and immediately afterwards they were to leave her in peace.

Wheeler and Ross left, aware that they had silently been dismissed.

Outside, Ross turned to her. 'That went well.' He slammed the car door and started the engine.

'Aye, well, it was never going to be easy but the old

woman's now got a vendetta against us for not protecting her son or his house.'

'Compensation. How the hell could she even think about that when she'd just been told her son has been murdered?'

Wheeler strapped on her seat belt. 'She's been waiting for the news for years. You heard what she called the kids at Watervale, feral brats who should never have been born. She's been working up to this moment since James Gilmore went to work at those schools.'

'She's going to be a fucking nightmare.'

'I know, it's a mess but the best we can do now, the only thing we can do, is catch the bastard who did it.'

'Any chance of a coffee before we go back to the station?'

'No chance.' She fiddled with her phone, sent a text. Huffed.

'Crisis?'

'Och, still the family drama. Nephew's determined to go off the rails; his mother's still going nuts down in Somerset.'

'And I guess you're het?'

'Aye, lucky me. I never wanted kids. Now I can see why. They're a pain in the arse.'

'Couldn't agree more.' Ross eased the car into the road and headed back towards Glasgow.

Chapter 15

An hour later and Wheeler was in the CID suite feeling like she'd been there all day. The team were all desk-bound. Wheeler stared at her computer and scrolled through the news links until she found what she was looking for. Grim's report was up to its usual standard.

Strathclyde Police have launched a murder inquiry after the body of a man was discovered on Monday evening. The shocking discovery was made in Glasgow's East End. The body is believed to have lain undiscovered since Sunday.

A post-mortem examination will be carried out later today but police are urging the public to come forward with anything, regardless of how insignificant it may seem.

Detective Chief Inspector Craig Stewart of Carmyle Police Station is leading the investigation and earlier today he had this to say:

'We would appeal for information relating to the murder which occurred in the London Road area on Sunday night. If anyone has any information they can come to Carmyle Police Station itself or phone directly and speak to one of my team. We would also like to appeal to anyone who may have seen anything unusual or anyone acting suspiciously in the past few days to come forward and contact the station. If anyone has any information at all which may help find the killer, then we urge you to contact us immediately. At present we cannot release the name of the victim until relatives have been informed, but more details will follow shortly.'

The report continued over two pages, but she had the gist. She also knew that whoever was feeding information to Grim was more than likely sitting in the station at that moment. She glanced around the room. Everyone was busy, answering phones, leafing through paperwork, scrolling down computer screens. Wheeler turned back to her own computer and finished the article. Stewart was a very effective cop. He used the symbiotic relationship between the police and the press well, but whoever had called Grim and tipped him off had crossed a line. She looked up as Stewart came into the room.

He stood in front of her desk. 'Anything from the mother?'

She told him about the St Christopher medal.

'Okay, well it's something. Anything else?'

She shook her head. 'Nothing helpful . . . only . . .'

'Let me guess, she wants to sue us over the fire at her son's house? I get it. Let's move on.'

'Yes, she was upset and—'

But he was out of the door before she had finished speaking.

Ross stood at the side of her desk. 'Read Grim's report?'

'Uh huh. Nothing we didn't already know; no one's come forward saying they had any information. Or saw anyone acting suspiciously.'

'Nothing.' Ross sounded disappointed and went back to his own desk, started typing up a report.

'It'd be a brave person who wanted to get tangled up with whoever did this. I'd say if anyone saw anything and wants to talk, odds are they'll do it anonymously.' Wheeler knew she sounded cynical.

'Wish they'd be quick,' said Boyd. 'Save me trawling through this list of schools. James Gilmore seems to have worked in every bloody school in Glasgow at some point in his career and some of them don't even exist anymore.'

'So quit whinging.' Wheeler flexed her fingers above the keyboard. 'You got anything positive yet?'

'Hardly had a chance, have I?' Boyd opened the drawer of his desk, peered in, shut it with a bang. Opened the second drawer, did the same.

Robertson was sitting at a table in the corner of the room, working his way through a long list of phone numbers from Gilmore's mobile. She called across to him. 'Anything?'

He looked up from the list. 'So far all the calls have been to the three schools where Gilmore worked, a couple to the home where his mother's staying. Not much of a result.'

'And no saved texts on his mobile. Weird.' Boyd slammed the third drawer.

'Very odd.' Wheeler turned from her computer.

'What is?' Ross asked.

'Doesn't everyone keep texts?' She looked around.

Ross shrugged. 'A couple, maybe.'

Boyd nodded. 'Loads – can't be arsed going through them all deciding what to delete.'

'Think he had another phone?' Ross asked. 'Or just no pals?'

'Just no life it seems.' Wheeler opened a bottle of water, took a sip. Wondered if it might be better if it was wine.

'Fits in with him being a ghost.' Ross swivelled his chair to face her.

'Maybe he deleted all his messages at the end of the day, kind of like emptying the in-tray,' Robertson offered.

'OCD.' Boyd raked through the pile of paperwork on his desk. 'Where the hell's my chocolate bar?'

'It's hardly obsessive to be organised – most of us function better that way.' Robertson turned away, dialled, spoke into the handset, leaving another message on an answering machine.

Boyd gave him the finger.

Wheeler stood and stretched. 'I'm done here. Need to get out into the fresh air.'

'Avoid the shit storm more like.' Boyd had found the half-eaten chocolate bar and had begun demolishing it. 'When Stewart realises we've nothing to give him.'

Wheeler glanced across at Ross. 'Let's take a drive out to Gilmore's house – we've an hour or so before the post-mortem. I want to see the house, see if it sparks anything.'

'Get it straight in your mind?' Ross was already logging out.

Wheeler pulled on her coat. 'Yep, get it straight and see if anything else crops up. I can't think straight staring at a bloody computer.'

Outside the cold air hit Ross in the face when he opened the door. 'Bloody hell, it's freezing.'

'It is winter, muppet.' Wheeler walked to the car, sleet settling for a moment on her face before melting and leaving a cold imprint across her skin.

They drove down London Road, took the turn-off on their left and drove to Gilmore's house. Parked. Stayed in the car with the heater on full. Tried to ignore the smell of stale sweat and chips that clung to the interior of the car. They stared at the remains of Gilmore's home.

The fire had ravaged the house, destroying most of the roof; the windows had been blown out and the old stone had lost its greyness and was now blackened and charred. The building had been secured and a notice prohibited entry.

'Looks like a set for a horror movie. Gives me the creeps.'

'What age are you, Ross – ten?' She leant forward, drummed her fingers on the dashboard. 'What are we missing?'

'About the house?'

'About the whole bloody case. There's something we're not seeing.'

'Back to the start?'

'Yep.'

'Apparently an innocent guy was beaten to death.'

'Then his house get torched.'

'He's a professional helper, no obvious signs of criminal behaviour, no drugs, no fraud, not even a bloody parking ticket. Nothing, clean as a whistle.'

'And the two boys' alibis held up. Both Alec Munroe and Robert Wilson were at a party the night Gilmore was killed – there are loads of witnesses who saw them get drunk on cheap cider and make arses of themselves. Most of them have it on their phones too. And of course it's plastered across Facebook.'

'So, the two boys weren't involved.'

'So who does that leave?'

'Known thugs?' Ross stared at the sleet lying on the windscreen and reached over to switch on the wipers.

'We know that at least two of them were out of the country when Gilmore was killed,' said Wheeler.

'Convenient.'

'Well, it seems that Jamieson was at his mammy's funeral. He couldn't have arranged for her to pass away at the same time as Gilmore died.'

'No but he could have arranged to have Gilmore killed.'

'True.'

'Tenant?' asked Ross.

'Big wedding anniversary – seems him and Nicky have been an item for twenty years. Treated her to a week in Vegas.'

'Classy. Means nothing though; they've got a whole team of thugs who could've done it.'

'I know.'

'Doyle?'

She looked out of the window – they were getting nowhere. Sleet was drifting gently over the charred remains of Gilmore's house, leaving a light dusting of white. 'Very festive, this weather. Let's get going. Stewart wants a clear slate for his Christmas holiday.'

'Still but it leaves us with—'

She smiled. 'I know. Absolutely sweet FA. Right, let's clear off then. The PM's at four o'clock – you ready?'

But he had already started the car.

Chapter 16

They'd only just left the burned-out shell of a house and were driving towards the city centre when he began whining, 'The smell of post-mortems clings – I can't wash the smell off, can you?'

'You're exaggerating. It's psychological,' Wheeler lied.

'And there's a game tonight. Don't want to go out smelling of death; it's not good for the reputation.'

'I'd have thought just turning up, they'd be overjoyed. Dead or alive. Who're they playing?'

'Plastic Whistle.'

'Any chance they might scrape a win?'

Ross shifted uncomfortably on his seat. Stared ahead, concentrated on the road. Said nothing.

'Too awkward a question?' She leaned over, pointing. 'Look at the state of you. You have gone and got yourself a wee pet, haven't you? Are you that lonely?' She picked the hairs from his jacket collar. 'Dog hair.'

'I'm just looking after a dog for a few days, that's all.'

'Poor mutt.'

'Does all right.'

'You're never there.'

'Old Mary across the road takes it round the block. Feeds it too.'

'You're a chancer, Ross – never met a bigger skiver.'

They drove towards Glasgow Cross. 'Any chance we could have a quick coffee and a bun first? Settle my stomach before all that gore.'

She checked her watch. 'If we're quick.'

They settled into their seats in the café, ordered two coffees and a couple of Danish pastries. When the food arrived, Ross started munching happily. 'It's that buzz-buzz that gets me.'

She picked up a Danish and bit into it. 'Mmm, these are lovely, nice and chewy, just the way I like them.'

'That wee Stryker saw they use?' Ross continued through mouthfuls. 'Christ, what an evil wee thing. It's like going to the dentist, then finding out you're in a horror movie. Turns my stomach.'

'Uh huh.' She chomped happily on the sugar pastry. Sipped her coffee, let the warmth of the café envelop her.

Later he paid and they walked out into the rain.

'Just a drizzle.' Ross sounded more upbeat as they got into the car and drove to the mortuary. He parked the car next to Callum's red BMW and killed the engine. Still he made no attempt to get out of the car.

Wheeler undid her seat belt. 'Now I don't want you to come over all sensitive on me, Ross.'

'I won't – I'm just saying, that wee saw's a bastard.'

She climbed out of the car, pulling her coat close around her. "Cause I'm not going to hold your hand if you keel over.'

He was close behind her. 'Perish the thought.'

'Aye, me too.'

Inside, Callum greeted them with a cheery wave. Behind him two young lab technicians were silently preparing the body and the photographer stood waiting. Everything would be recorded and photographed and the wounds measured while James Gilmore's body was neatly dissected.

'Well guys, let's get started.' Callum's voice boomed around the room, bouncing off the pristine white tiles.

Wheeler watched him work. He was always cool and businesslike, but then this was his business.

Callum switched on the microphone and recorded the date and time, then a list of everyone present. Finally he named the victim and began describing his clothing in detail before standing back to allow the photographer to do his job. Once the clothing had been photographed, Callum carefully began to remove it, before finally passing it to one of the techs, who bagged and labelled it.

There was no jewellery on James Gilmore's body, no sign of the St Christopher that his father had given him. Gilmore had no tattoos, no piercings and his body showed nothing out of the ordinary, unless you counted the bruises that criss-crossed his torso.

Wheeler stared at the dead body; it had become an object, a slab of meat to be stored in the cooling area of the mortuary. Exactly what Stewart had not wanted to happen in the newspaper report. People quickly forgot about a slab of meat. A few days ago, this body had been a professional man, and according to his mother, a gentle man, so how could this have happened? Wheeler stared at what was left of the educational psychologist and wondered if he could ever have imagined his death would have been so violent.

She watched Callum move around the table, measuring the length and depth of the injuries, still talking, still recording everything, and knew that what he had said at Gilmore's house had been right. The post-mortem wasn't going to give up any great secrets; this wasn't an American cop show, when the case would be solved in sixty minutes or less. Dissecting James Gilmore's body was only going to reinforce what they already knew – that he'd been battered to death. And that there were very few clues as to who did it.

'Did he even put up a fight?' asked Ross. 'Did he have any chance to defend himself?'

Callum shook his head. 'There are no signs of defence wounds.' He picked up one of the hands, scraped under the nails, held up the swab. 'Clean, no torn skin, no blood, no bits of clothing. Whoever it was came at him like a thunderbolt. And didn't stop hammering him until the job was done.'

Chapter 17

Tuesday evening

Wheeler was at home listening to Hank Mobley's *Soul Station* and getting ready to go out. The CD had just finished when a text came through from her sister. Wheeler read it: same old. She quickly sent a text to Jason.

CALL YOUR MOTHER.

A minute later she had a reply. *I already did.*

Liar.

She glanced at the clock; she just about had time. She called her sister, kept it brief and insisted that Jo did the same. 'So shoot – what's with all the texts?'

Five minutes later she had a clear understanding of what Jason was up to. He was stone-walling his mother and she was going nuts down in Somerset. Wheeler heard Jo's frustration.

'Okay, *just this once*, I'll go check on him. Where's he likely

116

to be, at home or out and about? Has he got a favourite pub?'

'The Vineyard.'

'Fine.'

Wheeler grabbed her boots and coat, pulled her hair into a bit of a quiff and within ten minutes was standing outside her flat in the wind and rain. She waited until the wrought-iron gates closed behind her before turning, head down into the wind and walking to Ingram Street. She stood in the entrance to a hotel and waited and watched four taxis pass, their orange lights dimmed, telling her they were not for hire. Eventually one turned off the High Street and made its way towards her, its light glowing. She flagged it down, climbed into the warmth of the back seat and settled herself.

'The Vineyard, Byres Road, please.'

The driver switched on the meter before driving off.

From the window she watched the festive crowds mill around the city centre, saw parties of office workers on their Christmas night out, the girls in tiny sequined dresses and bare legs flashing fake tan and sky-high heels, some walking like newborn colts as they navigated the icy pavements. Five minutes later the driver stopped outside The Vineyard and Wheeler handed him her fare, adding a tip. At last a smile.

Wheeler walked to the pub entrance. The Vineyard offered a healthy student discount and the music was loud. It was a bit of a long shot that he'd be there. There were at least a half dozen student pubs in a small area around Byres Road. She decided that if she had to, she'd at least look into them all.

Once inside the pub, she went to the bar and ordered a large glass of Chardonnay. If she had to babysit her nephew, she reasoned, then she might as well enjoy herself. She paid for her drink and strolled to the back area, sat in one of the huge red banquettes and made sure that she had an uninterrupted view of the bar and also that she could see out of the large window onto the street outside. Byres Road was one long road full of cafés, pubs and restaurants. It was close to the university and students seemed to spend most of their time in the area. If Jason was out drinking this would be the best place to find him.

The place began to fill up, mainly with students, killing time till they went back to waitressing or maybe just waiting until the clubs opened. Lazy sods, thought Wheeler. A few groups of office workers came in looking for a quick drink on the way home. She had almost finished her wine when she saw him. He arrived with a group of three others, two boys and a girl. Wheeler saw Jason's pallor, grey and wan. She hoped it was from studying hard but she doubted that it was anything as sensible. The trio with him were all as bad, all super-skinny, with sunken cheeks and attitude, *heroin chic* she'd heard it called. The girl was the thinnest, bony arms dangling from a black T-shirt. She wore a tiny miniskirt over thick black tights, a thick smear of black eyeliner and what looked like purple lipstick. She looked like a goth model, all long limbs and big doe eyes. On her head she wore a wee sparkly hair band. Jason was the tallest of the group, but the boys all wore the same uniform of skinny jeans, sloppy retro T-shirts, baseball boots, floppy hair tumbling over as-yet unlined faces. One boy wore a beanie hat fixed at a specifically cool angle.

Wheeler watched her nephew; he was smiling, looked happy, draped an arm casually over the shoulder of the girl. Mr Cool-as-Fuck with not a care in the world. She waited. After a few minutes she saw it, noted the car on the road outside cruise to a stop at the lights. She watched Jason peel himself away from the girl and slip out of the door. All very casually done, nipping out for a cigarette maybe, or darting round to the cash machine, perhaps taking a quick phone call? Any of the above, except that he wasn't. He returned a few minutes later, having leaned into the car and apparently done nothing more interesting than shake the hand of the driver. Maybe he was an old friend, a fellow student? Aye shite. The car moved away and the driver's purple Mohican created a distinctive outline. Weirdo. She caught a glimpse of another man in the passenger seat. Fat neck, greasy face. Smithy, Doyle's lackey. She slipped out of the back door, stood underneath the window and texted Jason.

Hi Jason, we need to meet up and have a wee chat. Where r u just now?

She watched him text back. Sipping from his pint, glass in one hand, phone in the other. A natural. Kids today. Multitasking.

Sorry, no can do, I'm still at work, have taken on another shift for friend who's sick. Holed up here, probably need to work an all-nighter. This sucks. Wish I wasn't here! I'd rather be down the pub. U ok?

It took her twice as long to text. *Me fine. Let's meet up soon.*

Read his reply. *Yeah. Defo! Whenever I get a min I'll be in touch. J xx*

She watched him tuck his phone into his jeans, laugh at something his friend said and drape his arm once again around the skinny shoulders of the gothic princess with the sparkly hair band. Well, Wheeler thought, she had given him a chance. She tucked her mobile into her jeans. Back in the pub she marched over to him, grinned at his look of surprise. Kept her voice the right side of fucked off: 'Jason, we need to have a word. Now.' She watched him go into action, put on the sheepish grin, duck his head down towards her face and peer out from underneath his hair, all moves that told her that her nephew had changed, had

119

morphed from an innocent wee boy into a handsome big shite who thought a smile would let him get away with murder. It probably did with his mother. Wheeler leaned towards him. 'You're a lying scumbag, you know that don't you? And to me of all people. I thought you'd know better.'

His friends parted to let them leave.

They stood on the wet cobbles in the back lane.

'I'm nearly twenty for God's sake,' his voice a tinny whine. 'I'm not having Mum get you to stalk me and report back to her. It's not fair.'

Christ, thought Wheeler, life wasn't fair. 'I'm not stalking you, I'm observing you. And I'm fed up with your mother hassling me 'cause you can't be bothered letting her know you're still alive.'

Huff. He stared into the middle distance. Handsome. Moody.

Well, maybe it worked on the goth girl. It was lost on Wheeler. 'Look Jason, I can't be arsed with this crap.'

Pursed lips, roll of the eyes, sourness in his voice: 'That makes two of us then.'

'I saw you with Weirdo.'

His hand went instinctively to his pocket. 'Don't know what you're talking about.'

'Look, I don't give a shit if you smoke the odd joint but Weirdo is involved with people who'd eat you up and spit you out all over Byres Road.'

Jason dropped the sour look and tried again for the cutesy smile, head down, floppy hair, big eyes. 'Look, Auntie Kat.'

Suddenly she felt a million years old. Auntie Kat sounded like she should be baking him cakes; instead she wanted to slap the stupid grin off his face.

'I hear what you're saying, honestly I do.'

'Really?' Could he be more patronising?

'But it's just a bit of dope, weed, or whatever you want to call it. Nothing stronger. I promise. Listen, scouts honour.'

She looked at him. Liar. It may be dope just now but she would bet money he'd go further. She was tempted to force him to turn out his pockets but stopped herself. He was old enough to take responsibility for himself, plus he was a law student and should know more than enough about the legality of drugs. Plus, she wasn't his fucking mother. She made to leave. 'At least text your mum now and again.'

'Yeah, yeah, no worries. It's all cool.'

She looked at him, took in the relaxed stance, the handsome face with its ready smirk, and she realised that for now he hadn't a care in the world.

Experience told her that would change.

'Anyway, I'm off – mind you call your mammy. It'll save me coming looking for you.'

'Cool. You going out yourself?'

She said nothing. There wasn't a hope in hell she would tell him she'd been set up by her friend Carol. A friend of Carol's was helping to organise a charity fundraiser later that night and Carol had suggested Wheeler hook up with him. An intellectual blind date – they were going to the fundraising lecture. Christ, what was she thinking? Still, she was near enough the venue. Half of Glasgow would be there, including her friend Imogen. It was hardly going to be intimate. She was meeting him at the Garden Bar for a quick drink first and if they didn't loathe each other on sight, they might make a late dinner after the lecture. At least there would be wine. She left Jason to go back to his pals and wandered out of the lane and along Byres Road. The bohemian feel to the West End, the constant thrum of rain and the buzz from the traffic gave the place an upbeat energy. The students walked alone, in pairs or in groups, all working their own look. Either casual in jeans, all-black ensembles or tweed jackets and Mumford and Sons hair. There were even a few punks. Chatter and laughter escaped from the pubs and cafés. There was a festive feel to the area, good times and nothing much to worry about. Jason and his pals had it easy, she thought – it was a different story for the kids at Watervale.

She crossed at the lights and headed up towards Ashton Lane. The rain had turned to sleet. There were three men waiting outside the Garden Bar. She glanced at them – one looked to be in his early twenties, another was closer to sixty. The third man was in his late thirties; she assumed it was him. Taller than her, broad shoulders, jeans, leather jacket. Strong features. Good-looking in an understated way, not pretty-boy. From a distance at least. She approached him, he smiled, held out his hand. 'Kat Wheeler? You're just as Carol described you. Paul Buchan, pleased to meet you. Shall we go inside for a drink?'

So far so good.

Chapter 18

The heavy sleet meant that Robertson needed to reach forward and switch on the windscreen wipers. He had parked
in the shadows across from the car park and sat in his car
watching the road. He began rotating his wedding ring, first
one way then back, as if the metal were somehow burning
his skin. He pulled it off and dropped it into the glove compartment. He waited until he saw his wife Margaret's old
Volvo approach and turn into the car park. He saw her get
out of the car, lock it and walk, head down against the sleet,
towards the building. She paused to pull down the brim of
her hat and pull the belt of her raincoat tight before disappearing into the building. When he was sure that she was
safely inside, Robertson put the car into gear, edged it out of
the layby and drove off in the opposite direction.

*

Inside the hall, Margaret Robertson chose one of the wooden seats in the second-to-last row. Heard the scrape of the legs against the rough of the wooden floor. It was a cold night out and just as bitter in the empty hall, so cold that she could see her breath mist in front of her. She pulled her coat around her and settled herself. On the wall to her right a framed Bible verse reminded her of what she already knew, that women were not permitted to speak during meetings; instead they had to have their own meetings, where they could speak freely to one another. *1 Corinthians 14:34–5: Let your women keep silence in the churches: for it is not permitted unto them to speak.*

The other men, women and children would arrive soon. She fingered her Bible, kneaded the worn leather cover with her hands. Waited. After a few minutes the others began to arrive. First came Mrs Harris, her red velvet beret damp with rain, her sensible heels clicking on the wooden floor. She was followed by her daughter-in-law Jennifer, her bobbed hair swinging out from under a blue beret, her advanced pregnancy obvious. The others arrived in ones and twos, all nodding hellos and complaints about the cold weather. The actual meeting would not begin for another five minutes.

Mrs Harris sat in the row in front of Margaret, settled herself then waited for Jennifer to do the same. Only then did they turn to Margaret. 'I read about the latest murder in the *Chronicle*. Dreadful. The poor man – he worked up at that school, didn't he? The school for . . .'

Margaret kept her eyes on her Bible. 'That's right, Watervale Academy.'

Mrs Harris tutt-tutted loudly. 'Awful business altogether.'

'Awful,' Jennifer echoed, unfastening her coat and patting her bump.

Margaret's eyes darted to the bump before quickly looking away.

Mrs Harris leaned towards Margaret. 'Your Ian will be kept busy with the murder. I expect all the police will. Do I remember your Ian doing outreach at that type of school sometime last year or the year before?'

Margaret nodded. 'He did visit some of the schools, and we had a couple of children who said they'd be interested in coming to a few Bible classes, but most of them weren't in the least bit interested. Not even in Sunday School.'

'Still, if he can get even a few along, it would make a big difference to their lives. It's a godless world and we have to do our best to help them. It's our duty.'

'I know.'

'A few more souls saved and you can't put a price on that, can you?'

Margaret kneaded her Bible, knuckles white, nails bitten to the quick.

Mrs Harris tutted again. 'Awful that the poor man died like that after spending a lifetime trying to help those children.'

Margaret looked at the floor, wished the meeting would begin. 'He wasn't at the school at the time. He was in his house. It might not be related to the school at all.'

'But still, those types of children.' Jennifer adjusted her beret and patted her hair. 'Scary, I'd call them.' She screwed up her face. 'Godless. They are lost souls.' She patted her bump, cooed, 'But you'll be okay.'

Margaret stared ahead. Sat in silence for the remaining minutes.

Then the meeting began.

About halfway through the sharing, Margaret did

something that she had never done before. She opened her Bible, cleared her throat and read aloud. 'Matthew eighteen, verses twenty-one and twenty-two: Then Peter came up and said to him, "Lord, how often will my brother sin against me, and I forgive him? As many as seven times?" Jesus said to him, "I do not say to you seven times, but seventy times seven."'

She closed her eyes, prayed that the Lord would forgive her for doubting her husband. Prayed that He would take the doubt and suspicion that plagued her and return her to His fold. She kept her eyes closed as some of the men shared, nodded in silent agreement with whatever concern was raised. Finally, when it was over, she opened her eyes.

Mrs Harris stood at her elbow, disapproval etched on her face. 'I wonder why you didn't wait for the women's meeting, Margaret, when you could have spoken out?'

Margaret stared at the floor.

'It would have been more fitting. Sometimes, Margaret, we have to fight our ego, not give in to it.'

Margaret swallowed.

Jennifer kept her voice light. 'Is Ian picking you up tonight?'

'No, he's working.' Margaret's fingers worried at the leather again.

Mrs Harris leant in close to Margaret, patted her shoulder stiffly, rested her hand for a minute. 'A wonderful man you have there, Margaret. See now that you look after him well. You are a very lucky girl. What else would you have done at your age?'

Margaret hadn't meant to blurt it out, but the words tripped over themselves: 'I need to speak with an elder.'

Mrs Harris drew her hand back and frowned. 'I'm not

surprised, after your show tonight. I think maybe you should go and speak with someone about your attitude. Maybe one of the women?'

Margaret shook her head.

'Then you'd better make arrangements to have a meeting with an elder. Perhaps Ian could come with you? That might be more,' she paused, 'appropriate.'

'No, it's not about what happened tonight . . . I mean Ian won't be there. I need to speak with someone alone.'

'You want a meeting with an elder, without your husband being present?'

Margaret nodded and bit her bottom lip. 'It's a private matter.'

Mrs Harris and Jennifer stared at her. At last Jennifer spoke. 'Go see Elder Morrison.'

Outside, Mrs Harris turned to her daughter-in-law. 'What was all that about?'

'I'm guessing that there might be problems in their marriage. Five years married and no children. Even at her age, she could have hoped for a couple of kids.'

'You don't think . . .?'

'What?'

'That she's thinking about a divorce? I mean, all this secrecy about seeing an elder and it being a private matter. What on earth could she say in private that she couldn't say in front of Ian? Unless it's about Ian.'

Jennifer kept her voice low. 'Margaret always wanted kids, no reason she shouldn't be able to have them and yet here they are, all this time and nothing.' She patted her stomach. 'Doesn't it seem odd to you?'

Mrs Harris looked back through the open door. Margaret Robertson was sitting with the Bible open on her lap. Her mouth was moving, her eyes closed. 'That girl's the odd one – Ian Robertson's a lovely man.'

Inside, Margaret hunched over the verse, the words already memorised, as if, by saying them, she might make them become concrete in the room. And things would be fine again between her and her husband.

'Luke six, verses thirty-six and thirty-seven: "Be merciful, even as your Father is merciful. Judge not, and you will not be judged; condemn not, and you will not be condemned; forgive, and you will be forgiven."' She breathed deeply and began again, giving special emphasis to the phrase 'forgive and you will be forgiven'.

Finally, when the caretaker stood in the doorway and flicked the lights on and off, she closed the Bible, stood and made her way out into the freezing cold evening.

Chapter 19

The lecture theatre was filling up. Wheeler sat in the front row, looked across the room, saw Imogen, waved to her and waited while her friend made her way towards her. Imogen squeezed into the seat beside her.

'Is your new date not coming?' Imogen scanned the crowd. 'I thought Carol said you were meeting him for a drink earlier on this evening?'

'God, do you two tell each other everything?'

'Pretty much – we're colleagues, remember. Unlike you and your chums at the station, we've loads of time to gossip instead of working. So, did you meet him?'

'I did meet him for a quick drink.'

'And?'

'And it's a friend of his who's giving the talk, so he's gone off to have a quick good-luck chat beforehand.'

'Lecture.'

'Aye, well, whatever.'

'It going okay then? He's not a nutter, a psycho or a miso?'

'A what?'

'Misogynist.'

'It's early days yet. I only met him an hour ago. His name's Paul and he's a psychologist.' Wheeler was aware of the seats filling up; the theatre was busy. 'He seemed okay.'

'Just okay?'

'Well, not an obvious nutter but as I said, it's early days.'

'Damned by faint praise.' Imogen sounded disappointed.

'Okay, you old romantic, it was like he was on his best behaviour. He seemed a bit reserved.'

'You want to see him on his worst behaviour on a first date?'

'Uh huh, if it's him being congruent,' Wheeler nodded, 'otherwise it's just an act put on to impress me.'

'Fair enough, although some folk would be happy if a guy was out to impress them,' she paused. 'There's someone standing in the doorway staring at you. That him?'

Wheeler looked up, smiled and waited as Paul Buchan made his way towards them.

'Good body,' muttered Imogen, 'nice shoulders, long legs.'

'You're gay, remember?'

Imogen smiled. 'But not blind, so what's your point caller?'

Buchan reached them as the lights dimmed. 'Took a minute to order us a bottle of Pinot Grigio for the end of the lecture. It'll be hellish to get served when everyone's streaming out at the same time.'

'Nice one.' Imogen sat back in her seat.

Wheeler smiled and hastily introduced them before the

lights flickered, telling them that the lecture was about to begin.

A few seconds later a man walked to the front of the theatre. He was small and wiry, his dark hair swept back from a tanned face and brown eyes glittered with intensity. He cleared his throat before beginning. 'Welcome, ladies and gentlemen, and thank you all for coming out on such a cold and miserable night. My name is Dr Matthew Barnes and I'm from the Keenan Institute.' He glanced around the audience as if hoping someone would recognise the name. No one stirred, so he continued, 'The Institute came into being last year and it will be, I hope, a place of sanctuary for troubled young people who have suffered neglect or abuse in some form in their young lives. At present we only have one facility, based in London, but given time, we hope to expand and have centres across the UK. As you may know, the local prison, Barlinnie, is overcrowded. This is a situation that is echoed across the UK and Europe. But I don't believe it has to be this way. I believe that many of the inmates have had a poor start to life; they were born at a distinct disadvantage. I am talking about severe neglect. I believe that we, as a nation, have created a society that is exclusive, in that we systematically exclude those who are the most vulnerable and most in need of our help. Children and young people are often left to cope alone – they are not parented properly nor are they supported. Often they grow up feral, having to fend for themselves. This in turn makes it difficult for them to find a place for themselves in society. They have no choice but to move outside of its perimeters, often turning to drugs, prostitution and crime. In time these children become homeless, or are incarcerated and then the spiral of crime continues.'

Wheeler was aware of the silence in the room. Matthew

Barnes held the audience's attention by force of will, his passion evident.

Barnes continued, 'I'd like to present a few thoughts about the issues and dangers of neglecting children in our society. Or if you like, more of the same-old-same-old, the nature versus nurture argument. I believe this is a crucial area and one which is woefully underfunded, so then afterwards,' he paused, smiling, 'I ask you for your money.' A ripple of laughter spread around the room. Then the lights went out.

'Ladies and gentlemen, let's begin right at the beginning.' He pressed a switch and the screen beside him flickered into life. An image of two brain scans flashed onto the screen, one brain noticeably larger than the other. Barnes crossed to the screen and pointed to the smaller of the two. 'This brain belongs to a child who was severely neglected from birth. The child's brain has much less tissue.' He pointed to the other scan. 'In this image, the larger brain belongs to a child with a normal upbringing – that's to say a child who wasn't neglected, a child who had their needs met. Notice the increase in both the size of the brain and the amount of brain tissue.'

Wheeler sat in the dark, listening to Barnes speak. She listened to the statistics and the theories about neglect and the proven link to delinquency. She thought about her own upbringing, a mother who had loved both her and her sister. Her father had died too early in her life for her to have any memory of him, but their mother had made sure they had everything she could manage to give them. The old adage had applied: they'd everything they'd needed but maybe not everything they'd wanted.

'And then there are these . . .' Barnes continued his lecture. Wheeler watched another set of brain scans, thought of Alec

Munroe and Rab Wilson and the other kids from Watervale Academy and wondered how a scan of their brains would match up against her nephew's. She wondered if the Watervale kids even had enough resources to cope with the world. Her nephew had been feted all his life. And from what Wheeler had seen, instead of this making him stronger, he had become an indulged brat.

'So, you see,' Barnes continued, 'children tell us from a very young age how much they are struggling to make sense of the world that we have created for them. And if they, literally, don't have the brain power,' the two disparate brain scans flashed again on the screen, 'if they don't have the brain power,' he repeated, 'due to neglect or abuse, to process the world they live in, then what chance do they have?'

Silence.

'University? Unlikely. A meteoric career? Doubtful. Successful relationships?' He peered at the audience. 'What do you think their chances would be?' He looked around the room, waited. No one offered an opinion. 'So, they learn to create their own smaller worlds, often outside of society. They become outsiders. We have created a sub-society of outsiders because from birth these children are massively disadvantaged. The question is, now that we are aware of this,' he slammed his fist on the desk, his voice rising, 'what the hell are we going to do about it?'

Silence.

Finally the lights went up.

Applause.

Wheeler sat, like most of the audience, wondering the same thing. What was to be done to help children who were so ill-equipped to deal with their surroundings?

Buchan turned to her. 'Maybe we need to distil the

lecture, let it settle for a while. Matt gets very passionate about the neglected weans and their needs.' He glanced at the doorway; people were filing out and making their way to the bar. 'Glass of wine?'

They followed him into the bar in silence, pausing only to write their cheques and leave them in the huge bowl with the rest of the donations. A pile of leaflets outlining the work of the Keenan Institute were stacked next to the bowl. Imogen took two and passed one to Wheeler.

'Pretty heavy stuff in there.' Buchan led them to a table with a cardboard place setting which had *Paul Buchan* scrawled on it. Beside it a chilled bottle of Pinot Grigio. He poured three glasses.

Imogen took hers. 'Heavy but interesting. I honestly didn't realise that the scans would look so different. I'm shocked at the difference in brain sizes. How can those kids cope?'

'Many don't – those are the ones Matt wants to help, before they move outside of society.'

'And into crime,' said Wheeler.

'And maybe onto the Bar-L?' Buchan leaned against the bar.

Wheeler sipped her wine, aware that Imogen sounded upset. She wondered if it was because Imogen's partner Alison was pregnant and the responsibility of giving a child a good start was playing on her mind.

Buchan touched her elbow. 'You look miles away. Glad you came?'

'Of course, yeah,' Wheeler nodded. 'Bit of a wake-up call, that's all. Not that I hadn't read up about stuff like that before.'

'But Matt's passion really sells it, doesn't it?'

'It made me think about my own childhood, how we

were brought up, fed, clothed and looked after pretty well. Then there are these kids who are trying twice as hard with half the resources. It just seems so unfair.'

'Excuse me, need a loo break,' announced Imogen, draining her glass.

'I hope it hasn't put a damper on our evening,' he said, changing the subject. 'You said you were in the middle of a big case at the moment.' Buchan topped up all three glasses, emptying the bottle.

'Not a damper. I think it's just reminded me of the reality some of the kids in our city are facing – not that there aren't some little shites out there, but, those images,' she gestured to the lecture hall, 'they make me uneasy.'

'But you help those kind of kids, don't you?'

Wheeler stared into her glass. 'I'm not sure. At least we don't always help them, not all the time. Sometimes there's no time to find out much about their background. It's just process them, place them in the system somewhere and then it's onto the next case.'

'You're being too hard on yourself,' he touched her arm, 'really. I think you probably do a lot of good for the kids you come into contact with.' He smiled at her, tried to lighten the mood.

'Is that right?'

'Uh huh, you do a great job. Changing the subject, do you want to go on somewhere for dinner?' He was definitely flirting.

'Might do.'

'Italian, Indian, Greek . . .?'

Imogen came back. 'I'm heading off home now – I've got a pregnant girlfriend who will be feeling neglected herself if I don't make a show.'

Buchan smiled. 'Just need to say a quick goodbye to Matt.

Won't be a sec.' He paused. 'Good to meet you Imogen, and safe journey home.'

They watched him disappear into the crowd.

Imogen pulled on her jacket. 'You going home with him?'

'I haven't decided yet.'

'Well either way, try to enjoy yourself. You need some down time with your job. And the lecture was great but pretty heavy. You need some fun.'

'Yep, I agree.' Wheeler sipped her wine, watched Buchan speak to Matt Barnes.

'Cute.' Imogen nodded towards Buchan.

Wheeler raised her glass. 'Abso-fucking-lutely he's cute,' but she heard the tension in her voice.

'Think you'll ever settle down?'

'Like you and Alison, do you mean?'

'Well, obviously not as perfect and loved up as we are, but you know, a committed relationship and emotional intimacy, that kind of thing?'

'Who knows? Maybe,' Wheeler lied.

'I hope he's not going to be just another one of your brief liaisons.'

'I'll try not to hurt his feelings.'

'What about you and Ross?'

'Ross?'

'You heard.'

'I hope you don't mean what I think you mean.'

'You fancy him.'

'What kind of a word is that,' Wheeler laughed. 'Are you still in primary school?'

'Cut the crap, Wheeler, just answer the question. You want to jump Ross, don't you?'

'Christ,' Wheeler spluttered, 'now you've graduated from primary to delinquent teenager. Jump him?'

'Just answer the question.'

'There is no question.' Wheeler held out her hand, counting off the fingers, 'one, we're colleagues, two, I'm a detective, three . . .'

'Ha, you do want to jump him.'

'Christ, any more of this and I'm telling Alison what a nutter she's with.'

'Mobile.'

Wheeler watched her friend answer the call, saw from her reaction it was her girlfriend.

Imogen finished the call. 'Need to go. You okay if I just push off now?'

'You're okay.'

'See you soon?'

'Definitely. Give Alison my love.'

'Will do.'

Wheeler sat, people-watching, until she saw Buchan cross the room towards her. Saw him smile. Saw that he was attracting glances from some of the other women. She knew if she went home with him and they had sex, that would be it, maybe one more date but then she'd move on. That was her pattern. Maybe Imogen was right; maybe she should give him a chance and at least try to get to know him. Wheeler drained her wine glass and walked towards him. 'Let's go for Italian. It'll give us a chance to get to know each other.' Even to her it sounded false.

Chapter 20

Ross closed the door behind him, threw the football scarf on the hall table and kicked off his boots. He padded towards the kitchen and almost skidded on the wet.

'Fuckssake.' He righted himself. Then he smelled it: sour urine. Dog piss. He switched on the light and saw that the puddle he had walked into had spread across his expensive parquet flooring. He squelched towards the sitting room just as the square-headed dog made a bid for freedom, charging past him, head down, on its way towards the door. Like a miniature bull. If the bull had three legs and wore a plastic cone around its neck.

'Christ, what a nightmare.' The dog turned and looked at him. Glanced at the door. Waited.

'Aye, you want out now, now that you've pissed all over the floor.'

The dog wagged her tail, tried to itch the gash on the side of her head but the plastic cone prevented her from reaching it. She whined quietly.

Ross pulled off his socks and walked into the kitchen, shoved them into the washing machine and slammed the door shut on the smell. The dog had followed him and stood watching from the doorway. He stared at her. 'You, in future, you keep it in until I get back. Cross your fucking legs if you have to.' He collected the bucket and mop and started the clean-up.

The dog stared. Wagged her tail some more, looked at the door. Whined.

'Oh for God's sake, I'm just in out the rain.'

The mutt waited patiently. Then whined again. Paused. Began again.

Ross dumped the mop. 'You're not going to give up, are you?'

More whining, this time softer but still insistent.

Ross decided that he couldn't be arsed going in search of socks, so he just pulled on his boots, feeling the leather harsh against his bare skin. He grabbed the lead. 'Well, pee-the-bed, let's go.'

Once outside the flat, he turned left and carried on down Argyle Street, towards the Kelvingrove Museum and Art Gallery. The huge baroque building was floodlit and impressive even in the rain. Ross had been inside often enough to see different exhibitions, though he tended to avoid it when the massive pipe organ was being played. He liked it best when it was quiet and he could be alone with his thoughts and whatever exhibition he'd gone to see. He walked across the grass, the mutt trotting happily beside him. He patted his pocket, checking for poo bags, and walked around the perimeter of the building. They passed the bronze sculpture of St Mungo, the patron saint of Glasgow, fashioned as patron of art and music, and continued over the bridge that crossed the River Kelvin.

They turned right into Byres Road, which was full of revellers spilling out of the pubs and restaurants. Music was blaring out from The Vineyard and Ross ignored a drunk who pointed to the dog and shouted, 'You walking that thing for a laugh?' Followed by, 'Should it no be in the circus?' They walked on, crossing Byres Road and stopped outside the chippy. Its windows were steamed up and the smell of frying food hit him; his stomach growled in response. He was on the verge of going in when the dog tugged on the lead, crouched down and deposited a steaming poo. Ross bent down, felt the rain run through his hair, knew his jeans were soaked. Grabbed the soft poo in a plastic bag and tied the tops, trying to ignore the smell. As he turned he saw Kat Wheeler coming out of the Italian restaurant opposite. The tall guy she was with was telling her something funny. She laughed up at him. Ross turned and dragged the dog back the way they'd come, depositing the plastic bag in the first bin he saw.

Once home, the dog shook herself over the hall floor before padding through to the sitting room. She jumped onto the sofa and turned in a circle a few times before settling down. She was asleep in seconds, a gentle wheeze emanating from her snout.

Ross was wide awake.

He stood in the hallway deliberating. Not for long. Ten minutes later he was heading east along Argyle Street, towards the station, windscreen wipers humming a rhythmic chorus. He switched on the radio; the sports discussion was midway through.

'Raith Rovers,' the presenter laughed, 'were they robbed

tonight, or were Partick Thistle just too good for them? You decide. Call us with your views on—'

'Fuck off,' Ross muttered, switched to a music channel, leaned back in his seat as *Fairytale of New York* began. 'Bloody Christmas music,' he leaned forward, his hand hovering for a second before he rested it back on the steering wheel. A few bars in and he was singing along.

Tommy Cunningham was behind the desk and smirked as Ross passed. Ross ignored him, took the stairs to the CID suite two at a time, pulled open the door and was pleased to find it empty. He grabbed a pile of reports that had been left on his desk and settled himself to read through the list of phone messages that had come through following Stewart's appeal. After the first few pages he crossed to the kettle and switched it on, scooped coffee into a mug and rooted around the room for biscuits. He found some in Boyd's desk, took two and settled back at his desk. There had been a number of responses to Gilmore's death but some would be bogus, some would be mistaken and others, well, Ross hoped that they would be helpful. Whoever killed Gilmore was out there watching, waiting and perhaps planning another attack.

Ross turned the page, read through another list of calls, making notes as he went along.

I did it. It was me. No, I didn't know him before, it was a random attack but it was me. Definitely. The caller had given his name, number and had cheerfully agreed to come into the station to be interviewed. How helpful. Ross put a question mark next to the name. The police had left out much of the detail surrounding the beating, in particular the fact that the body had been hung on a hook. That information was known only to the police and the killer and would help them sift through the time wasters.

Next message. *You need to be looking at James Gilmore and Arthur Wright. London. That's all I'm saying.*

Ross read on; the man had been asked for his name and a contact number. Both had been refused. He'd been calling from a public call box somewhere. Ross jotted down the name *Arthur Wright, London.* Underlined it. Beside it he wrote *trace the call.* Then he read on.

I think I might have known a guy called James Gilmore. Going back a while now mind you . . . wee guy, ginger hair? . . .

I knew James when he was doing his training. I think it was a James Gilmore, not sure now that I think about it, maybe his name was Jamie, that'd be much the same but . . .

I know something important about James Gilmore. He was one of the bad guys. He wasn't what he appeared to be; he was a fucking psycho. I don't want to give my name. I can't be implicated in this. But he's not what he seemed. Look at his history. Just look at his history. No name, no number. Public phone box. Again Ross wrote *trace call* in his notebook and read on. Two callers, both anonymous, had suggested that Gilmore hadn't been one of the good guys. Either they were muddying the waters for the police or Gilmore had a life that he'd kept hidden from everyone. Ross favoured the last idea. He fired up the computer, opened the police database and typed in 'Arthur Wright, London', pressed enter and waited.

A half hour later and he'd found nothing useful. Ross was closing down his computer when his mobile chirruped. A text. He glanced at the sender. Sarah, his ex-girlfriend. The broody one.

I'm lonely. Want to come over?

Ross thought about their last conversation. About her wanting kids, him not ever wanting them. Nothing had changed for him and he couldn't carry on seeing someone who so clearly wanted a family. Children would never be on his radar. Wife, kids, dog. He didn't want the package. Ross picked a stray dog hair from his jacket – well he'd been suckered into having one out of three, but that was it. He wondered idly if Sarah had changed her mind but he knew that there was no chance. If he were being honest, she was lonely and probably a bit bored and what she was offering was sex. He paused for a heartbeat before texting, *Will bring wine.*

A second later she replied, *Food?*

He sighed. *Chinese or Indian?*

Indian. Yum.

Ross stuffed the notes into the tray on his desk and switched off the light on his way out of the room. Good food and hopefully great sex; it was a decent end to a hard day. He even nodded to Cunningham on his way out of the station.

Chapter 21

'Well, for a start you can take these and shove them up your fucking arse.'

A can of lager split as the four-pack hit the wall behind him. Mason knew it had been a mistake to come home. Lizzie Coughlin was more than pissed at him. Well fuck her, he just needed to get his stuff, that was all, in and out. No messing. He heard the hiss of the lager as it ran down the wall and foamed onto the carpet. Then the bloody bird began tweeting. Fuck, he stared at the birdcage as he walked towards the bedroom door. The yellow bird blinked back. Duchess. Stupid name. Stupid bird. Same as Lizzie.

'You've been in the Bar-L for years, then you're out and you can't make it home and now, at this hour, you've decided to breeze back in. Where the hell were you?'

Hysterical. Voice trembling. Eyes bloodshot. She'd been on the vodka again.

Mason bared his teeth. 'I've been busy. Not that it's got anything to dae with you. I'm off. I'm going into business. A partnership. Fifty-fifty.'

Lizzie, hands on her hips, sneered, 'Oh aye? Doing what?'

Mason tapped the side of his nose with his forefinger. 'Nosy cow. Let's just say I've got a bit of merchandise and I'm standing back and waiting for the dividend to be paid.'

Lizzie's eyes narrowed. 'Whose merchandise?'

'You wouldnae know him.'

'Try me.'

'It's none of your business – keep your snout out of it.'

'You've wanted tae get intae the drugs scene for ever, but it's moved on since you went inside; you've nae chance. It's all sewn up.'

'That right?'

'Aye, Tenant, Doyle, Jamieson. Do you know nothing?'

'Like you'd know anything,' he sneered. 'Tenant's giving me a way in.'

'Wee Stevie Tenant's intae drugs and you've nae money, so where are you planning on getting your "dividend" from?'

Mason stared at her. Stevie Tenant was Davey's younger brother but there was no point in telling her she had the wrong brother. It had nothing to do with her and besides, there was something more important he had to say. 'You're staying out of it, Lizzie. You're no going to be part of it, so there's nae point in asking. See us? We're over. You're history. The lager was tae soften the blow, seeing as how I'm a gentleman, but as usual you've lost the fucking plot.'

'I'm dumped? Is that it?'

'Aye.'

'And you're going in with wee Stevie?'

'Correct in that I'm going into partnership with someone.'

'So who'll you be up against?' she asked.

He ignored her.

'It's got to be Andy Doyle.' Lizzie watched Mason swagger into the bedroom and emerge a few seconds later with his bag stuffed full of clothes.

'I'll be back for the CDs and stuff when I get settled.'

'So you think you can just walk out on me? Nae chance there. You're not walking out.'

It was like a white light when it happened, like a migraine beginning, but instead of being painful, it became energising. He dropped the bag and crossed the room in an instant. He was aware that Lizzie had stopped yelling and had started to tremble. He smiled reassuringly as he reached out to her, kept smiling as he raised his right hand and curled his fingers around her throat. Mason held her with just enough pressure to stop the air flow. Waited, watched her flail, arms flapping, mouth gurgling, eyes bulging. Kept his voice low, quiet, sincere: 'If you ever mouth off at me again, I'll kill you. Think on Lizzie, you get in my way and you're dead meat. And don't bother running tae your auld da. I've enough pals inside – I'll get him chibbed. He's an old timer, remember that. Yesterday's news. Just like yourself.' He waited a few more seconds then let go. Heard her retching and choking as he crossed the room, glanced back, saw that she was doubled over, gasping for air. Bared his teeth in a grin.

Mason grabbed his coat, picked up his bag and opened the door, then he paused, turned back. Opened the cage and took the bird in his right hand, felt its heartbeat quicken, squeezed it hard and used his thumb to flick its head back. Felt the heartbeat flicker, then stop.

Lizzie screamed behind him but it was a weak, snivelling scream. Mason slammed the door and walked to the car, started up the engine and rolled down the window. He turned his car away from Haghill. Next stop was a drink at the Smuggler's. He smiled, teeth bared at the night sky; it was good to be free.

Chapter 22

A waste ground in North Glasgow.

'It's got nits.'

'It's no nits, ya numpty, it's fleas.'

'Oh aye, so there's a difference?'

'Aye.'

Rab Wilson held the pigeon in his hands. 'And see, it's tagged – it's a racer.'

Alec Munroe stared at it. 'So, how come it's sitting here in the middle of the road?'

'It's knackered.'

'How?'

'They race them from a long way away – France, sometimes. The birds get as far as they can and they're just too knackered to go on, so they stop. Just stop for a lie down.'

'So they just die then?'

'Sometimes. Depends where they come down.'

'How come you know all this?'

'My Ma's ex-boyfriend was intae racing pigeons.'

'Hammy?'

'Naw, before him.'

'Thought his name was Billy?'

'Before Billy.'

'The wan that broke your nose?'

''Fore him.'

'Cannae remember that far back.'

'He was called Jock. He was okay.'

'Then how come your ma chucked him?'

'He got pissed and shagged my Auntie Tracy. Long time ago now. It spoiled my Christmas though, all the screaming and chucking things at each other. My Ma tells everybody she's no got a sister. But she has so.'

'Is that no what Christmas with the family's all aboot?'

'Aye, cannae wait to get away and get my own place.'

'Me tae.'

They stood watching the rain fall into dark puddles.

Alec broke the silence. 'Whit's your Ma's new boyfriend like?'

'Kenny? He's an evil bastard. I hate him.'

'Right.'

'Jock wisnae bad though but he's an old cunt an' now he's in hospital for an operation. Won't be oot for a month. He's got an allotment but.'

'You get tae go down?'

'Aye, he got me a shed. Padlocked an' everything. It's mine. Get tae keep all ma stuff in it.'

Alec sniffed. 'Whit about this then?'

'Whit?'

Alec looked down at the bird. 'See if we leave it here, Rab, will a cat no get it, or a fox? Or just the fucking freezing weather?'

'Mibbe.'

They stared at the pigeon. Rab spoke. 'Better to kill it here then than leave it to get scoffed by a fox. Get a brick and bash its heid in.'

Alec looked around the spare ground. 'Are ye sure?'

'Aye, it's the kindest thing. It'll be our good deed for the day. What did Ms Paton used to call it when she was rabbiting on in assembly?'

'Random acts of kindness.'

Rab waited until Alec had returned with the brick. The bird watched them with curious eyes. Blinking.

'Best to just cave its heid right in, smash it to bits quickly. It'll no feel a thing,' Rab said. He could feel its heartbeat through the soft feathers. The bird shifted in his hands, its claws curled around his fingers. It settled itself. Waited.

Rab and Alec walked to the edge of the waste ground. 'Here.'

'Okay.'

Alec raised the brick above the bird's head, paused, then brought it down quickly.

Rab stared at him. 'Ye missed it, ya numpy. How've ye managed tae miss it?'

Alec looked at him. 'Ah cannae dae it.'

'Christ, how no?'

'You dae it well!'

Rab sighed. 'It's a nice enough wee bird. Disnae deserve to die just 'cause it's knackered.'

'Disnae deserve tae be battered tae death cause it's tired.'

'Naw, mibbe no.'

'Naw,' agreed Alec, 'mibbe we should batter the cunt that raced it too far?'

'Aye, mibbe.' Rab laughed.

They stared at the pigeon. It stared back. Blinked. Curled its claws tighter around Rab's fingers. Held on.

'Whit noo?'

'Fuck knows.'

'Aye, right enough.'

Rab looked around. Derelict tenements stood waiting for demolition, and lined each side of the waste ground. A couple of flats looked like they might be home to squatters. Folk who shot up on a daily basis, given the number of empty syringes littering the pavements.

'We could get it up to the top windae in that place.' He pointed to the last tenement; its windows were meshed with metal, but a hole about two feet square had been cut into the closed door. 'It'd be safe up there. Nae foxes. Come on.'

On the other side of the waste ground a four-by-four trawled by slowly, its blackened windows reflecting the street lights and rain. It slowed to a pause. Stopped.

Alec and Rab stomped up the stairs, avoiding needles and tinfoil, discarded lighters. Vomit and shit. Up to the top landing. One flat had been burned out, the walls charcoal, the windows blown.

'Handy,' Rab walked into what would have been a bedroom. He stopped in the middle of the room and nodded to Alec. 'Gonnae clear that?'

Alec cleared the shards of glass from the window sill using the sleeve of his hoodie.

They placed the pigeon on the sill. Listened to it coo.

'Nae food for it, but.'

'Naw.'

'It'll be safe here?'

'Aye.'

'Will it go back tae its hame?'

'When it's rested a wee bit.'

They left the room, both looking back to check on it. The pigeon blinked and watched them leave.

Outside the wind was up; Rab pulled his fleece close to him. 'Fuck me it's freezing. Hame?'

Alec nodded. 'Hame.'

They walked down the street. The four-by-four was waiting for them; the window hummed as it was lowered. Smithy leaned out, pointed a fat sausage-shaped finger at them. 'Want a word wi you two wankers.' Alec and Rab didn't pause to answer – they bolted across the waste ground, their trainers squelching through mud.

Smithy smiled, let them get a head start before he started the car. He'd enjoy the chase.

Chapter 23

The Smugglers Rest looked exactly as it had on his previous visit. Maybe a little more depressing if that were possible. The twins, Heather and Shona, were perched on bar stools making one drink last them all night. They glanced over and smiled hopefully but Maurice Mason ignored them. The twins scowled, muttered to each other and turned back to their drinks.

Sonny nodded at him. 'You want your usual?'

Mason smiled. 'Naw, I'm having a wee celebration, Sonny, gie us a double vodka. And have one yourself.'

Sonny looked up quickly, eyes narrowed. 'Is that you won the lottery then or what?'

'No quite but things are looking up. I'm out of the jail, newly single and I'm coming into a wee bit of money soon. So, let's get the party started.' He raised his glass to the barman.

Sonny poured himself a shot, kept his voice low. 'Somebody die then?'

Mason tapped the side of his nose with his finger. 'I'm keeping schtum.'

'Aye, probably safer that way,' said Sonny.

'Anyway, a wee toast.'

'To whit?'

'To me being newly single, nae girlfriend, nae family, nothing tae drag me down. Let's drink tae that: absent family.'

'Christ, I hope to hell mine stay absent. Cunts they are, one and all.' Sonny raised his glass. 'Cheers.'

Mason glanced across at the twins, noticed that they were still watching him, saw Heather lick her lips, keep them parted while she stared at Mason.

'They two always working?'

'Aye, business is slow and they're trying to keep ahead of the influx for the Games.'

'The whit?'

'The Commonwealth Games.'

Mason was confused. 'It's no like they'll be going, is it?'

'Naw, but they had a wee read at Grim's article in the *Chronicle*. Depressed them.' Sonny shoved the paper across the bar. 'Be my guest.'

Mason glanced at the front-page article, began reading aloud, putting his finger under each word, sounding out the longer phrases. 'Fears are running high that Glasgow will fall prey to organised sex trafficking during the Commonwealth Games.'

'Nightmare,' Sonny said. 'The twins don't need the competition. No to mention it's a shite life for the wee foreign lassies that'll be trafficked through the city.'

'Pigs no dae nothing, is that no whit they're paid for?'

'Says in the paper the polis huvnae got much of a clue. Kind of down tae communication and according to the paper, there's no much between the different kinds of polis. Aye, everyone's got their problems.'

'Aye.' Mason jabbed his thumb in the direction of the twins. 'Here Sonny, you reckon it's BOGOF the night, seeing they might lose out during the Games to the wee foreign birds?'

The barman chuckled. 'Aye, just tell them you read what Grim said in the paper, see how it goes. You'll be lucky, you chancer. Mind you it's a quiet night, might be worth a try. Wouldnae get on their wrong side mind you – one punter refused to pay Shona last week. Arsehole tried to dae a runner.'

'And?'

'I've no heard how he's doing, but the last I saw was the ambulance crew picking up bits of broken bone from his nose before they carted him off to the Royal. Still a few wee shards out the back that they missed.'

Mason sipped his drink, let the alcohol warm him, knew the twins were still watching him, perched like two wrinkled hawks ready to pounce. 'Well mibbe I'll have a wee think about it, but the night's young yet, Sonny, the night's young.'

DREAMER

It's four a.m. and the Dreamer stirs in his sleep, puts a finger to his mouth and scrapes at the skin on his lips until blood seeps onto the pillow, then his fingers worry at the side of the sheet, kneading and pressing it into submission. His nostrils flare. It is the smell he remembers best, the coppery smell that drenched the room. The Dreamer smiles, remembering how he'd stood over the body and inhaled deeply as particles of airborne blood had entered his mouth and he'd held them there for as long as he could before forcing them far into his lungs, willing them to become part of his fibre. Gilmore's blood. The smell of coppers in his pocket, the smell of loose change. That was what Gilmore's blood had smelled of, loose change. But he was worth less. The Dreamer's hands clench and unclench, a frown flits across his forehead; darting in and out of his emotions are feelings of relief, of a spring finally being allowed to uncoil. The Dreamer's hands stop their fretting and he lets himself fall further into a deep sleep.

Chapter 24

Wednesday, 11 December

The Kelvingrove Art Gallery lies in the shadow of Glasgow University and the River Kelvin passes close by. Myth has it that the building was built back to front and when the architect discovered this he hurled himself to instant death from one of the towers. This is untrue but generations of Glaswegians have passed it down as fact, preferring the colourful lie to bald truth. A series of early-morning lectures, The Breakfast History of Art, was being piloted at the Kelvingrove.

It was seven a.m. and it would have been her day off had James Gilmore not been murdered, but Wheeler had booked the session months in advance and was determined to go. She sat in the semi-darkness of the building and listened. '. . . And voted Glasgow's favourite painting,' finished the guide, pointing a grubby, nail-bitten finger at the picture. Wheeler peered at Salvador Dali's masterpiece. The early lecture meant that she got to forget about dead bodies and traipse round the Gallery listening to ideas that were a million miles away from police work. Just her and other art lovers. As the lecture took place hours before the usual opening times there were no chattering school groups, no exhausted mothers with pushchairs sheltering from the weather, no folk who'd nowhere else to go and just wanted to be somewhere warm and quiet. They would all come later. For now, it was just her and peace and quiet and pictures. And the coffee bar for a caffeine hit.

Wheeler felt her mobile vibrate in her pocket, fished it out and surreptitiously glanced at it. Mobiles were to be turned off during the lecture. It was Ross.

U at that arty-farty thing? I'm close by. Fancy a coffee when it's done?

She managed just two characters.

OK.

She stared at the painting, Christ of Saint John of the Cross. Christ on the cross, with no blood, no gore, just as Dali saw it in his vision. Peaceful. The picture had an eerie silence about it, as if she were spying on God. She found it both beautiful and unsettling. She bent and looked at the painting sideways, felt herself sway. It was something about the angle. She gave up on the picture, preferring instead to sit in the silence and drink in the atmosphere of the place. To get it almost to herself was a delight. More than a million souls visited the place every year and during normal opening hours she'd been hard pressed to get anywhere near her favourite pictures.

She took a stroll along the corridors, the marble floor absorbing her footsteps, the dim lights casting a permanent calm across the arches, the huge blocks of sandstone glowing after their recent deep clean. She passed the bronze sculpture of Madame Renoir and on to the gallery hosting the Scottish Colourists. The gallery was empty, so she wandered in and stood in front of the paintings and once again wished that her police salary would stretch to her owning an original. Her flat was home to five large framed prints but it wasn't the same as having an original. She wondered about the tiny J.D. Fergusson drawing in Moira Gilmore's apartment – what would happen to it after she passed away?

Wheeler stood in front of Fergusson's *Torse de Femme* and studied it, saw the energy and the passion in the brush strokes, then she studied Cadell's *The Orange Blind*, felt the calm, reflective energy of the painting soothe her. She wandered among the paintings, noting colour, line and composition until, finally, it was time to go. She left by the Argyle Street entrance, turned left and waited on the Kelvin Way for him. After a few minutes she turned back towards the tenement flats and started walking. She soon saw him. Ross had a dog on its lead; in the other hand he held a pile of plastic poo bags. The three-legged dog looked like a cross between a pit-bull and an alien. Wheeler walked up behind him.

'God, but that's ugly. And it's got its head in a plastic cone. Nightmare.'

Ross turned, tried to laugh but couldn't pull it off.

'That your wee pet then?' Wheeler continued.

He nodded. Blushed.

'Not quite the babe magnet I'd envisaged. Still, I bet you've got a wee soft spot for it.' She bent down, patted the dog. 'Its head's awfully square, how's that?'

'Don't know.'

'Something happen when it was a pup?'

'Don't know. Haven't had it that long.'

'And it's got a nasty wee gash on its head as well.'

She straightened up, put two and two together. 'Let me guess. You got it right after you wrecked the car.' It was more of a statement than a question.

Ross shuffled his feet, stared at the dog. 'Can't be sure – it's a while back now.'

But she knew she had him, saw the blush start again, first at the bottom of his neck and then work its way up. 'Either you ran into the wee runt or swerved to avoid it. Which is it?'

'Avoid. Somebody chucked it out of their car. I never even got the registration. Scabby car, kicked in, think it was a Fiesta. It was a stormy night.'

'It had all its legs then?'

'What?'

'The mutt.'

'No, still just the three.'

'So you swerved, mangled the pool car, *police property mind*, and then went to rescue Fido, the three-legged, square-headed mutt? You're a hero.'

Ross turned away. 'It's not an it, it's a her. And the vet says the cone can come off in a week or so. Anyway, I need to be getting her back. We still on for coffee?'

'You're a soft muppet. I'll walk slow; catch me up when you drop it off.'

'Her.'

'Apologies, her. What's her name?'

'Haven't given her one yet.'

Wheeler looked at the dog. 'Is "I'm-a-lucky-wee-shite" too obvious? Or just too long?'

Ross said nothing. Turned and began walking back, the dog trotting obediently after him, her nose in the air.

Wheeler crossed the road and walked back along University Avenue, taking her time, ignoring the rain and thinking about the case. She had turned into Great Western Road by the time Ross caught up with her.

'Where to?' He was out of breath.

'Where do you fancy, Ross? My treat, since you rescued a wee dug, so you get to wear the hero's badge for the day. All day.' She couldn't help the smirk.

He stared at her. 'You wouldn't.'

'What? Wouldn't buy you breakfast?'

'Wouldn't do what you're thinking of doing.'

'Might do.'

'No, even you're not that evil.'

'What? You don't want your chums at the station to get wind of your heroics? Or a description of your ugly wee friend? Which is it?'

Ross walked ahead, just enough that she knew he was in the huff. But not so much that she withdrew her offer of breakfast.

They settled into the café, steam obscuring the windows. It was still early and the café wasn't yet full.

'A large latte and the same as what he's having,' Wheeler said to the waitress.

'Full breakfast, extra fried egg and extra potato scone and a tea for me, thanks.'

The waitress left.

'Peckish then, Ross?'

'Wee bit.'

'It'll be all that exercise with the three-legged one.'

They settled back. Wheeler picked up a copy of the *Chronicle*. They waited until the food and drinks had arrived, then began their chat.

'Gilmore's fading into the past a bit.' Ross bit into his egg.

'But there's been a couple of interesting phone messages. Came through to the station last night.'

'Who from?'

He sighed. 'Anonymous callers.'

'Saying what?'

'That Gilmore's one of the bad guys.'

'Anything else?' She sipped her latte.

'One of them mentioned a guy called Arthur Wright, London. That's all. I've looked him up, but we've nothing on an Arthur Wright. I've got a trace out on the calls.'

'Gut instinct? You think they're bogus or legit?'

'Too early to call. I'll keep on it.' Ross started on his toast. 'Either way, the case needs to be kept in the papers.'

'I know, what with Christmas coming and look at this,' she tapped the front page of the *Chronicle*, 'the heid high yins are running scared that Glasgow's going to get inundated with foreign girls for the sex trade now that we're getting the Commonwealth Games.'

'Read it already. Grim's right though, might be a bit of a nightmare.'

'I know.' Wheeler tucked into her fried bread. 'The thing is, we can worry about that later, but right now it's pushing Gilmore's murder off the news. There's hardly anything at all in the paper about his death.'

'Off the news and out of the public's mind,' agreed Ross.

'Exactly.' Wheeler chewed thoughtfully.

'Trouble is, he just doesn't have much of a profile. A middle-aged man, a psychologist at a couple of schools in the city who's a bit of a loner. No wife, no kids.'

'So no sad pictures or pleas from them,' said Wheeler.

'Exactly,' he paused. 'Maybe it points in one direction.'

Wheeler sipped her latte, paused. 'Paedophile?'

'Possible.'

'Facts?'

'Nothing yet, either way. I'm just saying it's possible.'

'I'll keep an open mind. Certainly he has a hell of a low profile. No girlfriend. No friends. All he has is an elderly mum in a care home.'

'And she's a bit of a bitch.'

'That's the trouble, Ross, it's not sexy. His life was pretty empty. Folk just aren't that interested.'

Ross wiped the egg yolk from his plate with a piece of toast. 'It's a bit of a sad day when being battered to death in your own home is a one-day wonder.' He finished the eggy toast and started on the potato scones. 'Maybe we need to look again at the kids at Watervale.'

'Because?'

'Because, well it's Watervale . . . you saw the scheme.'

Wheeler sipped her coffee. 'Yeah, kids living in a rough scheme. Some of them pretty neglected,' she paused. 'Brain scans.'

'Come again?'

'I went to a lecture about brain scans.'

'Talk about sexy.'

'Shut it. It showed the disparity in brain size between kids who've been neglected and kids who have had a normal upbringing.'

'Shocked?'

She nodded, recited the facts as best she could.

Ross listened and agreed. 'Hard for some of them. On the other hand they're not all neglected, those kids – some of them are just wee thugs. It's a deliberate career choice. Some of them are just evil wee shites.'

'You're going to make the best dad, when the time comes, you know that don't you?'

He smiled. 'You offering?'

'In your dreams, matey.'

He flushed, looked away. 'Got the report from the other two schools, St Austin's and Cuthbertson High. Boyd and Robertson did the interviews.'

'Yeah, I saw it already. Nothing much in it, same as our report.'

'Yeah,' he agreed. 'They described him pretty much the same as the staff from Watervale. The guy was a bloody ghost.'

She groaned. 'We've nothing. Stewart's going to love us.'

'In the biblical sense, do you mean?' Ross scraped his plate. 'Would that suit you?'

Wheeler left the rest of her breakfast. 'You've a mind like a sewer Ross, you know that, don't you?'

He nodded. 'Aye, but just so you notice me one way or another.'

She stood up. 'Let's go, muppet.'

Chapter 25

They were sitting in the CID suite by nine. Stewart was perched on her desk for one of his informal chats. Wheeler looked up from her computer and saw that once again he looked pristine in a dove-grey suit. She instinctively touched her own trousers – same outfit as yesterday. She felt slightly grubby, thought maybe the smell from the greasy breakfast she'd shared with Ross still clung to her. They were in their way to see George Grey but Stewart obviously wanted something. 'Boss?'

Stewart stared down at her. 'The Grim Reaper will be in my office in ten minutes. Make it worth my while seeing the little gremlin and throw him a bone. What have you got?'

Wheeler could smell his citrus aftershave, felt that he was sitting too close. She sat back in her seat, felt the blush creeping up her face. 'Love to, boss,' she tapped a pile of reports, 'but still sifting through the evidence. Going through the house to house again as you suggested, but it seems no one saw anything suspicious.'

'Uh huh.' Stewart waited.

'That's the thing. James Gilmore was nothing out of the ordinary. Apparently he was just a decent guy doing a decent job. But his death was completely out of the ordinary.'

'Unless . . .' said Ross.

'Go on.'

'Paedophile?' said Ross. 'Would account for the way he died – someone out for revenge?'

'Evidence?'

'There were a couple of calls that came in from pay phones—'

'From?'

'Haven't traced them yet, boss, but one caller warned us about Gilmore not being one of the good guys. The other linked him to Arthur Wright, London.'

'Who?'

Ross shrugged. 'Came up blank but I'll keep digging.'

'Get the calls traced.'

'Will do.'

'Any other theories?' Stewart waited.

'Could've been a dealer? He worked city-wide, so it's pretty good cover?' Robertson offered.

'Gilmore was a supplier?' Boyd sounded doubtful. 'And going up against the McGregors and the Tenants, not to mention the independent entrepreneurial nutters out there?'

'No, maybe not going up against them but working for them,' said Robertson. 'If Gilmore got himself involved in something that he shouldn't have, it may be that he paid the price.'

'Okay,' said Stewart, 'so, we've nothing. Let's start something.'

'Boss?'

Stewart cleared his throat. 'I'll tell Grim to write up an article about our zero-tolerance approach in the lead-up to Christmas. We'll make it known that we'll be targeting all known offenders.'

'Everyone, boss?' Ross was already doing the maths.

'We'll tell them it's everyone. In reality it'll just be the usual scum who'll be stopped and searched.'

Wheeler warmed to the idea. 'Make it difficult for them to do their not-so-legitimate business.'

Stewart smiled at her. 'Exactly, we make their daily life complete shite and so they'll need to get us off their back. Someone knows something about this murder; it didn't happen in isolation. The bloodied clothes the killer was wearing, the car he used. Someone must be boasting about it to their pals. Something has to give.' He crossed to the window, looked out at the grey sky. 'There's a dozen incentives already in place that this can easily dovetail in with.'

'Stop and search is never popular,' said Wheeler.

'We're not trying to be popular,' replied Stewart. 'We're trying to be a pain in the backside. This'll hit the dealers and if we hit them hard enough they'd grass up their own granny, never mind whoever did Gilmore.'

'So we hassle them until they snap?' said Boyd.

'Exactly. We know the main players and their teams – let's make them uncomfortable.' He smiled. 'Okay, let's go with that. I'll get the word out via Grim and the *Chronicle*. Might as well try to shake things up a bit.' Stewart adjusted his tie and marched to the door. Wheeler watched him leave the room, thinking that he was right. They had nothing new and they had nothing to lose by stirring up some bad feeling.

'You not going through to watch the performance, then? See the big man in action?' Ross grinned at her, fanning his hand in front of his face. 'You warm? Only you look a bit flushed.'

Wheeler stood, pushed the reports to the side. 'Shut it, you. I'm off to the loo, then we're having a chat with George Grey.'

When she passed Stewart's office, the door was open and he was sitting behind his desk. Grim was seated on a hard chair facing Stewart. She heard them begin.

'Good to see you, Grim,' said Stewart.

'Likewise, Stewart.'

Neither managed to convey even a hint of sincerity.

'Okay, enough with the pleasantries – let's get on. Grim, I want you to run an article on a police crackdown, a type of zero-tolerance, and here's why.'

Wheeler walked on, made a quick stop at the loo and marched back to her desk. 'Ross, we're off to see George Grey.'

Wheeler and Ross pulled up outside a row of tenement buildings that were not scheduled for demolition. But should have been. Ross killed the engine. 'Let's give it a second, see if the rain goes off a bit.' He looked at the houses. 'We need one of those wee sanitising units. This place is worse than the scheme at Watervale.'

'Can't all be trendy West Enders like yourself, Ross.'

'Right enough.' He turned to her. 'Rovers got beat last night.'

Wheeler laughed. 'So? Is that not a regular occurrence? Surely you can't be surprised?'

'Fair enough.' He paused, stared out at the rain. 'You out and about yourself?'

She looked at him. 'Well I wasn't out watching football, if that's what you're asking.'

He waited, 'And?'

'And what?'

'Good time?'

Wheeler stepped out of the car. 'I told you, I went to a lecture on brain scans.'

He waited.

She slammed the door.

He grunted, got out the other side, automatically smoothed down his hair.

She watched him. 'Don't think the photographers will be here today. Besides, there's another bit of dog hair on your jacket. Either your grooming's slipping or you're letting that mutt sleep on everything.'

'Shit.' He brushed the hairs from his jacket and was locking the door when the half-brick sailed by his head and smashed onto the bonnet of the car. Wheeler spun round and saw three boys running into one of the tenement buildings. The taller of them turned back, his voice ferocious, 'Fucking scumbag pigs!' A smaller boy shouted, 'Oink, oink.' The third wasn't quite so humorous: 'Next time the brick'll kill you.' He paused, spat on the ground then followed his friends into the close.

She looked at Ross. 'It's a welcome of sorts.'

Ross grabbed the brick and chucked it onto the ground. 'No point going after them, is there?'

'What for? We'll be led a merry dance round the houses. Come on, we've got work to do.' She walked into the mouth of the close. 'George Grey's house is on the ground floor, so we're probably not going to be ambushed.' Wheeler paused outside a wooden door; the paint was peeling and the central glass panel had been severely cracked and gaffa-taped back together, giving a warped mosaic effect. Wheeler grimaced. 'I'm thinking industrial chic – what do you think?'

Ross stood beside her and whined, 'I haven't even had a chance to digest my breakfast before that crappy wee welcoming committee outside.'

She patted his arm. 'Aw diddums is all sensitive again. The big boys upset you? Never mind, I'll buy you coffee and a bun later if you're good.' She knocked hard and waited.

A boy of around sixteen answered.

'You George Grey, son?'

The boy nodded, turned back and shouted into the house, 'It's the polis.'

Wheeler looked at Ross. 'Are we that obvious?' They flashed their ID but the boy had already turned away.

They followed the boy into a dank hallway, the wallpaper flaked and torn, and through into a cramped room. The smell of damp hung in the air. George stood in the filthy kitchen. 'I'm just havin' ma breakfast. That okay?'

'Of course.'

'You want some?'

They shook their heads. 'Thanks anyway.' Wheeler waited while he scraped the dregs from a margarine tub and smoothed it over two pieces of pan bread, then took a handful of crisps from an opened packet and laid them on the bread. Squeezed on a good dollop of budget-range tomato ketchup, put the two slices of bread together and scrunched down hard. Opened a can of Irn-Bru and slurped about half of it down before looking up at them. 'School said you'd come and talk to me.' He walked through into the sitting room. 'Whit aboot?'

Wheeler and Ross followed him into the room. Wheeler

tried to ignore the cloying smell of urine and stale vomit and walked towards the sofa. She perched herself on the arm, avoiding the worst of the damp and mould. She battled to understand why social services couldn't improve a place like this. Fumigate it maybe. But then what? Demolition would be an answer.

'We need to have a wee word about Mr Gilmore. But it can wait till you've finished your breakfast.'

She watched George Grey start on his sandwich. He was about five-five. Thin, greasy strands of hair fell in defeated layers over a bony forehead. He wasn't just skinny, he was painfully emaciated. He settled himself on a greasy beanbag and stared at her. Dark eyes peered out from his gaunt face. They were the darkest blue she had ever seen, but she had never seen an expression so lacking in hope, so soulless. If she had to name it, George Grey was the walking dead. She sighed; he was like other terminally neglected children, whose life was over before it had really begun. A part of him had already died. What remained was what she had to interview.

She shifted on the arm of the sofa, listened to someone retch in the bathroom above, heard the cistern flush, then a hacking cough sound, until finally she heard footsteps on the bare stairs. A skeletal man wearing a stained vest and jogging bottoms wheezed his way into the room and stood in front of her.

'I'm DI Wheeler and this is my colleague DI Ross.' They flashed their ID again.

The man ignored their cards. 'The filth? The school said you'd be round. Whit's the matter, you cannae solve sumthin' and you want to pick on George?'

'We just need to ask your step-son a couple of questions.'

'See, that's where you're wrong, right off, hen. I'm no his

step-da. His da scarpered long ago. My name's MacIntyre, William MacIntyre, and,' he pointed to George with his right hand showing the three stumps that used to be fingers, 'that there's no step-wean o' mine.'

Ross coughed. 'Guardian?'

'Ah live wi' his ma. Is that good enough fur you?' He leaned in towards her and Wheeler got the benefit of a mouth full of decaying teeth. She stared instead at the gnarled stumps. Wheeler wondered how he had lost the fingers; it didn't look like they had been created by professional medical intervention. She turned away and faced George, waited a second until he had swallowed the last of his drink, then she began.

'I don't know if you've heard, but Mr Gilmore was found dead at his home on Monday evening.'

George nodded. 'Aye, I heard he copped it.'

'Whit? Gilmore's deid?' MacIntyre flopped onto the sofa.

'You knew him, Mr MacIntyre?'

'No well – he worked with George though, didn't he?'

George nodded.

'Can you remember the last time you saw him, George?'

'Last week, I think it was Tuesday.' He paused. 'Aye it was Tuesday, 'cause right after I talked to him I had to go and get changed. We had P.E.'

'Was there anything unusual about him? Did he seem nervous or tense?'

'Naw.'

'How'd he croak it?' MacIntyre's voice was low. Feral, sleekit. His left hand rubbed at the stumps, massaging the wrinkled skin.

Wheeler stared at him. 'You didn't see it reported on the telly or read anything in the *Chronicle* about it?'

MacIntyre sniffed and then coughed up a ball of phlegm,

rolled it around his mouth, swallowed. 'Flu, hen, I've been out of the game for a few days.'

Wheeler had noticed the track marks, fresh, not old. Heroin, just as Nancy Paton had told them. If MacIntyre had been out of it for a few days it was because he'd scored enough to keep him in his own personal nirvana. 'Is Mrs Grey able to speak with us?'

He jerked a thumb at the ceiling. 'She's in her bed – she's got a dose of the flu as well, right enough.' He gnawed on his thumb nail. 'So, how'd he die, then? Whit happened?'

She heard the tremor in his voice. Noted it. Watched George take his empty can of Irn-Bru into the kitchen, heard him scrunch it into the bin, and she kept her voice low while watching MacIntyre's reaction. 'He was found murdered in his home, Mr MacIntyre.'

'Not very nice.' Ross stared at MacIntyre, watching his pale face turn yellow.

'Fuckssake.' MacIntyre shuddered, then he rounded on them. 'And you arses are trying to pin it on George, is that it?'

'Why would you think that?' asked Wheeler.

'Cause that's what pigs dae.' MacIntyre glowered at her like a malevolent gargoyle.

'We're just trying to find out if Mr Gilmore seemed in any way different over the past few weeks. It might help us with our enquiries.'

'Well, George's telt you he wis jist the same, noo beat it. Scram.' MacIntyre started shaking, first his hands, then his arms; finally his whole body was twitching. George stood in the doorway watching.

Wheeler stood. 'Can you remember anything unusual about Mr Gilmore, George? Hear of anyone threaten him or someone who might want to harm him?'

The boy stared at the stained carpet, his voice still. 'Don't know nothing about him. Hardly ever saw him.'

She tried for eye contact. 'You sure?'

George blinked at the carpet. 'Sure.'

Outside the weather had begun in earnest; sleet fell in horizontal sheets as they made their way back to the car.

'Well, William MacIntyre's a right ladies' man – what a charmer. Ross, he could teach you a thing or two.'

'Aye. I thought so.'

'He was awful freaked about Gilmore's death, considering that he never really knew the man.'

'Aye, I thought he looked a bit too shaken up about someone he'd barely known. Doesn't seem the type to waste time with emotions. Doesn't figure.'

'Agreed. He knows more than he's letting on.'

'Sometimes it's hard to tell with junkies. See the shaking – he needed his fix. And all that stuff about flu was complete bollocks.'

'Flu symptoms,' she agreed, 'otherwise known as withdrawal symptoms.'

Ross patted his stomach. 'Is it time for our coffee pow-wow yet?'

'You still needing a wee coffee after all that food earlier?'

'I was up early.'

'Running?'

'Running, then walking the dog – can't all be swanning about at arty-farty lectures.'

'Wimp.'

'I'm starved.'

'Your metabolism's out of whack.'

'It's pretty efficient,' he said proudly. 'It's all the exercise.'

She took out her phone. 'I'll phone in for a quick recce to see if there's been any developments.'

'Yeah, we can't be expected to do all the work.'

She stared at him. 'You're a skiver, Ross.'

'I'm hurt. I was at the station till late last night.'

'Turn up anything?'

'Just the two calls.'

She settled herself into the car, punched in the number for the station. 'I'm impressed, Ross. You'll soon just about have earned your acting DI.'

He ignored her, drove quickly but made sure he kept inside the speed limit. Listened to Wheeler speak with Boyd.

Twenty minutes later Wheeler and Ross sat in the back of the café. They ordered two coffees and two Danish pastries.

'I'll be back in a jiff.' Ross raced out.

He was back before the coffee arrived.

'What's wrong? Scared I'd ask you to pay?'

'Nope, just needed to get some of this.' He held up a small spray-bottle of hand sanitiser. 'Want some?'

She shook her head. 'Once again. You're a wimp.'

He squirted gel onto both palms and rubbed them together vigorously. 'No, but MacIntyre's house, bloody hell. I felt itchy just sitting there. Lice, nits and fleas, take your pick.'

'I know, but what the head teacher said was right – George Grey is a poor wee soul. Do you think he could have had anything to do with Gilmore's death?'

'Stranger things,' Ross said as the coffee and buns arrived, 'stranger things.'

Chapter 26

Doyle sipped scalding black coffee and then spoke. 'Yeah, Weirdo, he's on his way in to see me. Tell Manky good work.' He switched off the phone and waited. A few minutes later, he heard a knock on the door.

'Come in.'

Smithy waddled across the carpet, hands stuffed into the pockets of his tracksuit top, voice chirpy. 'Mr D, you needed to see me?'

Doyle studied the walk, thought he detected a hint of swagger. Kept his voice reasonable. 'Tell me Smithy, have you got a death wish?'

The hint of a swagger disappeared. 'I'm not with you?'

'Easy enough question, Smithy.'

Silence.

'HAVE YOU GOT A FUCKING DEATH WISH?'

Smithy looked at the carpet, then at the Gaggia, looking for an answer, any answer. Came up with none. Decided on the direct approach. 'No?'

Doyle stared at him. 'See, that's not how it appears. Unless I've got it wrong, I run this outfit. Right?'

'Right, Mr Doyle.'

'And so when I hear about a shitty fat toerag like you going it alone, ACTING SOLO, then I get concerned.'

Confusion. Panic. A flash of guilt. Tried to hide it. Failed. 'I never, I never sold anything on, honest.' He moved from foot to foot. Scratched his neck. Coughed.

'I'm not talking about the merchandise, Smithy.' Doyle waited.

Eventually, 'I never said nothing to Stella, Mr Doyle, honest. I mean she's a lovely lassie and all that but I never . . . honest . . . no' for a minute . . .'

'I'm no' talking about Stella. Take a minute, Smithy, have a think. When were you last a right arse? Care to hazard a guess?'

Doyle watched Smithy's face contort. Heard his breathing quicken. Could almost smell the sweat. Waited. Then waited some more. Eventually he put him out of his misery. 'See that's a worry, that you can't remember being an arse.'

Smithy rubbed a hand across the fold of fat that was his neck. His fingers glistened with sweat.

'I'm talking about scaring two wee boys half to death last night. Or can you not remember driving my four-by-four across waste ground? Does it not ring any bells?' Doyle watched the colour spread up Smithy's neck, waited until his face and neck were inflamed before adding, 'See, that makes me angry.'

'I was just showing some initiative.' His voice a squeak.

'You, Smithy, aren't paid to think. You're certainly

not paid to act out your own wee gangster fantasies. You're paid to do what I tell you. That's all.'

Smithy sighed, relieved. 'Aye, right ye are, Mr Doyle. Just thought the wee shits needed a scare.' Rubbed some more sweat from his neck. Wiped his damp fingers on the sleeve of his fleece.

'How so?'

'I asked them if they'd taken anything from Gilmore's. Said no.'

'You believe them?'

Relaxed smirk. 'Hard to tell with them wee pricks.'

'Is that right?'

Smithy heard the tone. Stopped talking. Stopped smirking. Almost stopped breathing.

'So you warned them off?'

Smithy nodded.

'So, what next? They'll go home and tell their wee pals, what exactly?'

'Not to squeal.'

'Or else, what?'

Chest out, flabby thumb prodding his chest. 'They'll get it from me.'

'And then the polis will come after you?'

'Mibbe.' The smirk was back in place. 'But I'll no say anything. I'll stay schtum.' Smithy made a zipping gesture across his mouth.

'Is that right?'

Again the tone.

Smithy swallowed.

'And when the polis can't be arsed wasting their time going after a fuck-up like you, they'll aim a bit higher. Mibbe they'll ask around, see who you work for and then mibbe they'll come and pay me a wee visit? Seeing as now they have a convenient link from me to James Gilmore via the two wee boys, thanks to you.'

Smithy tried to steady himself but the sway was way too obvious.

Chapter 27

The smell in the CID suite was of dust, dampness and old ghosts. Two uniformed officers had joined Boyd and Robertson, who were working slowly and methodically through James Gilmore's possessions. The seals on the cardboard boxes had been broken and the contents grouped into piles. Robertson sat at his desk in a fog of aftershave and began sifting through more papers. Old bank statements had been paperclipped together. 'Nothing much out of the ordinary – mortgage, electricity and gas all paid by direct debit. A few cash withdrawals, usually fifty or sixty pounds at a time. If anything was stolen, it doesn't look like they managed to get very far. Certainly, no one's hacked into Gilmore's account.' Robertson continued muttering to himself.

Boyd stood up, stretched and headed towards the kettle;

the uniforms had made their own coffee earlier so he turned to Robertson: 'You want a coffee?'

Silence. Robertson kept on reading.

'Hey, Robertson, you're miles away.'

Robertson glanced up. 'What?'

'You want a coffee?'

'No, I'm good, thanks.' He turned back to his box. 'You seen the secondment that's up for grabs?'

Boyd scooped two heaped spoonfuls of coffee into a greasy mug. 'Nope, but you have – can't wait for promotion to come around?'

Robertson shrugged. 'What can I say, I'm ambitious. Need to get on.'

'I'm too knackered to even think of it.'

'You look shattered.'

'Cheers for that. It's the new girlfriend – she's keeping me up all night.'

Robertson pursed his lips, turned away, busied himself. 'What about your wife?'

'I never mention the new girlfriend; it'd only upset her.'

Stewart strode into the room. 'Remember, you two, press conference in an hour. Mind and scrub up. Boyd, try to look less like a criminal waster and more like a police officer.'

Boyd smiled. 'Will do.' He nodded to a female officer in uniform who'd come into the room. 'You want to give me a hand going through this stuff?' He handed her a pile of papers, receipts, bills and envelopes. There was a stack of parking tickets on top. 'Sorry it smells a bit. His house was damp.'

She took the pile and sat at a desk, began sorting.

Boyd took his coffee and began flicking through the photographs in another box. There were old cards, scraps of notepaper that Gilmore had scribbled on. Boyd held up an old birthday card – the writing inside was thick, etched into the paper. It was signed, 'Moira and Murdo Gilmore. Your parents.'

'Who signs birthday cards "your parents"?' He showed it to the female officer.

'This it then?' A young constable had entered the room and stood amidst the boxes.

''Fraid so.' Boyd nodded to a box. 'Everything that was found has been recorded and now we get to have a nosy through.' He wrinkled his nose. 'Musty. Damp.'

'Depressing,' muttered the constable, looking through the contents of the box. 'It's not much to show for a life, is it?' He scanned the pile. 'Old bits of paper, parking tickets, stuff cut out of magazines. A pile of old photography magazines. Why bother? It's the digital age.'

'He seemed to be stuck in a different era,' Boyd agreed, dredging through more paperwork.

'Even my wee granny has a camera on her phone and she's ancient.' The constable kept searching.

'Maybe he liked the romance of developing his own photographs? Ever heard of Avedon, Arnold, Doisneau?'

'No,' replied the constable.

'Christ, that makes me feel old.' Boyd had stopped sifting and had begun searching through his desk for biscuits. Found some.

'This stuff seems to echo the house though,' said Robertson. 'Everything's kind of dying. I mean it's all so tatty, so tired.' Robertson sounded depressed. 'A life not lived to the full.'

'Garbage really,' the constable offered. 'Why did he even want to keep all of this?'

'People do though, don't they, they stuff it all in the

attic or the garage. Hoarders. It's a condition,' suggested Boyd.

'It's all rubbish though, isn't it?' the constable repeated.

'Garbage,' agreed Boyd, glancing through a dusty photograph album. 'Gilmore as a child on a bike . . . at school . . . class photograph . . . university graduation . . . someone's wedding.' Gilmore was five foot six, and was thin with wary eyes. In the photographs he wore checked shirts, grey ties, tweed jackets. Nothing bright, nothing stylish. It seemed that James Gilmore had never wanted to stand out. 'Nondescript.' Boyd closed the album. 'Just the same information we heard from the schools.' He glanced at Robertson. 'Anything else?'

'Nothing that stands out, no big gambling debts, no Sky sports package. Gets through a fair bit of cash though.' He flicked through the statements. 'Doesn't go into overdraft but cuts it fine every month. I didn't see much in the house to reflect this.'

'Maybe he paid for his mother's care?' said Boyd.

'No, she's a woman with means; seems her husband Murdo was a very successful academic – he's written quite a few textbooks and left her with more than enough for her care.'

'Bookies?' suggested Boyd.

'Then he was on a losing streak.'

'In more ways than one.'

An hour later and they had left the uniforms to continue. Boyd was working at his computer and Robertson was beginning to work on the set of keys.

Stewart strolled into the room, perched himself on the edge of a desk. 'I've put the press conference back half an hour,' he tapped one foot impatiently, 'so what've we got?'

Robertson patted the papers on his desk. 'Just finished trawling through this lot, boss. Nothing out of the ordinary. Next up I'll check the keys, see if I can locate where they were used.' He held up a key with an electronic tag attached. 'This looks like the most interesting.'

'A lock-up, maybe, or a storage unit?'

'Nothing about the company, no name.'

'Odd.'

'I'll call round, see if I can find out which companies use this kind of tag.'

Stewart turned to Boyd. 'Anything?'

Boyd put down his second cup of coffee and tapped the computer screen. 'Still going through Gilmore's diary. He was at a charity do last month at the River Hotel.'

'Expensive place,' said Stewart.

'Fundraiser for a kids' charity,' Boyd scrolled down the screen, 'the twenty-second of November.'

'And?' Stewart asked.

'High-profile dinner, auction and everything. Lord Provost and loads of high heid yins at it. But only a couple of folk we're interested in.' He scrolled down the page and clicked on the mouse. A slide show began and he clicked through it until he found what he was looking for. He turned the screen towards Stewart.

'What am I looking at?'

'Overview of the tables, see,' he pointed, 'here and here.'

Stewart looked at the picture while Boyd talked him through his find. 'Here's Andy Doyle holding court at one table.' Stewart stared at the picture; Doyle was chatting, hands mid-air, making a point to a thin man seated next to him. On the other side of Doyle, Stella was wearing an off-the-shoulder silver dress that showed too much cleavage. Her eyes were shining as she smiled at Doyle.

'And look at this,' Boyd continued. 'James Gilmore is at a table on the other side of the room.'

'Excellent, Boyd. Now all we need is to ID the guy next to Doyle.'

Boyd tapped the screen animatedly. 'I know who he is, boss. The guy Doyle's talking to is Jay Haddington. He's some kind of a big-shot producer – I heard he was trying to raise money for his next project.'

'I want to speak to Jay Haddington; get hold of him, Boyd,' said Stewart.

'Will do, boss.' Boyd reached for the phone.

'How come you know all this, Boyd? I mean about the producer guy?' Stewart sounded impressed.

'My girlfriend's in the business, boss.'

Stewart stood, brushed an imaginary fleck of dust from his pristine suit. 'Keep digging. I'll call Wheeler, update her on the development, get her to go speak to Doyle. And remember the press conference in half an hour – you two will be on show.' He strode out of the room.

Wheeler was finishing her coffee when she heard a text go through to her phone. Checked it. Her sister.

'Anything wrong?' Ross scoffed the last of his pastry.

'My nephew's gone AWOL again. I met up with him, told him to keep in touch with his mother. Promised he would. Lying wee shite can't be bothered.'

'Happens at uni all the time – first time away from home, everyone goes a bit mental. It's kind of compulsory.'

'You talking from experience then?'

'Of course,' he said.

'I know it's bloody normal, but try telling that to his muppet of a mother. She's imagining him lying in the gutter, with his head bashed in.'

'Bit unlikely, given he's only mixing with other students and probably the most dangerous thing he does is skive off lectures.'

'Well he's up to a bit more than that.' She thought of Weirdo. Said nothing. She deleted the text – her sister would just have to grow up. Her mobile rang; she mouthed 'Stewart' to Ross and took the call.

'Okay . . . Yeah . . . Will do.' She finished the call and sat back in her seat. 'Well. Boyd found something.'

'What?'

'He found a picture online, some big charity do at the River Hotel that Gilmore attended.'

'So Gilmore had a social life after all. And expensive tastes.'

'He wasn't the only one at the do.'

'Let me guess – he was there with a girlfriend?'

'No, he went as a representative of the education establishment.'

'And I'm guessing someone interesting was there, so, if not a girlfriend, a boyfriend?'

'You're rubbish, Ross. I'll give you a clue: who lives beside a big tip?'

'Andy Doyle was at the do?'

'Indeed he was, our very own community-minded local businessman.'

'We off to see him then?'

'Uh huh.'

'Glad I've had a coffee.'

She knew what he meant. 'Me too. Sets you up, doesn't it?'

'You driving?'

'In this weather, what do you think?'

Chapter 28

The press were gathered together in the biggest room at the station. At the front a large, gilt-framed picture of the Queen looked down on the assembled reporters. Stewart, Boyd and Robertson walked into the room. Stewart looked at the reporters, disappointed at the turnout. 'Looks like James Gilmore's old news,' he said under his breath. Boyd nodded as the three officers lined up behind the table. He introduced DCI Stewart, who looked straight at his audience and spoke clearly, enunciating each word. 'We have gathered a considerable amount of information and leads which we are pursuing regarding the death of James Gilmore. We are heartened by the response from the public and are appealing for witnesses to continue to come forward. We are particularly interested in two callers who wouldn't leave their names or their contact numbers.

We are appealing to them to please call back as soon as possible.'

'So, what's the update, chief inspector?' a woman called from the back of the room. 'Surely you have something to give us?'

'At this point we are still gathering leads and once we have solid evidence we will take it forward. For now we are still appealing for information.'

Grumbles around the room.

A young photographer stood at the back of the room watching. He stared at Robertson, waited until he knew that the detective had seen him, then he smiled. Robertson scowled, looked away, studied his notes.

Chapter 29

'Is that his house?' Ross had turned off the engine and they sat for a moment listening to the rain dance on the roof of the car.

Andrew Doyle lived in detached splendour in a stone villa in Mount Vernon. The area was close to one of the biggest landfill sites in Europe. Greenoakhill Quarry covered over 200 acres of land and buried half a million tons of waste a year.

'He's got a big dumping ground,' said Ross, 'right on his doorstep.'

They had parked at the bottom of the drive and looked up at what estate agents would call a substantial detached residence. The garden was big enough to be termed 'grounds' and a wide gravel path wound its way to the villa. A blue Mercedes, a black four-by-four and a silver Jaguar were parked outside.

'Well covered for transport,' said Ross.

'Aye and the M74 and the M8 are just over there,' Wheeler noted. 'He could be in and out of the city in a heartbeat.'

'It's quite nice, though. No quite your Brutalist architecture is it?'

Wheeler started up the drive. 'Think maybe the brutality goes on inside.'

She rang a bell that sounded way down in the bowels of the house. A few minutes later a skinny woman teetering in high heels opened the door.

'We're looking for Mr Andrew Doyle.'

The woman pursed her lipsticked mouth. 'Who's asking?'

Wheeler and Ross flashed their ID. Ross gave her his best smile. 'Mrs Doyle?'

The woman shook her head. 'Girlfriend. Name's Stella. Wait here.' She stepped back into the hallway. 'Andy's downstairs in the gym; I'll just go give him a shout.'

Ross took a step forward. 'May we wait inside?'

Stella opened the door wide. 'Suppose. Wait here in the hall though, and no snooping.'

She left them in the hallway. Glanced back as she went through the doorway, green eyes flashing, tight mouth set in a scowl.

A few minutes later Andy Doyle appeared at the far end of the hall and strode towards them. He wore tracksuit bottoms and a T-shirt stretched taut over his chest. Wheeler noted the cropped hair, the thick muscles, but it was his expression that troubled her the most. Andy Doyle looked like there was fire behind his eyes. She held his gaze, noted the brown of one eye was far darker than the other; heterochromia meant that it blazed black.

He stopped in front of her, too close. She could smell him, a mixture of expensive cologne and fresh sweat.

'Now what?'

'Mr Doyle,' Wheeler began, 'I'm DI—'

Doyle cut her off. 'Aye, so big deal, you're the polis. I could've told you that much from across the hall. What's the problem?'

Wheeler kept her voice neutral. 'We just want to ask you a few questions about a man name of James Gilmore.'

'Doesn't ring any bells.'

'You met last month. At the charity gala night, in the River Hotel?'

'Which night was that?'

She checked her notes. 'The twenty-second of November; there was a big gala do for a children's charity – the Lord Provost was there.'

Doyle shrugged. 'I go to a lot of functions. Hard to remember.'

'You were seen chatting to a producer, name of Jay Haddington,' Wheeler prompted.

'Oh aye, I remember now, the producer. Good food at the do but crap weather if I remember right.'

'Sorry to hear that.' Ross sounded anything but.

'So the producer guy, what's he done?'

'Nothing as far as I'm aware of; it's another man we're interested in. Mr James Gilmore? He also attended the event.'

'Him and a few hundred others. I do remember talking to the producer guy – what was his name again?'

'Jay Haddington.'

'That's it. Haddington.'

'Do you remember what you spoke about?'

'He wanted money for his new play. Investors. Thought I might give it a punt.'

'Didn't have you down as a thespian, Mr Doyle.' Ross kept his voice smooth.

'There might be a part in the play for Stella, so it's a win-win situation.'

Wheeler brought out the photograph of Gilmore she'd taken from the school records. 'Can you take a look at this please and see if it rings any bells?'

Doyle took the photograph from her, stared at it for a few seconds before shaking his head. 'Can't help you. As far as I can tell, I've never met him before. Mibbe he was at the charity do, but I didn't meet him.'

'Are you sure?'

'Aye, certain.' He gave her back the photograph. 'Why would I lie?'

She let the question stand for a minute.

'Aren't you curious why we're here?'

'Seeing as you're polis, I can hazard a guess. Either this Mr Gilmore's done something or someone's done something to him. You're not uniform, so it's a bit higher up the pecking order. A wee jolly for the CID, so let's say there's been some kind of an assault. Am I right?'

Ross nodded. 'In the general ball park. Amazing.'

Doyle warmed to the subject. 'Not one but two cops from the CID, so let's go "double or quits": he's either attacked or killed somebody or somebody's attacked or killed him. Am I close?'

Wheeler: 'You're psychic.'

'Sunday night. Would you mind telling us where you were?' said Ross.

'And since you asked about Sunday night, I'd imagine that's when it happened,' Doyle smiled, revealing too-even teeth, the result of expensive dentistry.

'Would you mind telling us where you were?' Ross repeated.

Doyle looked past them, studied the sky. 'Would I mind?'

Wheeler kept her voice calm. 'If you wouldn't mind.'

'Here. I was here with Stella, watching the telly.'

'What was on the telly on Sunday?'

'We watched a box set. One of Stella's – I think it was *Mad Men.*'

'And I'm sure Stella will back you,' Ross said.

'What do you think?' Doyle smiled and continued, 'And since I've told you I was home all night and it can be,' he glanced at Ross, 'corroborated, then you want me to help you. See if I can recall meeting James Gilmore anywhere?'

They waited.

'And after that, to see if I can think of any wee toerags that either he might want to harm or who might want to harm him.' Doyle laughed. 'Is that not kind of like me doing your job for you?'

Wheeler put the photograph back in her pocket. 'Not quite. It's called cooperating with the police. And a man has been murdered.'

'Has he now? I wonder what he did to piss someone off?'

'So, if you do remember anything, or think of anything at all, regardless of how small or insignificant it may seem . . .'

Doyle smiled and held open the door. 'Then you'll be the first to know,' he paused, Katherine.'

She spun round. 'It's Detective Inspector Wheeler.'

The smile had vanished; instead his dark eye glittered. 'Whatever you say.'

The door closed quietly behind them.

They turned back towards the car.

Ross: 'How come he knows your name?'

'He could've picked it up anywhere. I shouldn't have reacted. He was just playing games.'

'Very cocky guy, very sure of himself.'

Wheeler opened the car door. 'Folk that are too sure of themselves have more chance of slipping up.'

'Still think he's involved?'

'Let's just say I think Doyle is involved in many things. Meantime, let's go find out who else was on that list for the charity do.'

Chapter 30

They were back at the station within the hour. Wheeler paused at the desk to talk to TC. Ross headed up the stairs. In the CID suite Robertson's aftershave hung in the air but his chair was empty.

'Where's the boy wonder then?' Ross threw his jacket over his own chair and settled himself at his desk. The room was busy and hummed with the sound of both CID staff and uniformed officers talking on the phone, tapping at their computers, reading notes and compiling reports.

'While you were skiving off to visit Andy Doyle, some of us were doing the real police work.' Boyd finished off a chocolate biscuit and brushed the crumbs from his shirt.

'Oh aye, what's that then?' Ross said. 'Scoffing biscuits, chatting with our local reporters after the press conference?'

Boyd tut-tutted his disapproval. 'Nope, I've been collating vital evidence, Ross. Surely you must remember it? It's part of police procedure. Cast your mind back to what they taught you at Tulliallan. I know it's a bit of an ask but go on, give it a go.'

'Ho ho ho. Very funny,' said Ross.

'Aye, hysterical – am I not just Santa's little helper?'

'So what have you come up with apart from your "I'm a proper little helper elf" routine?'

Boyd swallowed the last of his coffee and licked his lips before replying, 'Forensics eventually got back to us. A fingerprint, well not a whole one, that would be too much to ask, but a partial turned up at Gilmore's.'

'You get a match?'

'Robertson's off trying to find a match, but it's quite an unusual fingerprint, so there's hope.'

'How so?'

'It's the shape of the whorl – it seems too flat, it's an odd shape.'

'You've lost me,' Ross said.

'Look.' Boyd pointed to the copy of the fingerprint. Ross went over to him, stood behind him, 'Go on.'

'Whorls on fingerprints are usually kind of like a spiral, going round; this one looks like it's been flattened. And also there's an old scar. So it looks pretty hopeful – if our guy's on file then we're onto him.' Boyd couldn't keep the enthusiasm from his voice.

'I hope we've got him on file.' Ross went back to his desk. 'Maybe we've turned a corner in the case.'

'If we have, you owe me one.'

'It's not a bloody trade-off. I was out talking to George Grey and seeing Andy Doyle – hardly a wee jolly.'

'Since when does skiving off for a wee chat count as work?'

Ross scrunched up a piece of A4 and lobbed it at Boyd's head. It struck home.

Boyd ignored it. 'As I said, we do the real police work here. Talking of the man, did you get anything from Doyle?'

'Not a sausage. He's the complete innocent.'

'Aye right, he just employs others to do his dirty work for him. Anything from the wee boy, George Grey?'

'Zero. Saw nothing suspicious, heard even less. The last time he saw Gilmore, he was the same as usual, nothing out of the ordinary.'

'Waste of time?'

'Guy who's living there, William MacIntyre, was freaked about Gilmore's death. Didn't strike me as the caring type. Did you lot find anything else or is the partial it?' asked Ross.

Boyd shrugged. 'Not much. Still wading through the boxes and Robertson's trying to identify all the keys. The poor wee lad's cross-eyed with concentration. I think he reckons if he can crack the case single-handedly then promotion will be the next step. If not that then a wee stint somewhere cushy on a secondment. The only flaw in his plan is he's underestimating just how much you'll miss him. I think he's inspired by you getting the acting job, Ross, and he reckons it's his turn next.'

'That'll be shining bright,' Ross huffed. 'He's got no chance of a secondment; the boy's a dreamer. He needs to put in the graft first, like I did.'

Boyd guffawed.

'And the keys could just be some old set,' Ross continued. 'Folk hang onto all sorts of rubbish.'

Boyd belched. 'Suppose. You getting any more grief about the accident? TC was going on about it again. He reckons that you should resit your driving test and that we should all get to watch. A wee afternoon of spectator sport.'

'He's an old shit-stirring git.'

'Is it going any further?'

Ross shook his head. 'They're letting it lie.'

'You're a lucky bastard Ross, you know that don't you? Teflon fucking coated.'

Ross sniffed, crossed to the kettle, switched it on. 'There was no harm done.'

'There was no one else on the road, you mean.' Boyd dropped his voice. 'Were you pissed?'

'What do you think?' Ross tried for his best hurt look. 'I'm a cop. Remember?'

'I'm only asking, so, what happened?'

'Nothing bloody happened – it was a dark night, stormy. Typical winter weather. End of story. Accidents happen all the time.'

'All's well that ends well, then?'

'Aye, will be if we crack this case. At least the partial fingerprint's a breakthrough. And there's a wee link to Doyle.'

'And Rovers might get promoted,' Boyd laughed.

'I'm not holding my breath.' Ross spooned coffee into the mug, poured boiling water over it.

'Best not to, given their form.'

'Ho ho ho.'

'Very festive.' Wheeler marched into the room, dumped her coat on the chair. 'That coffee for me?'

Ross handed it over.

'Got the full list of people who attended the charity do at the River Hotel.' She gave Boyd her best smile. 'It'll be painstaking work, sifting through it.'

'I'll bet.' He stared at his computer. 'I pity the poor sod that gets it.'

'But for the right candidate, the right kind of CID guy . . . an ambitious go-getter, who's also a team player . . .' she trailed off.

The penny dropped. 'You're joking, right? More desk-bound stuff? I'll be losing the use of my legs.'

'That's more to do with the new girlfriend,' muttered Ross.

'I'll stand you a bacon roll and a coffee,' Wheeler offered.

'Already had one earlier, thanks.' Boyd stared harder at his computer.

'And a biscuit a minute ago,' Ross added.

'Can't be tempted?' Wheeler held out the list of names to Boyd. 'As a big favour? You know I'm rubbish at lists.'

'Only the girlfriend's doing a sponsored walk,' Boyd said, changing the subject.

'That right?' Wheeler said. 'What's it for?'

'Local cat and dog home. She's a soft muppet for strays.'

'She must be if she took you on.' Wheeler glanced across at Ross. He ignored her but Wheeler saw the blush rise up his neck; he was waiting for her to tell Boyd about his ugly wee three-legged pal. She sighed, 'I'm surrounded by nutters – what's the damage?'

Boyd slid the sponsor form across the table. 'A fiver and we're on, a tenner and it'll get priority.'

Wheeler took a five-pound note from her purse. 'It'll be a fiver and it'll be priority.'

Boyd relented. 'Throw in a chocolate bar as well then. Looking at that lot I'll need another sugar hit in an hour or two.'

'You know I've got a soft spot for you, Boyd, don't you?' Wheeler handed him the list and signed the sponsor form.

'Aye,' he took them, 'it's a ditch in the Cathkin Braes, where all the bodies are buried.'

Ross opened his drawer and took out the notes, opened the search engine on his computer and typed in *Arthur Wright, London*. Waited. 'Shit.'

'What, you Googled him?'

'Yep.'

Boyd smiled. 'About a million hits?'

'Yep.' Ross scanned a few, closed the link. 'There must be thousands of links to Arthur Wright or Arthur or Wright.'

'Might be bogus – you know how many nutters there are out there. Trying to be helpful but muddying the waters instead. You get a trace on the calls yet?'

'Not yet,' Ross picked up the phone. 'I was just going to chase that up.'

In the corner a young uniformed officer picked up a file from the desk and made for the stairs; once outside he paused to quickly text.

In the offices of the Chronicle Grim read the text: *Found partial fingerprint, no one we know. Still searching database in hope of match.*

Grim smiled – he had more for his next article than Stewart had given the rest of them at the press conference. He texted back: *Keep at it and keep me informed – we have a deal remember.* Clicked send. Grim looked out of his office window; the sky was grey and the rain had started again. He grinned.

Chapter 31

Ivan Saunders sat in his office looking out of the window at the crowds streaming into Glasgow Central Station, their umbrellas bobbing in a haphazard dance. He held his mobile in one hand, clàmped to his ear, and a cigarette in the other, on which he puffed furiously between sentences. In his ten years as a private investigator, he had yet to encounter a tone as condescending as the one adopted by his newest client.

He listened to the old lady rant '. . . feral this . . . scum that'. Apparently she knew her son would wind up dead; she'd been waiting for the visit from the police for years. Saunders stubbed out his cigarette on a cracked saucer which was already overflowing with butts and began doodling some of the phrases the old lady was wittering about. He'd bet his fee that she'd hit the sherry bottle already. '. . . James

. . . worked with . . . underprivileged kids . . . tough area of the city . . . Watervale.' He gently placed the mobile on the desk top and quietly relit another cigarette; when he picked up the phone again, she was still talking. He puffed on his cigarette, greedily inhaling the nicotine as he listened to her talk out her rage, only occasionally interjecting, 'Yes, the police aren't the brightest bulbs in the box, are they? No, I agree, couldn't find a needle in the proverbial . . . Of course I'll report directly back to you . . .'

He ground the butt of the second cigarette on the saucer and wound up the conversation. 'Yeah, I'll start right now, I'll go along to the area, yep, I'll check out Watervale and ask around a bit, then take a look around the other areas . . . Yep, Mrs Gilmore, I've got it, but we already covered this when I came out to the Courtyard to see you.' He hadn't liked the old woman's tone then, even less now.

He ended the call, reopened his packet of cigarettes and lit his third. He was sure that the old lady was onto nothing and that he was wasting his time and her money: whoever battered James Gilmore to death was a professional and knew enough to cover his tracks. If the police had no new evidence – and Saunders presumed that they didn't – then he could easily bank on a few days' work from the old lady. He doubted that he'd find anything but he'd be earning money for a change. He picked up his keys, pocketed his cigarettes, turned off the lights and locked the office. He hoped, not for the first time, that Strathclyde Police wouldn't turn up with fresh evidence just when he was getting started. He badly needed a break. He would go to the Watervale scheme and ask around, but first he needed a wee detour into the city centre to the pawnbroker to retrieve his wedding ring. His ex had left him a message – she wanted to try again. Saunders sighed, a waste of time but he'd give it a go.

He'd parked his car in a piece of waste ground about half a mile's walk from the city centre but it was free and, with his finances, well worth the inconvenience. He walked down to Clyde Street and kept to the path that hugged the river. He heard the comment just as he passed the deserted area around the Jamaica bridge: 'Hey mate, any spare change?'

Saunders glanced at the man, took in the grubby outstretched hand, the skeletal face. Saunders walked on, not wasting his voice. He had only managed a few paces when the bottle hurled past his head, whistling softly before smashing at his feet. He spun round – the homeless guy had been joined by three mates and they were all walking towards him, their hoods up, faces concealed. Saunders glanced around him. The road was empty – there was nothing for it. 'Bastards' he muttered and started running, took a right along the darkened arches running under the bridge, felt his lungs explode with the exertion and cold air, heard his feet slam into the wet tarmacadam, heard the noise of traffic up ahead and took a second to look behind him. They were standing where he'd left them, just doing nothing. Only laughing. 'Taking the fucking piss,' Saunders gasped, letting himself bend over, catching his breath, spitting phlegm onto the wet pavement, 'fuckers were only taking the piss.'

He straightened himself, took another look – they were still there, watching, smirking. One gave him the finger. Useless jakies. Saunders felt the bile fill his stomach, felt every fear and frustration come back to him. Decided to slip back. Kept to the shadows, heart beating, put his hand in his right pocket and felt the rubber flex. He took a left and doubled back; now he was behind them. They stood huddled, numb with the rain, their sport over for now. Surprise always worked. He sprang at them, whipped out the flex and started on the backs of their knees, thrashing and whipping until they'd folded, screaming in pain, blood pouring from their wounds.

'Jakey bastards.' Saunders felt the laugh rise in his throat, slapped the flex into a face, saw blood spurt. Gone was the veneer of professional respectability he'd constructed for his clients; now he was back to Ivan Saunders, the boy from Barlanark, who as a youth was a local gang leader. All that was behind him now but he still missed the rush of adrenaline.

'Ivan Saunders isnae a coward,' he spat. He waited for a second but knew that they weren't getting up and so sprinted back towards his car, heart beating, adrenaline surging through him. He unlocked the door, slid in and started the engine, decided not to go back the way he'd come and nosed the car out into the traffic, turning left. He felt that he was flying. The visit to the pawn shop to retrieve his wedding ring was completely forgotten.

He drove straight to the Watervale school and parked the car on the main road. As he locked it he felt eyes on him, spun around, but there was nothing. The road led into the academy and he followed it, waiting for the inevitable gangs to secrete themselves from the buildings. But no one appeared, leaving him with the sensation of being watched. He walked to the youth centre; it was locked. Rab Wilson walked by, his hands stuffed into the pockets of his fleece.

'Hey son,' Saunders called, ''mon over here, I need a wee chat.'

Rab stood watching him.

'It's okay son, I just want a wee bit of info. You from round here?'

Rab nodded.

'Got a name?'

'Aye.'

Saunders waited.

Rab let him wait.

Saunders began talking. They stood in the rain and Saunders briefed Rab, told him how some poor old woman was in tears because her only son had been murdered. Asked Rab if he'd heard anything about it. Anything at all.

Rab shook his head, 'Nothin'. Only that it happened. You polis?'

'Private.'

'How come?'

'Gilmore's wee mammy doesn't trust the polis to find out who killed her son.'

'That right?'

Saunders nodded. 'See if you're from around here, maybe you can tell me who would know something? Who's part of the community, who'd have heard a wee whisper?'

Rab stared at the wet pavement. Said nothing.

'You not worried that there's a murderer around here son?'

Rab blinked. 'Shit happens.'

'What about the youth club – who runs it?'

'Malcolm Miller.'

'He around?'

'Mibbe. Later, when it opens.'

Saunders watched the boy walk off. He knew the boy was lying. Knew that the body had been discovered by two youths – that much his contact at the station had given him – but still he had to be careful. He couldn't be seen to be treading on polis turf, *compromising their investigation* as they liked to remind him. Still, he would check out the shops in the area, find out who knew Gilmore, get some insight into who the man was. Then later he'd come back and speak with Malcolm Miller.

Saunders knew after an hour of chatting to the locals that the word was out. They knew someone was looking for information. And would pay for it.

He just didn't expect it to be him.

He was two-thirds of the way down the road, going back towards his car to eat a greasy sausage roll, when they appeared, three youths, hoods up, scarves around their faces. Same old, same old he thought. Except these weren't tired old jakies. He stopped, waited for them to approach. At the same time he felt more than saw a couple of others move in behind him, cutting off his escape. He waited, his fingers on the flex. Tried to summon adrenaline. Failed. Balled the sausage roll into its wrapper and tossed it. Took a step forward and heard a car screech to a halt behind him.

Saunders turned and was felled by the man who was behind him, felt a solid boot crunch into his mouth, felt teeth loosen, closed his eyes as blood began to pour onto the street. Tried to grasp the flex but someone was standing on his hand, biker boot crushing bone. Saunders looked up through the wet and blood and saw a halo surrounding the man. He remembered his childhood, raised as a Catholic. The halo shone as it had in the picture books at his school, only this time it wasn't gold, it was purple. Saunders closed his eyes and let himself drift into unconsciousness.

Across the city, Doyle took the call. 'Our friend's not playing nice today? Okay Weirdo. And Weirdo?' Doyle paused. 'Make sure Rab stays in touch with you via Manky.'

'Will do, Mr Doyle.'

'I spoke to Smithy. If he pulls any more of his stunts, I want to know.'

'Okay, Mr Doyle. Manky was just saying he got a visit from the filth.'

'And?'

'He told them nothing.'

'Tell him to keep it that way.' Doyle put down the phone.

Chapter 32

The view out towards the Campsies was beautiful, the rain creating a fine mist across the countryside, like a watercolour painting, but it was lost on her. Had she looked up she would have seen the hills in the distance, a dark outline against stormy sky. An artist's dream scene. Instead, Margaret Robertson sat in her parked car and worried at the tissue in her hands, shredding and tearing and reducing it to dust. She listened to the thrum of rain on the car roof and the rhythm of the windscreen wipers for a few minutes before switching on the radio. She flicked through different channels, but there were limited options given the poor reception so she decided not to bother and switched it off again. Took another tissue out of her handbag and began the shredding process again. She was parked in front of the

Gospel Hall, blinking at the phrase in front of her.

THE LORD REWARDS EVERYONE ACCORDING TO WHAT THEY HAVE DONE

The two-foot-high letters stood beneath the huge wooden cross that dominated the front of the low, modern building. Rain lashed against glass and concrete, and the railings that surrounded the hall dripped with water. The hall stood in its own grounds at the foot of the Campsie hills, its gates firmly locked against both the elements and non-believers.

The sky had darkened to black and a storm hung in the air by the time the car pulled in behind her. Elder Morrison was behind the wheel. He was in his early seventies; silver hair hung at angles around a pinched face, a hooked nose and thin, tight lips.

Inside, the hall was cold, but she wrapped her coat around her and sat, waiting for him to join her.

'So, Mrs Robertson, you needed to see me?' His voice was cold, his words measuring out gravitas with every syllable.

She looked at his face, searching for kindness but instead found righteousness. Her hands kneaded themselves red raw. 'I need to talk to someone about my husband, Ian.'

'Yes, I know, the policeman. He's a good man. I know he works with our Outreach Team.'

'Yes, he does, but that's not why I'm here ... I mean he ... we ... I'm not sure how to begin.'

'The beginning is always a good place.' His eyes the eyes of a hawk.

So she told him. Starting with their marriage, how she had hoped for a family, how it had never happened.

'Perhaps it is the stresses of modern life. Your husband has a very demanding and stressful job. Be patient. Don't become a nag or a shrew. Never become a burden to him.'

She looked at her hands, saw the rawness, heard the

frustration in her voice. 'You don't understand; he won't talk about any of this. He just blanks me.'

'Then you must be patient, wait until he needs to talk. It cannot be all about your needs; the Lord warns us of our desires.'

She blurted it out. 'I think he's having an affair.'

Morrison steepled his fingers, pointed them heavenward, sat back in his seat and scowled, 'Because?'

'He doesn't seem to need intimacy; he won't even touch me.'

'Again. It's about your needs.'

Margaret sat in silence, listened to the storm rage outside. 'Do you love him?'

'I don't know,' her voice small, defensive. 'He won't ever say it to me and now I don't know if I do love him still. I certainly don't trust him.'

'Then why on earth did you marry the poor man?' It was more an accusation than a question.

'I don't know. It was different then – he was different. I think he really wanted to get married but . . .'

'But?' he prompted.

'But now I think he's seeing someone else. He goes out, won't tell me where he's going, he comes home late, goes straight into the shower and then goes to sleep.'

Elder Morrison pursed his lips. 'Then let's look for guidance.' He reached across for his Bible, flicked through it for a second, selected the text and read in a sonorous voice, 'Ephesians five, verses twenty-two to twenty-five. "Wives, submit yourselves unto your own husbands, as unto the Lord . . . For the husband is the head of the wife, even as Christ is the head of the church . . . "'

Margaret nodded her head, whispered, 'I know all this . . . but . . .' She began to cry.

'Then why are you doubting him? Does he beat you?'
She shook her head.
'Keep you short of housekeeping?'
'I have a job.'
'Abuse you in any fashion?'
'I told you, he never touches me.'

Elder Morrison rose. 'Patience is what is required, Mrs Robertson, rather than these continual, perplexing demands. Give it another few months – if nothing has changed, then we can talk again, but it's my opinion that you need to look at yourself and not to your husband.'

She stood and walked to the door.

He followed her, paused in the doorway. 'In the meantime, try to see things from your husband's perspective. Try to understand that he's doing his best, in all areas. Marriage is more than the demands of the flesh.'

She stared at him, tears rolling down her cheeks.

'I will pray for you.' He turned and began bolting the doorway. 'Goodbye, Mrs Robertson.'

Outside, Margaret stumbled to the car as the storm raged overhead. The clouds had gathered above her and seemed to follow her as she drove away from the hall, turning the car reluctantly towards home.

Chapter 33

The room smelled of sex. The sheets were damp and crumpled and the silver room-service tray lay discarded on the floor, the bottles of wine empty, the napkins stained, plates cleared.

Sometimes one just wasn't enough. Jay Haddington chuckled to himself as he lay naked on the bed of his London hotel room. He was rolling his third spliff when he remembered to dial his office answering machine and pick up his messages. He lit the end of his spliff and closed his eyes, inhaled and kept the smoke there until the message had ended.

'Mr Haddington? Detective Constable Alexander Boyd from Carmyle Police Station trying to contact you. Would you mind calling us back on . . .'

Haddington nodded at the phone, took another drag

and nodded again. The voice asking him to call the police station was far away, too far for him to reach. He listened to the message again, wondered vaguely what it was about and was still holding the phone when his twenty-year-old girlfriend came out of the shower, leaned across and took his spliff, took a long drag, then listened to the message.

'Jay, you need to speak to them.'

'Now?' he giggled, bit his lip in remorse when he saw that she wasn't laughing. 'After this one's finished?'

She took it from his hand. 'Not afterwards, you'll barely be able to speak. Do it now – it could be important.'

She scribbled down the number then tapped it into his mobile, handed the phone back to him. He got through on the second ring. Asked to speak to DC Boyd and was put right through.

'DC Boyd.'

'Hi, my name's . . . Jay . . . Haddington. I'm returning your phone call.'

Boyd heard the spaces between the words and recognised that he was talking to a stoned man. Decided to ignore it – instead he explained why he was calling. Jay Haddington told him everything he needed to know. No, he hadn't known Andy Doyle before that evening at the charity event. Nevertheless he was very impressed with both Mr Doyle and his lovely girlfriend Stella. He had been particularly pleased by Mr Doyle's decision to invest in his new play. And of course Stella's kind offer of playing a small part in return for the investment.

'No, Mr James Gilmore doesn't ring any bells either . . . he was in attendance that evening too? . . . Sorry . . . is he in the business? Oh, I see, murdered, how awful . . . no I'm sure I never met him . . .' and so the conversation continued until Boyd thanked Mr Jay Haddington for his time and hung up.

Haddington lay on the bed and closed his eyes.

'You okay babe?' His girlfriend stroked his arm, put the spliff back into his mouth, let him draw on it, 'only you look kind of upset.'

'A murder in Glasgow – seems the guy was at the charity do last month.'

'And?'

'And from the way the police constable mentioned Andy Doyle, I believe they think he may be involved.'

The two of them sat closer. 'Is he a criminal?'

Haddington drew on the spliff before answering, 'All I know is that he's an investor.'

His girlfriend did the mime, covering her ears with each hand, then her mouth and finally her eyes. Hear no evil, speak no evil, see no evil.

Chapter 34

Wheeler stood in front of Stewart's desk. Waited. Ross stood in the doorway, leaning against the jamb.

'Ivan Saunders was admitted to Accident and Emergency at the Royal Infirmary an hour ago,' Stewart told them.

Ross frowned, 'Isn't he the PI who works out of a crappy office across from Central Station?'

'Exactly the one.'

They waited.

'His head was split open because he sniffed around the Watervale scheme asking about James Gilmore.'

'Why was he asking?' By the time Wheeler finished asking the question, she had the answer. 'The old lady?'

Stewart drummed his fingers on his desk. 'The wee toe-rag was employed by Mrs Gilmore to investigate her son's murder. Seems she doesn't rate our chances of finding her son's killer.'

'Charming,' said Wheeler. 'Does she know she's messing up the investigation?'

'I mentioned it to her when I called but I'm sending a uniform out to see her, to tell her in the gentlest way possible to keep out of this until our investigation is complete.'

'No more hiring PIs,' said Ross.

'Meantime Mrs Gilmore has been contacted by the *Chronicle*.'

'Grim?'

'Grim,' Stewart said, 'offering a sympathetic interview from the grieving mother's point of view.'

'The grieving mother who doesn't rate the police,' said Wheeler. 'I can just imagine how the article would read.'

'So, that's the update. Oh, one more thing: I'm thinking of bringing in some outside help,' Stewart smiled. 'I want our department to be seen to be accessing every resource available to us.'

'You don't think we're working fast enough?' said Ross. 'It's been all of five minutes since we found the body.'

'This is *extra* help, Ross. It's no reflection on the team. It's doable, something we can access immediately and more importantly be seen to be doing.'

'By HQ,' muttered Ross.

'By HQ,' Stewart repeated.

'And we can afford to bring in outside agencies?' Ross didn't sound convinced. 'I thought overtime was cut. Budget, cutbacks, all that sort of thing. How come we can afford this?'

'Special budget, special rates.' Stewart sounded irritated. 'Trust me.'

'And who's the special rates guy?'

'He's a friend who used to be on the force. Does a bit of pro bono now and again.'

Ross groaned. 'An old timer.'

'No, he isn't retired – he chose to leave the force. He wanted to explore other avenues. Believe me, he's a professional. Remember the Blackwell case?'

Wheeler did. 'He got ten years, but it should've been double.'

'There wouldn't have been a conviction at all if it hadn't been for Pete Newton.'

'But bringing in an outsider?' Ross asked. 'Won't it damage morale on the team? All this "work as a team" stuff, and now we haven't got there fast enough, so you bring in an outsider.'

'Don't be so bloody sensitive Ross, Pete Newton's not just *anyone*. I mean he's a bloody good professional and by Christ, we need professionals around here.'

Ross huffed and said nothing.

Wheeler thought for a moment, before the penny dropped. 'He's a psychologist, a criminal profiler, isn't he?'

'Aren't they called BIAs now?' said Ross.

'Right,' she waited.

'Behavioural Investigative Advisers.'

'I'm glad we've got that settled.' Wheeler looked at Stewart. 'Whatever they're called, I'm right, am I not?'

Stewart snorted, 'We need to use every resource we have. Do you understand what I've been saying to you both?'

She nodded.

Stewart had Grim's article spread out before him and he jabbed his finger at the paper. '"Despite the horrific murder, Police have no new leads . . ."'

'With respect, I don't think the team want a BIA from outside to tell them how to do their job.'

'With all due respect, Wheeler, have you anything new on Gilmore's murder?'

She studied the floor.

'Are there any more suspects you've still to interview?'

'No.'

'And other than a partial fingerprint which doesn't seem to match anything on our database, and two anonymous callers, what do we have?'

Wheeler and Ross were both silent.

'Well then, we've nothing to lose by giving Pete a try,' Stewart looked at her, held eye contact, smiled, 'have we?'

She walked to the door, pushing past Ross.

'Give him a chance, he's a good guy,' Stewart called, reaching for the phone. A minute later he spoke into the receiver, 'Hi Pete. Yeah, I've spoken with the team and they're all very enthusiastic about a meet-up – they jumped at the chance of liaising with a psychologist.' Stewart waited until the laughter at the other end of the line subsided before continuing, 'Seriously Pete, we could do with the input; how quickly can you get here?' He paused, listened to his friend reply and then nodded, 'Great, looking forward to it. See you tomorrow.'

Stewart stood and crossed to the window. Outside it was dark; the lights of the houses shone in the distance and he could see the twinkle of Christmas lights. The orange street lights threaded their way down the London Road, casting a weak light into the darkness. Stewart crossed to his chair and pulled on his jacket. On the way out he hit the light switch before closing the door.

Chapter 35

Lizzie Coughlin opened the door, and a blast of freezing air hit her. 'Shit but it's cold,' she complained, ushering her friend Steffy inside before double-locking the door and putting the snib on. 'That bastard's not getting back here. Fucker tried to kill me.' Her voice rasped. She fingered the scarf that she'd tied around her swollen neck.

Steffy held up a bottle. 'I got us a wee vodka, hen. Thought you might need cheering up. He's a fucking waste of space that Mason.'

Lizzie eyed the bottle of vodka. 'Whit's this? Thought you'd nothing till next Wednesday? Did Kenny gie you child support at last?'

Lizzie snorted.

'Or wee Sammy or Vinnie?'

Steffy snorted, 'You're joking, right? Hell'll freeze over

A. J. McCreanor

before I see a penny from them fuckers. Naw,' she patted the bottle, 'I got this wee baby from the Co-op. Some poor wee auld soul fainted and they had to call an ambulance. So I just nipped in and helped myself. Wee drink to toast you being a single wummin again. We can go out on the razzle together next week when your neck's better. Be like old times.'

Lizzie was confused. 'Dae they no have CCTV in the Co-op but?'

'Smashed – that wee sod that tried tae ram-raid the place last week, he smashed it. Wee nutter, did us all a favour.'

Lizzie got two glasses and watched her friend pour vodka to the top of both. 'Cheers hen, but who's watching the weans?'

'Angelica's at my da's and Tamzyn and Nathaniel are at my ma's.'

'Where's the baby?'

'She's with wee Sharlene next door. That lassie's a wee pet. An' she's great with the kids.'

'Should mibbe have her own then.'

'Nae chance. I hope she's always there tae help wi mine. It's no likely though is it, Lizzie, that she'll have her own. You've seen her, right?'

'Aye well, she could dae more with herself, I suppose,' Lizzie suggested tactfully.

'And I repeat, Lizzie, you've seen her, right?'

Lizzie relented. 'Right enough, she's a pot-ugly wee cow. Anyhow, she's better off without men. I should know.'

'Is it no awfully quiet in here?' Steffy looked around. 'Where's the wee bird? Did you not have its cage in here?'

'The cage is in the shed in the garden.' Lizzie's eyes filled up.

'How's that then, hen?'

'That bastardin' shite killed her.'

'Mason killed wee Duchess?'

Lizzie nodded.

'How come?'

''Cause he's an evil bastard.'

'That much you knew already, but why did he kill the wee yellow thing?'

'Harmless wee pet, he just opened the door and grabbed her. Broke her neck.'

Steffy shuddered.

Lizzie sniffed, 'She never stood a chance against the fucker.'

'Naw, she'd have nae chance,' Steffy repeated.

Warmed by the vodka, Lizzie took off her scarf. Her neck was swollen and the purple bruises had begun to ripen. 'He threatened tae kill me.'

'And after you waiting for him to get out of the jail?' Steffy tut-tutted. 'That cunt's nae manners.'

'And, I spoke wi Sonny down at the Smuggler's. Mason's been in there flashing the cash and chatting up the twins.'

Steffy shuddered. 'Filthy, manky bitches – hope he catches something painful.' She took a long draw from her glass. 'Got any fags?'

Lizzie threw her the pack. 'Two-timing me with them slags.'

'But the cash, though, where'd he get it?'

Lizzie took a cigarette, lit it and inhaled deeply, 'Fuck knows, it's no like they hand them a load of cash when they get out of the Bar-L. He's got a plan. Thinks he's coming intae big money.'

'What's the plan?'

'No chance he'd tell me. Said I wis history. Something happened inside the Bar-L. He's got together with somebody.

Now he thinks he's going intae business with Stevie Tenant and he's come over all Mr young, free and fucking single.'

'He's a shite.' Steffy puffed furiously on her cigarette. 'You're better off without him.'

'I want to get him done, Steffy. It's him or me. I don't feel safe with him having it in for me. Wee Duchess was a warning. Next time he'll come after me.'

'But how? And mind you remember what he was in the jail for – you need tae be careful, hen.'

'Aye, I know what he did, but he's got this coming.'

'Right enough, but how?' Steffy repeated as she scratched thoughtfully at a scab on her arm, watched the blood pool, spat on her fingers and wiped it. 'You should go down tae the Royal, go intae Accident and Emergency. Go now, show them the bruises. Then call the polis. Get him done for assault and battery.'

'You mad, Steffy? That the vodka talking? Whit can they dae? It's a domestic – they'd no get involved. Gie him a warning, mibbe.' The vodka had hit home and Lizzie started to cry, 'I miss my wee Duchess.'

Steffy reached across and patted her friend's arm. 'Aye hen, I know but there's nae point in going to the polis about Duchess, it's only a wee bird. They'd piss themselves laughing. And even though they hate his guts, they can't really arrest him for killing it.'

Lizzie pointed to her friend's arm. 'Gonnae no get blood on my settee, Steffy, it's no even paid for yet.'

'Sorry hen.' Steffy licked the blood from her fingers and then sucked at the scab.

Lizzie sipped her drink.

Steffy studied the scab. 'Clean enough now?'

'Aye, fine hen, but I want revenge for him doing this tae me and for killing ma wee bird.'

'You're your father's daughter, right enough Lizzie.'

'Mason forgets I know where the bodies are buried.'

'Whit bodies?' Steffy's voice was too high.

'No literally, ya numpty. It's when you know a lot about somebody. Stuff that can get them into trouble.'

'So, how's that work then?'

'Speak to somebody.'

'Who?'

Lizzie blew a whorl of smoke into the air and watched it float. 'Andy Doyle. If Mason's going into business with wee Stevie Tenant, then it's got tae be drugs.'

'Thought you had tae marry intae the Tenant clan?'

'Stevie must be expanding, going out on his own. My guess is the two of them are going up against Andy Doyle.'

Steffy coughed up some of her vodka, 'Christ, Lizzie. Andy Doyle.'

'Aye, I know,' Lizzie agreed.

Steffy stubbed out her cigarette and reached for the bottle. 'Let me just fill us up again hen – if you're getting involved with Doyle, I think you're going to need it.'

Outside the storm had returned and a thick curtain of rain fell from the dark sky. A flash of light accompanied a siren as an ambulance sped into the night, illuminating the road for an instant before plunging it back into semi-darkness.

Chapter 36

Mason stood in the shadows behind The Fern Hotel. There was a smoking shelter and a bin for butts but most of the smokers had tossed them onto the concrete. Stella had driven around the back of the hotel and parked the four-by-four. In the distance, the sound of a police siren faded into the night. Stella approached him. He bared his teeth in a smile. 'Stella doll, good of you to come. Sorry we cannae meet in public.'

She waited.

He tried to make conversation, his voice friendly. 'Did you not used to be called Maggie?'

Stella's voice was sour. 'What's it to you?'

His tone changed as he tapped the video. 'Stella, Stella, star. That why you changed it, you wanted tae be a star?'

Stella chewed gum, stared at Mason through narrowed eyes, waited.

'Well, I suppose you have become a kind of a star, Stella,' he paused. 'You mind of Davey Tenant? Good-looking boy. Ended up doing time in the Bar-L?'

Stella waited.

'That's where we met,' Mason continued. 'He's got a nickname in the jail – they call him Pretty-Boy. It wisnae very pleasant, if you get my drift, so Pretty-Boy needed a bit of protection. See, he needed to pay me to keep the worst of the vultures away from him. A boy that good-looking gets passed around. My protection cost, though. And Pretty-Boy didnae have much. Only one thing that he thought might be worth something. And it was on the outside. Any ideas what your ex-boyfriend had, Stella?'

Silence.

'A wee home-made video. But I can get it copied onto a DVD. Anyway, I think the correct term for it is sex tape. You and him had a wee fling. Pretty-Boy Davey was specific about the dates.'

She waited.

'See and the dates mean that you were two-timing Andy Doyle. Can't think of him being pleased about that.' Mason's eyes shone. 'What do you think, Stella-star?'

Her jaw moved rhythmically, gum being pushed around her mouth. 'It was a long while ago. I was a different person then.'

Mason held out his hands palms up. 'Fair enough, then Doyle won't be too bothered that the lassie he's shacked up with has the starring role in a wee home-made porn movie. See if this gets out, every gangster in Glasgow will be laughing at Doyle. How do you think he'll take to that? Don't know about you, Stella hen, but I'm guessing, not very well.'

Silence. Stella chewed, stared at Mason unblinking. Ground the heel of her shoe into the ground.

Mason continued. 'The stuff ye get up to in that wee film, I wis dead impressed.'

'Davey's a bastard for recording us.'

Mason shrugged.

Stella chewed.

Mason kept his voice pleasant. 'You on the stage now an all?'

'What's that got to do with anything?'

'Mibbe it'll help them see you in a new way. For different roles, I mean. More exotic.' He cast a sly glance at her breasts, then held her gaze. 'Ye understand whit I'm getting at?'

'I'm already an actress, Mason.' The rhythmic chewing, the steel in her voice, the hate in her eyes.

'You did a good job of looking like you were enjoying it.'

'Everyone's had sex. It's not a big shock.' Stella's voice held. Almost.

'Aye, mibbe not, but you're Doyle's property now. And Davey Tenant's wee brother Stevie is up against Doyle for territory. Think it's getting a bit complicated? You having sex with the enemy?'

'It's not like Andy thought he was getting a virgin.'

'Aye but what happens in private is one thing – see, this wee video nasty makes it public. See, it'll look like you're soiled goods. Kind of second-hand.'

Stella looked hard at Mason. 'So, big shot, what is it you want?'

He reached across and stroked her arm. She flinched. 'Don't be like that, Stella doll, let's keep this friendly.'

Stella grabbed his hand, dug her nails in. 'Fuck off.'

Mason pulled back, saw that she'd drawn blood. 'Okay, you want to keep it purely professional? Fine. I want six grand for this tape. Or,' he held it up, 'Doyle gets a private screening and gets to know the dates.'

'So, what's the payback time, a few months? Six?'

'Oh no, Stella,' Mason winked, 'two days max. Forty-eight hours. It's not that I don't trust you but there's no point in giving you time to make up some dross for Doyle. This needs to be kept fresh. Forty-eight hours, hen.'

Stella turned, crossed the dark car park and climbed into her four-by-four, the red sole of her shoe flashing. When she put the key into the ignition, her hand shook. She glanced at the CCTV camera above the exit, put her foot down on the accelerator and drove, missing Mason by inches.

Twenty minutes later Stella parked the car in the darkest spot behind the Smuggler's Rest. She opened her mobile, punched in the number and waited for it to be answered. 'Sonny, it's Stella. I'm round the back. I need to ask a favour.'

A few minutes later, Sonny climbed into the four-by-four.

Ten minutes later he stepped out again and Stella drove off, alone.

Chapter 37

Wheeler sat on the sofa, a glass of wine in her hand, Sonny Rollins on the CD, the track 'St Thomas' playing. She had left the blinds open and a crescent moon sat in the dark sky. The storm had passed and she watched the raindrops fall gently against the window panes. She had been thinking about James Gilmore and how, other than his mother, no one seemed to care very much that he was dead. Where were the friends and lovers who make up the substance and fabric of one's life? She wondered who would be at his funeral. She had attended funerals where there had been standing room only and others where she had been one of two attendees. The other being the minister. She guessed Gilmore's would be more like the latter, although his colleagues at Watervale Academy, St Austin's and Cuthbertson High might get together to make a bit of a show. Maybe, but she hadn't sensed any real friendship or warmth towards him from any of the other staff, not even from Nancy Paton.

Wheeler shook herself; she was getting maudlin. She crossed to the wall where she had leaned a cork noticeboard. She did this with every case she worked on – it gave her both the space and the opportunity to think away from the station. She closed her eyes, remembering the scene at James Gilmore's house, remembering exactly where his body had hung, the distance between the body and the doorway, the distance to the window, and also the shape his outline had taken and its relationship with the other objects in the room. She had carefully stored all the images and the facts in her memory and would hold them there until the case was solved and her part in the process finished. Then it would be over to the authorities and the courts. The prosecution and defence lawyers would argue their points and the judge and jury would reach a conclusion on whoever had been charged. Then the bloody images stored in her memory would fade and finally disappear and she would be fresh for the next case.

'But not yet,' she reminded herself, speaking aloud in the empty room. 'Not just yet.' Covering a large section of the board were her scribbled notes on the case, a map of Glasgow with pins showing the locations they had so far. Gilmore's house, his mother's apartment at the Courtyard Retirement Home in Milngavie, Watervale Academy, St Austin's and Cuthbertson High. Watervale was obviously in the roughest area; the two other schools were both in the Southside and had a reputation of being 'good' schools.

Next, Wheeler looked at Gilmore's personal details; she'd placed a question mark against his sexuality. If he had been gay, he had decided to keep it quiet. Another question mark was next to the word 'partner'. There was no indication he'd had either a recent girlfriend or a boyfriend. Or was Ross right and Gilmore was an abuser? A number of children from all three schools had been spoken to, but nothing had ever been reported. Or even hinted at.

Wheeler sipped her wine, looked at her notes, followed the arrows from Doyle to Weirdo, from William MacIntyre to George Grey, who was in contact with Gilmore through Watervale Academy. Wheeler stared at the notes but nothing came from them. Nothing. This was unusual – she usually got some kind of a spark – something triggered her imagination. There was something about this case that was wrong.

'Right,' she said out loud, 'go right back to the beginning.' Top left in the diagram were Alec and Rab. Two boys, no convictions, would-be petty thieves perhaps, anything more? She studied the line diagrams, the links: they were both at Watervale but there was nothing linking Gilmore's death and the two boys, other than the school itself. And that would link him to all of the other members of staff, including the head teacher Nancy Paton. Wheeler discounted the staff. They had looked into the list of names. The most they had come up with regarding criminal activity had been a few speeding fines and parking tickets.

There was another list of names bracketed beside the school. Known offenders who'd attended the school in previous years. Not that unusual – most schools had at least a few kids who went off the rails after they left. She counted the names: twenty-three. That wasn't the impression she had received from either the head teacher, Ms Paton, or the deputy, Margaret Field. According to them, their kids weren't criminals. Were they just in denial? Or was Matt Barnes right, that kids from such a deprived area made their way outside of society? She checked through the list of their misdemeanours. It was mainly theft and gang fights. One had been done for murder and another two had been done for manslaughter. They were doing time in the Bar-L.

Her mobile sounded; she glanced at it. Another text from her sister.

I'm still worried about Jason – he's gone AWOL again. I think something's happened to him.

Wheeler deleted it. She'd looked him up; he was fine. Let them sort it out.

Then a call came through, but Wheeler ignored it, heard it go through to voicemail. Listened – her sister was near hysterical. Wheeler spoke aloud, 'What the fuck is it with mothers and their sons?' She deleted the message.

The CD ended. Wheeler went into the kitchen and topped up her wine, brought it back through to the sitting room and flicked on the telly. A documentary was about to start on a group of her favourite Scottish painters. She lifted the remote and turned up the volume.

'The Scottish Colourists . . . Fergusson . . . Peploe . . . Cadell . . . Hunter . . .'

She settled into the sofa, pushed thoughts of Gilmore's dead body and the deprivation of George Grey's life aside. Sipped her wine and let the presenter guide her through the formation of the Colourists.

Chapter 38

The building was a four-storey blonde sandstone close to the university; the top storey had a balcony and she had sunbathed there on the odd day Glasgow's weather had allowed. Lauren shared the flat with four others.

Lauren scrunched down on the sofa and pointed the remote towards the CD player. Rihanna thundered from the speakers. Jason was sprawled on the floor. 'And if we drive out tomorrow go easy – it's my car, remember, Jason. You're not driving it like you do your old banger.'

He turned towards her, gave her a mock salute. 'Scout's honour.'

'Right and why are you wearing those gloves inside?'

'My mum bought them for me; aren't they great?' Jason looked at the expensive leather driving gloves. They were a bit over the top, like his mum, but he loved them. They were a symbol of what he would become, a great lawyer.

'So, where are we going exactly?'

'Hamilton.'

'Because?'

'You said you wanted to hear it.'

'The echo?'

'The best echo in Europe.'

'Right.'

'It's true,' Jason said, 'there's this big fuck-off vault, which has the longest-lasting echo of anywhere in the world.'

'The whole world? All the canyons and—'

He cut her off. 'Well, maybe not them . . . I mean, it's got the longest echo of anything man-made.'

'So, you were lying!' She laughed, her head back against the sofa, her sparkly hair band lying askew. 'Why do you want to go there?'

'So I can sing to you, serenade you.'

'Seduce me more like,' she said.

'Lauren, it'll be amazing.'

'The seduction,' she laughed, 'or the singing?'

'From past feedback, I'm guessing both.'

'That'll be shining bright.' She adjusted her hair band, smoothed down her hair. 'Will we be able to get in?'

'We'll break in.'

She looked at him sideways, 'You're kidding, right?'

'Yeah, we'll just have a look tomorrow; I think you have to arrange special access.' He reached for the map which was lying beside him, traced the route they would take, follow the M74, on out through Glasgow to Mount Vernon and its sandstone villas and the huge Greenoakhill Quarry. On through Uddingston and Bothwell and then Hamilton. He fired up the laptop and showed her a photograph of the mausoleum. 'Looks phallic, don't you think?'

She peered at it. 'In your dreams, Jason.'

The dome stood over a hundred feet high. A ghostly reminder of the excess of Hamilton Palace and its long-dead duke.

'What's its story?'

'It was a burial chamber for the tenth Duke of Hamilton. He'd a big thing for Egypt so had himself interred in an Egyptian sarcophagus, and the rest of the rellies stored in a crypt underneath.'

'Charming.'

'It was all in vain though – they all had to be moved.'

'Nightmare. Because?'

'Flooding. The River Clyde burst its banks.'

'And so no quirky resting place?'

'Inside the dome are the whispering walls.'

'The what?'

'The whispering walls,' Jason explained. 'So, if you and me stand at either end of the walls, but facing away from each other, facing into the wall, we could still have a conversation just by whispering to each other – our voices would be amplified.'

'Uh huh.'

'Really, honestly, wait and see, but we might not be able to see the heads close up.'

'The heads?'

He flicked through the images on the laptop to show her. 'The heads are called Life, Death and Immortality. They're carved over the entrance to the crypt. It's amazing though, 'cause Life and Death have weathered and faded with age, but Immortality hasn't.'

'Immortality through death then?'

'Suppose so.'

'Cool.'

Jason moved across to the window, opened it and peered out. Dark clouds momentarily obliterated the moon. The wind seethed and howled.

'Jason and Lauren were bewitched by the dark beauty of the landscape.' Jason looked at her and laughed. 'Only one thing would improve this.' He closed the window and walked towards her.

She snuggled into the sofa. 'You've a one-track mind.'

'Not that; I've got something.' He reached across her and grabbed his rucksack, unzipped it. Heard Lauren start to laugh. Started laughing himself.

'What is it?'

'Liquid G.'

'GHB?'

'Yeah.' He placed a small plastic bottle on an empty CD case, went into the kitchen and returned with a glass and a bottle of cordial. He looked across at her. 'Want me to go first?'

'Yeah, but where's your glass?'

He reached into his rucksack and pulled out a hip flask. 'I keep this with me always.' He began to pour.

The song had ended and the next one had begun when Jason lay back on the floor and let the sensation wash over him. He looked across at Lauren – she was lying flat out on the sofa, a smile on her face, her eyes closed.

Chapter 39

The television was on in Ian Robertson's sitting room, the sound turned down. Images of the Scottish Colourists and their art flicked in silence as Robertson paced the room. Finally he heard the noise of a car outside. He was at the window in a second and stood watching his wife's car pull into the driveway. He drummed his fingers on the sill, frowning. When she saw him Margaret blushed, looked at the ground. It was then that he knew. He waited until she was in the hall before going to meet her. He kept his voice casual, neutral.

'Where've you been?'

She wouldn't meet his gaze; instead she concentrated on hanging up her coat. 'Out.'

'I can see that. Where?'

'I went for a drive.' She crossed to the kitchen, put on the kettle. Stood with her back to him.

'Margaret, we don't have secrets. We're not that kind of a couple.'

She turned to him, her eyes filling up. 'But we do have secrets, Ian. I feel as if I'm in this marriage alone. You come and go without even waking me sometimes. You go out at night and never tell me where you're going. It's as if I don't matter. Sometimes I feel I don't exist.' Her shoulders began to shake; the familiar sobbing began.

He reached out and held her, let her cry for a few minutes before he spoke. Kept his voice even. 'What brought all this on?'

'It's been building for a long while. '

'What has?'

She held out her hands. 'All this, me being kept out of your life. I've tried to talk to you about it, but . . .' Her voice trailed off.

He turned from her, looked out of the window, watched the outside light go on and illuminate the garden. A fox padded across the lawn, its bushy tail amber in the light. Robertson watched it disappear into their neighbour's garden. He could hear the noise it made as it ate the dog food his neighbour insisted on leaving out for it. Robertson sighed, turned back to her. 'I'll need to see to that fence. Get it sorted once and for all – it's like a zoo out there sometimes.'

Margaret said nothing.

The kettle had boiled and he went to the cupboard, took down two mugs. 'Tea or coffee, Margaret?'

Her voice was calm. 'I went to see Elder Morrison.'

He froze, let his hands fall to his side, struggled but failed to keep the anger from his voice. 'You went to see Elder Morrison? About what?'

It came out in a rush. 'I went to talk to him, about us,

about our issues. How we've not been getting on. How we barely see each other and we never talk.'

He waited. 'And?'

'And how we don't have any . . .'

'Any what exactly?'

'Just that we don't . . . we haven't, you know, in a long while.'

'You spoke to him about our sex life?'

'I was desperate – you won't talk to me, we hardly touch.'

'So, the best way to resolve this is to go and speak to someone outside of our marriage? To air our dirty laundry in public?' His voice bitter, accusing.

'I didn't mean to talk about it,' Margaret pleaded. 'I didn't know who to turn to.'

'I suppose you told the women at the meeting too; I suppose now the whole Hall knows?'

'No, just Elder Morrison.'

'I see. And what did he say?'

Her shoulders slumped. 'He told me to be patient, that you had a stressful job. That it's not all about my needs.'

'Your bloody needs! That's all you think about. Maybe you should never have got married – maybe being an old maid would have suited you better because you don't seem to be able to handle being a good wife, do you?'

The tears fell steadily. Margaret didn't bother trying to brush them away.

'Well, Margaret?' he bellowed.

'I want to have a baby.' Her voice a whisper, 'I want us to have children.'

'So then maybe you listen to him, maybe you think about me for a change and all the stress I'm under at work, instead of your own selfish needs. I work fucking hard to keep a roof over our heads.' It was the first time he had sworn at her.

'I work too, you know.' Her voice was quiet, losing conviction.

'You're unbelievable. Can you really compare your shitty part-time job at the bakery with my career? Do you know what it's like to work in the real world?'

She reached for the kitchen towel, began shredding it. 'I only took it until the babies came along. You encouraged me.'

'I encouraged you to take it to get you out of the house, to give you something to do instead of obsessing about children all day.'

'I'm not obsessed. Mum agrees that it's time I had a family of my own.'

'You've spoken to your mother as well? Well, that's just great. Is there anyone who doesn't know?'

Margaret was confused. 'But I always talk to Mum.'

'Then maybe it's time for you to grow up and be an adult for once. Anyway, how can we afford a family with our mortgage? You do the sums.'

'We could sell the house.'

'And live where?'

'We could ask Mum and Dad if we could stay there for a bit. They could help us.'

Robertson rubbed the back of his neck, flexed his fingers, stared out at the back garden. 'Listen, that is never going to happen. And I don't want you ever, do you hear me, EVER to go talking to others about me behind my back. Got it?'

Silence.

He turned to her, leaned into her face. 'DO YOU HEAR ME?'

Margaret nodded.

'And if anyone needs help it's you. You need to get to the doctor again, get some tranquillisers or something to calm you down. You're losing it, you know that don't you?'

She began sobbing again.

He grabbed his coat, slammed the door behind him. He drove as fast as the speed limit would allow, desperate to get away from her nagging and far away from their claustrophobic home. Robertson felt the familiar band of pain tighten around his head and press in on his thoughts. He gripped the steering wheel, fought the desire to press hard on the accelerator, kept driving, out of Glasgow, out to the Campsies, past the Gospel Hall and out into the dark hills. Far away from his wife, Elder Morrison and a marriage that was choking the breath out of him.

Chapter 40

Wheeler switched off the television and went through to the kitchen, put on the kettle and scooped a spoonful of coffee into a mug. While waiting for the kettle to boil she reached for the radio, switched it on and heard the start of the news. 'A body has been found in Glasgow's West End, believed to be that of a student from Glasgow University . . .'

The ringing wove its way through her concentration. Her mobile flashed a familiar number. 'Ross?'

'Boss. They've just found a body off the Great Western Road.'

'I heard it on the radio just now.'

'You want me to call them?'

'Quicker to go over?'

'I'll pick you up. Ten minutes.'

She was pacing the pavement when he arrived. She had texted Jason. Nothing.

Wheeler's stomach churned as she heard another text come through. She glanced at it. Her sister.

I'm worried. I think something may have happened to Jason.

Wheeler pulled on her seat belt. Christ, she hoped her sister wasn't psychic.

They drove in silence, arriving at the scene in a few minutes. She joined Ross inside the police cordon. Beyond, a crowd had gathered, muttering and staring at the ominous tableau. Police cars and an ambulance had killed their sirens but their lights still flashed danger. The shiny red BMW was parked nearby. Callum.

Wheeler felt the rain seep into her bones; she was freezing cold.

A stout DI marched towards them. 'Morag Bruce,' muttered Ross.

The DI smiled. 'Hey Ross.'

He nodded. 'What have you got, Morag?'

'Young girl. Poor kid. Out here in this weather. No place to die.'

Wheeler felt a rush of guilt at the relief which washed over her. It wasn't Jason. But still, the girl had been someone's daughter.

Bruce leaned across the cordon. 'Want to go see, Ross? Does it tie in with anything you're working on?'

Ross looked at Wheeler. She thought about it. 'No,' she turned to the woman, 'we'll leave it to you. She doesn't belong to us.'

Bruce nodded. 'It's an awful shame to go like that. Looks like she fell from her balcony.' The policewoman glanced up at the fourth-floor window; bright lights illuminated it. The police were already inside.

Wheeler thought about Jason and his friends, all of their lives ahead of them. She nodded to Bruce. 'A bloody waste.'

'Aye. Poor lassie, horrible way to go. And wearing a wee sparkly hair band.'

Wheeler felt sick. She swallowed. 'Maybe a quick glance, see if I can shed any light on it?'

'Be my guest. Looks pretty straightforward though.'

Wheeler trudged towards the body. Her mobile rang and she snatched it from her pocket, expecting her sister. Saw that it was Paul Buchan. She paused for a second, aware that rain was trickling down her neck. Then she switched the phone to mute and stuffed it back into her pocket before following Ross through the throng.

Callum was coming towards them. 'Just finished. Tragic.'

'Uh huh,' Wheeler agreed.

'So why are you here?' Callum was curious.

She walked on. 'Christ knows.'

He called after her. 'Any further forward with our Mr Gilmore?'

She told him the truth. 'Going round in circles and getting nowhere fast.'

She stood over the body. She had known when she had heard about the hair band. Must be hundreds of them sold, but she had known. She'd just wanted to make sure. She turned to Ross. 'Fucking nightmare.' Knew she should say it. Knew that she should tell them the girl was a friend of her nephew Jason. Said nothing.

Ross finished reading the notes and handed them back to Morag Bruce, who stood waiting. 'Student ID says her name's Lauren Taylor.'

Wheeler nodded. Kept waiting to find her voice and tell Ross that Jason knew the girl. Tried to still the voice that told her, so what? Half of Glasgow University must have known Lauren. Why drop her nephew in it? A student death wasn't unknown. Then she came to her senses – what the fuck was she thinking? Wheeler pulled Ross aside, found her voice and told him she'd seen Jason with the dead girl. 'And he had his arm around her minutes before he scored from Weirdo.'

Ross shook his head. 'Fuckssake, Wheeler.'

'I know. He swore it was just dope.'

'And you believed him?'

'Students take dope all the time – doesn't mean he's involved with this.' She pointed back to the scene.

'Doesn't mean he's not. So, what're you going to do?'

She walked ahead of him. 'Check the facts.' She spoke to Bruce: 'Thanks for letting us take a look. You sure it's straightforward?'

Bruce nodded. 'Looks like she fell or . . . jumped maybe. There was no sign of a struggle, but we're keeping an open mind. Investigation will be thorough. There was only one glass on the table inside, nothing to suggest anyone else was there – looked like she'd been drinking.'

'Definitely alone?' Wheeler asked.

Morag Bruce peered at her. 'Looks that way but . . . as I say, the investigation's just getting started.'

Wheeler stood in the rain, felt it soak into her skin. Said nothing.

'Got what you needed?' Bruce had already turned back towards the body.

Wheeler wasn't sure what she needed. She fingered the mobile in her pocket, thought of calling the station. Getting them to pick Jason up. She called Jason again, left another message on his mobile. Told him to call her ASAP.

Ross was waiting for her at the car and he did the universal mime for going for a drink. She realised she was still gripping her phone. She let it drop into her pocket and gave Ross a firm nod. A few minutes later they were back in his car.

Chapter 41

He started the engine. 'That give you a shock?'

She nodded. 'More ways than one.'

'You wondered if it might be Jason lying out there?'

At the mention of his name she winced. 'What if he's involved?'

'You think he was there?'

'He did at least know the girl. I just don't want to jump to conclusions. I'm getting as bad as my hysterical sister.'

'Peas in a pod are you?'

'No chance, we're opposites. She's prone to melodramatic outbursts.'

'While you're perfect?'

'That too, but I am calm and rational. And physically we're opposites – she's small and fragile.'

'You're not huge.'

'No, tall. Athletic. I'm happy with it. We've just nothing in common.'

'Why don't you call Jason?'

'Think I haven't tried?'

'Go round to his digs?'

She sighed. 'Yeah.'

He indicated and turned the car into the road. 'Let's do it together, now?'

'Thanks.' She gave him the address and ten minutes later they hammered on a student residence which was deserted. Wheeler glanced at the empty flats, all in darkness. 'I know most of the students have gone home for the holidays but I thought maybe one or two might be around.' She shoved a note through Jason's letterbox and a few minutes later they were back in the car and driving towards Byres Road.

Ross parked the car; they checked the Vineyard and a few of the other student pubs. Finally, Wheeler said, 'That's it, let's take a break.'

Wheeler and Ross were settled at the back of the café bar. Once again he ordered food and organised the drinks. 'You look shattered.'

'Cheers.'

The food arrived and they ate for a few moments before he spoke. 'Morag Bruce said there was only one glass in the living room; what makes you think Jason's involved?'

'I just want to be sure that he's not in any way involved.'

They continued the conversation, exploring the what ifs, the maybes, until they had exhausted every angle.

'And maybe it was as it looked – a poor girl who accidentally fell from her balcony after having a bit too much to drink,' Ross suggested.

Wheeler nodded. 'I know.' She sipped the last of her wine. Finally she sat back. 'Feel a bit better. Thank you for this.'

Ross polished off the last of the chips before pointing to her glass. 'Another?'

She paused, allowed the wine to hit the spot and herself to feel normal. 'Only if there's more food coming.'

'Christ, I'll be bankrupt. Bloody West End prices.'

'I'll pay.' She dug around in her purse.

'You're all right. Just think of it as a bribe for when I go for promotion. Having the acting DI is okay but I'd prefer it to be permanent. You can mentor me.'

She looked at the empty chip bowls in front of her. 'Christ, if that's a bribe for me mentoring you, you're not aiming very high.'

He ignored the comment, went to the bar. Reordered. Glanced back at her, saw that the colour had returned to her face.

It was late when he dropped her home.

Chapter 42

It was two a.m. and the rain battered the pavement and icy drops chilled the bones of anyone caught in its downpour. Jason walked on, not caring in which direction he was headed. Twenty minutes later he found himself in the city centre. It was quiet apart from a few disparate groups of revellers looking for taxis or late-night buses. Deserted stores burned their lights brightly, illuminating gifts and items on Christmas displays. The city had closed down; streetlights cast eerie shadows in back lanes and doorways. As he walked, Jason's jacket flapped open around him – he was oblivious of the rivulets of rain coursing down his neck, soaking his skin. His shirt was glued to him. His jeans were heavy with water but Jason was floating on a drug-induced high. He heard his footsteps squelch on concrete, marvelled at the sound. He walked down Buchanan Street, past the statue of Donald Dewar and on down to St Enoch Square. He moved quickly but wondered what it would be like to fly. He looked up at buildings and imagined soaring from the rooftops. He giggled to himself, wondered if he should call Lauren. Maybe he shouldn't have left her? He danced across the road, moving towards the River Clyde, its banks swollen, its waters high. Ahead was the Jamaica Street Bridge, one of many bridges which crossed the river. Underneath, the arches were in complete darkness. The concrete walkway led him past a small group of jumpy addicts huddled around a short, fat dealer. Their transaction almost complete, they turned to stare at Jason. Soon, their shakes would be temporarily stilled and their lumpen shapes would rest on cold concrete or damp doorways. Jason passed some of the homeless of the city who had swaddled themselves in thick cardboard. He strolled on, smiling. He passed a statue standing high on a plinth, the figure's arms outstretched, informing the city dwellers that it was 'Better to die on your feet than live forever on your knees.'

Then it hit him.

Somewhere in the recess of his mind he remembered and the memory gathered momentum and rushed past the euphoria and into his consciousness and Jason huddled under the statue, blinking back tears. He couldn't call her; she had gone. He took out a half bottle of rum and drew on it until he was gasping. Tried to stop the tremble in his hand. Failed. Cursed himself. Cursed Lauren. Mostly though, he cursed Smithy for introducing him to Stevie. Jason wondered what the fuck was going to happen to him if the police found out he'd given Lauren the drugs.

He started on again, walking and reciting curses in time with his footsteps, ignoring the wet, on and on under arches and through alleyways, always sticking to the shadows, only stopping now and then to draw from the bottle. By the time he'd reached Charing Cross and the Mitchell library the bottle was empty. 'Fuck this.' He hurled the bottle at the library, listening to the glass shatter as it hit the wall. He swayed. The vast building stood in front of him. The biggest public reference library in Europe was floodlit, the distinctive dome glittering against the black sky. He watched the rain batter in vain against the huge structure. Jason's eyes filled with tears of self-pity as he whispered, 'It's all fucking useless. There's no point to any of it.'

He moved off, walked down Sauchiehall Street to where it joined Argyle Street. Above him the sky was dark and heavy with rain. He reached the Kelvingrove Art Gallery, the building looming out of the dark; beyond the gallery, the spires of Glasgow University pointed to a stormy heaven. Finally Jason stopped on the Kelvin Bridge and stood, bloodshot eyes watching the River Kelvin surge beneath him. He listened to the noise of the water, imagining an underwater world where the inhabitants of the Kelvin dance an aquatic ballet on their urgent way through the city. Decided he would join them. A glance behind him; there was no one. This weather, no one was out unless they had to be. Overhead the trio of lights from the Victorian lamp cast a sombre glow. He looked up at the university buildings, shrouded in darkness. Wondered why he'd ever gone in the first place. Stared at the silent buildings, willed them to call to him. Heard nothing but the roar of water beneath his feet. Imagined instead that it was the river that was calling to him.

A few minutes and it would be over. Four minutes max if he allowed the water to take him, if he refused to struggle. He closed his eyes, relaxed his shoulders, listened to the rush and swell of the Kelvin, felt himself pulled towards the water. He put his hands on the bridge, breathed in the icy air, reasoned to himself that he was already soaking wet and so was halfway there. He stood on tiptoe and began climbing onto the bridge. Felt it slippery under his wet fingers. Felt his mobile vibrate. He stopped climbing, pulled out his phone, glanced at the name. Kat Wheeler. Auntie Kat had texted him earlier. He ignored it, stuffed the phone back into his jeans pocket and felt his stomach churn, felt the alcohol sour in his gut and then watched as his vomit cascaded into the water. He stuffed his fingers back into his pocket and grabbed his mobile, cursed loudly before hurling it into the air, where it hovered for a second before plunging into the water, barely making a splash. Jason took a deep breath and turned back towards the city centre.

DREAMER

His fingers worried at the sheet. Although asleep, he heard the noises clearly. His memory had stored them and would keep them for ever. As he slept he let the sounds overwhelm him. They began with the whoosh of the bat when it first made contact with James Gilmore, then there was the clumsy noise he made when he fell. After that there were his cries of pain, then the pleading, before, finally, the soft moan as he slipped into unconsciousness. The sound the bat made when it made contact with skin and a different sound altogether when it broke bone. Then the silence, watching Gilmore's skin break apart and blood leak from the wounds. Hearing Gilmore's breath leaving his body for the last time and knowing it was over. Then the silence in the room with only the distant sound of lorries on the London Road to shatter it. Lorries which were moving on, leaving the city and its dead behind. The Dreamer sighed in his sleep, his fingers stilled, their worrying over. He breathed deeply and rhythmically and dreamed of standing in a field full of sunshine and flowers.

Chapter 43

Thursday, 12 December

At five a.m. Wheeler sat in her kitchen with a cup of coffee and scrolled down the list of news articles on her phone until she found the one she wanted.

Grim had gone for a discreet heading.

Tragic Death of Brilliant Student

The body of Lauren Taylor, 21, was found late last night outside her flat near Great Western Road in Glasgow's West End. The Glasgow University student is believed to have fallen to her death.

A dog walker discovered Lauren's body and called an ambulance. Paramedics tried to resuscitate Lauren but she was pronounced dead at the scene. Lauren was a popular member of the university and was studying English

Literature. She had also enrolled in the exchange programme at the university and had been scheduled to spend a year at an American university.

Lauren's family are devastated by the news and have asked for their privacy to be respected at this time.

A spokesperson for Glasgow University issued this statement: 'We are all greatly saddened by this news. Our thoughts go to Lauren's family at this tragic time. They are in our prayers.'

Friends have also opened a condolence page for Lauren on Facebook.

But it was the photograph that depressed Wheeler. She stared at it over her coffee cup. The doe eyes, the long hair. The picture had been taken recently; she looked no different from when Wheeler had seen her in the pub with Jason. Only twenty-one with her future ahead of her. Wheeler poured the remainder of her coffee into the sink. Her stomach had curdled.

She knew it was useless but she called Jason anyway. It went straight through to voicemail. She would speak to Stewart about getting him picked up. Either he'd seen Lauren that night, in which case he needed to talk to the police, or he hadn't, in which case they could discount him from the investigation.

She pulled on her running shoes, opened the door and headed out into the cold, dark morning. She needed to let go of her frustration about Jason and also the lack of progress in the Gilmore case, and pounding the streets was as good a way as any to refocus.

Five miles later and she was back. She kicked off her running shoes and stripped naked, padded through the hallway into the bathroom and turned on the shower. The steam rose through the air and she slathered on rose-scented oil. In the hall the buzzer sounded. And again. She heard the commotion outside. A voice shouting, calling her name. She grabbed a robe and darted through the hall and across the sitting room. She peered out of the window. Below in the street a solitary, soaked figure stared up at her. Jason.

She crossed to the hall, slammed her hand against the buzzer and tried to stop her heart from thundering.

A moment later he stood dripping wet on her kitchen floor. He looked exhausted.

'Fuckssake, Jason, I nearly had a heart attack. Where have you been?'

He stared at the floor. Said nothing.

After a minute he spoke. 'You didn't answer your buzzer.'

She heard the slur in his voice. 'Wait there.' She ran to the wardrobe, grabbed an old sweatshirt, collected more towels from the bathroom and threw them at him. 'Sort yourself out; I'll put on some coffee.'

When she returned he was sitting on the sofa, sniffing.

She studied him, saw the tremor, the downturned eyes. Nothing remained of the bravado she'd seen in the pub. The night he had been with Lauren. 'You know about Lauren Taylor?'

He nodded. 'I heard about it from a friend. He texted me.'

'Have you called your mum?'

'No, not yet.'

She'd trust that to be the truth. 'Think maybe you should.'

'Don't have my phone.'

She tossed her mobile to him. 'Call her now, while I pour the coffee.'

When she came back, he'd made the call. 'Told her I'd call later for a longer chat.'

'Yeah?'

He nodded, 'Yeah.' He sipped his coffee. Said nothing for a long while.

'So, about Lauren Taylor's death? When was the last time you saw her?"

'I didn't know her that well.'

'Wasn't she the girl in the pub with you?'

He stared at the floor. 'We were just drinking buddies, like half of my lecture class. You know, just hanging out. Nothing special. I haven't seen her since.'

She listened to the tone of his voice, to the timbre. Decided that, once again, it wasn't authentic. Lauren Taylor had meant more to him than just a drinking buddy and she was pretty sure that he was also lying about having not seen her again. 'You had your arm around her in the pub.'

'Yeah, so?'

'You were friends with her and now she's dead and you say "yeah, so"? Were you there when she died?'

'NO!'

'You were buying from Weirdo; you're already taking drugs. Why should I believe you?'

'Only dope, I told you. Not the hard stuff.'

'Was Lauren taking drugs?'

He looked at the floor. 'No idea.'

Her eyes narrowed. 'Really, you've no idea?'

He stared at the floor. 'Maybe, I don't know. I didn't know her that well.'

'Well, the cops'll pay you a visit. Anything you want to tell me before they talk to you? Might be better for you to volunteer the info.'

'Like what?'

'Like if you were there with Lauren?'

'I told you, she was just a pal and I wasn't with her when she died.'

'Was she suicidal? Depressed?'

'How the fuck would I know?'

Wheeler balled her right hand into a fist but kept it at her side. 'You were supposed to be her friend.'

Again, he stared at the floor. Said nothing.

'Well? Lauren's dead, and you seem very accepting of it.'

'What do you want from me? Shit happens. I thought you of all people would know that.'

She stared at him. 'Why didn't you phone? I left messages. Went to your flat.'

'I lost my phone.' He yawned. 'I'm shattered.' A sly glance. 'You going to tell Mum about seeing me with Weirdo?'

'What do you think?' The truth was, she didn't give a shit. Jason was going to get a visit from the CID; that would be scarier than his mother.

'Mum'll go ballistic if she knows I smoke dope.'

Wheeler looked at him, couldn't believe that he could be so naive. 'You've no idea the trouble you could be in, have you?'

'You know what she's like. You're lucky.'

'That right?' Unclenched her fist; let him rot in jail if they found anything linking him to the girl's death.

'Not having parents.'

Wheeler wondered who they'd send to interview Jason, or would they drag him into the station? She would request the latter. Scare the shit out of him. 'How come not having parents is now a positive?'

'Well, at least they're not here to nag you.'

Wheeler stared at her nephew. What a fucking charmer.

Jason cleared his throat. 'I need to get back home.' He waited.

She let him wait.

He paused, looked at her from behind his fringe. 'I've no cash on me though.'

Finally she got it, the hesitation, the waiting. So this was how he played his mother. Wheeler went to the door, opened it. Waited.

'A tenner?'

She shook her head. 'You've got Weirdo on speed dial, a young girl is dead and you want money?'

'I need it. I've no food in the flat . . . and—'

'And tell it to someone who gives a shit. And Jason?'

He waited.

'I can take you to the station but it would look better if you went in yourself.'

'But you're . . .' His expression told her what she'd expected: the only reason he'd come to see her was he thought that she'd protect him. Little shit.

'Yeah?' she looked hard at him. 'I'm what?'

'Nothing. I'll go myself.' He left, slamming the door on his way out.

She stood at the window and saw him walk head down into the rain. Saw him check his pockets then hail a taxi. Her nephew. An addict. And a liar. Fucking great.

Wheeler was still thinking about him when she reached the station.

Chapter 44

They were midway through the session. Dr Moore sat quietly, waited until Doyle settled again after his outburst. 'So, that's why you decided on twice-weekly sessions?'

'Might as well get it over and done with.' One eye blazing black, the other cold.

Moore smiled warmly. 'I'm delighted that you're willing to put in the psychological work, Andy. It's sometimes painful work but ultimately it's healthier to get it done, and then usually we can move on.'

Silence.

'What I'm saying is you should be proud of yourself for coming to therapy and embracing challenge and change.'

'Aye right, whatever. Let's get on.'

'Okay, so last time we talked about your need for people to be loyal.'

'Uh huh.'

'Can you give me an example?'

Doyle thought about it. 'The guys who work for me, I need to know they won't join the opposition. I need to know that they'll be loyal.'

'You need to be able to trust them?'

'Trust is mibbe taking it too far; I need to know that they'll be loyal. End of.'

'Has anyone ever let you down?'

'A couple of guys in the early days.'

'And how did you react?'

'Don't get your drift.'

'What happened?'

Doyle clapped his hands together and made a sharp noise. 'Whoosh . . . Gone.'

Moore waited.

Doyle stared at her. 'Nothing sinister, just that they decided to . . . relocate.'

'So you demand complete loyalty?'

Doyle nodded.

'There's no room for people to make mistakes? After all, we're all human, we all mess up.'

'You mess up, you move on; that's my motto.'

'Does this include Stella?'

'Aye.'

'So, what if Stella was to be disloyal?'

'If she was fucking around behind my back?'

'I didn't mean specifically in a sexual way but okay, what if she was to have an affair?'

Doyle sat back in the chair, considered it. 'If she had an affair then that would be it. Game over.'

'You wouldn't want to try to work through it? Perhaps go for couple counselling?'

'I told you, it'd be game over. Done. She'd be dead meat.'
Moore stared at him.

He corrected himself. 'I mean she'd be history.'

'You wouldn't give her a second chance?'

'Fuck no.'

'Okay.' Moore waited.

Silence.

Eventually she spoke. 'You look angry.'

'The thought of Stella fucking around with somebody else makes me bloody angry.'

'Okay, so we've established that you have a need for people around you to be loyal.'

'Aye,' said Doyle.

'This was one need you identified quite quickly. Can you remember when this idea of loyalty began, when the need for it became so important?' Moore waited, saw conflicting emotions flit across his face. Saw him struggle to find answers. Finally he spoke. 'At the home.' His voice small, embarrassed.

'Stobwent-Hill Children's Home where you grew up?'

'Aye.'

'Go on.'

'What?'

'Loyalty, what did it mean to you at the home?'

'Like a foundation, like it was a stable thing when my life was . . .'

'Unstable?' she offered.

He nodded.

'Go on.'

The anger was back. 'Shite, it's textbook psychobabble isn't it?'

'Is it?'

'I didn't have a family, so I felt like I had no foundation.

You know how family is always there as a kind of a foundation or an anchor?'

'Yes.'

'Even if they're a shite family?'

'Go on.'

'Well, I wanted to have this foundation but I didn't have it, so I needed to create it. I needed to create a family.'

'And how did you do this?'.

Doyle shifted uncomfortably in his seat, stared at the wall. Moore watched the anger dissipate. Eventually he answered, 'I made them up.'

'Okay, how did you do this?' she repeated.

'There were boxes of old photographs in the TV lounge at the home, a load of shite mainly, but I liked looking through them.'

'Because?'

'Because there were loads of pictures of families, and in the pictures they were all standing together, arms linked and smiling into the camera. Rubbish stuff, but I liked it.'

'Why did you like it? What was it that appealed to you?'

'Fuckssake, you're the therapist, is it not bloody obvious?' Anger again. Knuckles beating against leather and chrome.

Moore blinked, watched Doyle, finally asked, 'So why don't you tell me then?'

'I used to look at the photographs and fantasise that those families were my family and that they'd had to go away for different reasons, but they would come back to collect me. Loads of stories, one to fit every photograph. Over the years I made up a million stories about families who all wanted me as their son.'

'What kind of families did you create?'

Doyle drummed his hand on the side of the chair.

Moore waited.

'Christ, this was Glasgow in the eighties and I was in a fucking children's home. I made up a family that were so far away from the dysfunctional cunts that I saw around me. All the fucked-up shit on offer, I didn't want. I wanted smooth, clean, powerful people to be in my family.' He peered at her. 'I suppose you think I'm nuts. Do you even get this?'

'I get it. So who was your favourite fictional family?'

'Fuck knows.'

'You know.'

Silence.

Finally he answered, 'A mismatch of characters from the telly.'

'Okay, but who? A mismatch of which characters from the television?'

Doyle stared out of the window, eyes calm. 'They were outsiders mainly, kind of like me. Folk who didn't fit in but didn't give a shit. Folk who did it their way.'

'Who?'

'I feel stupid saying.'

'You were a child in a home – why would you be stupid to imagine a family? That's what you're here for, to sort things out before you decide about having a family yourself.'

'Okay,' he sighed, 'I watched a lot of telly – it was the eighties, remember?'

'Go on.'

'I imagined my family would be kind of like the A-team. Folk with the balls to change things.'

She noted the grey pallor, the hopelessness in his voice as he revisited his childhood. 'Why was that so important?'

'Why do you think?'

'Because you couldn't change things?'

'Not then.'

'But you can now?'

'I used to sit in the stinking TV lounge and watch the A-team and plan what I would do when I was an adult. I'd make a list of people who'd pissed me off and figure out ways of getting revenge on them.'

'Do you still have the list?'

Doyle nodded. 'I've managed to . . .' he paused, 'delete a few names over the years. Then again I've added a few.'

'Recently?'

'It's an ongoing process.'

'And do you still want revenge on these people?'

'It's pretty much what makes life worth living.' Doyle glanced at his watch. 'Time up, I'm out of here,' his voice suddenly energised, his eyes sparkling, one darker than the other. He stood, straightened his jacket and strolled towards the door.

'Time up,' agreed Moore, but the door had closed behind him. She sat for a few moments. She noted that Doyle's body language had confirmed what she had suspected, that he felt most alive when he was engaged with the idea of exacting revenge. Moore knew for certain that she had found Doyle's passion and understood that it was this that had propelled him from a children's home into adulthood and the semblance of a successful career. She was in no doubt that Doyle was withholding information about his business and that he had the demeanour of a man of violence, but, she reasoned with herself, that wasn't why he was in therapy. He had come to confront his demons, to let go, to move on. He was ambitious and wanted to enter into what he called 'acceptable society' and maybe have a family, knowing that at present, in his own words, he 'stuck out a mile'. Part of Andy Doyle craved acceptance and wanted to fit into a society he mistrusted. He wanted to leave the poor, orphaned boy behind, but that would be difficult. At their initial meeting Moore had been clear about the boundaries of the client/therapist relationship and he understood that if he told her anything that compromised either himself or another individual she may have to contact the police. So far this hadn't happened, but Moore wondered about the spaces between the words and what had been left unsaid.

She'd told Doyle that in order for therapy to be successful there were certain requirements, including self-reflection, challenge and ultimately the desire for change. At the time he'd seemed confident, excited even about the possibility of change; now, however, she wondered about him. Was Andy Doyle willing to do what was required to make those changes?

Chapter 45

'Okay TC, I'm on my way down.' Wheeler stood and rubbed the back of her neck, easing a dull ache. She made her way into the corridor and headed for the stairs. She knew that Stewart had contacted Morag Bruce and that Jason would be interviewed at the station in the West End. Other than what she had told them, Wheeler was not to be involved. Meanwhile Stewart had asked her to collect the profiler when he arrived. She wandered down the stairs, still rubbing her neck and wondering what, if anything, this guy could bring to the investigation. Whoever Pete Newton was, she doubted that he'd be popular with the team; she only hoped they'd be at least civil to him. She turned into reception and Cunningham pointed to the man in the waiting area.

He was standing with his back to her but turned as she walked towards him. Wheeler offered her hand. 'DI Kat

Wheeler.' When he took it his was a firm, solid, handshake which stopped short of causing pain. 'Pete Newton,' he smiled. There was something about him, something familiar. The aquiline nose, the green eyes, the haircut that matched her own – short at the sides, a quiff on top. A gold pentagram glinted at his neck. She squinted up at him. 'Have we met?'

He leaned towards her, his aftershave heavy in the air, and whispered, 'The play.'

Wheeler took a step back. 'Sorry?'

'I think I saw you at the play the other night.'

She stared at him, noted the dark lashes, the height. Remembered that she'd had to push past him. Remembered the stubble around his lipsticked mouth and the Adam's apple. 'You were in the red dress?'

'A particular favourite,' he laughed, his eyes creasing.

She said nothing.

'Shocked?' he asked.

'No,' not quite the truth, 'surprised maybe.'

He pursed his lips, tapping his index finger against them. 'Shh then, it'll be our wee secret. I don't think the boys in blue would appreciate my particular brand of sartorial elegance, do you?'

Wheeler shrugged her response and headed up the stairs. Newton followed close behind.

Upstairs, Ross was meandering into the room. Robertson followed behind him and looked to be in a particularly sour mood. In the back row, four uniformed officers were chatting quietly. Wheeler turned to Newton, 'I'd bet that there isn't a cross-dresser among that lot.'

'You'd think so, looking at them now, but you'd be surprised – we're an eclectic bunch. There's more of us around than you think.'

'Right.'

'See that tall guy with the leather jacket? He'd look great in light blue. It would bring out his eyes.'

She looked at Ross, who was settling himself into a chair. 'He could certainly take advice. Maybe approach him after your talk? I'm sure he'd love it.'

'Let's leave it to his girlfriend, if he has one. Mine certainly keeps me on my toes.' He paused. 'She thought the red was too much. What did you think?'

'It seemed okay,' said Wheeler.

'Okay for a cross-dresser or okay lovely?'

'Let's just say it brought out your eyes.'

He sniffed, tried for a hurt look, failed, laughed instead. 'You hated it. Fair enough.'

She watched Newton laugh, saw his relaxed stance. A man at peace with himself. Wheeler saw Stewart come into the room and head towards Newton. She left them chatting and walked across to Ross, sat down beside him and waited.

After a quick chat with Stewart, Pete Newton strode to the front of the room. He was six foot two with broad shoulders and hands the size of shovels. He knew that most of the team would think that he was a twat, so first off he fixed his glare on the guy he thought looked to be the most anal.

Robertson sat in the front row, a notepad resting on his lap, a silver and black ballpoint pen tapping on the paper. He looked up, caught Newton's eye. Robertson smirked. Newton held his gaze. The smirk faded. Newton looked at the team, whose body language told him that they were already bored. He cleared his throat and began, his voice filling the room. 'Hi, my name is Dr Pete Newton.' His voice was deep, husky. 'Thank you for inviting me.'

Smirks, a few coughs. A few shared glances, just enough to let him know that they hadn't. Well, that much he knew already.

'And while I'm no longer a detective,' he continued, 'I do feel that I can contribute something to this investigation.'

The team waited. Arms folded. Waiting for him to tell them something they didn't already know.

'DCI Stewart has asked me to share my thoughts on the recent murder of James Gilmore.' He glanced at his notes. 'And since I have some experience in researching the criminal mind, I agreed.'

The female uniform beside Robertson nudged him, kept her voice a low. 'Yeah, we have a bit of experience in that area too.'

Robertson ignored her, stared ahead. Pen tapping on notepad.

Newton continued, 'Right then, in the case of James Gilmore, his injuries are typical of a certain type of killer. With this kind of guy, it is not enough just to kill his victim, he endeavours to create the *absence* of the person. Killers like this are compelled to completely obliterate their victim and consequently their humanity. They want to reduce their victim to a piece of meat.' He paused. 'Hence Gilmore's terrible injuries.'

Boyd spoke. 'Why the additional effort to eradicate someone when surely the time spent doing so would make it more dangerous, there being less time to escape? Why wouldn't it be enough just to kill them?'

Newton nodded. 'Good question. Why would our killer bother to put in the additional time and energy when he could have killed Gilmore quickly?' Newton looked around the team.

'To murder in this way reinforces the killer's belief in his superiority?' offered Robertson.

'Yes, but also to destroy the very presence of James Gilmore himself.'

A young uniformed officer from the back of the room spoke. 'Do you think it could've been an ex-partner?'

Newton pursed his lips. 'It's possible that it could be an ex-partner, but in my opinion it would be unlikely to be a female. I believe that it was a man who murdered James Gilmore.'

'Because?' asked Wheeler, aware that she was arguing for the sake of it.

'Because, statistically speaking, you would be looking for a male. And also, the degree of violence inflicted on the victim would indicate a male.'

'A woman could have done it, or two working together?' the uniformed officer said. 'Remember Nikki Fullerton?'

'Of course, I read about the case.' Newton waited for her to continue.

'She killed her husband and kept bits of him stuffed into handbags. She stored them in the loft.'

'Yes, I know, and psychologically Fullerton's a very interesting case, but nevertheless I'm certain that our killer is male. So moving on, firstly, why kill? What would motivate our killer?'

'A grudge?' said Boyd. 'And if not a girlfriend then maybe a boyfriend?'

'There were no signs that he was gay.' Robertson twitched as he spoke.

'There was no evidence of penetration, anal or oral. Before or after death,' agreed Newton. 'But that doesn't tell us much. What do we know about the victim's sexuality?'

'A complete lack of any recent relationships,' said Wheeler. 'Other than a fiancée who died years ago, there's been no mention of either a girlfriend or a boyfriend in past decades.'

'Okay.' Newton waited. 'Any theories?'

'It's what it could point to,' said Ross.

'You think he was a paedophile?' asked Newton.

Ross shrugged. 'It's a possibility.'

'Of course. Any evidence?'

Ross shook his head.

Newton carried on, 'Okay. Let's keep an open mind. But what I want us to focus on is not the physical but the psychological aspect of the murder. The killer needed to feel powerful.'

'Don't they all?' asked Boyd.

'Not always.'

'You think he's a local man or someone from out of town?' asked Wheeler.

'I would definitely say that the killer lives and works in this area. He's a local man, I'm certain of it. Whether or not they were a couple, I don't know, but whoever killed him knew him intimately. The nature of the beating was in itself extremely intimate. There was no sense of the man left. The killer was involved either physically, psychologically or emotionally with Gilmore,' Newton paused, looking around the room, 'and we know that the killer will be following developments closely.'

Most of the team nodded. It was well known that killers liked to monitor their notoriety.

'Some killers need to read about their progress in the newspapers or listen to people discuss the murder in the street or on the television. He may even compare himself with other murderers, try to gauge the level of his notoriety. The more audacious prefer to communicate with the police force directly, to prove to themselves both how clever they are and how stupid the police are. One of the most important attributes of this section of society is their ego. They feel intellectually superior to others. And especially the police.'

'If you have profiled him correctly,' said Ross.

'Of course, it's not an exact science.'

'But this is nothing we don't know already,' Boyd said. 'This is all good in theory but textbook cases aren't really going to help us.'

'Anything else?' asked Robertson, still tapping his pen on his notebook. So far he hadn't taken a single note.

'Okay, so we have a local man who in some way was intimately involved with James Gilmore. What sort of man might he be?' Newton looked around the room, waiting for answers.

'A psycho.' Boyd slouched in his chair, sounded bored. 'Obviously some psycho nut job.'

'Not necessarily,' said Newton.

'How come?' Boyd chewed on the inside of his cheek.

'Define psychopath.'

'Christ, everyone knows what that is: somebody who can't feel guilt about what he does, somebody who can't empathise with his victims and also somebody who shows no remorse.'

'And?' prompted Newton.

'And what?' Boyd said. 'It's enough, isn't it?'

'Anything else?'

Boyd sat up, eyes darting to the left, remembering the research paper he'd read. Found it somewhere in his memory, scanned it quickly before replying, 'Okay, it usually starts at school. He might be bullied, then he goes on to become the bully himself, maybe increasing the violence and intimidation as he gets a taste for it. Also he might mangle a few animals along the way, just to help him find his feet. Then as an adult he finally emerges as a fully fledged psycho.'

Subdued laughter.

Newton smiled. 'Not bad. But you're forgetting something: they are also extremely focused, can be incredibly charming, charismatic and good-looking. And they are great at manipulating people. They can also make brilliant business leaders, so they can be difficult to spot.'

'Right.' Boyd wasn't convinced. 'We're looking for a good-looking, successful guy?'

'In all probability.'

'But not definitely?' said Boyd.

Newton was patient. 'The study of human behaviour isn't an exact science.'

Boyd looked at the floor. 'Blinding insight,' he muttered.

Newton ignored him. 'Let's move on. Let's look at what makes a killer function, his motivation if you like. There are some generalities we might look at. Killers, on the whole, but not always, tend to come from dysfunctional backgrounds. They often come from homes lacking in love, validation or support. They learn at an early age to escape into dream or fantasy worlds, which enables them to feel empowered when they are disempowered. Later they begin to resent the society which they feel rejected them. They may direct that hate towards the mother or father figure for having brought them into the world. As they mature, they may continue to feel inadequate, despite having achieved what, on the surface, may constitute success. They long to be included but persistently feel excluded. Deep down they feel unloved and unworthy of love. Neglected. Rejected. Abandoned.'

'Neglected?' Wheeler repeated, thinking of the Watervale kids and also remembering the brain scans from the lecture Matthew Barnes had delivered. The Keenan Institute was all about helping those kinds of children.

'Yes, neglected, definitely. And although in his mind he

274

is a *loner,* in terms of how society judges him, he could be a great success. But as a child he would have been left alone. He would have been neglected, perhaps by both parents, but definitely by the mother figure.'

'Oh for goodness' sake,' said Boyd, 'he murders because his mammy left him?'

'She *ignored or neglected* him. Perhaps even abandoned him.'

'So someone with a grudge against his mother?' asked Wheeler.

'A grudge against society, *originating* with his mother.' Newton paused. 'Another aspect is that since at his core he feels disempowered, it is by killing that he becomes empowered. God-like. The rush of adrenaline he would have experienced during the beating was an opportunity to experience power.'

'Sick bastard,' said Ross.

'So, who are we looking for?' Robertson asked. 'Theories are interesting but surely we need substance.'

'Many killers can and do outwit the police. And psychiatrists and psychologists. Psychopaths, if he is one, are clever and learn what they should say, what they should do, how they should act and, under scrutiny, they do it. But internally they are their true selves. They may be introverted or paranoid, with a fixation that the world and people are against them. Yet, externally they may successfully hide this. In fact, they may be prominent people in our society.'

'Like politicians?' suggested Ross.

A ripple of laughter from the team.

'Like anyone. You or I, for instance.'

'Not a copper, though,' muttered a uniformed officer from the back.

'Why not?' said Newton.

The officer glared at him but said nothing.

Newton continued, 'You see, that's his cover. He can merge into any society. That's why we can't identify killers when they stalk our streets. He is an outsider, someone who doesn't fit in. But he has learned to.'

'And you think he might be liaising with the police?'

'In some way he will be communicating with you. That would feed his ego. I would go as far as to say you may well have spoken to him directly. I can only offer an insight into the man's mind. It's for you to uncover the pattern of his movements. I would say someone who appears confident but internally is lost. A lost soul.'

A poor wee soul, thought Wheeler, wasn't that what Paton had called George Grey? 'What about the two boys?'

Newton glanced at his notes. 'Munroe and Wilson? I think that they stumbled, literally, across Gilmore's body.'

Wheeler nodded.

'Could it be one of the other kids from the school?' Boyd asked.

Newton paused. 'He'd have to be quite a complex character, have the ability to present himself in a positive light while being capable of this. Of course there is a third way.'

'Which is?'

'That emotionally he's not just detached but dead. In that case, this would have been merely a mechanical deed.'

'And?' prompted Boyd.

Newton pursed his lips. 'And he is emotionally dead because anger, violence and death may be all he knows.'

'A lost soul,' said Wheeler.

'Might be quite a big section of the city,' said Ross.

'I know, but it's a start,' offered Newton.

'So, are you directing us back to Watervale?' Robertson sounded irritated.

'I don't believe so; this wasn't done by kids.'

Wheeler thought about the list of ex-Watervale pupils who had landed in trouble with the police.

Stewart strode into the room. 'Thank you, Dr Newton. Now if you're finished, a word in my office?'

'You're very welcome. I hope it maybe gives a bit of room for thought but, as I said, it's not an exact science.'

Wheeler remembered her previous conversation with Stewart. *Special budget. Special rates.* She watched Stewart and Newton leave the room together. Did that mean 'mates' rates' and what had Newton meant by 'there're more of us around than you'd think'? She saw the back of Stewart's pristine suit, knew the hit of his aftershave was floating around the room. Suddenly the unwanted image of Stewart in a bright red dress, wearing lipstick and high heels, flashed across her mind. She quickly turned away. Too late, the image had registered. Wheeler shook her head and wondered if she would ever lose it.

Chapter 46

Wheeler went back to her desk and fired up her computer. Checked her messages. There was an email from Callum Fraser asking her to call him.

So she did.

'Lauren Taylor had gamma hydroxybutyrate in her system.'

'GHB,' Wheeler said, 'the date rape drug?'

'Except that she wasn't raped. Hadn't had sex recently, which means—'

'Which means,' she finished for him, 'that she took it recreationally.'

She listened while Callum gave her the specifics. Wheeler jotted the information down in her notebook.

'So, the side effects, if I remember correctly, include hallucinations?'

'Hallucinations and often a sense of euphoria.'

'So she could have been hallucinating and walked out onto the balcony?'

'It's certainly one possibility.'

'Anything else, Callum?'

'The individual may feel dizzy and their vision may become impaired.'

'Could she have been pushed?'

'There were no signs of a struggle, no defence wounds. Nothing much under her fingernails to suggest that there was a scuffle.' He paused. 'My other phone is ringing, Katherine – may I email you the results later?'

Wheeler agreed, thanked him quickly and put down the phone.

Ross was at his desk. 'GHB?'

Wheeler nodded.

'Jason?'

'West End are interviewing him later. I'll email them the results Callum sends through.'

'Was there anything at the scene to link him to Lauren?'

'Nothing.'

Later, at his interview, Jason omitted to mention that after he had left Kat Wheeler's flat he had gone home and calmly showered. Then he made sure that there was nothing incriminating in his flat. He had washed out his hip flask, put the gloves in a drawer and had made sure that he had his story completely straight before he met with the cops. He hadn't been with Lauren that night – she'd been there by herself – so, unless they had evidence to the contrary?

They had none.

Chapter 47

Since her meeting with Maurice Mason, Stella had not stopped thinking about him for a heartbeat, but she was smart enough to carry on her daily routine and for her this meant shopping. She had just pulled her car into the underground car park in the Buchanan Street Galleries when her mobile rang. It was Doyle.

'You in town?' He knew she was; she had told him where she was going before she'd left that morning.

She kept her voice soft. 'I've just pulled into the car park, babe. You need me to pick up something for you?'

She waited, heard the hesitation in his voice. 'No, I don't need anything. I've just had a phone call . . . it feels all wrong.'

'Yeah?' Stella heard her breathing quicken a pace, tried to keep her voice casual. 'Anybody I know?'

'Lizzie Coughlin.'

Silence. Stella's chest tightened for a second. She inhaled then exhaled, calmly. Took her time.

'You there, Stella?'

'The reception's bad here, babe,' she lied. 'I didn't catch the name – who was it again?'

'Lizzie Coughlin. You remember her?'

'Vaguely. Isn't she big Kenny's daughter?' *And Maurice bloody Mason's girlfriend. Fuck. Fuck. Fuck.*

'She wants to talk to me,' said Doyle.

'Lizzie wants to talk to you? She say what about?'

'No, she wants a one-to-one. In private. Thought you might know what about. Fuck knows, I've got nothing to say to her.'

'I could come home, babe, and speak to her?'

His voice suspicious, 'No need, it's me she wants to see. I was just wondering if you had any bloody idea what it's about?'

'Haven't heard from Lizzie in years.' Stella kept her voice calm. 'Maybe it's something about Kenny. He still inside?'

'Yeah.' Doyle sounded bored. 'Just thought I'd check it out with you. I'll sort it. See you later.'

The phone went dead.

Stella sat in the car, drummed her scarlet nails on the dashboard. Glanced at the phone, dialled, waited a heartbeat for an answer. 'Sonny, about that favour? It's needed ASAP.' She ended the call without waiting for a reply.

She crossed the car park, heels clicking on concrete, a flash of red sole. She took the lift to John Lewis and stood at the entrance to the store and breathed deeply, allowing the calm and order of the shop to comfort her. The place was as close to a spiritual home as Stella had and she felt almost reverential. She glanced around, noted that everything on display was ordered, arranged neatly and looked beautiful. Stella felt herself calm. Breathed deeply again and stepped over the threshold. Once inside, she made for the kitchen department and began browsing, running her fingers over the knives on display.

A few seconds elapsed before an assistant approached her. 'Hello, may I help you? Are you looking for anything in particular?' The assistant was middle-aged and enthusiastic and managed a smile which seemed genuine.

Stella returned the smile. 'As a matter of fact I am. I'm looking to buy a knife, a big boning knife,' she held her hands out, a foot apart. 'You know the kind butchers use?'

'Of course.' The smiling assistant led the way. 'What kind of meat will you be preparing?'

'Tough meat. Usually that's the problem isn't it, meat that's all bone and gristle? You have to hack your way through it. Gets messy.'

The assistant had stopped in front of a display. 'There's quite a difference in price range and weight – some of the knives are very heavy.'

Stella reached across and took a fifteen-inch, stainless-steel knife in her right hand, felt the heft, curved her fingers around the handle. 'Beautiful.'

'That one's pretty heavy—' The assistant looked doubtful.

Stella cut her off. 'No worries, I'm stronger than I look.'

The assistant pointed to another, smaller knife. 'There's one over here which might—'

Stella smiled sweetly. 'Where do I pay?'

The assistant nodded and led the way.

Chapter 48

The Gaggia hissed steam and gurgled and Doyle waited patiently until the thick black liquid had poured into his cup before turning to her. 'You want a coffee?'

Lizzie shifted uncomfortably in her seat. 'I wouldn't mind, Mr Doyle, if it's not too much trouble.'

Doyle turned back to the machine. A few seconds later he settled himself. 'Right, let's get started. Stella says you're an old pal of hers from school.'

'Aye, well, I was a few years ahead of her. Knew her as Maggie then, before she changed her name to Stella and she went intae all that acting stuff. Before she left the area . . . our families kind of knew each other.'

Doyle stared at her; she was rambling.

She stopped rambling, sat quietly, sipped her scalding coffee. Smiled.

'You're big Kenny Coughlin's daughter.'

She blushed with pride, looked at the floor. 'Aye, that's ma da alright.'

'How's he doing?'

'He's doing okay, Mr Doyle.'

'You see him often?'

'Every week.'

'When's he getting out?'

'Not for a while, good few years yet.'

'Right.' Doyle sipped his coffee. 'So, you said on the phone you've got boyfriend trouble; is that right?'

'It is.'

'And your boyfriend's Maurice Mason?'

'Right again.'

'Is he no a bit old for you, more your da's age?'

'Thought I'd go for the more mature man; turns out he's an immature wee prick.'

'That right?'

Lizzie removed her scarf. 'Mason tried to kill me.'

Doyle was calm. 'Nightmare. All the same, what's it to do with me? Your da's pals not help you out?'

'Da's clumsy – he's only got one way of doing business.'

'So I heard.'

'Claw hammer.'

'That's it. Your da's a traditionalist. Old school.'

'Mason thinks he's coming intae money.'

'So?'

'So I wondered where he thinks he's going tae get it. Says he's got a deal going with Tenant. I think it's got tae be wee Stevie Tenant.'

Doyle's eye darkened. 'Has he now? What do you know about it?'

'Nothing except he's going to get some money soon and

it's because of a partnership with someone called Tenant. That's about all I could make out. Mason wasn't giving much away.'

'So, Mason and Tenant are going intae a wee partnership together? You any ideas what the pair of them might be doing?'

Lizzie sat forward in her seat. 'It's got to be drugs, Mr Doyle. See, that's where I thought you'd come in . . .' She looked at him. Read the expression correctly. 'Sorry. I'm sorry.'

'First off Lizzie, I don't know what you're on about. I run a respectable business.'

'Sorry Mr Doyle, but I just thought if . . . He's got off with loads. I gave him my best days . . . went up to the jail every week. Thinks he can just come out and dump me – well that'll be shining bright. I know too much about him; I could get him banged up again.'

Doyle shook his head. 'You watch too much telly, Lizzie. We're not all gangsters, you know. Go home. Forget about Mason; you're right, he sounds a prick. But he's a useless prick.' He gestured to her throat. 'If he tries that again, get the polis involved.'

'But—'

Doyle stared at her for a second.

'Sorry, Mr Doyle.' Lizzie crossed the room and closed the door quietly as she left.

Doyle dialled, waited. A few seconds passed before it was answered. 'Weirdo, come over.'

Weirdo stood on the carpet, his purple Mohican damp from the rain. He had sprinted from the car and was panting quietly like a well-behaved dog. He waited patiently.

Finally Doyle spoke. 'Got a visit from a lassie called Lizzie Coughlin.'

Weirdo waited.

'You know her?'

Weirdo shook his head.

'She's big Kenny Coughlin's daughter.'

Weirdo looked blank.

Doyle nodded. 'Okay, not everyone's a networker like me, and Kenny's last week's news. Been inside a long while. Big, clumsy man. No refinement. Old school. Likes the claw hammer. Disnae understand that things are getting more sophisticated.'

'Lizzie causing you bother, Mr Doyle?'

Doyle shook his head. 'No, but Maurice Mason's her bloke and she's pissed off with him. Any ideas what he's up to?'

Weirdo shrugged. 'Don't know Mason myself but Sonny down at the Smuggler's said he'd been in, looking jammy, like he'd hit the jackpot. Splashing the cash and gobbing about coming intae money.'

'You've got my interest. Go on.'

'Said he'd come into some merchandise which would give him a wee income. Said it could roll and roll.'

'Merchandise?'

Weirdo nodded. 'Aye but he never told Sonny what it was, said it was secret.'

Doyle sounded bored. 'Right, well it's probably got nothing to do with me or my business interests, but I need to be sure. You keep an eye out, speak to Sonny again. Tell him to find out what Mason's up to.'

'Okay, boss.' Weirdo waited, then realised he'd been dismissed. Biker boots marched silently to the door.

Chapter 49

Rab stood outside the door of his house, his key in his hand, listening. He heard his mother's voice, heard her curse her boyfriend. Heard the boyfriend curse her back, only he was louder and more aggressive. Heard the bottle smash against the wall. He knew where she would have been standing, in front of the television. Heard the pause, the seconds it took the boyfriend to cross the room, the sound of his mother's head being rhythmically bounced off the living-room wall.

Better just leave them to it.

Rab zipped up his anorak, put his key back in his pocket and began walking to the bus stop. He huddled inside the deserted shelter, shifting from foot to foot, trying to keep warm. Somehow the air in the shelter seemed colder – he shivered, heard his stomach rumble. It had been four hours since he'd had the cheese sandwich at Alec's house. Rab checked his pockets, came up with thirty pence, not even enough for a bag of chips. He glanced back at his home. At least there might be a packet of cheese and onion crisps in the kitchen. He wavered, thought of his mother and her boyfriend, decided against it. Saw the lights of the bus in the distance. Rab waited.

Twenty minutes later he jumped off the bus and began running. He heard his breath rasp into the cold, felt his muscles respond to his desire to quicken his pace, heard the sound of his trainers landing on concrete. Soon he would warm up, he would overcome the elements, he would succeed in conquering the hunger eating at his belly. Rab clenched his fists as he ran, thought about his last boxing match, how he had wanted to pulverise his opponent's face. How Keely, his trainer, had forced him to stop. Later, Keely had told him to take some time out. Anger-management issues, he'd said. Rab smiled. He didn't need boxing now. That had been his training as a child and an adolescent; it had kept him safe from bullies, including his mother and the succession of bastard boyfriends. Now he was old enough he would move out and his life would begin.

He turned into the allotments, raced through the deserted paths until finally he slowed his pace, stopping outside the hut, his hut, panting. He bent down, reached around to the side of the building for the plastic bag containing the torch, switched it on, flicked the beam around the area. Nothing. No one. He slipped the key from the pocket of his anorak and unlocked the padlock. Rab paused, listened. Other than the rain and the distant noise from traffic on the main road, there was nothing to suggest that there was another living soul in the area. The wooden door of the shed opened with a creak; the smell of damp and rotting vegetation clung to the air.

There had been another smell, one that had interested Rab much more than any of the others. He stepped into the damp space, closed his eyes and let the rush of adrenaline hold him, squeeze him until he could hardly breathe. He inhaled deeply, let the memory of the smell come to him, feel its way into his nostrils, snake its way to his heart. He could feel his heart quicken its beat in response. Rust and iron, the metallic smell of blood. Rab could almost have tasted it when the bloodied bat had first arrived. He'd been told to get rid of it. He shone the beam from the torch into the corner of the shed – it was still there; he couldn't get rid of it. It lay hidden behind boxes. Rab closed his eyes and tried to imagine the night it had been used. In his mind a series of images began playing. He imagined the initial resistance a body would have to the bat, resistance which would evaporate as the force increased. He imagined the crack of wood against flesh, the sound of bone breaking. Imagined first curses, then screams, then the pleas which would have reverberated around the room. He imagined the heft of the bat and how the weight of it would increase the damper it had become, at its heaviest when it was coated with thick, sticky liquid. He wished that he'd been there to see Gilmore suffer. He wished he'd done it.

Afterwards James Gilmore's blood had still clung to the bat, with particles of flesh and hair. Rab had touched the bat, brought it to his face, closed his eyes and inhaled again. He had smelled blood, sweat and definitely fucking tears. He'd been told that Gilmore had grovelled for his life. It hadn't been worth saving.

Rab opened his eyes and leaned into a dusty box he'd salvaged from a skip, rummaging around until he found it. He brought out the gold chain and medal. Looked at the motif, a man with a child on his shoulders and a staff for walking. Rab heard his stomach growl. He turned the chain around in his hands, flicked the medal over and over. Rab made up his mind. He needed to eat. He would sell it. Weirdo or Sonny at the Smuggler's would take it on – he'd offload it to one of them. Then he'd fucking take Alec and they'd go for a pizza and lager. And sit in, not just a takeaway to eat outside in a piss-soaked bus shelter. Rab tucked the gold medal and chain into his anorak pocket. He made sure the bat was still hidden in the corner before locking the hut and double-checking the padlock.

When he got home the house was empty. There must be a party on somewhere and the two of them had fucked off. Rab crept into the kitchen, took the last slice of bread from its greaseproof package and spread margarine on it, looked about for crisps. There were none. He reached up and took down a bag of granulated sugar and sprinkled some of it over the margarine. He folded the bread over and wolfed the sandwich down. He checked the cupboards and the fridge to see if there was anything else. Nothing except a four-pack of cheap lager; he grabbed one. He'd get battered for it but he was past caring. Rab closed the door behind him and slipped back out into the cold night. He'd go to see Alec and explain his plan. Maybe they'd go to see Sonny together; maybe Rab would go on his own. He'd need to pick the right time – the Smuggler's could be dangerous. As Rab walked he wondered about the wee bird, the racing pigeon. He hoped it had managed to get back home. Remembered that that was the night Smithy had chased them. Rab had told Manky, who'd told Weirdo. He knew that he'd relay the message to Mr Doyle. Rab walked on through the freezing night. Hoped that Doyle would sort Smithy out.

Chapter 50

If you were to place an equilateral triangle on a map of Glasgow, the Royal Infirmary would be in one angle, Wheeler's flat in the second and, in the third, Buchanan Street bus station. The station replaced the old one at Anderson and was built in keeping with Glasgow's modern image. At this time of the night Buchanan Street was floodlit, illuminating the buildings in a cool blue light. At the top of Buchanan Street stood the Buchanan Galleries, John Lewis dominating the smaller shop units. Outside in the freezing cold night the bronze statue of Donald Dewar dripped rain while the wind screeched around it.

Inside, the bus station was brightly lit. When the overnight coach to London pulled into the stance, a sleepy group of passengers stood stretching and yawning and made their way in an orderly queue towards it. Some had plastic bags with sandwiches for the journey, bottles of Irn-Bru or Coke tucked into pockets with crisps and chocolate. Others had spent a few hours drinking and would sleep for most of the overnight journey, awakening to a new day at London Victoria cramped and sore and mildly hung over. One passenger stood at the end of the line, clutching a new holdall containing a pile of shop-bought sandwiches, a packet of crisps and a bottle of sparkling water. In the pocket of his anorak there was a new leather wallet containing ten twenty-pound notes and the phone number of a man he'd never met. Weirdo had made sure George Grey had everything placed in the holdall before he handed him the ticket to London. It was one-way. Weirdo had shaken his hand and left him at the bus station.

The four-by-four waited a short distance from the station. Doyle watched the last of the passengers climb onto the coach. Watched until the driver had loaded the luggage and settled himself behind the wheel, closed the doors and reversed out of the stance. Doyle watched the coach pull out of the station. As it passed the four-by-four, George Grey lifted a hand in recognition, smiled quickly at Doyle before turning away from the window and closing his eyes. Leaving Glasgow had been Doyle's idea; George Grey had listened, followed instructions and felt that for the first time in his life he could trust someone. The coach pulled into a lane and George opened his eyes and stared out of the window, watching as Glasgow passed him by, understanding that he wouldn't see the city again or at least not for a long time. Thought of his mother, wished that she were dead. Wished again that he had never had a mother. It might have been better, he decided, if he had never been born in the first place. The coach was warm; he closed his eyes again and scrunched down in the seat. A few minutes later he was sleeping, dreaming the now-familiar dreams. His finger, the one with the scar cutting across the fingertip, twitched throughout the long journey.

Chapter 51

Not long after the coach had pulled out of Buchanan Street bus station Weirdo was standing in the piss-soaked living room of George Grey's house. Weirdo smiled and cracked his knuckles more flamboyantly than was absolutely necessary, seeing as he already had William MacIntyre's full attention.

'See Wullie, we find it awfully fucking difficult to understand, so mibbe you could explain it to us?'

'Us?'

'Me and Mr Doyle. He wanted a word but seeing as how this fucking place needs fumigated, he sent me on tae have a wee chat.'

MacIntyre's already grey pallor faded to white. 'Doyle's coming here?'

Weirdo shook his head. 'You can appreciate why he

wouldn't want to come here in person, seeing as it's a fucking cesspit, and you'll also twig as to why he's reluctant to invite you to his place, what with you smelling like the arsehole you are, can't you, Wullie?'

MacIntyre shifted uncomfortably on his chair. Reached for a half-empty packet of cigarettes, took one, watched his hands shake as he tried to light it. Felt the sweat running down his back, pooling at the base of his spine and turning cold. He shivered. Tossed the packet of cigarettes onto the floor.

Weirdo paced across the sitting-room floor. 'You listening to me Wullie?'

MacIntyre coughed, drawing phlegm from deep in his throat and spitting it into a discarded coffee cup. The dark globules landed on the green mould clinging to the cup and mixed with the dregs of cold, black coffee. He rubbed the three stumps on his hand into his back, trying to knead the pain from his kidneys. He failed. He failed also to keep the fear from his voice. 'You gonnae tell me why Andy Doyle's so interested in me?'

Weirdo's phone rang. 'Yeah? Right Mr Doyle, sure thing, no problem, I'll tell him.' He paused, listened, then responded, 'Yes, he's here. He's playing the innocent. I'll explain the terms of your offer.' Weirdo paused, listened again, then spoke, 'Oh aye, Mr Doyle, I'll make sure it's made very clear to him. There'll be no room for any misunderstanding.' Weirdo finished the call, turned to face MacIntyre. 'Let's begin.' He held up the forefinger of his right hand. 'First off, wee George Grey.'

'That wee shite's no here.'

'Correct.'

MacIntyre shrugged. 'Fuck knows where he is. Could be anywhere.'

Weirdo nodded, muttered under his breath, too low for
MacIntyre to hear, 'Best that you know nothing.'

'Whit?' MacIntyre screwed up his eyes, peered at Weirdo.
'Whit did ye say?'

'I said let's back up a bit. Let's have a wee think about
George. Think mibbe you might want to tell me about whit
was happening to him?'

MacIntyre slid further down in his chair, made himself
small. 'Nuthin. Nuthin wis happening tae him. If he says
anything else, he's a lying wee bastard.'

Weirdo bent over him. 'See I cannae hear any conviction
in your voice, Wullie. You're a shite liar.' He shook his head.
'Fuck, have you nae talent at all?'

MacIntyre squeezed himself further into the chair. Weirdo
continued, 'Tell you what, I'll make it easy for you. James
Gilmore, care to tell me about whit was happening?'

MacIntyre shook his head. 'There's fuck all tae tell.' But
the tremor in his voice contradicted him.

Weirdo waited; eventually he bent over the cowering
man and whispered, 'We know.'

Silence.

Weirdo repeated himself. 'We know.'

Silence. MacIntyre began shaking, tried to stop, failed.

Weirdo smiled. 'See Mr Doyle keeps a wee list of cunts
that need annihilated and Gilmore was on it.'

'How's that then? How was Gilmore on it?'

Weirdo paused, said nothing. Waited. Saw that MacIntyre
still didn't get it. Shook his head. Went back to his original
point. 'Have a wee think about Gilmore. Then have another
wee think about how he met wee George all those years ago.'

MacIntyre flinched as if he had been hit.

Weirdo paused and watched while the penny dropped
before he continued, 'Now guess what?'

MacIntyre stared at him.

'You guessed it,' whispered Weirdo, 'now you're on Doyle's list too.'

MacIntyre closed his eyes.

'So, the thing is Wullie, given that you're now on the list and given that Mr Doyle has been nice enough to warn you, what are you going to do about it?'

Weirdo left the house, pleased with his behaviour. He heard MacIntyre whimpering and congratulated himself that he hadn't used his fists. Hadn't needed to. Mr Doyle was right, Weirdo thought, he was getting better at this; he was ambitious after all. He smoothed his Mohican and clicked the metal stud in his mouth in time with his footsteps. He stopped walking when his mobile rang. 'Mr Doyle.'

'You finished with that cunt MacIntyre?'

'Aye, I've just left him.'

'And he understands?'

'Aye, he's shitting himself.'

Weirdo listened to Doyle laugh. 'Great, let him.'

Weirdo heard Doyle cover the phone, heard a muffled 'Christ Stella, I told you I'll be there the morrow night, but then I'm having to work late okay?' Then he was back on the phone. 'Stella's got a part in a panto starting tomorrow night Weirdo, so I want all of this stuff done with; it's not going to spoil my Christmas, got it?'

'Aye.'

'But after the panto, I want you and me to have a wee chin-wag about you moving up in the business. Okay? Stella's going to be off celebrating with her actor pals, so it'll just be the two of us.'

'Great Mr Doyle.'

Doyle paused, lowered his voice. 'Next wee job for you,

Weirdo, I need you to check out a few things, then tomorrow I want you to get up to studentville. Understand?'

'Sure. Students' residences up by Maryhill?'

'You'll know the area well.'

'Aye, of course, like the back of my hand.'

'Pay a wee visit, discreet mind.' Weirdo listened for the address, then the name of the student. Recognised the name. Waited while Doyle continued, 'A wee lassie's dead. GHB. Find out where it came from and if he had anything to do with it.' The phone went dead. Weirdo turned and walked quickly towards the car park. Outside the rain had turned to sleet. In George's Square the huge Christmas tree twinkled in the dark and festive songs rang out, wishing everyone peace and happiness, reminding the citizens of Glasgow to 'Have A Very Merry Christmas!'

The residence Weirdo was looking for was out towards Maryhill. But that was tomorrow. First he had some errands to run in the East End. He nosed the car out into traffic, flicked the heat on full and switched on a Christmas compilation CD. He began belting out 'Santa Claus is Coming to Town' followed by 'White Christmas'. He'd sung along with the other songs while he cruised through the sleet, windscreen wipers beating their own rhythm. The city centre was full of revellers, out partying, laughing and skidding on the sleet-soaked pavements. Happy days.

Chapter 52

The sleet hammered down over the deserted street in the north of the city. Robertson slowed the car to a crawl, stopped and listened to the steady rhythm of the windscreen wipers for a few minutes before finally killing the engine. He twisted his wedding ring from his finger and threw it into the glove compartment. He felt his heartbeat quicken, felt the tremor in his hand begin. He heard the thrum of rain on the roof of the car, the dying sounds of the engine as the heat escaped. He licked his lips, tasted mint toothpaste and bitter mouthwash. He felt adrenaline work its magic as he waited expectantly. His mobile rang and he glanced at the name: *Margaret.* He switched it off. Within minutes there was movement from the bushes. Robertson watched as the shadow of a young man left the cover of darkness and sauntered towards the car, hips thrust out, hands in pockets.

As if he were only on a night stroll. As if this was the perfect weather for walking. He looked as if he was in his late teens, but early twenties was more probable. His jeans were skin-tight, revealing the outline of his legs and his crotch. He wore a tightly zipped leather jacket and dark trainers. His dark hair was mid-length and swept back from a pale face. Robertson waited. The man approached, opened the door, settled himself in the passenger seat. Robertson inhaled the ocean scent of aftershave. He glanced at the young man, took in a strong profile, a large nose, plump lips, a diamond stud earring. Robertson reached forward and started the car.

They drove in silence to the industrial park. It was deserted and huge metal buildings blanketed the space. Aside from his car, the car park was empty. Robertson did what he always did: he leaned across and began. Gently at first, touching, exploring, pressing. Later he pursued his desire more aggressively and felt adrenaline fly through his body until finally, when he was sated, he stopped and leaned back in his seat, sweat saturating his shirt. He pulled up his trousers, ran a sweaty hand through his hair and sat waiting, until his breathing returned to its regular pace.

They drove back in silence, the sweat on Robertson cooling to a deep chill. The young man combed his hair, adjusted his clothes and stared out of the window. Robertson's mouth tasted sour – he swallowed a few times before he finally slowed the car, opened the window and spat into the sleet. When they came to their earlier meeting place Robertson leaned over, pushed open the door and shoved the young man into the freezing cold night, then threw the notes after him. Before driving off, Robertson reached into the glove compartment and retrieved his wedding ring. Then he switched on his phone. Saw another missed called from his wife. Ignored it.

Chapter 53

In the East End of the city, in the empty CID suite at Carmyle Police Station, Boyd was answering the phone. 'Hello, Mrs Robertson . . . no Ian's not here. As far as I know he left a few hours ago. Of course I'll tell him to give you a bell if he comes in. Bye.'

The strip lighting glared across the room, blinking now and again as if trying to induce a headache. He stood, walked to the window and stared out. In the distance he could see the M8. Cars were crawling through a fresh downpour, their tail lights creating a hazy, meandering path into and out of the city. He thought of the landfill site beside Doyle's house and wondered why Doyle, with his kind of money, had chosen to live so close to it. He crossed to the kettle and switched it on, glanced across at his desk; on top of the pile of paperwork was a list of some of the items retrieved from

Gilmore's house. Everything that had been removed after the discovery of the body had been analysed for fingerprints, stray hairs, small particles of fibres, anything that would help identify the killer. But apart from an unmatched partial fingerprint and two anonymous callers, they had nothing.

He heard the kettle click, turned from the window and was spooning coffee into a mug when Robertson came through the door, coat damp, hair dishevelled.

Boyd raised an eyebrow in surprise. 'You're late back. And by the way, your missus is just off the phone. You need to give her a bell.'

Robertson ignored him.

'You okay?' Boyd asked, 'only you look drookit.'

Robertson looked at him. 'I didn't expect to find anyone here at this time.'

'Doing a bit extra, couldn't sleep.' Boyd held up his mug of coffee. 'You want some? Think I might have a packet of biscuits somewhere if that thieving git Ross hasn't swiped them.'

Robertson shivered. 'No thanks. Just came in to pick up . . .' he paused, looked around. His desk was, as ever, an altar to neatness. 'I thought I'd forgotten something.'

'Anything important?' Boyd looked at his colleague's desk, at the neat rows of pencils, three pens evenly spaced apart, all paperwork aligned. Anal, Ross had called it. Certainly it was organised.

Robertson sighed, ran his hand through wet hair.

Boyd saw that Robertson's hands were trembling. 'You okay?'

'Me?' asked Robertson. 'Why wouldn't I be okay?'

'Fuck knows, I'm only asking.' Boyd paused, stared at him. His tie was off and despite his obvious chill he was sweating. 'You getting the flu?'

Robertson said nothing.

Boyd took his coffee back to his desk and flicked through the paperwork he'd laid out. There was a list of the phone messages that had come in after the police appeal for information had aired. There had been dozens of sightings of 'suspicious' people who'd been seen around the area at the time Gilmore had been killed.

He tried again. 'You seen the number of dodgy sightings that've been called in?'

Robertson nodded.

'Trouble is, it's not that unusual to see people acting suspiciously in Glasgow. I guess we're like most cities – we have our fair share of suspicious characters.'

'We just need the right one,' Robertson said.

'True,' agreed Boyd. 'What we need is a very particular type of character, a murderer and preferably seen on Sunday night carrying a bloody baseball bat dripping with James Gilmore's DNA.'

'Aye right.'

Boyd flicked through the updates. 'Nothing much of interest here.' He sipped his coffee and once again read the neatly typed notes taken from the staff at St Austin's and Cuthbertson High. 'Word for word the notes from the other two schools could have been from Watervale Academy for all the insight they offer into who James Gilmore was.'

Silence. He looked up at Robertson, saw that he had pulled his shirt collar around his throat, held it there with shaking hands, struggled to keep his voice steady. 'I'm off then.'

'Did you get what you came in for?' Boyd nodded to Robertson's desk.

Robertson looked blank for a second before muttering, 'It doesn't matter.'

Boyd watched him leave. 'Okay, see you in the morning.'

But Robertson had gone.

Boyd settled himself and began scrolling down the new list of messages. He was on the third message when he saw one that might actually be helpful.

'Hello, I saw your appeal about James Gilmore. Me and James . . . we went out for a while. It was years ago though. Not sure it matters much. Haven't seen him in donkey's – maybe it's wasting your time? Anyway, here's my number. I could tell you a wee bit about him. Not sure it would be anything you didn't already know. But let me know if you want to talk. Bye-bye.'

The woman's name was listed as Ms Debbie Morgan and her home address was in Sighthill. She'd supplied both her home telephone number and her mobile. Boyd jotted them down. They could call her but it was always more helpful to meet with an individual; sometimes it was what they didn't say that was the most useful. Boyd wondered why Gilmore's mother hadn't mentioned the woman. Maybe Gilmore had a secret life after all? He flicked to the next message.

DREAMER

The Dreamer sleeps fitfully. He dreams of that night, of the storm. He dreams of leaving the house just as the big man was arriving. Both of them had had the same intention, had wanted the same outcome. Gilmore dead. The Dreamer hadn't known that; he had felt that he had to do it. The Dreamer's eyelashes flutter against his face, tears fall and his hand automatically rises to brush them away. He dreams of walking through the graveyard, of the storm soaking the blood from his clothes. Listening to the voice above the storm, being told what to do. Understanding that everything had changed.

Chapter 54

Robertson parked his car in the driveway and as the overhead security light came on he saw a fox disappear through the hedge. He walked to the front door and put his key into the lock, turned it, pushed open the door and went inside. Despite the two painkillers he felt the headache spread across his skull.

He stood in the hall and knew that she was behind him before she spoke.

'Where have you been?'

'Out.'

'I called the station.'

'I know.'

'You haven't been at work, have you?'

'No.'

'Where then?'

He stared at the carpet. It was over. 'Out, driving around, thinking.'

'About?'

'Us.'

She waited.

'We're over. I'm leaving.'

Saw her look at him; she was hollow-eyed from crying. She started to shake. Robertson left her in the hall and went to the bedroom, took the case out of the cupboard and began packing.

Heard his wife crying, heard her anger rage into words, then sounds. Ignored it; it was white noise in the background of his journey.

A few minutes later and he was in the car again, driving through the empty streets, finally stopping at a cheap hotel. For the time being, it would do. He heard his mobile shrill, checked the number. It was Margaret. He switched it off.

Chapter 55

Friday, 13 December
Morning

It was the constant buzz that unnerved him, like the sound of a million hearts beating as hard and as loudly as his own. George Grey gripped his holdall and walked behind a young couple who'd also been on the overnight coach. They walked into the sea of bodies, their heads down, marching resolutely towards the exit. The young man was adamant. 'It's a different scale here altogether. London's massive compared to Glasgow.'

His companion buttoned her coat up to the neck, shivering. 'You're not wrong there. Glasgow's population is around what? The half million mark?'

'Wee bit over but that's the ball park.' He walked beside her. 'It's a village in comparison.'

'What's London then?'

'Seven point five million and still growing.' The man hoisted his bag over his shoulder. 'As I said, it's a different scale.'

They followed the sign for the tube station. George Grey did as he'd been told and turned towards the taxi rank, where he queued for a quarter of an hour before climbing into the back of a black cab. His hand shook as he gave the piece of paper to the driver; the address had been neatly written out. He sat back in the cab and gnawed at the nail on his thumb. The nail was ragged and torn and his fingers were translucent with the cold. Forty-five minutes later they drove through wrought-iron gates and down a long gravel driveway. Huge oak trees lined either side of the drive, casting shadows over an already cold day.

'This used to be the lunatic asylum.' The driver pulled up in front of the building and switched off the meter. 'What's it now then?'

George Grey blinked, said nothing, thrust the notes into the driver's hand and stepped out of the taxi and into a wind that whipped his face and tore at his clothes. The icy rain made his face feel raw. He waited until the taxi had driven off before turning towards the house. The place was in darkness save for a single light upstairs. The huge wooden door was closed; a bell on the left rang far into the house. He heard footsteps on a wooden floor, then the door opened. George Grey stood on the step in the rain and blinked at the man.

'Come in George; I've been expecting you.'

George heard the door close behind him and the lock fall into place.

Chapter 56

Wheeler opened the door and a blast of heat from the station hit her. She took the stairs to the CID suite two at a time and walked into the room just in time to overhear something positive.

'Well, it's a result.'

'Cheers, boss.'

Stewart was perched on the edge of her desk, still talking. 'We'll get someone out there to interview her.' Boyd was finishing his morning coffee and was looking very pleased with himself and she guessed it wasn't just because he was scoffing the last of a Belgian bun and was on a sugar hit.

Boyd brushed the flakes of the bun from his shirt.

Wheeler dumped her coat over her chair. 'What?'

'Boyd's traced an ex-girlfriend of James Gilmore's,' said Stewart.

'And not Angela Meek,' added Boyd.

'Aye, right.' Stewart smoothed his tie and fiddled with his cufflinks. 'Well, Angela Meek was cremated thirty years ago and her ashes scattered on the Clyde, so no, not her.'

'His mother didn't seem to think he'd dated again,' said Wheeler.

'This woman says she dated him a while back, but she phoned in, left a message. Mammies don't always know best,' said Boyd.

'So, go see her, Wheeler.' Stewart stood and arched his back, groaned. 'Bloody squash.'

'On my way.' As she watched Stewart leave the room, she tried to shake the image of him in a dress. Failed.

'I'll drive.' Boyd pulled on his padded anorak, stood waiting for her like an eager puppy. A very round puppy.

'No chance. I've seen your driving; it's worse than Ross's.'

'That bad?'

'Uh huh. And don't sound so pleased about it.'

Beside her in the car, Boyd was dipping into a bag of crisps. 'We going past the stone circle?'

'Come again?'

'The stone circle up by Sighthill.'

'You kidding me?'

'Nope. There was a stone circle built in the 1970s up by Sighthill. Properly aligned and everything.'

She peered at him. 'Glasgow's very own Stonehenge?'

He tucked into the last of the crisps. 'You mind?' He pointed to the radio.

'Go ahead.'

Boyd turned the dial to hear the sports discussion. Wheeler tuned out, thought about a Glasgow stone circle and decided she might check it out at some point, see if it really existed. Right now she needed to get to Gilmore's ex-girlfriend. Debbie Morgan lived in a flat on the thirteenth floor of a high-rise in Sighthill. One of the remaining high-rises which had so far escaped demolition. Wheeler drove through the city, towards the Tron theatre, turning up the High Street and driving on past the Royal Infirmary.

A few minutes later she turned the car into the car park. The weather meant that they trotted from the car to the entrance to the building. They took the lift; it smelled of cheap air freshener. Boyd sniffed. 'Could be worse.'

The thirteenth floor was immaculate; potted plants lined the corridor and little welcome mats sat outside doors.

The woman who opened the door was in her late forties, bleach-blonde, skinny. Smelled like a smoker. Sported a black eye. 'You the polis?'

Wheeler and Boyd flashed their ID cards.

They followed her into a sitting room that could have rivalled Santa's grotto. A huge silver tree stood in the corner of the room, every branch dripping with baubles, tinsel, ropes of glittering beads and multicoloured fairy lights. A pink angel sat on top of the tree, one eye winking. Boyd stared at it. 'That thing winking at me?'

Debbie flushed with pleasure. 'I know, it's brilliant, isn't it? Runs off a wee battery.'

'My girlfriend would love that,' Boyd said.

'I got it from the Barras . . . and—'

Wheeler cleared her throat.

Boyd flushed. 'Sorry boss, just stuck for a pressie and—'

Debbie tried to save him by changing the subject. 'Yous two want coffee?'

'No thanks, we're fine.'

'Wouldn't mind, thanks.'

They'd spoken in unison.

Debbie Morgan looked at them. 'What's it to be then?'

Wheeler spoke. 'Nothing for me but if my colleague here wants something.'

'It's okay,' said Boyd.

Debbie patted Boyd's arm. 'It's no problem, I'll make us a coffee. I fancy a wee Bailey's coffee myself. What about you?'

Boyd glanced at Wheeler. 'Maybe just the coffee then.'

'On duty? Ach I'm sure your boss'll no mind,' she stared at Wheeler, 'will you?'

'Actually I do.' Wheeler smiled. 'No point in drinking this early.'

Debbie shot Boyd a sympathetic glance. 'I'll away and make you a straight coffee. No wee treats,' she stared reproachfully at Wheeler, 'even though it is nearly Christmas.'

When she returned with the tray, she joined them on the sofa, slotting herself neatly between the arm of the sofa and Boyd. It was a tight squeeze. 'So, I read about James, that's why I phoned you and left a message. I read that he got killed last Sunday but I've been away for a few days or I would've called in straight away. I had a wee accident.' She touched her blackened eye.

'You okay now?' Boyd asked.

'Fine, ta.'

'I'm sorry about how you heard of James Gilmore's death.' Wheeler kept her voice compassionate. 'You said in the message you'd been dating.'

'Ages ago, I mean years ago. It didn't last long.'

'We spoke to his mother,' said Wheeler. 'She seemed to think he'd only ever had one girlfriend.'

'Never met her. Didn't even know his mum was still alive – he never mentioned her. James didn't talk about much; he was a bit secretive. But also a bit of a show-off.'

Boyd leaned forward. 'In what way?'

'He wouldn't talk about his work much, said it was confidential. And we hardly went out on our own, you know, just the two of us? He always wanted to go to the same places his work cronies would go to; it was kind of like he was proud that we were dating. It's not that he especially liked them or anything. But . . .'

'But?' prompted Boyd.

'But he never really wanted to spend time with me on my own, only if we were out and about being seen by others. He was a cold fish at home.'

'How long were you dating?' asked Wheeler.

'On and off for about six months.'

'Why did he break up with you?' asked Boyd.

'Oh, he never broke up with me,' Debbie laughed, 'I chucked him.'

'Can I ask why?' Wheeler recognised something in Debbie's tone. Resignation, disappointment. Something had been far wrong. She wondered if Debbie would tell them.

'He couldn't get it up.'

'Sorry?' Boyd had gulped his coffee so quickly it had burned his mouth.

'Happens to most men now and again; I suppose you'll be aware of that,' she nodded to Boyd. He studied the pattern on the carpet.

'Go on,' said Wheeler.

'Well he could never do it – it was never on the "on" button if you get my drift, it was always on the "off", so I told him to sling his hook. Us girls need a bit of fun, don't we?' she grinned at Wheeler. 'And I wasn't having any.'

'How did he take it?'

'Badly. He proposed.'

'Marriage?'

'Aye.'

'Why would he do that?'

Debbie sat back in her sofa and drained the last of her coffee. 'I've thought long and hard about that over the years. Me, I was working in the local chippy; he was a graduate. He never loved me, I knew that.'

'So why the proposal?' prompted Wheeler.

'I don't know for sure, but I reckon he might have needed a . . .' she put her hands in the air and made the shape of quotation marks, 'a wee wifie.'

'Because?' Wheeler asked but she already knew the answer.

'Because, I reckon he was gay and needed a wee wifie to keep up appearances. Had to be – couldn't have sex, didn't fancy women. Couldn't even fake it.'

'Not many men can,' muttered Boyd.

'Anything else?' asked Wheeler.

Debbie paused. 'Nothing else that I can remember.'

'Thanks very much for your time.' Wheeler stood to leave.

'More coffee?' suggested Debbie.

'We'll let ourselves out. Thanks again.' Wheeler offered her hand, Debbie shook it then turned to Boyd, winked at him. 'You mind visit any time you like. I reckon we're a couple of kindred spirits you and me.'

In the corridor the smell of air freshener seemed to have intensified. 'Let's take the stairs.' Wheeler strode on. 'You were certainly a hit back there.'

Boyd had the decency to blush. 'You think Gilmore was gay?'

Wheeler took the steps two at a time. 'Or maybe he just didn't like his girlfriend that much.'

'She's a bit scary right enough but he still wanted to keep her as a cover. What was he hiding?'

'I know, it looks quite suspicious.'

'Or sinister.' The word hung in the air.

She paused. 'But there was nothing in his past to suggest . . .'

But Boyd was there before she finished. 'Kids?'

'Yeah.'

'Nothing turned up in any reports; there were no accusations. Nothing.'

'Uh huh.' They both knew that meant very little.

'Pete Newton said the killer hated his mother. Sounds like Gilmore wasn't so keen on his old dear if he never mentioned her in the six months that he was dating Debbie.'

'I've met his old dear and she's anything but a dear.'

'Gilmore's ghost is taking on form.'

Outside the cold hit them. 'Where to now?' asked Boyd.

'Back to the station to carry on our sleuthing work. I've got a gut feeling.'

'Go on.'

'Something's changed in this case. The station will be a hive of activity.'

Chapter 57

The CID suite at the station was dead, deserted except for Robertson and some uniformed officers who were frantically typing at computers. Wheeler could tell something had happened but the atmosphere was all wrong.

'Well?' She looked at Robertson, took in the faintly creased suit, the tired expression. He looked like he hadn't slept. 'Where is everyone?'

'Clydebank.'

She could tell by the flatness of his tone. 'And?'

'Nothing yet, except this.' He handed her a slip of paper with an address scrawled on it. 'Stewart says to get out there ASAP. We found the address on two of Gilmore's old parking tickets at the bottom of one of the boxes. Finally called them; it turns out that the key's for a steel storage unit in Clydebank – Solid Steel Solutions.'

Wheeler noted the expression, the tone. This was the breakthrough they'd been looking for but something was wrong. Robertson's tone and the fact that the team had *all* taken off. For a visit to a storage unit. Gilmore had a big house in Glasgow – why did he need a storage unit too? And why was it way out in Clydebank?

She was at the door before she thought to ask, 'Robertson, anything else happen?'

He nodded. 'Better ask Ross.'

Minutes later Wheeler and Boyd were driving out of the city. Clydebank was out at West Dunbartonshire, about thirteen miles from Carmyle, and the journey would normally have taken them around half an hour.

'Shit,' Wheeler cursed again as they sat in traffic which was backed up on the M74. Sleet was falling fast and visibility was poor. Boyd sighed, switched on the radio, switched it off again. Tried not to appear agitated but failed. Drummed his fingers on his seat belt. Swore under his breath.

The A814 was the same: traffic was backed up and nothing was moving. Wheeler drove cautiously when they were moving, careful not to let the car slide. Eventually after almost an hour they got to their destination and saw that 'Solid Steel Solutions' was set in a remote area on the outskirts of Clydebank. The secure storage on offer was rows of steel shipping containers around ten feet by eight feet. Each had its own padlock. Wheeler looked at the entrance; it would usually be accessed by sliding the electronic key tag over the pad which would activate the huge metal gates. Once a car was inside, the gates would automatically close behind it. Right now the gates were permanently set on open to accommodate the police cars. She glanced around and guessed from the lack of an on-site office that the site was not usually manned, but she

318

could see four personnel in suits standing in the sleet talking to Stewart.

As Wheeler and Boyd approached, Stewart broke off to acknowledge her and point to a storage unit at the end of the row. He needn't have bothered – it was crawling with CID and uniform.

Ross came out of the unit as she approached. Shook his head, walked on.

Stewart finished with the men in suits and stood beside her. He touched her elbow.

She looked at him. 'Boss?'

'A quick look, Wheeler,' he instructed her. 'Don't linger.'

Inside, her footsteps echoed on the concrete floor. There was metal shelving running the length of the unit. On the shelves in neat, ordered packs, were thousands of photographs and pictures. James Gilmore had been methodical in his storage. There were bundles of images, scribbled locations. She glanced at one of the older packages: *Stobwent-Hill Children's Home, Glasgow.* As far as she knew the home no longer existed – it was long gone, its child residents scattered across the city. Other labels simply described the images as *Downloads 2008–2009, 2009–2010, 2010–2011.* On the shelves there were thousands of pictures, some developed, others downloaded. All dated, sorted chronologically, the most recent at the front. All revolting. Gilmore had been a paedophile for decades. He was in some of the photographs – she guessed that he was the man in the mask, holding the chains. Wheeler glanced at one, saw the bleakness in the young boy's eyes, the leather collar tethered around his thin neck, and felt her stomach heave, her mouth fill with bile, her forehead break out in a cold sweat. She turned away, headed for the exit and was grateful when she stood outside taking in gulps of cold sleet. She tightened both hands into fists. Walked over to Stewart, who was talking to a group of officers. Her throat was sore and she wanted to throw up. 'Boss?'

'Right, get this lot dusted for prints, bagged and tagged and shipped out.' Stewart's face was grey, his knuckles white as he spoke to the officers. He looked at her. 'Back to the station. We can't do any more here and I think you've seen enough.'

She had.

Boyd was staying put, so she drove back, insisted on it. Said that she needed to concentrate. Ross sat beside her. She waited until they were out of Clydebank before she spoke. 'You were right.'

'Bastard.' Ross stared out at the River Clyde. 'Fucking bastard.'

'Robertson said there was something else.'

'Yeah, I finally got a reference for Arthur Wright. And a phone trace for the two calls about Gilmore.'

'The ones about Gilmore being linked to him and not being a good guy?'

'Yeah.'

'And?'

'They were from a payphone in the Watervale scheme. Near the youth club. Someone had done their homework. Maybe they didn't want to talk to the polis but they found out about Gilmore and passed the info along.'

'Took us long enough to find it though.'

'It was a long shot. Arthur Wright had been deported from the US, went back to his original name, then an alias. It was cross-referenced, but it took forever to trace.'

'And?' her voice trailed off.

'Same as back there.' He jabbed his thumb back the way they'd come.

She drove to the station, parked, and they were in the CID suite, taking off their damp jackets, when Stewart arrived. 'Meeting in my room in ten.'

She nodded but knew that the atmosphere in the suite had lost its charge. James Gilmore had been murdered but now that he had gone from victim to perpetrator, the energy for a conviction had dissipated.

'Changes everything, doesn't it?' Ross pushed a cup of coffee in front of her. Slid a wrapped chocolate beside it. 'Eat.'

She ate. 'It shouldn't change anything though, should it? Gilmore was brutally murdered and we still need to find out who did it.' But she heard the weariness in her voice, the lack of emotion. An image from the storage unit flashed into her mind, a young boy's face. The dead expression in his eyes. She sipped the black coffee, sighed, swallowed the chocolate, felt a rush of sugar and warmth. 'Fuck, fuck, fuck.'

Ten minutes later and they were crowded into Stewart's room.

Chapter 58

Friday night

The strip lights in the Royal Infirmary were too bright for him. William MacIntyre half closed his eyes and watched while the doctor chatted to each patient in turn. He cursed under his breath as he waited for her to make her way around the ward. He clawed at his arm, felt the shakes begin again. Forced himself to lie down on the bed. Closed his eyes, prayed that the pain would disappear. Cursed again, this time loud enough for the man in the next bed to hear and respond. 'Christ, will you shut up. You're not the only one suffering.'

MacIntyre ignored him, focused instead on the progress of the doctor. He thought she looked about sixteen but he knew she had to be older. He studied her: she was small, about five two, but she had an athletic build and a fresh, open face and her long blonde hair was tied back in a pony-tail. She looked like a different species from him. Healthy. He felt his stomach spasm. Took a deep breath. Felt into the pain. Watched her smile at another patient, touch their hand. 'Fuck,' he hissed; the pain was worse. He closed his eyes. 'Fuckssake,' he whispered.

'Shut it you,' the man in the next bed snarled. 'Think you're the only one in pain, you junkie tosspot.'

Eventually she came to him, read his notes. A wee lassie telling him what he should be doing, what he should be taking. What a cunt. MacIntyre sat up in the bed, screwed his eyes at the name badge. Dr Susan Armstrong was still droning on.

'Mr MacIntyre, we can help you with a withdrawal programme. I can get you signed up today if you like. It might not be available right away, it might take a week or so, but there are agencies that could help you. It would be a managed withdrawal, with plenty of support, including counselling. It wouldn't be like going cold turkey on your own.'

He shook his head. 'I'm no interested.'

'Because?'

He shrugged – why bother going into it?

She moved closer to the bed. 'You don't understand. After an attempted suicide, we need to put help and support into place.'

He glared at her. 'Mibbe you don't fucking understand hen.'

'I won't put up with bad language.' Her voice cold.

'Well then shut it.'

The doctor took a step back, frowned, started again. 'Mr MacIntyre, I'm here to help you. At least try to be civil.'

He felt his fingers twitch. Felt the ache deep in his bones. 'How long have I got? How long can I stay here?'

'In this ward?'

'Aye, in the infirmary.'

'Until tomorrow morning. Then I'm afraid we need to move you on. Which is why I'd like to get you signed up to the programme.'

MacIntyre shut his eyes. His voice cracked, 'I took a fuckin' overdose, could you no have just let me be?'

She glanced at her notes. 'You were at home when you took the overdose.'

'Aye, so?'

'Your neighbour found you and called the ambulance.'

MacIntyre closed his eyes. 'The neighbour's a thieving git. Should never have been prowlin' about ma hoose in the first place.'

'That may well be but he saved your life and now I suggest that you accept help in managing your addiction. We have outside agencies who can help you. In the meantime I can get you on a methadone programme.'

MacIntyre gripped his hospital gown around him and sniffed. He heard more questions but ignored them all. He waited until the young doctor had moved off, exasperated, before he opened his mobile and dialled home. It took a while ringing before she answered.

Her voice was slurred. 'Yesh?' She didn't have her teeth in.

'I'm no coming back.'

'Who's thiss?'

'Who the fuck dae ye think it is, ya daft cow?'

A long pause. 'Wullie?'

'Aye.'

'Are ye no still in the Royal?'

'Aye but I'm meant tae be out the morrow.'

'Hame? You're gonnae be hame in the morning?'

'I'm no coming back but.'

'How'ss that then?'

'The fucker that got Gilmore's coming for me next. I'm oan the list. I'm oan Doyle's fucking list. Weirdo told me. Ma name's right under fucking Gilmore's and look what happened tae him.'

A long pause, the penny dropping. 'How doess he know, how doess Doyle know? How doess Weirdo know?'

'I don't know. But they fucking know. And George has disappeared. I think he told them about whit was happening.'

'Fuck.' Her voice a whisper.

'Aye, I'm fucked. And I'm no letting them dae tae me whit they did tae Gilmore.'

Silence.

'You still there?'

'Aye.'

'So I'm off, away oot of it.'

A long pause. 'But where will you go?'

His voice hardened. 'There's no a lot of choice is there? Whit I'm saying is my options are very-fucking-severely-limited.'

'Well. Jist come hame then? Ish that no the besht thing?'

'Fuck off.'

Silence.

'That'ss no nice.'

'Well, the-games-a-fucking-bogey for me.'

'Kin ye no sort it?'

'How? It's over fir me.'

Silence.

'You hear me?'

'Aye.'

'So.'

'Aye. That's me on ma own now?'

MacIntyre switched off the phone. Lay on his back, felt the tears come, hot, salty. Turned onto his side and faced the wall. Closed his eyes. He felt the ache in his kidneys begin again and he stretched his right hand around to the soreness. The three stumps on his hand kneaded uselessly against the searing pain. MacIntyre knew about the list – Christ, everyone in Glasgow knew Doyle had a list. And now MacIntyre's name was on it. MacIntyre knew it was over. Knew where he had to go.

The bridge.

He waited until the shift change had started, watched the nurses congregate around the desk at the far end of the ward. Looked at the clock: it was eight p.m. Through the window he saw sleet hammering down on the city. He crossed the ward, stumbled down the corridor to the lift. A few minutes later he was walking past a group of smokers at the hospital doorway; one of them spat on the ground as he passed. MacIntyre ignored them and walked out into the cold night and kept walking until he reached it.

The bridge.

He waited until the bus was in sight before he stepped off the bridge.

Chapter 59

It's Friday night, surely you have some time off . . . are you around for a drink?

Wheeler read the text from Paul Buchan. Pressed delete. She sat alone in the CID suite; it was silent apart from the distant thrum of traffic. Even the sleet outside had ceased battering against the window panes and had lessened to a drizzle. The overhead strip of fluorescent light was turned off. Wheeler sat under a halo of light from the desk lamp. There was just enough light for her to read the reports, to examine the evidence bags. The photographs had been dusted for prints, everything had been logged, recorded, noted. In the still calm of the night Wheeler reached for one of the bags, noticed the tremor in her hand as she pulled out the photographs and stared at each one in turn. Finally she began to stuff them back into the plastic bags. A few remained. Holding one of the pictures in her hand, she tried to imagine the reality of life for these boys. The boy in the photograph had his back to the camera and was completely naked, his skin blue-white with cold. The room was empty, only the boy standing alone, his skin pale but for the smear of red that seeped down his thighs.

Wheeler put the photograph back with the others.

Downstairs, Tommy Cunningham was at the desk sipping coffee and finishing off a chocolate biscuit. He looked up as she approached. His voice was soft when he asked, 'That you done, then, for the night?'

Wheeler glanced at him. 'I'm done, TC. I've had more than enough of this case for today.'

'Aye,' Cunningham agreed, 'I think we all have.'

'Goodnight TC.'

'Night hen.'

She pulled on her coat, shoved a hat over her damp hair and wandered into the rain. She could feel a tension headache start at the base of her neck. Her mobile rang. She glanced at the name. *Ross*. When she answered there was music in the background. 'Wondered if you fancied a drink, maybe a chat about the case?' Ross paused. 'But maybe you're shattered. And we'll get the official debrief from Stewart tomorrow.'

'It's okay, I thought you were off to see your girlfriend?'

'Ex-girlfriend.'

'Thought you went round there the other night?'

'It was a relapse for both of us. It's over. Sure you don't fancy coming into town for a drink?'

Wheeler felt the rain run down her neck, felt the cold of the wind against her face, felt her headache retreat. 'Maybe. Depends. Where are you?'

He paused. 'Bar 99.'

She laughed, 'Could you have aimed any lower?'

'There was supposed to be live music.' He sounded defensive.

'Is there a band on?' she groaned. 'I couldn't face music tonight.'

'It was cancelled.'

Bar 99 was right next to the River Clyde. It was a pub to get lost in. Usually crowded, dark and with enough nooks and crannies to talk without fear of being overheard. A place where you could talk about a case without anyone hearing. So ideal in some ways.

'Tempted?'

'Okay. Let me drop the car off first.'

She drove home, parked the car and walked through Candleriggs and its ropes of twinkling fairy lights and glowing Christmas decorations. She passed the Bluestone Theatre and turned, kept going until she heard the roar from the River Clyde. A few minutes later and she walked into Bar 99, all low ceilings, dark wood panels and a warm atmosphere. It was busy in the back but there were stools free at the bar. She looked around, saw Ross ensconced at a corner table with two heavyset women. Both women wore thick eyeliner, even thicker foundation and painted smiles. Wheeler nodded to Ross, he rose, and the smiles on the women's faces turned sour. Wheeler settled at the bar and ordered a Chardonnay.

'Medium or large?' asked the barman.

She had to stop herself asking for a bottle. 'Large, thanks.' She watched it being set in front of her.

Ross shuffled onto a stool beside her. 'Out of your depth there, Ross,' she smiled as she sipped the cold wine.

'Christ, you're telling me. I just came in for a quick pint and they pounced.'

'You're fresh meat.' She glanced back; the two women looked like they wanted to kill her. 'Sure you don't want to go back, be the meat in their sandwich?'

He shuddered. Nodded to the barman. 'Pint of heavy please.'

The barman began to pour. 'No interested in the two lassies back there then, son?'

'No way.'

'They'll be gutted – they must've thought it was their lucky night.'

'Think they'll get over it,' said Ross, paying for both his pint and Wheeler's wine.

'Think they already have,' the barman grinned.

They turned to look. A small, thin man in his late sixties wearing a pencil moustache and a freshly pressed tweed suit had perched himself at the table, fitting snugly between the two women.

'Carnage.' Wheeler shuddered and turned back to the bar.

The barman gave Ross his change. 'Och, he'll die happy, hen. Ye cannae begrudge him that.' He left them alone and went to the far side of the bar.

They sat in silence for a few minutes; the new development in the case had robbed them of their adrenaline. Both of them knew they would have to find it again.

'So, what brings you out on a night like this?' Ross gave her his smarmiest smile.

'Is that your best chat-up line, Ross?'

'Would it work?'

'Tell me, has it ever worked?'

'True.' He sipped his pint. The music was loud, Snow Patrol.

She kept her voice low. 'So what are we left with?'

'James Gilmore died because he was abusing children. There are hundreds of victims and it could be any one of them. And to be honest, Wheeler, I wouldn't blame them for killing the bastard.'

'That's it exactly,' she sipped her wine, 'I think the whole of the station wants to just let this one go.'

'Yeah.'

'But that's not our job.'

He studied the clientele in the pub. Said nothing.

Wheeler continued, 'We've nothing new and eventually Grim will write up what was found at the unit in Clydebank. No one will come forward and there's no chance of a conviction, is there?'

'Some folk will believe that it's a waste of taxpayers' money to go searching for whoever did this; they'll believe the killer did us a favour in the long run. And I can't blame them.'

'You think Andy Doyle had anything to do with it?'

'Evidence?' asked Ross.

She looked at her glass. 'Nothing, other than they met at the charity do.'

'Him and a few hundred others; it's not enough, is it?'

'No.'

'I think Doyle maybe knows who did it, but whether or not it was him . . . who knows? We have no motive.'

She sipped her wine. 'I know. And Lauren Taylor's death, just horrible. It's been a fucking awful week.'

'You got the update on Jason?'

She nodded. 'They dragged him into the station in the West End. He swore he wasn't involved. Eventually they let him go. They're convinced that the evidence points to her getting off her face and accidentally falling from the balcony.' She paused. 'Do we know where she got the GHB?'

Ross drained the last of his pint. 'We're pretty certain it came via someone in the Tenant clan.'

'Wee Stevie?'

'Maybe, if he's trying to go it alone.'

'But he doesn't operate near the university. Could Weirdo have supplied it? So then it would be Doyle that we'd be looking at?'

Ross shook his head. 'No evidence to point that way.'

Wheeler drained her glass, waited until Ross had ordered again and the fresh drinks sat in front of them before she spoke. 'Even if he's not involved, Jason's a heartless fuck.'

'You reckon he gave her the stuff at some point in the last week?'

'Highly possible.'

'But he's denying it?'

'But I already know that he's a liar.'

'You sure about the drugs though?'

She sighed.

'Burden of proof?'

She nodded. 'And I'm not allowed to investigate because he's fucking family. He's involved in some way, I'm sure of it, but he's going to get away with it. He could be done for supplying.'

The barman switched CDs. Van Morrison sang about a brown-eyed girl. The bar was getting busy and people were crowding in from the street. Ross nudged her. 'Let's get a comfortable seat.'

She followed his gaze; the two women and the thin man were disappearing out of the door, leaving their table free. 'Result,' the barman smiled as he followed them to the table and collected the empty glasses.

Wheeler's phone chirruped. A text from her sister: *I demand to know what's going on.*

'I bet you fucking do,' Wheeler muttered, deleting the text.

Her mobile rang. 'Let me just take this quickly, Ross.'

Her sister sounded hysterical. 'I want to know what the problem is, Katherine.'

Wheeler kept her tone the right side of pissed off. 'There's a big problem, Jo. Fucking Jason.'

Silence, then, 'He's in trouble?'

'Big trouble.'

'Tell me.'

Wheeler told her.

Jo's voice rose. 'He won't be involved – how can you even think that?'

'He knew her. He knows a lot more than he's saying.'

'So? You need to clean up this mess.'

'How come it's now my mess?'

'You're police. You can sort this.'

'Think Jason already tried that approach. It failed.'

'And he's family.'

'He's *your* family.'

'You've never cared about family. I suppose you think that it's my problem and you can't be arsed helping us.'

Wheeler held the phone out in front of her, shook her head in disbelief. Let her sister rant for a few minutes, heard key phrases – 'you were always rubbish at emotions', 'hopeless at being part of a family but then . . .' a pause as if she was holding back. Then a new list of why Wheeler wasn't a good sister, hadn't been a good daughter, blah, blah, blah. Finally Wheeler clamped the phone back to her ear. 'You finished with the character assassination?'

Jo hadn't. 'How would you even know how a mother feels? You've no idea what I'm going through.'

'You've no idea how clichéd you sound.'

'Let me explain something: it's like a physical pain. An actual pain.'

'Oh, for goodness' sake get off your cross.' Wheeler was losing patience. 'A young girl has died and Jason could be involved. He's certainly lying through his teeth about something.'

But her sister still hadn't finished. 'I'm suffering, Katherine.'

'Yes you are,' Wheeler paused, 'from a terminal case of melodrama.'

'You fucking cow!'

The phone went dead. Wheeler looked up, caught Ross watching her. 'Played that one well, didn't I? Didn't exactly get her on board.'

'Could've been better, I suppose. You going to call her back?'

Wheeler shook her head. 'First time I heard her swear.'

'You must have touched a nerve.'

'She said I was rubbish at emotions and family. This coming from a woman who's produced a fucking psychopath for a son.'

'Charming.'

She sipped the chilled wine. 'But I'm right.'

'You think she'll come round when she realises the trouble he could be in?'

'I doubt it.' Wheeler looked at him. 'I think he's like his mother; it runs in the family. Besides, officially he's off the hook.'

Chapter 60

'Now it's your fucking problem you little prick, so you should start worrying.' Weirdo slammed his fist against the wall, narrowly missing Jason's head.

'I didn't give it to her. She took it herself.'

The second punch hit Jason hard in the stomach. He doubled over and began to cry. Weirdo kept his voice low, controlled, professional. 'Doesn't fucking matter does it, you lying to yourself? Or the polis. Important thing for me is to find out where it's from. See, I know you didn't get it from me. You got it from some other cunt and now you're going to tell me who, or I'm going to cut your shrivelled balls off and make you suck on them like sweeties. Understand?'

'I need to remind you . . . you need to watch it,' Jason wheezed. 'You know I have a contact in the police force.'

Weirdo paused his fist mid-air. 'Aye, so you said.'

Jason tried to hold the stare. Failed. 'It's true, I do have a contact, so you better stop this now.'

Weirdo leaned into Jason's face. 'You trying to scare the shite out of me?'

Jason misread the signs, gathered himself, tried for some bravado. 'I already told you, my Auntie Katherine is an inspector with the CID.'

Weirdo laughed; Doyle was right – it was like taking sweeties from a baby. 'And I care . . . because?'

Jason gave his answer the gravitas he felt it deserved. 'A detective inspector can arrest you and put you in jail.'

Weirdo paused and pretended to think for a moment. 'Doesn't ring any bells with me; what was the name again?'

'Detective Inspector Katherine Wheeler, Carmyle Station, CID.'

'Oh aye, I remember now. I passed on that wee snippet to my boss already.'

Jason began to relax.

'It's just,' Weirdo leaned in closer, his spit landing on Jason's face, 'that *Katherine's* already been round to see my boss. My boss didn't seem too upset.' Weirdo continued, 'And as for me, well I don't give a flying fuck who your wee auntie is, get it?'

Jason got it. After the next punch hit the wall, again narrowly missing his head, Jason slid down onto his knees and knew that it was over.

'Well?' Weirdo stood back. Waited.

'Stevie,' Jason whispered.

'Go on.'

'Stevie Tenant. Guy said his name was Stevie Tenant.'

'And how the fuck did you get to meet him?'

'Your friend.'

'My friend?' Weirdo asked but he already knew the

answer. Jason would never have seen Weirdo with Doyle, but he had seen him with Smithy.

'The fat guy who was in the car with you.'

Bingo. 'And now you're going to go snivelling to your wee auntie?'

Silence.

'Well?'

'She already knows . . . that I knew Lauren.'

'And?'

'I said nothing about the drugs. She didn't believe me though.'

'Because?'

'The West End cops already had me in. She told them to interview me.'

'Go on.'

'I told them I didn't know anything about the drugs and they believed me. I never mentioned Stevie, honest.'

Weirdo shrugged. 'I don't give a fuck if you dob wee Stevie in it but there's a few things you might want to be aware of.' Weirdo bent down again and stuck his mouth next to Jason's ear. 'So, a word to the wise wee man, if you think I'm a scary fucker and I see from the wet on your jeans that you do, just try wee Stevie aka Crusher Tenant. If you want tae try and dob him in it with your wee auntie, you might want to stop by the undertakers' and choose a nice wee burial plot for yourself first. And maybe one for your wee auntie *Katherine* as well. Happy shopping.'

Jason sniffed, wiped the snot from his top lip and stared at the carpet. Ignored the mess on his jeans.

'See, now you've lied to the polis. Told wee porkies. I could mention it to them. I reckon the polis could have you banged up for supplying. And you might want to have a good think about what happens to little pricks like you in the Bar-L.' Weirdo held up a finger. 'One, your fuck-off English accent is going tae have them wetting themselves with joy.' Another finger. 'Two, the shit you supplied killed a wee lassie.' A third finger. 'Three, and this is the bull's eye, why they're really gonnae love you. You're the nephew of a polis. The polis who maybe put them behind bars.' He leaned into Jason's face so far that spittle hit Jason's cheek again. 'And when I say they'll love you, I mean it in the raw, physical way. Loving you until it hurts. You get my drift?'

Weirdo stood, stared at Jason for a few seconds, saw the tears form, then shook his head, 'Fucking wean.' As he closed the door quietly behind him, he heard the sound of Jason sobbing. Weirdo pulled out his mobile, punched in the number. Waited. 'Hello, Mr Doyle?'

Silence.

'It's me.'

'Go on.'

'Just paid a visit to the student.'

'And?'

'He gave the Lauren kid the gear.'

'Where did he get it?'

'Wee Stevie . . . via Smithy.'

'That right?' Weirdo heard the edge in Doyle's voice sharpen.

'And,' Weirdo continued, 'he went on about his auntie, the CID cop, Wheeler.'

'Did he now?' Doyle's tone had changed. 'How much did he tell her?'

'He didn't tell her he gave the kid the drugs, but he says Wheeler suspects.'

'Because?'

'She got the cops to get him in for interview. He says they believed him.'

'But Wheeler didn't? She's CID and her nephew's just given a wee lassie drugs and she died?'

'Yeah.'

The silence lasted for half a minute.

'You still there, Mr Doyle?'

'Okay Weirdo. Good work. Let's keep this to ourselves.'

The line went dead.

Chapter 61

Sonny looked up. 'You're no allowed in here son, away hame and come back when you're eighteen. Or at least when you look it. I'm closing early the night.'

Rab stood at the bar. 'I only want an Irn-Bru. Need to talk to you, Sonny.'

Sonny glanced across at the twins, kept his voice down. 'You're not supposed tae be here son. Were ye no told tae keep away? You shouldnae be here.'

Rab nodded. 'I only wanted tae get rid of this.' He put his hand in his pocket.

'Stop right there.' Sonny held up his hand, horrified. 'Round the back for fuckssake, dae you know nuthin?'

Rab followed him to the rear of the building, handed him the St Christopher medal and chain.

'Aye, wee George told me there was a bit of tinsel round the old cunt's neck. This it?'

Rab nodded. 'I need tae eat, Sonny. I'm starving.'

'Right ye'are, son. Ye'r ma still with that ugly cunt?'

Rab nodded.

Sonny pocketed the St Christopher and chain. Reached into his waistcoat and took out two ten-pound notes. 'Take this meantime. This is too hot tae flog here; best it goes across the water. I'll get the rest tae ye, less commission of course.'

Rab nodded, folded the notes and stuffed them into his jeans. 'Manky said if I was stuck to go to see him. So I told him Smithy chased us. Me and Alec. He said Mr Doyle would sort it.'

'Aye, well Andy Doyle has sorted a lot, you've got that right. But it's over, wee man. Forget it now.'

'But . . .'

'Sshh.'

'I've got the bat.'

'Right. Where is it now?'

'Allotment.'

'I'll get it rehomed.'

'But George said somebody came intae Gilmore's hoose and told him not to worry, that if he hadn't done it then he was there to do . . . was it Mr Doyle? Was he there tae kill Mr Gilmore only George got there first?'

Sonny paused. 'It's best you forget what you heard, forget what you're thinking now.'

'Only George wouldnae say who wis there, who put Mr Gilmore on the hook . . . wis it Mr Doyle?'

'It's over. You know nothing, son. Nothing.'

Rab nodded. 'That's what I told the polis.'

'Good.'

'How come me and Alec cannae go tae London with George?'

Sonny peered at him. 'Did Gilmore touch either of you two?'

'Naw. But I hate where I'm living and Alec dis tae.'

Sonny sighed. 'It's no jist as easy as that, son. See it costs a lot and I mean a fuck load of money tae get the kind of therapy wee George is gonnae get. Wi it being residential and that, it means he lives in and gets fed and stuff.'

'Aye, okay. I see whit ye mean.'

Sonny knew that Rab didn't understand why one wean had got out of it but the rest of them were left. Gilmore might have been discovered abusing George but Rab and Alec were being neglected too. 'Christ,' Sonny shook himself, 'I'm turning soft. Away round the front, I'll get ye a wee vodka tae heat ye up, then you fuck off tae the chippy or for a pizza with Alec. Understand?'

Rab nodded and followed Sonny back into the bar.

Chapter 62

It was after midnight and the rain had momentarily stopped battering the city. It was only a light drizzle by the time the Smuggler's Rest closed. The twins had left earlier after Sonny had tipped them off about a lock-in at another pub. The Hangman's was equally as salubrious as the Smuggler's and Sonny had assured Shona and Heather that they would be welcome at the lock-in.

Sonny rinsed the few remaining glasses and left them upturned on the draining board for the morning. He moved quietly around the bar humming tunelessly to himself. He had his usual routine and he liked this time of the night, when it was quiet, when everyone had gone home or elsewhere. He poured himself a double vodka and sipped it as he wiped down the tables. He left the table in the corner to the last as one customer lay slumped on the chair, his body sagging, his head resting on the scarred table, mouth open, a stream of saliva dripping its way onto the table. Finally, when he had tidied everywhere else, Sonny went over to the table.

'You're out for the count, Mason.' Sonny wiped around Maurice Mason's head before leaning over and checking his breathing. It was regular and shallow. It was as if he had fallen asleep. Or maybe he was just a happy drunk who'd nestled down after one too many. Or perhaps he had simply fallen unconscious naturally. Instead of being dosed with Rohypnol. Either way Mason was snoring contentedly. Sonny went to the bar, searched underneath and pulled out a pair of rubber gloves. He walked back to the table, hauled Mason into a sitting position and patted down his coat. He opened Mason's wallet, removed most of the contents, left the loose change and smiled, 'This is for wee Rab in exchange for the bling.'

The video was in the right-hand pocket. Sonny slid the packet out, checked to see that the video was in place before letting Mason's face crash back onto the table, breaking his nose in the process. Then Sonny tut-tutted, 'Careless, Mason. You need tae be more careful or you'll hurt yourself.' He took out the St Christopher medal and chain and fastened it around Mason's neck. 'I wis going tae flog this, Mason, but it's your lucky day, you get tae wear it.'

Sonny strolled to the counter, reached underneath and took out a large black holdall, unzipped it and unfolded a thick tarpaulin and spread it on the floor, found the ropes he'd stored earlier and placed them all together.

Then he got to work.

Outside at the back of the pub, a battered blue van was reversing quietly into the deserted car park.

Chapter 63

'Think of it as a wee road trip for Mason.' Stella winked at Lizzie as Sonny loaded Mason into the back of the van.

'You jist after doing your stint at the panto?' Sonny asked, noting the silver dress, the high heels and heavy make-up. He didn't mention the wig and dark glasses she was holding.

'Aye Sonny, it went like a dream.'

'You and Doyle not out celebrating?'

She shook her head. 'He thinks I'm out with my pals; besides, him and Weirdo are having a wee meeting. Business.'

'You sure you want tae dae this Stella? I could've done it for you, no problem.' Sonny sounded solicitous.

Stella smiled at him. 'Definitely, Sonny. We need to say a wee cheerio to him ourselves, don't we Lizzie? You and me, we both need closure.'

Lizzie nodded. 'But I went tae see Doyle . . . will the polis no think that—'

Stella cut her off. 'The polis don't know that you went to see Andy. No one knows.' She turned to Sonny. 'Who saw Mason in here earlier?'

'Only the twins and they left before I put him out. Anyway, they'd never talk to the polis.'

'No chance,' Stella agreed, helping to heft the body into the van.

Sonny stooped to test the rope tied around the body. 'He'll be out for a good few hours.'

'He go under okay?' Stella asked.

'Aye. Easy enough, although his nose is busted so his breathing's already fucked. And I put the wee bit of tinsel round his neck for luck.'

Stella looked at him. 'Tinsel?'

'You don't know about it doll, but it'll come in handy.'

Stella smiled. 'Feeding time for the fishes.'

Lizzie whimpered.

Stella looked at her, pointed a warning finger. 'Once it's done, it's done, Lizzie. End of. Move on. Lizzie Coughlin, you're not your father's daughter. I'm disappointed.'

Lizzie hiccupped softly but nodded her head. 'No, I thought I could dae it . . . but . . .'

'But what, Lizzie?' Stella's voice was harsh.

'Nothing, Stella. Whatever you say.'

Sonny and Stella exchanged a look. Sonny kept his voice low. 'She gonnae be okay? Cause, you know if not . . .'

Stella stared hard at Lizzie. 'Well?'

Lizzie nodded. 'I'm okay.'

Sonny continued, 'We can't take any chances; it wouldn't be . . . safe to leave any loose ends hanging around.' He let the meaning hang in the air.

Lizzie shivered and pulled her jacket closer around her. 'I'm fine. Honest. You can trust me.'

Sonny said nothing. He slammed the van door and stood back, nodded to Stella. Ignored Lizzie.

The two women climbed into the van, reached for their seat belts and secured them in place. Only Lizzie's hands were shaking. She glanced at Stella. 'Maggie, I mean Mags ... sorry I mean ...'

'It's Stella. Lizzie, what the fuck is the matter with you?'

'Sorry, I'm just nervous,' Lizzie muttered. She tried to steady her voice. 'I thought Margaret was a lovely name.'

'It's no special enough, is it? I always knew I was going to be a star, that I'd go stellar. So I got in there first and changed my name. Stella means star and I'm going to be one – that reason enough for you?'

Lizzie nodded, gripped onto her seat belt and stayed silent.

Stella nodded to Sonny and pulled out of the car park, carefully nudged the van onto the road and they set off. The roads were fairly quiet, other than a few cars, late-night buses and taxis. The rain had stopped and a full moon shone pale and cold over them as they drove out of the city. Stella stayed close to the roads running beside the River Clyde, knew that the river was swollen, its banks in places fragile and ready to burst. She knew that the Glasgow Humane Society would be patrolling the Clyde, rescuing those they could find or recovering cold bodies with dignity and compassion.

Stella drove carefully, avoiding as many CCTVs as she knew of. No matter, she wore a wig and glasses and her manicured hands were carefully ensconced in gloves. She gripped the wheel and chewed hard on gum for a few minutes before reaching over and turning on the radio.

'And now we have Michelle Makepeace on line one to introduce her favourite song. Ever.'

'So, like this is the best song ever. I love it . . .'

'Thanks Michelle and here it is, Robbie Williams with "Let Me entertain You".'

Stella smiled, turned up the volume, tucked the gum into the side of her mouth and sang along.

Lizzie waited until the karaoke had finished and cleared her throat. 'You not worried Stella, that the polis will know it's us? Trace the van tae us?'

Stella sighed. 'Van was stolen to order – they're gonnae find it burned out in the morning. Abandoned on a wee bit of wasteland over by the Watervale scheme. No worries, hen.'

'And James Harris requested this one for his wife Alexandra, who's due to give birth to their first baby in a few days. Good luck with that! Now here is,' the presenter paused, *'here is the song James requested: let's hope it's not a message to Alexandra! Here's "Suspicious Minds" by the late, great, Elvis Presley.'*

Eventually Stella turned off the road, drove down a deserted dirt track and into a narrow lane. Kept driving.

Beside her Lizzie was quiet and pale; she stared out of the window as they left the roads where the streetlights glowed orange and drove into the dark of the country. She didn't ask where they were going.

Stella drove for half an hour before she turned off the lane and drove through a sodden field. The van lurched as it crossed the uneven ground. Stella rolled down the windows, heard the roar of the Clyde, knew that they were close to the river bank. Stella put the van in reverse. They both sat in silence listening to the sound of the water, the spray hiss into the cold dark air. The smell of the river.

Stella had picked out the tarpaulin herself, industrial-strength, which was helpful as they had to drag Mason's body across the last part of the field. She changed into wellington boots. At the water's edge, Stella took out her new knife and cut the rope Sonny had secured around the tarpaulin. She watched Mason's body slide onto the sodden ground.

'See, he might get washed up, Lizzie, and we don't want it to look bad. We need it to look just like he's fallen in after having one too many drinks.'

'But the—' Lizzie began.

Stella cut her off. 'The roofies will be long gone from his system unless he washes up in the morning. And what are the chances of that?'

The drop was long, the splash muffled by the hiss of the river. Stella threw the knife in after him.

Lizzie cried softly.

'Shh hen, there's no one to hear.' Stella paused for a second, shone the torch down where they had dropped the body. There was no trace of it. Mason's body had slipped neatly underwater. Stella grinned.

Lizzie began snivelling again. 'It's gonnae be awful for him, waking up and being under the water and stuff. Cold and dark. Horrible.'

'Shite, his heart would've stopped when he hit the freezing water. A wee heart attack before he even went under. Never even woke up. We did him a favour. He wouldn't have felt a thing.' She patted Lizzie's arm. 'He'll be sleeping like a baby now.'

Lizzie blinked. 'You sure that they always have a heart attack, right away, so they feel nothing?'

'Always,' Stella lied.

'Best that way.' Lizzie stared at the water, comforted. 'Well, if he had to go . . . probably best that way.'

'Mon.' Stella grabbed the tarpaulin and strode back to the van.

Lizzie trotted along beside her. 'That it?'

'Aye, that's it. The cunt's gone.'

'What now?'

'Nothing, you know nothing. Let it be. You forget all about that wanker. Okay? Polis come looking for him, tell them he's scarpered. You've no idea where he went. Besides, there's no reason the polis should be looking for him.'

Lizzie shivered as she climbed back into the van. 'I've not done anything like that before.'

'Aye, so you said earlier. It's not like I plan on making a habit of it.'

'I've never though. Even though ma da . . . well, you know.'

'Then you need to man up, Lizzie. Get over yourself. Mason was a fucking waste of space.' Stella put the van into gear. 'You know that, don't you?'

'Aye but still, it's murder and . . .'

'Shite, it's a service to society. The cunt's gone AWOL. That's all the polis will know. That's all anybody needs to know.'

Lizzie stared out of the window and watched the sky. Dark clouds rolled across the moon. Her eyes filled up; she brushed the tears away.

'And Doyle never gets to know about our wee trip, okay?' Stella said.

Lizzie nodded.

On the way back to the city Stella sang along with every song on the radio, her hand thumping the steering wheel loudest to Cheryl Cole's 'Fight for this Love'. Stella sang like her life had just got better; she felt for the video in her jacket pocket, imagined Mason at the bottom of the Clyde and grinned as she sped through the sleeping city. She dropped Lizzie close to a taxi rank before abandoning the van, keys still in the ignition. It would be picked up and burned out. The polis would just find another burned-out vehicle, nothing to get excited about. Sonny had it all arranged. Stella left the gloves, wig and glasses on the seat. Threw the wellington boots in the back and slammed the door behind her.

Once home she poured herself a drink, took it through to the TV lounge and slipped a *Mad Men* DVD into the player. By the time Doyle had returned she was on her third episode of the drama and her fourth vodka.

He poured himself a double.

Stella smiled. 'A good business meeting with Weirdo, babe?'

'Aye, but I heard that there was an unexpected death the night.'

Stella gripped her glass tight, swallowed hard, 'That right, babe? I never heard anything. Who died?'

'No one important, guy called MacIntyre jumped off a bridge.'

Stella sipped her vodka. Breathed deeply.

'You okay?' Doyle looked at her. 'Good night?'

Stella smiled, raised her glass. 'Fabulous.'

DREAMER

George Grey turns in his sleep, fingers worrying at unfamiliar sheets. Unfamiliar smells. He sighs, eyelids flickering, lashes damp with tears. Remembering. It had been his sixth birthday when MacIntyre had first taken him to Gilmore's house and left him there. That's when it had all started. George whimpers in his sleep. Eventually he awakens. There is a low light on in the room, the kind of night light a child may have in their bedroom.

There is a knock on the door. A voice asks him, 'Are you okay, George?'

'I'm okay.' George feels calmer and soon he closes his eyes again and falls asleep. Now he dreams of the future. He is standing in a field. He can hear birds singing; he feels the grass beneath him. The sun is shining and the tears dry on his face. George smiles.

Outside the wind rages through skeletal trees and rain lashes at the brass sign. The Keenan Institute.

Chapter 64

Saturday, 14 December

Doyle sipped his coffee and didn't bother to rearrange his face into any kind of civil. That kind of shite could wait. He heard footsteps walk towards his office, then pause. The knock on the door was slight, tentative, respectful. Aye, well it had better be fucking respectful.

Smithy inched his way into the room. Tried to say, 'Okay, Mr Doyle?' but his voice had deserted him. Stood, hands clasped together, shaking. Blubber glistening, pools of sweat cooling.

Looked like his bowels might let him down.

Doyle shook his head sadly. 'You like robins, Smithy?'

Smithy shifted uncomfortably. Said nothing. Eyes darting.

'What about sparrows?'

Smithy stared at the thick carpet, clenched his buttocks. Concentrated.

'You deaf, Smithy?'

'Is it like a trick question, Mr Doyle? If you want me to like them, aye, fair enough. But if no, well that's fine as well. Jist, you know, jist tell me.' He licked his lips. 'Whit's the right answer?'

'You tell me, Smithy.'

Smithy bit his lip. Hard. Drew blood. Sucked it back into his mouth quickly.

'I find wee birds handy, you know?'

'How's that then Mr Doyle, you one of them . . . things . . . no sure of the name . . .?' Smithy tried hard, like he was fighting for his life, 'A tweeter . . . a twitcher?'

Doyle smiled. 'An ornithologist, is that what you mean Smithy?'

'Aye Mr Doyle, that's whit I mean.' He sounded unsure.

'Well, see a wee bird told me that you've been, now, what's the right word here?'

Silence.

'*Fraternising*, yeah that'll do. See the wee bird whispered in my ear that you and that bollocks Stevie Tenant have been seen having a wee get-together.'

Smithy turned white, started to shake. 'I jist bumped into him in a pub, couple of times, Mr Doyle, honest.'

'Is that right?'

'Honest Mr Doyle. I jist nodded tae him. Couldnae ignore him could I?'

Doyle sat back in his chair, rested his hands on his boat of a desk. Watched Smithy try for a smile, his face a tangle of spasm. Waited some more. Saw the attempt to smile die on his face. Watched the face grow pale. Kept his voice low, reasonable. 'See there's something I don't like. Any ideas?'

Smithy didn't trust an answer, shook his head.

'I don't like it when folk are lying to me.'

Silence.

'But worse than that, way fucking worse is something I hate.' Doyle paused. 'Care to hazard a guess Smithy?'

More silence.

'I'll take that as a no then. The thing I hate most in this fucking world is disloyalty.' Doyle dropped his voice, held his palm out towards Smithy. 'Can't make it any clearer can I?'

'But Mr D . . .'

Doyle held a finger to his lips. 'Shhh, Smithy, it's too late for excuses. Thinking back on it, there was the night that you chased the two wee boys. Seems to me like it wasn't just a mistake, looks awfully like you were laying a trail for the polis. A trail which started at Gilmore and led to the wee boys, then to you and finally it ended at me. And now there's a wee lassie lying dead. Now I'm no angel but a dead student isn't good for business. Can you at least stretch your pea brain around that point?'

Smithy nodded. Look genuinely contrite. Relaxed a little.

A bit too premature.

'So, what I'm saying is, if her drugs didn't come from me via Weirdo, then they came from Tenant, McGregor or an independent. But, see, here's my problem. That wee lassie was at Glasgow Uni, in the West End. Am I correct?'

Smithy nodded. Looked at the floor. Waited.

'And who supplies the West End?'

'You do Mr Doyle.'

'But it wasn't my gear – see my problem? Which brings us back to the wee bird that told me they'd seen you with Stevie Tenant.'

The penny dropped. Smithy knew that this wasn't just a slap on the wrist.

'You know your options?'

Smithy nodded, his Adam's apple bobbing erratically.

'Relocation's always the safest bet. Edinburgh's mibbe too close, Aberdeen's nice at this time of the year, or further up? Otherwise . . .'

'No!' Smithy held up his hands. 'No. Please Mr Doyle, I'm out of here. Honest. I've a mate in Aberdeen I can stay with. First thing tomorrow morning . . .' He stared at Doyle, saw his expression. 'Just wanted to say cheerio to ma girlfriend?'

Saw that Doyle disagreed with that plan of action.

'Aye, okay, I'm on my way to Buchanan Street bus station. Last bus . . .'

Doyle shook his head.

Smithy waited. Eventually asked, 'I've no to go to Aberdeen?'

'Aberdeen's fine but you'll be going by train. Faster. I want you gone. Understand?'

'Next train leaving. Honest, Mr Doyle.'

'You see be on it. Otherwise . . .'

But Smithy was already out of the door. His bowels had moved.

Chapter 65

Later on, when she'd thought about it, when she had traced the events of that morning back to the beginning, Marjory Watkins decided that it was all the fault of her husband, Rory, like so many of the other things that had gone wrong in her life. It had been Rory's idea to get the dog in the first place, a small border collie. A very handsome dog with a gentle face, a long nose, soft brown eyes and neat paws. Answered to the name of Prince. There wasn't much wrong with Prince, Marjory thought, but he was a dog and dogs needed to be walked. Daily. That morning Rory had complained of flu again and that was why at 7.15 a.m. Marjory had been trailing after Prince in the cold morning drizzle.

Marjory had crossed the bridge and had been walking along the Clydeside when she'd spotted it. She'd stared at it for a few seconds but her eyesight was impeccable and she knew what she saw. The shape bobbing head-down in the freezing water was a human being, a man. Marjory gave a short cry and pointed, but other than the dog there was no one else to see the floating body. Marjory had not taken her phone with her that morning and so had to run into the road and flag down an early-morning bus. The driver called it in and had the kindness to pour her a cup of sweet tea from his flask as they waited for the police to arrive. Marjory had never cursed in her life, but that morning she called her husband a lazy bastard in front of the policeman. The policeman had nodded.

Chapter 66

Weirdo stood in the train station sipping a takeaway coffee from a cardboard cup. The station was open-plan, which meant every chill from the weather outside travelled through, keeping the place about the same temperature as a freezer. He blew on his coffee and watched the steam rise through the cold air. He checked the timetable again; the train to Aberdeen was due to leave in ten minutes. So far no Smithy. His mobile rang. 'Mr Doyle.'

'He there yet, Weirdo?'

'No, he's not shown a face yet.'

'Stay there.'

'Aye, will do.' He paused. 'Is Smithy definitely meant tae be in this station, Mr Doyle?'

'Aye.'

'Only he's cutting it fine – the train's already in.' Weirdo watched the rest of the passengers step onto the train. He glanced up and down the platform; there was still no sign of Smithy. He listened to Doyle speak.

'And you know what to do if he doesnae show?'

'Aye, Mr Doyle.' The line went dead. Weirdo resumed his wait. Two teenagers passed, staring at his Mohican. Weirdo gave them a second then turned, staring hard at them as they passed, forcing them to look away. He sipped his coffee. Then he saw him. Smithy waddled towards the train, dragging an overstuffed holdall behind him.

Weirdo watched Smithy get on the train, waited until it had pulled out of the station. Checked that he hadn't jumped off. Then he called Doyle. 'All okay Mr Doyle.'

'He's definitely gone?'

'Aye, wee prick left it to the last minute but the train's away.'

'He alone?'

'Aye.'

'Good.'

Chapter 67

Wheeler was sitting at her desk in the CID suite doodling on a piece of paper. She hadn't needed to be at the station – the team's meeting with Stewart wasn't for two hours – but she'd decided to finish up some paperwork. But instead of staying focused, she was finding it easier to waste time. She saw a text from Jo.

I spoke to a counsellor at university. She agrees Jason is traumatised by the death of his friend. He will be getting extensions on all of next term's deadlines. Also counselling/extra time in exams. They will have support in place for him when he returns after the break. Jo.

Wheeler stared at the text. *Fuckssake*, she thought. Jason would have his day though, one day. She'd make sure of it. She deleted the text, then she checked her emails; nothing urgent. Finally she scrolled down the news link on her mobile, saw another article by Grim. Read on.

Dead Body Discovered in River Clyde

A man's body was discovered in the River Clyde around 7 a.m. this morning.

The body was spotted by a passer-by. Mrs Marjory Watkins, 64, had taken her dog for an early-morning walk and made the gruesome discovery. Mrs Watkins, a receptionist at the Green Leaf Medical Centre, immediately raised the alarm.

The police were contacted and police divers recovered the man's body. The man has yet to be identified and a post-mortem will be held later today to establish the cause of death. Police are appealing for witnesses and are at present continuing their enquiries.

Ross stood in the doorway, carrying two takeaway coffees and a greasy paper bag. He placed one of the coffees on her desk, opened the bag and offered her a pastry. 'Any news?'

She took one and was chewing on it before she answered. 'Another body's been washed up in the Clyde.'

'Suicide?'

She shrugged. 'Too early to tell.' She sipped the hot coffee. 'Thanks for this, Ross, it's lovely.'

'You're welcome.' His voice was tired, flat.

'Still down about the case?' Wheeler took another bite of the pastry.

Ross glanced around the room, checking that they were alone. 'Yeah, but a bit of news on the personal front.'

Wheeler waited.

'Sarah thinks she's pregnant.'

The pastry turned to cardboard in her mouth. 'Pregnant?'

He nodded.

'But I thought you'd told her you didn't want kids?'

'I did.'

'And that it was over?'

'That too. She came off the pill a month ago. Didn't bother letting me know.'

'Right.'

'I can't see us together long-term. It was only ever going to be a temporary thing.'

Wheeler sipped her coffee. 'What are you going to do?'

He looked across to the window. Studied the weather.

The phone on her desk rang; she ignored it. 'How do you feel?'

'Trapped.'

'She definitely plans to have the baby?'

He nodded.

The phone continued ringing. She sighed and grabbed it. 'Yes?'

'Not having a good day, Katherine?'

'Callum, I'm sorry, I was miles away. How can I help you?'

His voice boomed down the line. 'It's I who can help you.'

'Go on.' She watched Ross, saw his miserable expression. Felt for him.

'Some interesting news: the body washed up in the Clyde early this morning?'

'Yes, I just read Grim's report.'

'It was someone known to you.'

'Go on.'

'It was Maurice Mason.'

Wheeler perched her backside on the edge of her seat. 'Maurice Mason's dead?'

Ross overheard, put his coffee down. Listened.

'Oh completely dead and has been for some hours,' said Callum.

'How'd he die?'

'He drowned.' She could hear Callum snort down the line.

'Excuse me a sec.' She put her hand over the receiver and spoke to Ross. 'The body they found in the river this morning? It's Maurice Mason.'

She returned to her conversation with Callum. 'I got that he was in the water; tell me more.'

'There were no obvious wounds, no knife or bullet wounds. His hands weren't bound. He did have a broken nose, but that may have happened after he was in the water. He simply drowned.'

'But did he fall or was he pushed?'

'Immersion in water leaves the body in a particular state – for example swelling, and also the skin may become wrinkled. Kind of like when you spend too long in the bath.'

'Prune-like?' suggested Wheeler.

'Exactly,' Callum agreed, 'and from what I've seen of his inner workings, I'd suggest that he was alive at the time his body entered the water.'

'Could it have been suicide?' Wheeler didn't believe that Mason would have killed himself but she needed to ask.

'Oh absolutely – he could have jumped in.'

'Or he could have been pushed?'

'That too. There's Rohypnol in his blood.'

'Is there now?' She mouthed *Roofies found in Mason's blood* at Ross. 'So he could've been drugged and tossed into the water?'

'Possible. Or he jumped or fell. I can't prove conclusively either way.'

'But if he . . .'

Callum finished her sentence for her. 'No, I'm afraid it's not possible to conclusively prove it, Katherine. All I can tell you is that he was alive when he went into the water.'

'But he was drugged.'

'He had taken drugs. And he had also been drinking. It's not unknown for people to mix both, is it? Fell, jumped or was pushed, that's your department. The police get to figure it out.'

They carried on for some minutes, until Wheeler said in frustration, 'So we don't know for certain?'

'There's no scientific evidence to point either way, as far as I'm concerned. It'll be down to what the police uncover.'

She was about to thank him and put the phone down when out of habit she asked, 'Anything else?'

'For example?'

'Anything Callum, anything at all.'

Callum sounded as if he were reading from his notes. 'He was wearing a shirt, trousers, coat, all the usual items of clothing, shoes, underwear. His wallet and other belongings have been bagged. There wasn't much in his wallet, just loose change. Also, included in his effects was his jewellery, a gold bracelet and another piece which was quite distinctive.'

'What?'

'A thick medal of St Christopher – I haven't seen one of those in years; they used to be very popular—'

'Stop,' she cut him off. 'Back up, Callum – describe the St Christopher.'

'A chunky piece – it looked to be of very good quality. Maybe half an inch in diameter. Good solid chain. Why?'

Wheeler quickly explained, checked the similarity again and then put the phone down.

Ross had heard enough. 'Mason was wearing Gilmore's St Christopher, wasn't he?'

She nodded. 'Looks like it.'

'So Mason was our man all along? He killed Gilmore?'

Wheeler nodded unconvincingly. 'Maybe. Maybe not.'

'Because?'

'He ended up dead after he had taken Rohypnol. Or at least it was in his system.'

'Took it? Or was given it?'

She shrugged.

'So, he murdered Gilmore, then killed himself? Convenient.'

'Mason didn't strike me as the suicidal type. He was a career criminal. They're not usually the reflective kind.'

Wheeler spent the next two hours arranging for the medal to be identified by the only person who would recognise it: Moira Gilmore.

The team eventually reconvened in Stewart's room.

Stewart updated them. 'Moira Gilmore has been given a general outline regarding the images we found in her son's storage unit.'

'How did she respond, boss?' Ross asked.

'Classic denial. She's flatly denied that it could have been his storage unit.'

'She still going to sue us, even considering what we found in Clydebank?'

Stewart shrugged.

'And the medal, boss?'

'She did however positively identify the medal as belonging to her son.'

Stewart looked at Wheeler. 'Update on the body in the Clyde, please.'

She nodded. 'I spoke with Callum. Maurice Mason had a broken nose but it could have happened in the water, hitting against the bank. The only thing Callum could tell me with certainty was that Mason had been drinking and that there were traces of Rohypnol in his system. He was wearing a gold bracelet, Gilmore's St Christopher and there was some change in his wallet. '

'Anyone speak to his ex, Lizzie Coughlin?'

Boyd said, 'I spoke to her. She's very bitter about the break-up. Says once he got out of the Bar-L, he chucked her and left their house. She didn't seem too upset to hear that he'd died. Told us he often used roofies.' Boyd checked his notes. '"Mason used uppers and downers all the time; he used anything he could get his hands on."'

'Where was she the night he died?'

Boyd glanced at his notes. 'She was with her pal, Stephanie Roberts. To quote Lizzie, "Me and Steffy got absolutely blootered."'

'And Steffy backed her?'

Boyd nodded.

'Right, so Grim's on his way. What do we have for the press?' Stewart looked around the room.

Silence.

Ross summed it up. 'Unofficially, we're not looking for anyone else in connection with James Gilmore's murder? Case closed?'

Stewart pursed his lips. 'Officially we are still continuing with our investigation and the case remains open until we conclude. But realistically, Ross, that would be a nice neat ending, wouldn't it? HQ would be delighted with that. We have a suspect who was recently released from jail, who was wearing jewellery that had been taken from a murder victim when he was killed. It's a result.' He looked at Wheeler. 'Anything more from the PM on Mason?'

'Callum says there's no way to tell if Mason was pushed or jumped. Or simply fell in.'

Stewart looked around the room. 'What's the consensus?'

Ross spoke. 'I think Mason was framed.'

'Evidence?' asked Stewart.

Ross shook his head. 'None.'

'So, we spend time and resources trying to clear his name?' said Boyd sourly. 'And even more time trying to find out who killed that evil bastard Gilmore?'

'Or just be glad that both Gilmore and Mason are gone and we have a result.' Ross looked out of the window. 'It's the obvious way forward. Why carry on throwing resources at the case when it's already been resolved?'

Stewart sighed. 'Let's just keep an open mind on it.'

They filed out of his room in silence.

Chapter 68

Saturday evening

Wheeler sat in the empty CID suite, the photographs spread out in front of her. The case was closing, there was nothing new to add and the team had a result. Grim would eventually write an article about James Gilmore and what police had discovered in his Clydebank storage unit. Public perception of the murder would change to outrage. The next article would report that Maurice Mason, a convicted killer who had recently been released from prison, had murdered again. This time his victim was the paedophile. A few days after the murder, Mason had been high on drugs and alcohol when he accidently slipped and fell into the Clyde. What could be neater? A feel-good story for Christmas.

She crossed to the kettle, switched it on, and while she was waiting for it to boil she looked out of the window.

Outside, a busker was doing a half-decent rendition of 'Have Yourself a Very Merry Christmas'. Wheeler stood at the window and watched the lights from the trail of cars going along the A74. She thought of the M74 and the huge landfill that existed between the two roads. She stared at the Glasgow sky and watched as the weather changed and it started to snow.

Behind her the door swung open and she heard snuffling. First through the door was the mutt – its plastic cone had been removed – and behind it Ross came into the room carrying a large carrier bag stuffed with Christmas decorations. 'These are for you.' He sat down, tied the dog to his chair and smiled at her.

'What?'

'Nothing, I'm just happy to have some time off. What are you up to over the holidays?'

She paused. Paul Buchan had texted, asking her for dinner – she still hadn't replied. 'Not sure, what about you?'

'Sarah wants to give it another go.'

She looked at his face, saw the tension. 'And?'

'I'm not sure. Need some time to think. She lied to me.' He sighed. 'Anyway, you fancy going out for dinner, celebrate the end of the case?'

'Not much to celebrate.'

'Still.'

'You paying?'

He smiled. 'Might do. Take it as another bribe towards my promotion.'

'You're on. You take Fido back first, okay?' She bent and patted the dog. It wagged its tail.

Ross nodded. 'Okay.'

'Meet you outside Kelvingrove Art Gallery in an hour?'

'You're on.'

'And thanks for these.' She gestured to the Christmas decorations.

'No problem. See you in an hour.'

Wheeler watched Ross and the mutt leave before returning to the photographs. She flicked through them for a few minutes, wondering about the children, what had happened to them, where they were now. She looked at their faces, saw a range of emotions: hope, despair, fear. Finally she gathered the photographs together and started to pack them away. Then she stopped. One photograph was left on her desk. She looked at the line of children, all staring at the camera. Some smiling, some looking nervous; one was scowling into the camera. The boy had faced the camera head on, one eye blazing darker than the other. Wheeler checked the back of the photograph. It was labelled Stobwent-Hill Children's Home. She checked her notes. Gilmore had worked at the home in the eighties. The children would have ranged in age between three and eleven. She studied the photograph again, noted the direct gaze of the boy, the bitterness behind his scowl. The flash of aggression in dark eyes. She reached for the phone. Called Ross. 'Listen, there's something about the case, can you come back to the station?'

Acknowledgements

Gratitude and love go out to Jack Oakman, Michael Dacre, Don Storey and Hania Allen.

Big thank you to Jane Conway-Gordon, Krystyna Green and everyone at Constable & Robinson.